The Winds of Change

Tony Mead

Published by New Generation Publishing in 2021

Copyright © Tony Mead 2021

First Edition

The author asserts the moral right under the Copyright, Designs and Patents Act 1988 to be identified as the author of this work.

All Rights reserved. No part of this publication may be reproduced, stored in a retrieval system or transmitted, in any form or by any means without the prior consent of the author, nor be otherwise circulated in any form of binding or cover other than that which it is published and without a similar condition being imposed on the subsequent purchaser.

ISBN   978-1-80031-081-0

www.newgeneration-publishing.com

New Generation Publishing

Part Four
Guilty of Honour

Tony Mead.

*Dedicated to my friend, Adela.
Thank you for your help.*

Contents

1. The winds of change… 1
2. Find Quigley 15
3. Christmas 1821 24
4. Pelican Sets Sail. 35
5. Joys of Spring. 42
6. Swing the Lantern 52
7. Cartmel...60
8. A New Vicar. 67
9. Surprise in the Churchyard. 73
10. Kidnapped 80
11. Off the coast of Argentina..90
12. Come quickly… 107
13. Find Emma 113
14. Desperate Actions 121
15. Cattle Thieves. 126
16. Temptress..137
17. Compton Island 144
18. The letter. 154
19. The Flight of the Raven 166
20. Van Diemen's Land 179
21. Captivity...188
22. Sail Away 194
23. The Spice Islands. 201
24. Against the wind. 221
25. Life goes on..230
26. The Reckoning. 234
27. Christmas Day 1825...241
28. New Arrivals. 255
29. The return of the Pelican..262

Books in this saga..268

1. The winds of change...

"That should hold it," Ben called from the roof of the new dairy. For three hours, he had been repairing several broken roof slates and now he was thirsty and ready for a break.

Ben laughed, he was enjoying his new life as a farmer and stockman; he had put away his Royal Navy uniform determined that after their last adventure he was finished with the sea. The memories were not so easy to put away, the reality of his past deeds often haunted him.

He stood up to stretch his back and a sudden gust of wind caught his hair, blowing it across his face; with the flat of his hand, he brushed it away. He stared out across his land and reflected a moment; he could sense that there was to be a change in the weather. A deep rumble of thunder, like the stomp of a fairy-tale giant across the land, shook the ground. Ben watched the plum coloured clouds slowly approach, their bellies were so heavy that they could hardly clear the distant hills. There had been endless days of summer heat, and now even with the approaching storm, it was hot and muggy. Ben mopped his brow and took a drink from his hip flask; he considered as to whether or not they should take a break. His mind was made up when the skies lit up and another deep murmur of thunder echoed down the valley.

He decided that they had done enough; he allowed himself a smile of satisfaction as he knocked the dust from the front of his clothes.

"We'll soon know if we've fixed it or not," Tim said looking up at the heavens.

He pointed up the lane to where it joined the main road into the village.

"That's unusual," Tim said under his breath. He was perched on the steep, tiled roof of the dairy. Pondering the situation, he wiped the dirt and sweat from his face with a cloth.

"What is?" Ben inquired, "What's unusual?" He was further down the roof trying to fix where the rain was getting in.

"Sergeant Parker's on his way, I wonder what he's after?"

"Perhaps we should ask him, I should think that that will give us an answer."

They watched the police sergeant from their rooftop vantage point. Tim slithered across the tiles to be beside Ben.

"He looks to be suffering in the heat, it's most unlike him to have his tunic flapping about," Tim whispered to Ben.

Tony Mead.

Sergeant Parker constantly mopped his brow with a large red cloth, it was clear that the summer heat was getting the better of him. However, as soon as he neared the farm and thinking that he was unobserved, he slowed his mount, buttoned up his tunic, and adjusted his cap to conform to regulations. Dan Parker was a stickler for regulations. After fifteen years as a constable, he had recently been promoted to sergeant and considered himself a cornerstone of the community, which brought with it the responsibility of setting an example.

"You look to be cooking in your tunic," Tim called out to him.

The sergeant seemed a little startled by the sudden voice from above, his mind had been far away on something else.

"Greetings, Mr Burrows, Tim," he politely nodded to them. "It's damned hot, but it looks like the weather's going to break. What are you doing up there?"

"Fixing all the leaks in our new roof," Tim said. "Jenny is driving me mad complaining about them," He guiltily checked over his shoulder to make sure that she was nowhere within hearing range.

"Looking at those clouds, you'll know soon enough if you've fixed them."

"Not before time, Dan," Ben said. "What can we do for you?"

Ben and Tim scrambled down from the roof and into the yard.

"I'm afraid I'm the harbinger of bad tidings." He stepped down from his horse as he spoke. He straightened his uniform and polished the toe of his riding boot on the back of his trouser leg as he walked. "Your old adversary Quigley has absconded from Lancaster Gael."

Tim took the horse, patted its neck, and then tethered it near the old stone water trough. The horse gratefully bowed its head and drank from the trough.

"Come in," Ben said. He led the way into the kitchen and offered Dan a chair.

"It appears that the deed was organised from outside," Dan explained, "He was being moved ready for transportation, a gang of black-hearted scoundrels, about ten men in all attacked the Black Maria. Two of the wardens, both God-fearing family men were killed and Quigley was away like a scalded rabbit. I just thought that you'd be interested because I remember that when we caught him, he was dead set on taking his revenge on you."

"They are out looking for him I assume?"

"The militia has its orders to find him. However, where do you start? The man had money and connections."

The Winds of Change.

"Yes, there are some high-ranking ones amongst them. His involvement in the slave trade amongst other things has put him in bed with folks of all ranks."

Jenny, Tim's wife entered; she was a pretty woman with long flowing auburn hair, bright sparkling eyes, and she wore a smile with comfortable ease. The atmosphere in the kitchen suddenly seemed lighter and the day much brighter.

"Hello, Mr Parker, I saw you ride down the lane," she said and handed him a small package wrapped in brown paper. "Some butter from our new dairy. The kids will love it. She poured everyone a cup of tea. "How's your wife? The last time I saw her at the market, she was looking poorly," Jenny said carefully handing Dan his tea.

"She's doing well, thank you, it was the summer fever. When it's dry for a long period she gets dreadful bouts of sneezing."

There was an embarrassing silence as they drank their tea. Another rumble of thunder filled the gap and rattled the teacups on the tray.

"I'd best get on," she said and left.

Dan looked on edge, he was obviously uncomfortable. "You've certainly done wonders with this place," Dan remarked, "I remember how dilapidated it was before you bought it. Old, Harry Toyne, was not a man easily parted from his coins. After his wife left him, he seemed to just give up on life," Dan said.

"It was the view across the bay that sold it; Emma sits out there and loves to paint."

"Well, I should be going, take care and I must advise you not to take the law into your own hands and try to seek out Quigley."

Ben smiled and nodded, but he knew he had to do something. Jenny returned and showed the sergeant out.

"I thought Emma would be back by now?" Ben said with a worried look.

"She's taken Dorothy and little Walter over to Emily's. Don't worry, they'll be all right," Jenny said.

Ben went upstairs to change his clothes. He stared at himself in the tall mirror on the bedroom wall. He stared long, and hard as if sensing that trouble or something like it was on its way. The prefix of 'young' had ceased to be attached to 'man' where Ben was concerned, but at thirty-two, he felt to be in the prime of his life. His complexion was dark and weathered from his time at sea, however, he felt that his youthful looks had tarried and there were only a few malevolent grey hairs amongst his otherwise raven black locks that gave a slight clue to his age. He still bore a thin scar across his left cheek, for years it had glowed white against his otherwise tanned face, but now it was more like a hairline crack. Neither had he lost his charm nor the good looks that at times had been his downfall, and he could still turn a woman's head when he was out shopping in the town, which would usually earn him a nudge in the ribs from Emma. Shopping was one of the things he had recently been introduced to by his wife. He did not particularly enjoy the experience of aimlessly walking along city streets staring in windows and trying to skip through the filth of the roads, but he silently endured it to keep the peace and his wife happy. This was just one of many changes in his life since giving up the sea; he had also acquired a farm, a son Walter and his teenage ward: Dorothy.

Ben went and saddled his mare. Out in the yard, he was met by Mould his faithful steward from his sea days. "Where are you off to in such a hurry?" Mould said.

"I'm riding over to see Mr Barraclough."

"Shall I come along?"

"No stay here, I've just found out that, Quigley is on the loose and I'll feel safer knowing where everyone is. I'll go to make sure they're safe. The mere mention of Quigley's name makes me nervous after what he did to us last time."

Mould steadied Ben's horse as he mounted. "Be careful, it's a while since I had to get out my sewing kit for you."

Ben usually enjoyed the ride to Cartmel, but this time he felt sick and nervous. Since the drama of the wedding day, things had settled down and the last four years had been almost idyllic. As he reached the fell top, he glanced out over the bay, instinctively keeping his eye on the weather he thought about how threatening an approaching storm with plum coloured heavy clouds would have seemed when he was at sea. It would have meant a great deal of work for the crew, sails would need adjusting, and anything that moved had to be securely lashed in place or be lost overboard.

It was not a long ride, and he was relieved when he finally reached Cartmel. His heart soared when he spotted Emma walking in the garden with Dorothy and Edward. *I wonder where William is,* he thought.

"Ben, good to see you," Edward Barraclough called out, "are you alright, you look a little anxious?"

Edward and Ben had served together for over ten years in the navy. During that time, they had become close friends and they had retired at the same time to take up farming and try to find a little peace and quiet after the maelstrom of their service.

"Quigley's out of gaol, we need to get the old crew together and go find him," Ben said.

The Winds of Change.

Emily, Edward's wife stepped forward and held Ben's mount as he stepped down. Ben smiled at her and once he was down, they embraced.

"It's good to see you, my dear," Emily said.

"Yes, you too, we'll be able to come over more often now that the dairy is finished."

Emma and Dorothy ran to meet Ben and they all embraced. He felt much better knowing that they were here and safe.

"Where's Walter?" Ben enquired.

"He's tagged along with Glenda's boys, they've gone fishing in the beck," Emma replied.

"Are the constables searching for Quigley?" Edward asked.

"They are, but I think we might have more success."

They all went into the house together: Edward poured Ben a glass of his favourite port.

"I presume you have a plan, you usually do; although I seldom like it," Edward said. He smiled as he offered the glass.

"Lancaster Gaol will still hold some of his gang, I suggest we go there and find out what we can."

"About what?" Edward asked.

"He must have favourite haunts; he can't go home, he's not that stupid."

Emily placed her arm around Ben's neck. "Now why didn't I think that your plan would be just to let the constables find him?" Emily gave Emma a knowing look and a sly wink.

"My dearest, Emily, it seems that you know me all too well," Ben said.

"My dearest Benjamin, I do know you. Ever since you arrived here as a scrawny stray with a bullet wound in your back and afraid of everything."

Emily's first husband, Reverend Jeremiah Linton had a knack of picking up waifs and strays, his pilgrims he called them, all of whom needed care and attention. Ben was one of those waifs a young teenager in need of shelter, who needed a safe place to rest and to rebuild his strength and revitalise his energy to face an uncertain future. This was when he first met and became friends with Tim, who was in a similar position.

Ben was becoming agitated and annoyed that the others were being so calm about the news. "We need to get the old crew together and warn them to be vigilant and look out to see if we can find him," he said impatiently.

Dorothy picked up her tennis racket and went back out into the garden. "Well, I'm not searching for anyone; we're playing tennis on the lawn. Come on all of you and watch us."

They all obediently followed. Ben and Edward found themselves a shady place to sit and finish their drinks. The thunder clouds had blown east, taking with them the threat of the storm and allowing the sun to return.

Ben smiled as he watched Emma chasing after the ball and then hitting it high in the air for Dorothy to return.

"She's a fine looking woman," Edward said, "she seems to have blossomed since having William, I can't imagine what she sees in you."

Ben gave a broad grin. "I never thought I'd find such happiness. We've been married four years now and I love her more with every day," Ben said proudly.

"It's a damn good job we have all that prize money, with the amount they manage to spend on their excursions in search of new dresses they could easily bankrupt a man."

Edward sat back with a contented smile, "This is the time I've experienced family life. I was ten years old when I was enlisted into the navy, being the third son there was no family fortune to inherit. My ship, crew, and fellow officers are the only family I've ever had." He took a large swig of his port. "Until moving in with you here, I never have had a picnic or celebrated Christmas, I've lost count of how many Christmas days I've been at sea."

Emily joined the men in the shade; she mopped her forehead with a handkerchief and sat close to Edward linking arms with him. "Did I hear you mention picnics? Once that storm blows over, I think that it will be perfect picnic weather; we've not had one for ages."

"We've been so busy recently," said Ben. "We should make more time for the family, after all, we don't need the money from the farms."

"Maybe so, but these days, so many people rely on us for their living, maybe twenty or more families," Emily said.

"We were just discussing your shopping trips," Edward said.

She looked at Ben. "Is he complaining about how much we spent last week in Leeds?"

"He may have mentioned something in passing," Ben said.

Like a whirlwind, the three-year-old William suddenly dashed across the lawn and let out a wild scream of delight when he saw Ben. He was carrying a glass jar that was tied around the neck with a length of cord to form a handle. By the time, he reached Ben, most of the water and the sticklebacks had bounced out.

"Pa, look what I've caught for tea." He proudly held the jar aloft.

The Winds of Change.

"That's not enough for tea, poor old Uncle Edward will have to go hungry," Ben said lifting his son onto his knee. "What about a picnic next week if the weather holds?"

The lad was off running again. "We're going to a picnic." He shouted excitedly and then jumped onto Edward's lap. "What's a picnic Uncle?"

Dorothy threw down her racket. "It's much too hot for sport. Did someone mention a picnic?"

"Ben did," Emily said.

"Good I need something to brighten my life," she sighed. She was suffering the usual agonies of being fifteen, which was being intensified by the emergence of several large pimples on her face.

"Me too," Walter agreed, he usually did agree with whatever Dorothy said.

"We cut the hay up in the top meadow this last week," Ben said

"Oh, that sounds promising," Dorothy chirped up, "so does that mean we can have a picnic up there?"

"I hope so, it's a favourite place of mine," said Emma.

Dorothy moved and flopped down at Emma's feet. "You and Ben met at a picnic," she said. "Tell me the story again."

"You've heard it before," Ben said impatiently, he had more important matters on his mind.

Emma gave Ben a secretive smile as she remembered that moment in time when she first saw him. She thought that he was the most handsome man she had ever seen, but it was more than that, when their eyes met, she felt a stirring inside that made her catch her breath, there was something about him. She had guessed that he was stubborn, but there was much more, was it naivety, no she decided that it was honesty. She knew instinctively that she could trust him and although her experience of men was limited to her late husband whose crude attempts at lovemaking were enough to put her off men for life, she knew that she wanted this man for the rest of her life. In fact, she made all the first advances, and completely out of character, she asked him if he would like to go swimming with her.

Emily smiled too; she had been there when they first met and remembered the day as though it was yesterday. She ran her fingers through Dorothy's hair. "We were sat having a picnic in the top meadow when…"

Ben interrupted her. "A rude young woman, riding on a very large hunter tried to order us off our own land," he said.

"I was not rude," Emma protested.

"A little bit," Edward said with a knowing wink to Emily.

Emma playfully slapped his arm. "Edward! You are usually such a good ally in these disputes; anyway, I thought that you were a gang of gipsies."

"You and Ben met there and fell madly in love," Dorothy said theatrically fluttering her eyelids, "Aunt Emily said that you couldn't take your eyes off each other."

"I don't think it was that obvious," Ben said.

Everyone laughed aloud at his statement; Emma hugged him.

Glenda, Emily's housekeeper, brought out a tray of fine china and served tea. The tea set was made of the finest bone China; a new acquisition of which Emily was very proud.

"My, how we've all come on, tea, in delicate china cups sat out on the lawn," Edward said shaking his head in disbelief.

"I suppose you would prefer navy grog out of old pewter tankards," Emily said scalding him. "I bought this tea service in Manchester, it's made by that reformist, activist, Mr Wedgewood in Stoke."

Ben still had his mind on his old adversary Quigley. "We need to get the old crew together this week."

"He'll not stay around here, not if he's any sense, he's too well known," Edward said.

Emily placed her arm around Ben's shoulders. "They'll all be here this evening for their suppers. Why don't you stay too, you've not seen them for a few weeks?"

Ben thought about it for a while.

"Oh please, Ben; I love it when your crew's all together," Dorothy said.

"Very well, I'll ride back to Fell Cottage and bring Mould back with me; he can help with the meal, and Jenny would never forgive me if she missed out on one of our get-togethers."

On the ride back to his farm, Ben wondered if he was being over cautious about Quigley being on the loose. Things had been moving so well, but he knew from experience that life was a precariously balanced commodity and that things were apt to turn turtle at any minute.

Mould was delighted when he heard the news that there was to be a supper at Emily's. He loved their suppers together, it was a chance to reminisce and have some fun. He hummed an old shanty as he harnessed up the trap so that they could all travel together.

"It'll be like old times, we had some fun, and you can't deny that, Skipper," Mould called from the stable.

Jenny did not need to be asked twice if she wanted to go, but as she was about to climb into the trap she suddenly ran back to her cottage. "Wait for me, I'll just be a moment," she called enthusiastically over her

The Winds of Change.

shoulder as she went. Minutes later, she reappeared in a different dress and carrying a blue bonnet.

"I couldn't go to a party in my work clothes," she said.

She jumped into the back of the trap and as they rode over the fells, she pulled her hair into a ponytail.

"How's that?" she asked Tim.

"Very nice," he said without much enthusiasm. As usual, his mind was on his dairy and cows. He enjoyed the old crew get-togethers, they were always such lively affairs, but his life seemed so boring when compared to their adventures.

From the corner of his eye, he secretly watched Jenny, he loved to see her happy he smiled, thinking about the attention Jenny would receive from the crew; when they were first married it had made him jealous, but he soon knew that it was harmless and she thrived on the extra attention. However, at times he was jealous of the way he would catch her eyes following Ben around the room, and how when he was there she seemed so much brighter and happier.

The crew had reached Emily's house by the time Ben and his party clattered into the market square. The crew gave a loud cheer when they saw the trap arrive and crowded around it.

"I must say, Mistress Jenny, you are looking bright as a new coin," Fletch said. He held out his arm to escort her into the garden.

"Thank you, Mr Fletcher, you are looking rather dapper yourself," Jenny said, giggling as she took his arm.

Ben went in search of Mitchell, and Snow who were seated in the parlour.

"Good to see you both, how are preparations coming along?" Ben said as he shook Mitchell's hand.

"Yes, everything is going to plan, the carpenters have been busy below decks installing cells for the prisoners, it's been a hard task to relocate the guns and make room for everyone. I think it will take until after Christmas before we are completed." He shifted awkwardly in his seat. "I hope you realise how thankful I am to be given the chance to captain a ship again. We'll look after her for you," Mitchell said.

"I know you will, Pelican couldn't be in better hands. I wish I was going with you, but I've promised Emma no more adventures."

"Your skills and company will be missed, Mr Burrows," Snow said.

"Thank you, Mr Snow that's very kind of you to say. I'd like to remind you both that there is always a place for you here whenever you get back," Ben said. "And so, down to business; what is your plan?"

"Obviously, we must wait for the conversions to be completed. It's a new experience for me, I've never sailed the Pacific. I must confess that I can't say I'm looking forward to the transportation side of it, I'm not even sure that I agree with it."

"The Admiralty gave us very little choice in the way we were conscripted by them," Ben said, trying not to get angry over the situation. "I'm pleased that you were available to help me out by captaining the ship for me, otherwise there would have been Hell to pay with Emma if I was to set sail again."

"There is an upside to this, and I must admit I could never have turned down the chance to circumnavigate the globe. Once we've picked up our passengers in Liverpool, I intend to sail southwest and follow Magellan around the cape," he said with a broad smile. "We know how vast the Pacific Ocean is, but we'll still find Van Diemen's Land without trouble our cargo of convicts will not be in a hurry to get there. Once our duty is done, the exciting part of our journey will begin." He paused to take a drink. "We'll sail north to the Spice Islands and India."

"What are your feelings, Mr Snow?" Ben asked.

"I don't like the transportation idea, but I have to admit that the thought of the journey is stirring, and it will add another great milestone to my career."

"Not to mention the fact that you will make a very handsome wage from it," Ben said with a smile.

Outside there was a large makeshift table set up ready for them all. Mould was in his element, he loved a party with his old shipmates. Straight away, he was helping Emily to fill the table with food and drinks. She always had a good supply of smoked and preserved meat and recently since the completion of the dairy; Ben had been able to keep her well supplied with cheese and butter.

Everyone mingled, laughing and joking glad to be in each other's company again.

"I understand you've bought a fishing smack," Ben said to Ezra. They had been part of the same crew for over ten years and were good friends.

"Aye, Skipper, this farming work's all right, but I prefer to be on the water. I still love the feel of the wind in my hair, what little of it I have left." He laughed as he rubbed his almost bald head with his hand.

"Maybe I'll come out with you one day," Ben said.

Jamie Douglas, the farm manager who as usual was smartly dressed in his beloved Douglas tartan, arrived with his Ghillie Ian Douglas. "I thought this might make an acceptable offering." He handed Emily a haunch of smoked venison. Mould added it to the food stacked on the table and after sharpening his knives, he began to carve generous slices of meat for everyone.

The Winds of Change.

Quite soon, the meal turned into a high-spirited party; as usual, a great amount of beer, and rum accompanied the non-stop banter being exchanged across and around the table.

Ben stood up and banged loudly on the table with his tankard. "I've some bad news; Quigley is out of gaol," he said and paused a moment to let the news sink in.

"We'd best all be on our guard after last time," Jamie Douglas said, his voice was calm, but he remembered the hurt Quigley had brought to them all.

"Who's Quigley?" Dorothy asked.

"Don't you worry none Miss, we'll handle that blackguard, no problem," Fletch said with a wink to her.

They finished off a barrel of ale and grew quite merry, which was usually the time when they would 'swing the lantern' which meant someone would tell a tale. Edward was usually first up, but on this occasion, he was beaten to it by Jamie Douglas.

"Seeing as how that son of the devil, Quigley, is out, I thought I'd remind you all of that terrible night when we lost the old Fell Cottage." His voice was deep but not gruff; his Kirkcaldy accent flowed like warm molasses. "Whenever I pass it and see its sad state now, I curse Quigley and his gang."

"Don't go frightening the ladies," Fletch said.

"We'll not be frightened," Dorothy said. "Please, Mr Douglas, tell us the story."

"Very well, young Mistress," he glanced over to Ben to make sure it was all right to carry on. "When we were signing on the crew for Pelican, before her first voyage, you'll all remember Quigley turning up with several what he called indentured workers, slaves more like." There was a chorus of 'aye' from the listeners. "Mr Barraclough and Mr Burrows rightly objected and didn't want any part in transporting slaves, saying that they had fought for years to try outlawing slavery and putting an end to that despicable trade of misery."

"Aye, Mr Douglas we'd fought storms and high seas, pirates and outlaws in that quest," Jones said. "As a child, I was transported by one of those slave ships; you'll never get nearer to hell this side o' dying if you ask me."

There was a roar of approval. Ben remembered when they captured a slave ship after a fierce battle with the ship's crew. The slave ship was loaded with frightened, desperate people who were being transported in dreadful conditions after being snatched from their homes. It was the first time that he had sailed with Jones and instinctively liked and trusted him. When they had overcome the slavers he gave Jones the honour of opening the hatches to free the slaves.

Mould as usual was busy looking after everyone and despite it still being warm; he lit a fire in a metal brazier to keep away the chill of the evening air.

Jamie continued. "There was a bit of an altercation between, Mr Burrows and Quigley and as he left the building, he cursed us all and gave us fair warning that the affair was not concluded."

There was a general murmur as everyone remembered his parting words.

Jamie tugged at his beard as he usually did when he wanted to say something. "First, he burnt down the barn on Christmas day, nearly killing my man, Douglas…"

"Then the water for the cattle was poisoned," Jenny, blurted out. She gave a weak, apologetic smile to Jamie for butting in.

"Indeed, Jenny, but then worse was to follow. As we slept in our beds like innocents, they torched the house with us all in it. Fortunately, Mr Burrows, you were at sea with Emma and the lads in Pelican."

"Aye, from my ship's log, we were sailing off the Cape Verde Islands at that very moment," Ben said.

Emma, who had just downed a large glass of champagne stood up a little unsteadily. "I seem to recall, that I'd asked Ben what time it was here," she said with a knowing smile. "He has a watch that tells the time for wherever in the world he is."

"I seem to remember you had stowed away on that ship and should not have been there at all," Ben said. To everyone's amusement.

"Well, it's a good job that I did… otherwise I might have been caught in that fire," Emma said and then sat down rather abruptly. Walter climbed on her knee and fell asleep instantly.

Douglas looked annoyed, his story had been so interrupted that he had almost lost the thread of what he was saying. "If I can finish…"

There were murmured apologies from everyone.

"Quigley was caught and sent to Lancaster Gaol; never has there been a more fearful place or a more just sentence for a rogue. Only his money and connections saved him from taking the drop, but now it seems that he has also escaped from being transported."

"As it is currently Pelican's mission to deport such villains, it would have been a curious coincidence and no mistake, if he had been shipped by us," Fletch said.

"I still don't condone shipping souls to their doom," Ben said, his speech was slightly slurred.

The Winds of Change.

"Aye, well, he's out now and we should be wary. I don't think that he'll be stupid enough to bother us again, but best be cautious," Jamie said.

Despite the hour being so late, the sky was still quite light when Ben and his family returned to Fell Farm.

"The summer sun barely seems to set at this time of year," Ben called to Emma riding in the trap. He and Mould were riding alongside the trap. They were all in a merry mood and soon they were singing at the top of their voices, even Ben had managed to put the news of Quigley's escape to the back of his mind for a brief moment. The mention of a picnic had brought back memories for him too; he remembered the first time he gazed into Emma's face. Everything there was to know about her was right there in those misty blue eyes.

"I'll put, Walter to bed," Emma said. He had fallen asleep on Jenny's knee and made only the slightest of murmurs as Emma lifted him up to carry him indoors.

"He's a grand lad," Tim said, "let's hope that he has a better start in life than we all had."

Jenny hugged Tim's arm it was only a few steps to their cottage. "He already has a good life, so many friends to look out for him. We just had enemies when we were his age."

"Should I see to the horses? Tim asked.

"I'll see to that," Mould said, "you all run along and get some sleep."

Jenny pecked Mould's cheek. "What would we do without you," she said.

She linked up with Tim as they made their way to their cottage. "Goodnight," they called over their shoulders.

The sun had finally set and a tranquil peace surrounded them. Ben watched them from his kitchen doorway before he went in; making certain that they arrived home safely. Inside, he threw a few split logs onto the main kitchen fire and then sat in his usual chair with his legs sprawled out. He stared at the flames and like a mountain waterfall rushing over a cliff, a jumbled mixture of memories tumbled through his mind. Each thought only stayed an instant, and then it was flushed away by the next one. There had been dangerous and sometimes frightening episodes during his time in the Navy, but none seemed quite as fearful as the thought of Quigley, or anyone else for that matter hurting his family. He stared into the fire, almost hypnotised by the leaping flames, as they wafted like exotic dancers in the hearth.

Emma appeared in the doorway. "Shall I light a candle?" she said.

"No, I like just the firelight. Once these logs catch alight, then that will be enough."

She had changed out of her clothes and she was wearing just a flimsy nightgown. She tucked it under her legs and sat at his feet on a thick sheepskin rug resting her head in his lap.

"You're worried about, Quigley aren't you," she whispered.

"Many years ago I had a run-in with a man called Mace; he didn't seem to have any other name, it was at the time that I first met Jenny." The thought of their time together brought a smile to his lips. "He was a bully and an evil character with a mind like a bull terrier's, once it was set on something he'd never let go."

"Do you think Quigley is like that?"

"I'm not sure, but I fear that he may be, and that's what worries me, he'll not let go."

Emma went to fetch some drinks pouring Ben a generous amount of his favourite Port. They drank in silence until the flames began to die down. Ben nudged the fire with a poker; it sent a shower of sparks swirling up the chimney.

"Why not ask my Papa to help; as a magistrate he has a certain amount of influence, and maybe we could get him to contact the Governor of the prison so that you could question one of Quigley's gang."

"Yes, as soon as Pelican sails we'll do that."

"I think it's time for bed," Emma said.

"Yes, you're right."

"I think it's time, Walter had a brother or sister," she said with a girlish giggle. She threw her arms around him and playfully bit his ear.

2. Find Quigley

The following morning the heat was stifling; with only occasional light gusts of a salty breeze, blowing from the bay to bring a little temporary relief.

Ben sat out on his favourite wooden bench sipping his morning tea, which as usual was laced with just a drop of rum. The bench had been carefully positioned so that in one direction, there was a view across the bay and out to sea; in the other a hazy blue line of the distant mountains. He tilted his head back to take a deep breath; it smelt fresh and clean; it reminded him of so many days at sea. He was interested in the weather across the bay; he could see the ragged bottomed clouds that indicated that it was raining out to sea and that a fresher wind was on its way.

Emma came to sit by him; she took his hand and pulled it around her shoulders.

"What are you thinking about?" she asked. "Are you watching that weather? It must have been a worry when you were at sea."

"Yes, I've got my eye on it, I'm wondering how long it will be before we look for cover. It will be welcome; the fields are bone dry, if we don't get some rain soon we'll not get to cut the hay again before winter and then we'll have to buy in fodder for the animals, which will be expensive."

She sat on his knee. "What are you really thinking about?"

"It reminds me of a storm that Edward and I went through when we were sailing on Adventurer. She was a good-sized ship, but that storm threw us about like matchwood. It started with a few distant clouds and then the sea went as flat as a pancake and the barometer dropped like a stone, next thing there were waves so tall the lookouts on the mastheads couldn't see above them. It went on for days; I don't think I've ever been so wet in all my life," he said with a smile.

"You must still miss the sea, I often watch you staring out across the bay. We are lucky to have such a view." They held hands and life stood still for just a fleeting moment. "Do you wish you were going with Captain Mitchell and Pelican, whenever it's ready?"

"Not really… maybe a little bit of me would like to go, but I have too many responsibilities here, and anyway I'd not like to be separated from you for such a long time."

"Will Pelican be away for long this time?"

"Perhaps two or three years, Van Diemen's Land is right around the other side of the world. We've discussed diverting the ship to Ceylon and perhaps Madras on its way home, there's no point sailing so far with an empty hold."

"We need to ride to my parents this morning, but I think we'll leave Walter and Dorothy here, it seems ages since just you, and I went for a ride."

Ben smiled at the thought of them riding out together. "Yes, you're right, plus the weather's going to break."

The smell of breakfast cooking in the kitchen interrupted their thoughts, turning their minds to food. As usual, Mould was busily preparing them breakfast; he had been up since first light baking bread and biscuits for them. "Morning, Skipper, Ma'am, looking at those clouds, we're in for a blow and a ducking later."

As soon as they sat down, Tim and Jenny followed them in obviously drawn by the smell of breakfast cooking. Jenny came with gifts of butter from the dairy and freshly baked loaves; she did her usual round of kisses for everyone and then helped Mould serve the food.

"Shall I get Walter up for you?" Jenny said.

"No, leave him and Dorothy in bed awhile, we all had a late night," Emma said, "we're going over to the Grange to see my parents."

"There'll be hell to pay with, Master Walter," Mould said. "You know he loves to visit his grandpa."

"You'll just have to keep him amused, but keep your eye on him, this news about Quigley has worried me," Ben said.

They ate a hearty breakfast, and as usual, the topic of conversation was the new dairy and the tasks waiting for them around the farm. After breakfast, Mould saddled their horses; he also took time and great care to prime both of Ben's saddle pistols.

Out on the open moorland, their thundering hooves brought a sense of freedom as they raced to the top of the meadow. It gave them a clear view of the bay and the surrounding distant hills.

"What a glorious view," she said, pointing across the landscape.

"I can see a better one," he answered, his eyes fixed on her. He leant across and they kissed.

"I understand why you've fetched me up this direction," she smiled.

Quite suddenly, the trees around them came magically to life; their limbs shook and their dry leaves rustled and danced as a strong gust of wind raced in from the sea.

"I think we'd best hurry," Ben said. "It's going to rain soon."

No sooner had he spoken, than the heavens opened. A clap of thunder followed by a deluge of ice-cold hail and rain took their breath away and soaked them to the skin.

"Come on, I know where we can shelter," Ben said.

The Winds of Change.

They galloped through the rain, screaming their laughter until they reached one of their shepherds' lambing shelters, and although it was not very big, they managed to get the horses in and out of the weather.

"I'm absolutely drenched," Emma said. She laughed as she tried to shake the rain from her jacket. She sniffed the air. "I love the smell of the rain; it reminds me of my childhood and picnics we used to have. They always seemed to be rained off."

Ben opened out a bale of straw for them to sit on.

"Here get out of those wet clothes or you'll catch your death," he said.

"Ha-ha, so I was right, you did have an ulterior motive for bringing me this way; I'll even bet you've arranged for the rain to catch us," she scolded him.

Ben had already removed his shirt. "Are you complaining?"

"Hmm," she purred, rubbing her hands with delight on his bare chest. "I'll tell you if I've any complaints in a while, but first..."

The sudden and surprising romantic break, as well as the rain, put them both in a good mood and they cuddled together in the straw on one of their horse blankets.

"I always feel safe when I'm with you," Emma said with her head resting on his chest.

"I don't know why I always seem to have trouble lurking somewhere around me."

"When I was in Canada, with my late husband, it always felt dangerous. The scenery was spectacular, high snow-capped mountains, seemingly endless lakes and salmon-filled rivers, but there were dangers too, wolves, bears, big cats, and unfriendly natives, not forgetting the French."

Ben toyed with her hair a moment. "I was once somewhere like that; it didn't have the bears and wolves, but very unfriendly natives," Ben said with a wry smile.

"Oh, where was that?"

"London, the natives there were very unfriendly." They both laughed loudly.

Ben gently kissed the nape of Emma's neck; she shivered slightly. "Don't ever stop," she whispered.

After the rain, they stood naked in the sun their bodies glowing with pleasure and satisfaction. Still naked, they embraced, and it was as if they were one, their flesh seemed fused together, they tingled right to their souls and for a moment they were the only inhabitants of the earth.

"Oh, that feels good," she said and turned her face to the sun and stretched her arms out as wide as she could. "I feel to be the luckiest woman alive."

Reluctantly, they dressed and then continued their journey, stopping on a hilltop to take in the idyllic view of the Grange with its ancient parkland. A large herd of red deer were grazing peacefully; they wandered amongst the huge, majestic, old oak trees scattered across the landscape. The sun was out and the scene was animated by the moving shadows of clouds and beams of bright light chasing across the fields.

Emma pushed her horse close to Ben's so that her leg touched him. "I was wicked at times when I was young; I used to love to ride through the herd and scatter them across the park," Emma said.

Ben spurred his mount forward. "You're a terrible person, I need to reform you," he said.

"Ha, that's not what you said earlier." She galloped away at full speed.

Lord Levante, Emma's rather eccentric father was in the courtyard to greet them. "Toot-hoot-a-hoot," he bellowed his favourite hunting cry skipping about with childish excitement. "What a nice surprise."

"It's only a week since we saw you last," Emma said.

A groom came and took their horses.

"Give your old Papa a big hug," he laughed heartily to Emma. "Goodness, you're wet through. Up and get changed before you catch your death."

He shook Ben's hand. "I'll get you a change of clothes too," he said to Ben.

In the parlour, Lady Levante sat serenely before the fire. Ben and Emma embraced her.

"Mama, do you need the fire, it is summer you know," Emma said.

"It's always cold in this room, anyway, I do feel the weather these days, I'm not as young as I once was." She moved across to the other side of the fireplace to sit on a large upholstered sofa. "So, to what do we owe this honour?" she said, patting the cushion beside her for Ben to sit down.

Ben explained about Quigley's escape, but some of his gang were still being held in Lancaster Gaol. "I was hoping that you could use your influence to gain me access to one of these characters."

His lordship looked as if he was studying the proposal. "There will be a price you know."

Emma looked shocked. "Papa!"

Her lady-ship butted in. "What are you talking about you old duffer?"

The Winds of Change.

"There has to be a price, and it is that you all come for tea tomorrow. Bring Dorothy and young Walter and I'll get Cook to make something special."

Lady Levante suddenly looked up as if she had just woken up. "Oh, I forgot to tell you I've received a letter from Roland's widow Annabelle, she wasn't aware that Ruth had died."

"Where was she?" Emma asked.

"Portsmouth, she's been staying with her family down there, although I believe her father, Admiral Hunter is still in the West Indies. Did you ever meet the Admiral, Ben?"

"Yes, he was on the panel that promoted me to lieutenant. It's over four years, surely she knew."

Ben glanced at Emma, she knew about Ben's short affair with Annabelle, which was long before they met, but he was still slightly embarrassed by the mention of the woman's name.

"She was always a bit of a troublemaker, I was surprised when Roland said that they were to marry, I know you were good friends at school with her Emma darling, but I never took to her," Lady Levante said. "You never invited her to your wedding, but there again, we never invited, Ruth either, but she turned up and nearly killed us all," she said with a hearty laugh.

"Don't puff up your stories mama, she only injured the statue of St Anthony," Emma said

"He lost his finger poor man, and you nearly lost a lot more of your man." Her lady-ship gave Ben a nudge and a saucy wink.

They stayed for lunch before riding home and as was inevitable, Walter was in a mood because they had left him.

"Well, I think that you are very cruel going to Grandpa's without me," he said indignantly.

"So what have you been doing?" Emma asked as she lifted him onto her knee.

"We baked a cake," he said enthusiastically his bad mood was now a thing of the past. "Jenny let me help her make butter; I turned the handle for her."

"And where is your sister?" Ben asked.

"She's grooming her new pony if she combs it much more its hair will drop out."

Lord Levante's influence was such that they received a letter of permission to visit the prison within four days.

Ben, Edward, and Mould left the same day as the letter arrived and pushed hard to cross the bay at Kent's Bank in time to beat the tide.

Although it was a dangerous place to cross because there were patches of quicksand and an incoming tide that was said to be faster than a racing horse and could soon drown the unwary, it saved many hours of travel rather than going around the bay

Along the main street leading to the castle were rows of vendors selling a whole host of wares and food stalls filling the air with tempting smells.

"This is a frightening place," Ben said as they approached the formidable towering gates of the castle.

Edward stirred uncomfortably in his saddle. "Yes, the sooner we are away from here the better," he said.

Through the high gate towers and into the courtyard they seemed almost afraid to speak. A uniformed guard carrying a musket armed with a long bayonet approached them.

"You must dismount here; leave your mounts over there. State your business," the guard said suspiciously. He pointed his musket at them giving them directions with the tip of his bayonet.

"Not the friendliest welcome I've ever had," Edward whispered to Ben.

An officer in a dazzling red uniform exited from a doorway in the castle wall. Ben offered him his letter from the Sheriff. The officer made a deliberate point of reading the letter holding it at chest height so that he could still keep his eyes on Ben.

"It seems in order. Will you follow me please, gentlemen?"

Mould stayed with the horses while Ben and Edward followed the officer. The Sheriff gave them a warm, friendly welcome, which was probably more due to Ben's association with Levante than his being pleased to see them. His plush office had polished wooden wall panels and neatly stacked bookshelves along the walls. He offered them a seat near a large oak table.

"So, gentlemen, how can I help?" the Sheriff asked. He was a lanky man with a dusty wig that seemed to be on the verge of falling off his head.

Ben explained to the Sheriff why they needed to talk to one of Quigley's gang.

The sheriff did not look pleased he squinted his eyes as if in pain as he thought about the proposal. "Very well, I can arrange an interview room for you. His gang is to be deported anyway," the Sheriff said. "We want Quigley caught too; I have a platoon out searching for him. I hope that you have more luck than us getting anything out of these vermin."

The interview room was a depressing shadowy oblong with dark green walls and flaking paintwork, which was lit by the light of a small,

The Winds of Change.

barred window six-foot up one wall. The only furnishings were a single rather battered table in the middle of the room that had four chairs placed around it.

Ben and Edward sat at one side of the table; they felt anxious and when the far door lock clattered and the latch was lifted, they sat forward expectantly.

Two wardens roughly handled the man and made him stand in front of the table.

"Stand up straight, hands behind your back," a warden bellowed in the man's ear from close range. "This good for nothing, worthless piece of excrement is, Harry McGuire," the warden said.

"You must be annoyed with Quigley; he never thought to help you escape when he fled," Edward said.

The man stood sullenly at the table refusing to speak.

The warder standing close behind him clipped his ear with a flick of his hand. "Speak when the gentleman asks you a question," he whispered menacingly into the man's ear.

"Sit down, please, Mr McGuire," Ben said he indicated for the man to sit opposite him.

The prisoner looked fearfully over his shoulder and then gratefully took a seat, after an approving nod from the warder. The man seemed to be shivering as though he was cold, he placed his trembling hands on the table and then thought better of it and tucked them under his leg to sit on them.

"A judge might look favourably on a fellow who helped catch a known felon," Ben said holding the other's gaze. "Where could we find Quigley?"

"My lips are sealed. How long do you think my life would be if I was to answer such a question?"

There was a pause as they tried to decide how to deal with this standoff. Edward's many years of dealing with awkward customers gave him an advantage over the man.

"Oh dear, you see, you've got a problem now, because we might let it be known that you've helped us anyway," Edward whispered.

"But I've said nowt!"

"The warder behind you thinks that you did. Is that not right, officer?" Edward gave him a wicked smile.

"I'm sure he said something, in fact, I'm certain that he did. I'd be forced to pass on my understanding of the situation to anyone asking."

The man spun around to face the warder. "No! Please, no."

"If we said that we might find you somewhere safe to go and spend a long, happy life, you might tell us where his favourite haunts were," Ben said.

There was real panic on the man's face. "He'll kill me."

"Not if we catch him," Ben said.

"He has contacts everywhere, even here. I'd want your word that I'd be moved or maybe paroled early, and I'd want that safe place you mentioned." He nervously turned around again to stare at Ben.

"It might be arranged," the warder said.

"Get me transported to Van Diemen's Land, not the Caribbean."

"Now why would you not want to go there?"

The man clammed up again, he sat hunched over and tightly folded his arms, with his head bent down staring at his feet.

"You'll need to see the Governor for his approval," the warder said. "We'll take him back to his cell."

In the governor's office, Ben placed a small purse of gold coins on the table.

"Don't consider for one minute, that I think that you could be bribed. Therefore, the contents of this small purse do not in any way constitute a bribe, but let us say a donation, for a charity of your choice. I need, Mr Maguire to talk and the only way he'll say anything is if we have something to offer him and if we promise to protect him."

The governor weighed the purse in his hand and peeped inside it; he smiled when he saw the gold. "He's doing hard labour; sometimes men escape from the gangs working in the quarry. It's a sad fact that we don't have the manpower to go searching for them."

"He said that he would prefer van Dieman's Land."

"There is a ship bound for there next month; I can make sure that he is on it."

"Then perhaps we could talk with him again, perhaps we could guarantee that he will be transported to the place of his choice," Ben said.

"I believe that you have a ship being converted for the purpose of transportation."

"Yes, she's almost ready, we've some final adjustments to make, and a crew to set on."

"You should have many contacts in that area, crewmen that is," the Governor smiled at them. "Will you take tea before you go?" he asked politely.

"No thank you, Sir, we've to get back across the bay, so need to sort this out with all haste."

The Winds of Change.

"Give my regards to Lord Levante; he and I have been in parliament together for some time."

Ben and Edward were edging towards the door, but the governor kept talking to them until finally, Edward spoke out. "We must be going, thank you for your hospitality."

They went back to the interview room where a warder waited, his stern expression warned them of bad news.

"Can you bring that prisoner back?" Ben said.

The man shifted awkwardly from one foot to the other. "We took him back to the main cell," the man struggled with his words. "Unfortunately, somehow someone knew that he was speaking to you about Quigley."

"Well, get on with it man," Edward said impatiently.

"We only left him in the main cell for a few minutes; we found him slumped in the corner with his throat slit open. It was too late to do anything, he was dead as can be."

Ben, was so angry, he thought his head would explode. "We've only been an hour, not even that," he bellowed.

Edward caught hold of his sleeve to control him. "Calm down, there's nothing we can do. Come on, let's go back to Cartmel."

They rode north towards Carnforth hardly exchanging a word.

Eventually Ben could not hold back any longer. "We've just been very naïve, I said that he had friends everywhere, either the warder or his men, maybe even the Sheriff is protecting Quigley. I thought he was acting suspiciously. We are on our own with this venture."

"It might have been one of the other gang members, either way, I think we'll not get much help from there," Edward said, "Let's go home, we should catch the tide and be able to cross the sandbanks to Kent's Bank."

3. Christmas 1821

A long dry spell in September brought about a colourful autumn, the fells turned from a lush green to a multicoloured patchwork of reds and oranges. However, all too soon this was followed by a very dark but surprisingly mild grey winter when mist and cloud hung around the hills and filled the valleys. Several cold frosty mornings froze the ground solid and adorned the trees with jewel-like crystals; they looked picturesque, but they meant extra work. Each day the ice in the water troughs had to be broken so that the animals that were still outside could drink and because the ground was frozen, the feed had to be put out for the cattle and sheep.

All too soon, it seemed that they were making preparations for Christmas. However, uppermost in everyone's mind was the need to have everything ready for the beginning of the lambing season just after Christmas. The threat of Quigley still being on the loose temporarily slipped to the back of everyone's mind.

At Kirkley Grange, that Christmas Eve, Lady Levante was in a panic, she loved to host the Christmas feast but things were not going to plan.

"Where is the butcher," she wailed as she dashed along the corridor towards the kitchen.

"Calm down, Mother, if you do not, then you will surely make yourself ill," Emma pleaded as she tried to catch up with her.

"Calm down! That's easy for you to say. What will people say, if we can't provide good fayre at Christmas, what if there is… no meat?" There was desperation in her voice.

Emma dashed so that she arrived in the kitchen at the same time as her mother did. They ran into a fog of hot, fragrant air filled with the aroma of spices, roasting meat and citrus fruit.

"Mrs Cairns, how are you managing?" Lady Levante cried as she entered the kitchen.

Mrs Cairns, the head cook looked up from the worktop where she was making delicate adjustments to her latest gastronomical creation. She had worked at the Grange for over twenty years and she was quite used to her mistress' annual panics.

"Everything is under control ma'am, Mr Banks has sent one of the lads to find the butcher, I'm sure it's only the weather delaying him." She wiped her hands on her apron. "We already have the game; we've two stags, supplied by Mr Douglas, and countless birds and rabbits thanks to his man Ian. We have almost everything we need m'lady."

The Winds of Change.

"Come on, Mother we're in the way here, everything will be fine, Cairns is an old trooper, she'll make it right," Emma said.

Mrs Cairns gave Emma an appreciative nod; they were old friends and allies. "Not so much of the old, if you don't mind, Mrs Burrows," she said with a smile and secretive wink.

Lady Levante could not leave without first inspecting the geese and wildfowl hanging by their feet in a neat row from a dark oak beam ready to be cooked. She picked off a couple of tiny feather quills that had been left from the plucking, which made her feel much better.

Mid-afternoon the guests and their baggage began arriving; many of them intending on a long stay over Christmas. Ben and Edward were dealing with the logistics of organising them to make sure that they and their entourage were all given suitable accommodation. The old Grange crackled with excited chatter as the guests were ushered to their rooms, and there was further excitement when they met up with old friends in the corridors.

Walter dashed about and was constantly in the way, but his enthusiasm was relentless, in contrast, Dorothy had the usual detachment of a teenage girl; she refused to show her excitement, even though she was burning up inside with anticipation of the Christmas Eve Dinner which was always a dazzling affair at the Grange.

There were several children brought by the other guests and Walter was friends with them all. They knew that tonight they would be allowed to join the adults outside for the lighting of the Yule Log and then tomorrow there would be gifts, presents, and sumptuous food.

Mould was also in his element. Mrs Cairns had given him permission to be in her kitchen, but more than that, he was being allowed to help, which gave him a chance to show off his skills as a pie maker. There were rumours that quite often on his days off from his duties as Ben's steward or valet as he liked to say, Mould could be found helping Cairns in her kitchen. Despite their age difference, Mrs Cairns was probably ten years his senior, they had a blossoming friendship and could sometimes be found sharing a glass of sherry beside the kitchen fire.

Ben was delighted to greet Mr McHenry his longtime solicitor and confidante and his wife. "Glad to see you," Ben said, "are you staying for the holiday?"

"No, we'd love to, but we promised to go meet my sister in Gretna for Hogmanay, but we'll stay a day or two. Jamie and Ian are travelling north with us. I've no doubt Jamie will give his blasted bagpipes a good outing."

"Oh, that's right, I remember Jamie telling me," Ben said. "They've corralled all his precious cattle and arranged for Tim to watch them for a day or two."

"He's never looked back since joining you here, I've never known him so happy or so obsessed with his work," McHenry said.

"He's looking forward to the lambing this year, everything is prepared, let's hope he gets back from the north before they start. Must dash, duty calls, I'll leave you to mingle," Ben said.

Outside the bonfire was being built, Ben helped heap the wood and finally, they placed a large spruce log on top, which was to be the Yule Log. Braziers and glowing brightly around the yard, fine sparks and wispy smoke filled the air.

At eleven-thirty, the guests were invited outside; it took a while for them to wrap themselves up in woollen scarves and heavy winter coats. When they were all gathered outside, Reverend Bright, who was now acting as the vicar of Saint Anthony's church led everyone in prayer and then in song. Ben noticed a late arrival; a modern, sleek carriage drawn by four horses and guarded by footmen came along the gravel drive. Its arrival went unnoticed by most of the guests and few gave it a thought as it slipped into the coach yard and then out of view behind the stable block. He was curious as to whom it might be, but with all that was going on around him, it slipped from his mind.

At twelve o'clock, the fire was lit, and Lord Levante blew three great toots on his steam engine whistle, which he had primed all evening ready for the occasion.

The children danced and played around the fire and as if by arrangement, and on cue, flurries of feather-like broad flakes of snow fluttered down, caught in the dancing light of the fire they added the final touch of magic. Toffee apples were served to the children and warming mulled punch to the adults.

"Cheers, Merry Christmas, good health," everyone called.

Emma hugged Ben. "Have you bought me a wonderful present," she said.

"No, I thought to have me was enough," Ben said with a broad grin.

When they moved back inside, the children were allowed two dances and then they were dispatched to bed in anticipation of the Christmas day feast. The adults warmed themselves by the fire and kept recharging their mugs of mulled wine. One of the large pine logs was carried carefully into the main hall where it was ceremoniously placed smouldering in the fire grate and where it would remain for the rest of the Yule Time Festivities.

The Winds of Change.

Despite the crowd, Lieutenant Snow seemed to be alone. He desperately wanted to join in and be part of it, but he never seemed to be able to relax in this sort of company. He nodded and smiled politely as people came near and yet inside, he wanted to scream and cry, but most of all he wanted to be noticed. He stared into the leaping, dancing flames, his mind was elsewhere and he was caught off guard when Lady Levante approached him and then linked arms with him.

"Come, let us walk Mr Snow you have a look of melancholy about you and I cannot tolerate that at my Christmas Event. How do you like our fine company?"

"I'm a little overwhelmed; I have spent too many lonely Christmas Evenings on hard wooden decks. The heat from the fire is welcome, but it also brings back some sad thoughts."

"I think that I understand, Mr Snow. You are to accompany, Captain Mitchell on, Pelican's next expedition," she walked him around the fire, "and how are your preparations going?"

"Pelican is almost finished. Our final plans and arrangements are well underway thank you, ma'am." He straightened his shoulders and allowed a smile to curl the corners of his lips. "The carpenters and blacksmiths have been working for months, the holds needed alterations, and part of the upper gun deck has been cleared to make the cells that are necessary to hold our cargo of convicts."

"It must have taken a lot of organising."

Now his mind raced with the details, it had been an enormous task; he was pleased that at last they were almost ready and they could begin the voyage.

"I hope that you Don't mind me chatting with you," she said, "We see you about but rarely do we speak, I hope you feel welcome here."

"Of course, my Lady, everyone makes me feel at home," he said shyly. "I must confess that I will certainly miss everyone this time away."

"How long will you be away?"

"Perhaps two years, because after we reach Van Diemen's Land we will be travelling to the mysterious land of India in search of spices and goodness knows what else."

"It sounds wonderfully exotic, but a huge undertaking. And what are your thoughts on shipping convicts around the world?"

"I just do my duty, but I don't see that what we are doing is any better than the slave trade was; we have fought for so long to try to end that terrible trade."

"Ben told me that you had a different vocation before joining the navy."

Snow smiled, it was a surprise to him that anyone should discuss him. "I trained as a priest but it never felt right for me, so as a last resort my father managed to find me a place as a midshipman."

"You've found your true calling in life now; Ben says that you were his most reliable officer and friend."

"I doubt that I was," he chuckled at the thought.

"So where will you take them?"

"There is a new penal colony at a place named, Macquarie Harbour, it is somewhere on the west coast of that distant place."

"I wish you a safe journey. You are not thinking of sending out the press gang to take, Mr Burrows or, Mr Barraclough with you?" she laughed loudly at her own little joke.

"They will be sorely missed on this venture Ma'am, it felt strange to be without them on our last voyage."

"They were needed to rescue you from the French if I remember rightly," said Lady Levante.

"To my embarrassment you are correct; I pray that we will find our own way home this time. We are sailing into unknown waters, not even Captain Mitchell has sailed into the Pacific Ocean before. It is unimaginably big and so little is known about its islands or its people."

Ben stirred the fire and then went to find Emma, who was dancing with a young army officer. "May I," he said and led Emma away.

"Are you jealous?" she said.

They found a quiet corner in the parlour and snuggled together on a rather well-used sofa that was comfortably baggy. Ben handed Emma a small package. "Merry Christmas," he said.

She carefully began to unwrap it, slowly removing the several layers of coloured paper.

"The lady in the shop kindly packaged it for me," Ben said.

Emma gave him a smile. "Well, I didn't think it looked like your handiwork," she said, "I've never seen such fine packaging, what a clever bow." She tugged at the ribbon to untie it.

Finally, hidden within the package, she reached a leather-covered casket, but it was locked and she could not open it.

"Stop teasing me, you wicked old pirate," she said, "where's the key?"

Ben held out his closed fist, she prised his fingers open to reveal the tiny key. Her hands were shaking so much that he had to help her fit the key into the lock. She cautiously lifted the lid to reveal a golden locket; a single diamond surrounded by tiny emeralds and rubies covered the lid. A delicate gold chain surrounded the whole thing. With trembling

The Winds of Change.

fingers, she carefully opened the locket and read the inscription, which simply said, Thank you.

He carefully placed it around her neck and she threw her arms around him.

"It's you that deserves the thanks," she whispered, "My life was very dull, and grey until you brought colour to it," she whispered.

Edward and Emily joined them, and before long, the whole crew was together again seated in a circle close to the fire.

"Do you remember one Christmas Day off St. Kitts; you said it didn't feel like Christmas because it was so hot? Well, I'd love for some of that heat here, right now," Edward said.

"That was on the good ship Adventurer, she was a fine vessel. Despite the number of years we were in the Caribbean, I never quite got used to it being eighty degrees on Christmas Morning."

"It was the first time you invited me to come to live here instead of going back to Bristol to live," Edward said with a smile.

"Well, I for one am very glad you took up his invitation," Emily said as she squeezed Edward's hand.

"I think that was the time, Captain Mitchell had that run-in with, Admiral Atkins," Ben said.

"Aye, and he wanted to poach you to be his navigator when he headed north to the Keys," said Edward.

"It was the first time Mr Snow came aboard," Fletch recalled, "and we all thought he was there to spy on us for Atkins."

"So what happened after the Captain had this run in?" Emma asked.

"We lost our two escorts and were ordered south to join a large fleet on its way to attack and recapture Martinique."

Edward was obviously studying something as if trying to get his thoughts in order. "I'm sure that we all remember our good fortune on our return journey last time out, when the French Captain of the frigate that had hunted us down, then let us sail away, even though he could have taken us prisoner?" he said to Emma. "That came about because one time before when we sailed with Adventurer, we were hunting for French ships along the coast."

"It came from nowhere, it looked huge, and it far outgunned Adventurer," Fletch added.

"It certainly did," said Bruce, "but thanks to Captain Mitchell's skill, we outmanoeuvred them and we won a memorable victory."

Emma looked confused. "So, years later, why does that same French Captain let us sail away with Pelican?"

"Because," Edward said as if giving away a great secret, "A certain, Lieutenant Burrows, led a boarding party onto the Frenchman's decks and then risked his own neck to save a young French Midshipman trapped by a fire below."

Mitchell joined them; he wanted to add something to the story. "The blaze was being fuelled by a leaking barrel of lantern oil, the flames were creeping ever nearer to the ship's powder magazine, and anyone with any sort of sense is retreating. But, after getting the French Matelots to drench him, Mr Burrows goes through the flames, getting his hair singed on the way, he then picks up the wounded lad and carries him to safety."

Mould joined in. "For once my sewing kit wasn't needed, but I'd to trim the back of his ponytail."

The crew laughed heartily, but Emma was still not satisfied.

"And the connection is?" Emma said impatiently.

"The young lad was the French Captain's son, and because he was an honourable man he made good a promise he had made to Ben, which was, that if he could ever return the favour he would. So, when we ran across him on our way home, he paid back the debt he felt that he owed Mr Burrows," Mitchell said.

Dance music was playing soft melodies and couples were swaying to their beat.

"Let us dance," Emma said. As they stood up to take a few steps, they were hit by a bombshell that stopped them dead in their tracks. Annabelle stood before them. From Emma's point of view, her sister-in-law and a one-time friend looked annoyingly stunning; her clothes and glittering jewellery was modern and blatantly very expensive.

"Ben," she purred, "Emma how delightful to see you again. How are you both?" she said with real friendly enthusiasm.

"Annabelle… how good to see you, still spending my brother's legacy I see," Emma said, fingering the expensive silk of the other gown. Immediately, she wanted to bite her tongue.

"Oh yes, why not?" Annabelle laughed, and with a sarcastic smile said, "You are farmers now I understand, I never imagined you for a farmer's wife Emma, how fortunes can change. You have a son as well as Ruth's bastard to look after."

"Are you here just to cause offence?" Ben asked. The muscles of his face stood out in tight knots.

"I don't usually come to these events a little boring for my tastes, but I thought I should help lift the tone of the party with my presence. I can see that you're cross," she said with a coy smile. "I have every right to be here, sister-in-law," she said to Emma.

"I thought that you would have remarried, it's more than five years since our husbands were killed in battle," Emma said.

The Winds of Change.

"Perhaps, I'm still waiting for the right man to sweep me off my feet." She smiled and stared provocatively at Ben. She lightly touched his jacket lapel as if straightening it.

Just in time, Lady Levante arrived; she had seen Annabelle move across the room and guessed that there could be more fireworks.

"Annabelle darling, how wonderful to see you," her ladyship said and pulled her into a hug. "You never responded to my invite, I didn't expect you, I'll have your old room made up, we've not seen you since… I can't remember when."

"I've been in the Caribbean, the climate there suits me."

There was a deafening silence between Emma and Ben as Annabelle was led away. Emma looked worried and a fit of sudden jealousy nipped her skin.

"Come on, let's not let her spoil our Christmas," Ben said.

They talked until the early morning, and without going to bed that night, they set off for the morning service at the church. The snow had cleared, but it was frosty with a bright blue sky as they rode the short distance to the church.

Reverend Bright welcomed them all; he was delighted to see his little church so full. He had taken over at St. Anthony's after Linton died and despite his advanced years, he worked tirelessly to keep the church in good order. To improve the Christmas decorations, he had commissioned a local potter to make characters for a large Nativity scene that was the centrepiece in the naïve. A large single candle burnt brightly above it to remind the worshippers of the reason they were there on that day.

Ben and Emma sat with Walter and Dorothy sandwiched between them. Their thoughts drifted back to their fateful wedding day. Emma caught Ben looking at the wounded statue of St. Anthony, who lost a finger on that day. They exchanged a knowing, secretive glance. Emma was not a regular worshipper, her past life experiences had severely dented her faith, but she felt some comfort now as she offered, a prayer of thanks, for although their wedding day had been surrounded by tragedy, it could have ended much worse than it did.

A blur of sad memories clouded Ben's thoughts; he stared at the statue, but his mind was far away. He thought he had long since put away the memories of Ruth, but now they escaped from deep within his mind. The sad images of her face as she lay dying in his arms surrounded by the cold water seemed quite real to him. He trembled slightly as he remembered the softness of her skin and the sweet taste of her lips. As her life slipped away, he gently kissed her eyelids as he had so often done in life. He remembered their first meeting when they were children and how beautiful and exotic a creature she had seemed to him; little was he to know the impact she would have on his life.

Emma sensed the change in his mood; it was as though a dark thundercloud had drifted across his soul. She could only guess at the reason for it, and although he eventually gave her a reassuring smile, she saw through that and thought that she could guess the reason for the change.

Could it be that after all this time, and after all Ruth had put him through he still loved her, she thought? Her seemingly settled and peaceful life was somehow under threat from the past and with the re-emergence of Annabelle, another of her school friend rivals, she felt another pang of jealousy like never before. She glanced at the statue and then at the bullet hole in the pulpit and began to weep, tiny tears that had been locked away for many years. Dorothy looked at her in surprise, but Emma gave a reassuring smile and all seemed well.

For two hours, the little church bubbled with the excitement of Christmas. Local children enacted the Nativity; a touch of realism was added by providing a baby donkey for the eight-year-old Mary to ride on. They had positioned the nativity stable where the light from the main window fell, and so the whole thing was bathed in a soft, warm glow from the coloured glass.

Then it was back to the Grange after the service for more eating and giving of gifts. Ben shook off his glum mood, but somewhere deep down there was a little pain niggling him.

Emma took Ben aside into the library. "Do you think that you will ever be shut of her?" She sounded angry but it was more that she felt hurt.

Ben sat down as if he bore a great weight on his shoulders.

"Forgive me my darling, I can't help myself. Rest assured I never, ever, loved Ruth in the same way as I do you. She was the catalyst, the reason for so much of what has happened in my life. In a way, I suppose she sculptured who I am."

"What about Annabelle?"

"You cannot be seriously thinking that Annabelle is in any way a rival…" he took a deep breath. "She was a one-off fling; she was my revenge on Ruth for her marrying, Compton, nothing more. I've not forgotten that it was she who betrayed me by telling her father, Admiral Hunter my true identity and he could have sent me to the gallows."

Emma looked sad she sat down beside Ben. "I've never felt like this, I know your past better than I really need to, I've never been jealous before," she said trembling and with tears running down her face she took his hand. "But… oh, I don't know why I'm so upset."

The Winds of Change.

"Not everything I've done in my life has been bad," he said simply. "Meeting you was another part of that journey; it has been the very best part. Perhaps it was meant to be and this was the route I needed to take to eventually find you."

It was the first time since their marriage that they had really faced the past. Emma did not mind sharing him with the children, but there were ghosts that she could never exorcise for him and it hurt her to know that.

He carefully wiped away her tears and kissed her cheeks. "I can't forget my past life and experiences, they happened and I can't change that, but I don't cherish them anymore. None of it means as much to me as my life does here with you."

The celebrations continued; each day there was a new theme, on Boxing Day; the weather was crisp and clear with a bright blue sky and so to fill their time before that day's feast they rode around the grounds and over the fells either in carriages or on horseback. It was a fun event with people shouting and waving to one and another before they retreated to the warmth of the Grange to enjoy more feasting.

The entertainment changed to outdoors where a timber stage had been constructed and large straw bales were piled high against its sides to give some protection from the weather. Other bales were arranged as seating, lanterns were hung, and braziers charged ready for lighting as soon as it was dark. In the great hall, they ate a hearty supper of beef stew and dumplings to keep them warm. There was lively chatter and raucous laughter; everyone was thrilled and excited by the prospect of the entertainment to come.

A horn was blown; it echoed loudly across the fells and gathered everyone outside. The professional team of actors marched proudly into the centre of their makeshift theatre to present themselves. Their two-hour performance was a combination of pantomime, slapstick comedy, bawdy jokes, and songs filled with near the knuckle innuendo. There were circus gymnastics, the highlight of which was a young woman walking a high wire that had been rigged between two tall poplar trees.

"They want to try that when it's blowing a force seven and the ship's bouncing about like a cork in the water," Fletch said laughing loudly at his own joke.

Emma tugged on Ben's sleeve. "I'm going to take Walter down to the front where he can get a better view." She disappeared into the crowd.

Ben felt someone push up against him. "I thought you might need warming on this chilly evening," Annabelle said, she linked up with him and snuggled against his arm.

"You don't give up do you?" Ben said.

"One way or another I usually get what I want," she moved even closer to him, "and I... want you," she said confidently her slightly husky voice barely audible above the sound of the pantomime. In an instant, she was gone, back through the throng.

When the Christmas celebrations were over and the New Year was in, there was a great deal of work to be done around the farm. Traditionally the ploughing of the arable fields started on New Year's Day and the barns were prepared for the lambing.

4. Pelican Sets Sail.

There were mixed emotions for everyone as they said their goodbyes on Pelican's quarterdeck, as she finally was ready to sail. The new crew were ready and impatient to begin their journey. Mitchell and his officers were busily checking over the final details as they waited on deck for the ebb tide to carry them out to sea.

"Good luck Captain," Ben said.

Mitchell took his hand. "Do you wish you were coming with us?"

"Yes, of course, but, I don't fancy the task of shipping convicts. However, the prospect of sailing to India and the Spice Islands is very tempting. I wish I had some better charts to offer you, but at least the ship has an excellent timepiece which will help, and of course, Mr Snow is a very able navigator."

Edward took Mitchell's hand. "It's tempting, but I must admit that farmhouse cooking and living have a lot going for them," Edward said, "Emma would kill us both if we even thought about sailing with you."

"I see that you've managed to track down some of Seagull's old crew," Ben said.

"Yes," replied Mitchell. "You remember, Mr Gill my purser, and Dr Harvey, they have both joined me again, they were working in Bristol."

"Try not to fall into enemy hands this time we don't have a spare ship to come and find you," Edward said.

Mitchell laughed loudly. "Aye, but if I know Mr Burrows, as I surely do, he'll find a vessel of some sort, I'm certain of that."

They all shook hands, it was a tense moment; reluctantly Ben and Edward disembarked. When Pelican cast off, they stood silently on the waterfront, both of them awash with a flood of emotions.

"She's as sound as any ship that sails today," Edward said, "and I know Mitchell, he'll look after her."

Ben agreed, "On his return from India, we should turn quite a profit on the venture, perhaps we should buy more ships."

Edward gave him a sideward glance but said nothing.

With the aid of two tugboats, the ship slowly moved away from her berth towards deeper water. As soon as the sails caught the breeze, the ship seemed to come to life. Everywhere there was action and movement; high above the decks, the yards were filled with sailors balancing precariously as they let out the sails. Orders were bellowed, ropes and lines were hauled upon so that the sails caught the wind. The haunting sound of a sea shanty could just be heard from the deck crew tramping around the main capstan raising the main yard. When she was set free by the tugboats, it was like setting, a young foal out into the meadow for the very first time she bent before the wind and crashed through the waves in her headlong charge for the open water.

The westerly wind soon took Pelican along the coast and out to sea. Mitchell watched Barrow disappear with mixed feelings; he had enjoyed his time on the farm away from the madness of life at sea, but every so often, the urge to stand on the seashore and watch the tide ebb and flow had been overwhelming. *Perhaps next time it will be my time to stay,* he thought.

"Mr Snow, I'll be below if you need me," he stopped as he reached the steps down to his cabin and turned back to check on his First Lieutenant.

"How are you, Mister? Would you have preferred to stay?"

Snow, who was usually a man of few words, nodded his head. "No, or perhaps yes, Captain, I thought that I might enjoy being a landlubber for a while, but I was wrong, it's not yet time for me to hang up my sea-boots."

"Well, at least we are no longer directly responsible to the Admiralty, we are free agents and once we are rid of the convicts there will be countless adventures waiting for us."

"Aye Captain, but knowing the ship belongs to Mr Burrows and our friends puts us under more pressure to get her home safely," Snow said with a worried expression.

"Let me know when we reach the Mersey."

Mitchell sat back in his chair as he studied one of his charts, he smiled when he recognised Ben's writing in its corner, it was just a simple note, mostly about some depth readings he had taken and logged.

He opened a letter of introduction about his new Ship's Master's mate: Peter Hardy. The letter was from an old and trusted Captain with whom Mitchell had sailed when they were both Midshipmen. The letter was a glowing report of the young lieutenant's abilities and reliability, and although it admitted that, the young man still had much to learn, it was still a very good recommendation.

There was a knock at his door and his steward entered with the new Lieutenant.

"Mr Hardy to see you, Captain."

"Thank you, Mr Cott."

The young officer stood to attention before the Captain's desk; he hardly moved a muscle despite the motion of the ship.

"You are well recommended, Mr Hardy," Mitchell said.

The Winds of Change.

"Thank you, sir, I'm afraid the service with the Royal Navy has become a little dull. My last ship I spent two years sailing around Scotland defending the outer islands."

"You wanted more action than that, perhaps."

"Yes, sir, my Captain recommended you, I'd also read of your exploits during the last campaign against France."

"We did seem to attain a certain amount of notoriety, which I must say was mostly due to the exploits of my Second Lieutenant, Mr Burrows. It was a big step to resign your Royal Navy commission."

"I felt it was worth it to gain experience working under your guidance sir. I intend to put in for my Ship's masters certificate on our return."

"I like a man with plenty of ambition. I'm about to inspect below decks, would you like to accompany me."

The lower deck looked a strange place; most of the armaments had been replaced by the metal cages ready for the convicts. There were only a few oil burners lit along the deck, their light was soft and warm, but the sound of the ship's timbers creaking and moaning made it an intimidating place. They walked the full length of the deck, and then down a flight of steps to what had been the main hold, where there were even more cages.

"I'm looking forward to this place being full of spices after we reach India," Mitchell said.

They descended into the bowels of the ship, here, amongst the straw and hay bales were two cows and a calf, plus numerous hens in cages. The Stockman dressed in a fawn smock and looking like a character from a painting by Constable suddenly appeared out of the hay.

"Morning Captain," he said with a cheery West Country accent that seemed to complement his attire, "any problems sir?"

"No, Mr Broughton, I just thought I'd bring our new Master's Mate down to where the real work is done."

"Ha-ha, oh aye Captain, I've always a spare shovel for mucking out if you feel the need young sir," Broughton said with a broad grin.

"I'll remember that should I feel the need for such exercise, thank you, Mr Broughton," Hardy said.

"I'll get you a couple of the convicts to help you; they'll probably be glad to be out of those damn cages," Mitchell said huffily.

Further along, was the brick-built oven that occasionally doubled as a fire for the ship's blacksmith. The baker with a small boy both of whom were covered in flour dust was hard at work kneading dough.

"Everything alright for you, Master Baker?"

"Indeed, yes sir, thank you, my son is a great worker, we'll give you a steady supply of bread and biscuits as long as we have the flour."

"We'll be stopping in the Caribbean; you must make sure you replenish your supplies there. Have you worked on a ship before?"

"Indeed, I have sir; I was your baker on the Seagull in eighteen o' five," the baker said and using a long-handled peel brought out of the oven a batch of biscuits. "Here you are Captain, try some, but be careful they're hot."

Hardy picked one up and immediately let out a yell and threw the biscuit down.

"I warned you, Mr Hardy," the baker said, he picked up two of three with his bare fingers. "Get used to the heat after a while," he said and handed Hardy a cooled biscuit. The young man still needed to juggle with it before he could taste it.

"Very tasty Mr Baker, I could be a regular visitor down here, when the Captain's not looking," he said with a wink.

Two days later, they sailed along the Mersey until they reached where they were to dock in Liverpool. By the time, they had secured the ship; lines of convicts surrounded by armed guards were being marched along the stone quayside toward them. Several officials preceded them and then stood impatiently on the dockside, one, in particular, looked highly agitated his hands were filled with paperwork. Eventually, when the gangplanks were down, the officials tried to come aboard and were surprised when they were stopped by Captain Brand's marines.

Mitchell took his time arriving at the gangplank head.

"What's the meaning of this," the prison official said indignantly, "they are refusing to let us aboard?"

"It is customary to ask permission to come aboard a ship. I am the ship's master and this is my domain; I have the right to bar or allow anyone I wish onto my ship."

"You're working for us now," one of the officials said. "And why are you so blasted late, we said eleven o'clock not…" he checked his pocket watch, "one fifteen."

"You may have given us a compulsory order to move these people for you, but that does not give you the right to board my ship or flout maritime tradition without my permission," Mitchell barked at the man.

There was an embarrassing silence, the men trapped on the gangplank fidgeted nervously.

"Very well, Captain Mitchell, could we have permission to come aboard."

The Winds of Change.

Mitchell stepped back and nodded for Brand to move his men back and allow the officials aboard.

They offered the paperwork to Mitchell who in turn ignored them.

"Mr Gill, please take care of these matters and make sure that all the paperwork is in order. I'll be in my dayroom." With a curt nod to the officials, he left them standing with open mouths.

Snow took charge, he knew his captain very well, and he realised that acting, as a transportation vessel would be a rather onerous task for him. Not that he agreed with it, but he knew they had little option other than to comply with the summons. He studied the list of convicts' names and their crimes. As they came aboard, they were checked off. Once most of them were aboard, he went to the dayroom.

"Excuse me, Captain, we are almost finished. I've been studying this list, our convicts are hardly the world's most heinous of criminals. Stealing bread, a yard of cloth, vagrancy, blasphemy; these things barely warrant an arrest let alone shipping around the world."

"There is big money in providing labour in our colonies, and this is a simple solution to our crime problem. You mention stealing cloth, console yourself with this fact, not many years ago, they would have been sentenced to the gibbet and would have been beheaded for something so trivial, at least now they have a chance, however small of starting over again."

"I'll report back when we are ready to sail," Snow said. "There is some sort of clerk waiting to see you; apparently he is to sail with us to Van Diemen's Land.

"Send him in."

The man entered rather unsteadily due to the ship's motion despite it being still tied to the dock.

"Good morning, Captain, my name is, Tristan Booth, I'm the Deputy Judge Advocate of the New Territories," he said with a pompous tone.

"You are to sail with us, sir? I was not informed; I shall have a cabin prepared for you."

"I understand that you do not approve of the transportation of convicts," Booth said.

Mitchell studied the man a moment. "There are usually some underhand political reasons for these things, but I will not allow my personal opinions to influence my judgement. We will without doubt transport these individuals for you to the best of our ability."

Snow returned. "We're casting off now Captain, three tugs alongside to free us from the river sand. Will you be coming on deck, sir?

"Very shortly, I'm afraid that you and Mr Hardy will have to yield your cabin to Mr Booth for the duration of the voyage. Make sure the prison guards are settled into their quarters. Let us make this trip as pleasant as possible for all concerned."

There was no ceremony as Pelican left the Mersey; she just slipped away with her forlorn and unhappy cargo who were trying to come to terms with their fate. Mitchell called his officers and the Ship's Purser to him on the quarterdeck. It was the first time he had captained this vessel and already he liked it; it was immediately apparent why Ben had been so pleased with it. The last time he sailed on it, was not a happy memory for him, as it was when Ben and Edward had rescued him from the French prison in Martinique.

"Gentlemen," he said, "we shall be calling on the island of Madeira where we can take on fresh supplies. I want the prisoners to be exercised every day by walking two circuits of the main deck."

"I'm not sure that's wise," Booth said.

"Mr Booth, do not presume to tell me what is and what is not wise. How many guards have you brought?"

"Ten, sir."

"If the prisoners are shackled to each other, then my marines will help with security and there will not be a problem. My orders are to deliver as many of these souls as I can in a well and fit state."

"It's just easier if you keep them below," Booth said. "This is my third trip with convicts and I know how difficult and troublesome a cargo they can be."

"I'll remind you, that these people are prisoners and not cargo."

There was a tense moment as the men sized each other up, they both knew that they had to get along somehow, but for the time being, some hostility remained between them.

"Your men will have their own mess below, you are invited to take your meals in the ship's officer's mess," Mitchell said. "Mr Hardy, Mr Snow I'd like you to accompany me below to inspect the prisoners."

In the dingy lower main hold, two rows of cells separated by iron bars had been installed. The prisoners had a forlorn weariness about them, and it was apparent that they were suffering from seasickness even though the ship had not reached deep water. Mitchell looked in on them and could not help feeling a certain amount of pity.

"Mr Booth, I don't want these people in chains below deck, it's against all maritime procedure," Mitchell said.

"I don't understand, Captain, they have to be chained."

"And what if the ship was to run aground, how would they escape? I'll remind you, sir, that they are sentenced to deportation, not death."

"Well, I'm not certain what to say," Booth stuttered.

The Winds of Change.

Snow stepped in front of Booth he was so close that their noses were almost touching.

"It is not your place to say, sir, the Captain's word is the law here and you had better get used to it or else," Snow said in a harsh whisper.

Mitchell was rather surprised at Snow jumping to his defence. "Thank you, Mr Snow; I'm sure that, Mr Booth, who is not familiar with our ways will soon get the hang of it."

Booth looked flustered; he was not used to being spoken to in this way.

"Mark my words, I shall write a full report about this incident," he said.

"That is your prerogative, but I will remind you that this is a private ship and I am responsible to the owners for her safe return."

As ordered, the prisoners were freed of their chains and exercised each day morning and evening. Doctor Harvey was as busy as the sailors were trying to treat the endless flow of seasick convicts.

"How are you doing?" Mitchell asked at dinner at the end of the first week.

"It seems to be settling down; the lower decks were awash with vomit up to yesterday, which makes the thing even worse. There are many other illnesses due to the terrible conditions that they've been exposed to in the prisons, some even have scurvy, we should improve them even on our meagre rations.

5. Joys of Spring.

Everyone at Fell Farm was in high spirits; a mild winter with very little snow had allowed the lambing to go well and for nature to take its course as it had done for countless centuries on the fells. There were a few sad moments when a new lamb died or was stillborn, but mostly it was an absolute joy to watch the new arrivals with their wagging tails suckling from their mothers. The young heifers also started to give birth just after the lambs began to appear, and everyone worked flat out night and day to make sure that everything went well.

The whole family were out picnicking in the first warm spell of the spring. Using straw bales as windbreaks, they sat on large woollen blankets watching the newborn creatures frolicking in the meadow.

"You've been in your element recently, Mr Douglas," Emma said, handing him a hefty slice of the pie.

"These wee beasties are my pride and joy these days," he said with a proud smile. "Our new herd of Highland Cattle with their long, shaggy, ginger coats and handlebar horns look at home here on these windswept fells."

"How's Hamish doing?" Dorothy asked.

The pride and joy of this new herd was a fine-looking bull, whom they had named Hamish. The animal strutted proudly around his harem.

"He's doing well, I was concerned after the drive down from Carlisle that he'd lost form but just look at him. If he's done his work, then all our Scottish ladies will bear calves. I'm looking forward to a great increase in the numbers of the herd."

For months, Jamie had been working tirelessly hour after an hour out in the fields making ready for the new arrivals. Fresh straw and sweet-smelling hay were stacked in the new timber shelters preparing them for the new season. Ben joined Jamie to watch the arrival of yet another calf.

"Just look at that!" Jamie exclaimed as a fine young bullock still wet from its birth struggled to straighten its gangly legs and stand up. Jamie wiped the animal down with clean straw making sure that its airways were clear of the birth fluid. This was the tenth healthy calf of the season and a real cause for celebration. Leaning over the gate, they watched the young fellow stagger to its feet and then take the first of its mother's milk.

"You've made a great difference here Jamie, we couldn't have made the steps forward that we have done without you," Ben said.

The Winds of Change.

Ian was helping with making sure that the calves were fed properly. "I'm sure I must be an uncle to some o'these beasties, we've got the same hair," he said tugging at his own auburn locks.

Walter sat in the straw with Dorothy, he was completely mesmerised by the miracle of birth that was happening in front of him. He studied long and hard. "I'll be a farmer when I grow up, perhaps next year," he said confidently.

"You've plenty of schooling to do first, you can nay be a farmer without it," Jamie said.

"I thought you wanted to be a sailor like your Papa?" Dorothy teased.

"Maybe I'll be like, Noah, and take my animals to sea," he shouted.

Almost as quickly, as it had started, it was over; life at Fell Farm suddenly felt very calm after the hectic months since the New Year. Physically and mentally, it had taken its toll; everyone looked exhausted by the time the last of the animals were put out on the fresh meadow grass.

Most days Ben and Edward would do the rounds going from one pasture to the next checking that all was well. The work meant long days and sometimes hard physical work, but they loved it.

Ben was leaning on the meadow gate with Edward watching the new lambs as they danced about enjoying the mild weather. "The Herdwick sheep have done well."

"Aye, the flock has more than doubled in size," Edward said, "this tough breed could almost look after themselves out here, but we need to watch for foxes, we lost quite a few lambs to them last year."

They parted at noon and Ben went back to his farm, Edward was under strict orders from Emily that he had to be back to take her shopping in nearby Dalton.

Ben kissed Emma as he entered the kitchen. He pinched a biscuit from the pile she had taken from the oven.

With a mouth full of biscuit he said: "It's time we had a housekeeper and cook, why don't you ask in the village? Emily has Glenda."

"I like doing things myself... anyway, Jenny is always somewhere about and I think that Mr Mould would be offended."

"I don't think I've had a full night's sleep for the last two months," he said and collapsed into his chair. He looked exhausted; his overalls were bloodstained and spattered with mud. "I thought we were going to lose that last ewe, her second lamb was the wrong way around and truly stuck. I'm not sure when I last changed my shirt," he said trying to wipe some of the stains from his smock.

"I don't think any of us have had much time for sleep," Emma said. "There's something else to think about too; it's Dorothy's sixteenth birthday in two weeks and we should have a special party, you know how the old crew loves a get-together, and it would be a nice way of thanking them for all their hard work."

"She's been a great help with the lambing, she's organised the Leicester's lambing shed on her own. The lads did the heavy work, but she pitched in, I think she'll make a great farmer one day," Ben said and then promptly fell asleep. He did not stir when Emma removed his boots and threw a blanket over him.

Emily's new house in Cartmel reverberated with music and laughter on the day of the party. The weather was dry and warm, but a few menacing clouds were threatening to spoil the day. There was a large marquee, big enough for all the guests to dine in was erected in the meadow, and coloured bunting dangled from trees and decorated the walls around the field. Emma, Walter, and Dorothy were greeting people at the gate as they arrived. There was a real sense of carnival as smoke from the roasting spit and music from the band blended to fill the air.

"My words, Mr Fletcher, you look quite dapper," Emma said as she greeted him, "I think that one day you will make your tailor a very rich man."

"I've had this specially made for today," he said, he stood back so that everyone could see him better. "All my life I've been jealous of the refined gentlemen in their fancy clothes, and I always promised myself that if I ever could afford it, I'd have a wardrobe of the finest suits and shirts." He pulled the jacket straight and showed off the waistcoat beneath. "Harris Tweed, the material's all the way from the Orkney Islands of Scotland."

"Oh, Mr Fletcher, be careful, or else Mr Douglas will be jealous," Dorothy said.

She reached up and kissed his cheek. "Thank you for coming today."

Fletch blushed a little. "I'd not miss it for the world. I've got a small gift for you too."

He handed her a small jewellery box, which she took excitedly. She carefully opened it and let out a squeal of pleasure as she lifted out a small golden sailing ship on a delicate chain.

"It's the Seagull, a ship we all served on. The gold came from a few old pirate doubloons that I had to hand. Whenever you want to hear a good yarn, ask your Uncle Edward about our adventures sailing her."

Ben arrived from out of the house where he had been trying to help with the preparation of the food. He was also dressed in a smart three-

The Winds of Change.

piece suit and looked every bit the gentleman farmer. Emma had insisted that he have a new suit for the occasion, which also gave her an excuse to go on a shopping spree in Lancaster with Emily and Dorothy.

"Ahoy there, Mr Fletcher, welcome," Ben said.

"Skipper, are you well?" They embraced and exchanged a few shoulder slaps.

"Yes, but we're run off our feet at the moment with the dairy."

"I've been busy up at the old cottage; the lads have replaced the walls around the top meadow and the old dormitory barn is back in use."

Dorothy cut between them linking arms. "For a couple of old pirates, you've cleaned up very well," Dorothy said, she laughed loudly.

"Don't be cheeky young mistress or there'll be no supper for you," Mould said. As usual, he was attended to everyone's needs carrying a tray of drinks.

"Have you seen Walter?" Emma asked she felt a brief flutter of panic.

"Yes, he's been helping me," Mould said with a smile. Sure enough, the lad appeared with a tray precariously balanced in his hands. With each step, it looked more likely that his cargo would end up on the floor.

"Hindering more like, if I know him," Dorothy said.

It was unusual for Walter not to be clinging to either Jenny's or Dorothy's hand, but he did like to help Mould with his jobs. With all his favourite uncles gathered together and the bonus of grandma and grandpa's arrival imminent, he was thrilled to bits.

Emma's parents arrived in a grand chaise and four, almost before it had stopped the footmen jumped down to unfolded the steps for Lord and Lady Levante to step down. The couple were modestly dressed and as soon as she was able, she found Ben and linked up with him and they walked towards the marquee.

"Now then, my boy, I understand the lambing went well," she said. "I do hope that we have lots of dancing and some good yarns from the crew tonight."

"You've been to plenty of our parties in the past, you can guess how the night will end," Ben said with a broad smile.

"Indeed, yes, I do hope that Mr Douglas entertains us with his pipes."

When evening arrived, and the light began to fade, everyone gathered in the marquee, where roasted meats and fresh bread were being served. A band brought all the way from Skipton began playing lively dance music. Around a makeshift dance floor, several torches and braziers were lit.

Ben and Edward sat like lords of the manor drinking port and smoking very large cigars. Suddenly, Walter charged out of the throng towards Edward, but twice he managed to fall headlong over the same tussock of grass before hurling himself onto Edward's lap.

"Be careful, your Uncle Edward is quite delicate these days," Ben laughed.

"His knees are not as bony as yours are Pa," Walter said cheekily. He loved all his uncles, but Edward was the one he always ran to first, he was the one to be shown the butterfly they had caught, or the newt out of the pond.

Sam the Labrador came and sniffed at the boy and then began licking his face with his great wet tongue. Walter loved it, but Ben pulled the dog away.

"Both of you sit down and behave," he said to the boy and the dog, "or you'll spend the night in the barn."

"Where do you think, Pelican will be now?" Edward said he had been busy calculating Mitchell's voyage using some of his old charts.

"I think, they should be nearing the Horn and making ready to go through the Magellan Straights by now," Ben stopped to make a few mental calculations, probably off the coast of Argentina by now. He's still a long way from home."

"Do you envy him?"

"Of course, I'd be a liar if I said any other, but I've promised Emma that my seafaring days are well astern."

"I don't think Emily would talk to us again if we were ever to set sail again."

The lively music was enticing people out of the marquee and on to the dance floor.

"This brings back a few memories of nights in the Caribbean," Edward said shaking his head. "You must sometimes think of Ruth. She was a spectacularly handsome woman." He nervously looked around to make sure Emma was not nearby.

"Each time I see Dorothy, I can't help but think of her," Ben sighed, "she was a real mystery, but unfortunately her beauty was only skin deep."

They finished their drinks and watched Walter happily playing with the dog on the grass.

"Walter, go find, Dorothy," Ben said.

The boy stood to attention. "Aye, aye, Captain," he said, trying to imitate Edward's accent, and then set off clinging to Sam's ear.

"He's a fine lad, Ben. Let's hope that he never has the urge to set sail."

The Winds of Change.

Lord and Lady Levante, Emma's parents loved the parties and they were always the first to join in with the dancing. Her ladyship caught hold of Ben's sleeve and dragged him onto the dance floor.

"Come along, Mr Burrows, you've not danced with me tonight," she said with a hearty laugh.

Despite her finest ball gown, she was happy to dance on the temporary boards laid down for the event. Ben went willingly to accompany her. He liked his mother-in-law and they always enjoyed at least one dance at a party.

"I understand that you've been invited to become a magistrate," she said as they passed on the dance.

"Yes, I think that you might have had something to do with that."

"You're an ambitious man, and it might help with your plans for the future were you to take up such a post."

"It's not something that I'd ever envisaged for myself; I think Edward would be a better candidate."

Dorothy felt exhausted and decided that she needed to find some peace and quiet. She often felt like that, one minute enjoying the crowd, then she was filled with a half-sad, melancholy, and she needed to find solace on her own. She went to find her favourite place in the garden; a wide garden bench with a latticework back and sweeping arms that had been suspended from the bough of an ancient oak to form a swing. She often sat there as still as an artist's model; her mind racing with memories of her mother, their life in the Caribbean and then their sudden departure for England. She hummed quietly to the music as she set the swing in motion, throwing her head back she closed her eyes and dreamt of the past.

She loved her new extended family; she had never had so many uncles and friends to care for her. She studied the golden ship Fletch had given to her; it brought back more memories of her earlier life in Jamaica and her mother. She sometimes missed her mother and their life in the Caribbean, but many of her memories were not good ones, particularly after her mother became sick. She distinctly remembered Ben and Edward visiting them, she was only about ten at the time and although she was not sure which island it was, she was sure that it was not when they were at home in Jamaica. She remembered thinking that Ben was the most handsome man she had ever seen, and she was sure that her mother felt the same. There was a distant, vague memory from when she was quite young and living in the Caribbean, of playing on a lawn with her mother, in the warmth of the midday sun. Unexpectedly, two tall, handsome naval officers approached them and she remembered how excited and pleased her mother had been to see them. Her mother had said that they were old friends, but she knew now that it had been Ben and Edward.

Sam the Labrador joined her and hopped up onto the seat, he wriggled until he was pressed hard up against her in the hope that she would pet him. She could not resist his charms and very soon, she had her arm around him and gently caressed his flank. She knew to expect Walter who would not be far behind his loyal friend. One of her favourite stories that her mother often told her was how she and Sir Arthur had been kidnapped by pirates and how it had been Ben and Edward ship that had come to their rescue.

The music from the party drifted through the air, she remembered how her mother loved to dance, and how on the day of a Ball before the guests arrived, she would be tirelessly dashing about to make sure every last detail was perfect. On the evening of the event, she would make a grand entrance, posing for a moment at the top of the long sweeping staircase until she was sure that she had everyone's attention, and then she would descend the stairs with such flowing grace that she appeared to be gliding down them. The women would watch with green-eyed jealousy and the men with desire and lust. She passed through the crowd like a queen with her court, smiling and benevolently nodding to her guests.

"Aha, there you are," Ben said, "I thought I'd lost you."

He took the ship from her. "What a lovely present, we are lucky to have such friends."

He placed the chain around her neck and smiled. "Pelican has never had a more beautiful mooring." As he sat down beside her, he kissed her cheek. "Are you happy with us?"

"Of course, there's nowhere else I'd rather be, I do like to go see grandpa in Bingley sometimes, but I don't miss Jamaica or my father, he was very cruel to us before we left. I was just remembering seeing you and Uncle Edward with my mother, but what island was it?"

"I think it was Barbados if my memory serves me right, we were all there for a harvest festival of some sorts."

They glided through the air on the swing. Dorothy cuddled up to Ben and interlocked her arm with his. Sam shifted slightly to readjust to her new position.

"Come on, I think we'll be missed," Ben said. "Were you thinking of your Mama? I know you do sometimes."

"Just a few minutes more," she said, "we'll wait until the next tune begins."

The Winds of Change.

When the music ended, there was a gentle ripple of applause and Ben gave Dorothy a squeeze. "Come on birthday girl, your audience is waiting."

Sam bounded away in the hope of someone else making a fuss of him.

They linked their arms and walked back to the dance area. "Excuse me, my dear," Ben said. "There is a certain duty that I have to perform."

He noticed that Mrs Cott, the postmistress and her stout husband were looking rather lost near to the dance floor; her tapping foot showed that she was desperate to join in with the dancing.

Ben approached her and said as he made a courteous bow: "Excuse me, Mrs Cott; will you do me the honour of a dance please?"

She was flustered for a moment, but quickly recovered her composure and did not need to be asked twice, a lively tune was playing, and she danced with obvious glee clinging to Ben's arm. They made two full circuits of the dance floor before the music ended.

As was usual on these occasions, Jamie and Ian Douglas prepared to perform a traditional Scottish dance. Jamie was resplendent in his Douglas tartan kilt and jacket; his grey hair was neatly plaited with its ends tied with tartan ribbons, all of which protruded from beneath the edge of his Tam O'Shanter. Over his left shoulder, he carried his pipes ready to begin accompanying Ian's sword dance.

The guests cheered enthusiastically as the couple stepped like ancient heroes onto the dance floor.

"Oh, would some Power the gift give us, to see ourselves as others see us." Jamie quoted Burns whenever he had the opportunity. "This is for you, Mistress Dorothy, to offer homage and our love to as we would say in Gaelic, our Bhana-Phrionnsa of these fells, our princess. Princess of Fell Farm," Jamie announced in his broad accent. "It's a dance, we've performed for ye before, but it is special and Ian loves this dance."

Everyone in hearing distance was amazed when Ian suddenly spoke up. "The dance is called, Ghille Chaluim, which means 'the servant of Calum'," Ian said proudly. "One story says that King Malcolm III Canmore, of Scotland, killed a fellow chieftain in battle, and celebrated by dancing over his own bloody claymore crossed with the sword of his enemy."

His dancing was a subject that he was passionate about, and so with great ceremony, he laid out his matching swords. He placed them down on the ground with great care and then adjusted their position until he was sure they were inch-perfect.

For a moment there was almost absolute quiet, only the crackle of the fires dare to make a sound. Each bar of music increased in tempo and volume until it swirled through the air like a typhoon. The hand-clapping of the guests and the sound of the pipes accelerated almost to fever pitch and then with a single yell Ian flung his arms out wide and began to dance. His feet stepped lightly over the blades, his kilt swirled as he turned on his toes and his arms stretched out with the grace of a ballerina. His audience yelled and clapped until they were almost exhausted. Eventually, Ian fell to one knee panting heavily. He lifted up one of the swords and saluted Dorothy with it.

There was rapturous applause and loud cheers for Ian and his dance. Jamie presented Dorothy with a garland made from heather, spruce and ferns, in its centre was the Douglas motif with the words 'Jamais Arriere' [never behind] and the red heart that represented their loyalty to Robert the Bruce.

"You have the love and loyalty of our wee Douglas Clan here on these bonnie fells," Jamie said proudly.

Very soon, the band was playing again and the dance floor filled once more.

An elaborate firework display was next on the agenda. The crew had spent two days organising it, the theme was a sea battle, two canvas ships had been erected, and the idea was to fire rockets between them as if they were fighting. The rockets they had made themselves, and to add authenticity they had brought a small swivel cannon from their warehouse to add sound effects.

Everyone gathered so that they could watch the spectacle safely out of harm's way. Fletch lit the first rocket which whooshed towards one of the ships before bursting into a bright blast of sparks. More rockets were exchanged and suddenly one of the ships caught light its sails blazed and flapped in the wind sending glowing embers in all directions. Unfortunately, some of the hotter embers landed in a box containing twenty rockets and some Catherine wheels and bangers. The display suddenly went to another level of excitement as the rockets from the box all set off together but in all directions. There were screeches and bangs, whistles and howls as great showers of sparks flew everywhere. It took a moment for the audience to realise that this was not part of the show and they began to panic and dive for cover as rockets screeched over their heads.

Brendon decided that he would fire the cannon anyway, despite the mayhem that was brightly filling the night sky. Suddenly, the blazing mainsail from one of the ships broke free and danced through the air like a ghostly spirit. The cannon shot caught everyone by surprise and there were several sharp intakes of breath. It was over just as quick as it had

The Winds of Change.

begun and there were spontaneous cheers and a great deal of laughter and applause as the audience showed their relief for surviving the ordeal.

Dorothy threw her arms around Fletch. "Thank you, that was the best surprise and display I've ever seen, even in the Caribbean we didn't have such amazing displays."

Lady Levante linked up with Ben as she often did.

"I hope my daughter is looking after you properly," she said with a smile.

"Yes of course," Ben said.

"You must have been lonely when you were at sea."

"I never really had time to be lonely; there was always so much to do."

"When is it time to, 'swing the lantern' as your crew like to refer to telling a good story."

"Perhaps the time is now, mother-law dear."

They built a bonfire and made sure that everyone had drinks and food; there was a buzz of anticipation because everyone knew what was to come.

Edward stepped into the light of the fire. "Ahoy there one and all it is that time when we like to spin a yarn, tell a tale, or swing the lantern."

6. Swing the Lantern

There were a number of the old crew always ready to tell a story, but they were all outmanoeuvred by Mould, who stood up and walked to the middle of the dance floor where everyone could see him.

"Swinging the lantern as we old salts like to say builds strong friendships, it is how we remember our past dramas, losses, and our fears, times good and bad, our memories softened by the passage of time. We've made them a regular feature of our get-togethers and we all enjoy them I'm sure." There were several 'ays' and other comments. "The fact is these stories are all about our lives, the characters we've met, and their effect on us. Sometimes, as rough, tough sailors, we can't find the right words to express our love for each other." There were a few catcalls, which made everyone smile. He paused a moment and then took the time to walk around the dance floor to find a better place to deliver his story.

"I remember one young man, still a teenager he was, and invited aboard Seagull by the lads of the pressgang. Pressed into service is not usually a good start, but he reluctantly joined our gun crew and seemed to fit right in. They put him with us because when he was working in the rigging he was a danger to everyone and had nearly been the cause of his own demise."

"And not just the once!" Fletch called out.

All the old crew knew to whom Mould was referring. He took out of his waistcoat pocket a worn canvas roll tied with two lengths of plaited hair.

"This is my sewing kit," he said and held it above his head, "it should be for the repairing of sails, but after this young man joined us, it was always being used for another purpose." He replaced it in his pocket. "Should he ever be knighted," there was another round of whistles and cheers. Mould raised his voice above them. "Then the sewing kit should be part of his coat of arms because he was the one who stitched us all together and brought us all here to join him and his loved ones." He smiled at Emily and bowed to Emma. "It was clear almost from the start that this fellow was a born leader and very soon he moved on up the ladder of success, but not before I needed to use my sewing kit on him a few more times."

There was more laughter, but people sensed that the story was coming and moved closer to listen.

Mould took a huge swig of ale; with the back of his hand, he wiped the froth from around his lips. "We were on a mission to relieve the

The Winds of Change.

garrison on Martinique. We thought that Napoleon's fighting fleet was all tied up in Cadiz by Nelson's fleet, but we were wrong. If I remember rightly, it was a blistering hot day, so hot the ship's timbers had to be soaked to stop them cracking. We knew that we were in deep trouble when some French warships all of which outgunned us were bearing down on us." He paused to drink. "We huddled beside our gun, perhaps hoping that it would shield us from any incoming shot. In the midst of that bloody and ferocious battle, we became locked to the enemy by our fallen masts and rigging that tangled with theirs. The men were exhausted as they tried desperately to free us from the grips of that enemy ship, but with God's help they found the strength to keep going, and to keep shooting and fending off the enemy with sword and musket." Mould turned toward Edward. "Our brave Captain standing high on the poop deck suddenly went down, the worst sight the crew can see. Mr Barraclough went to his aid, but then he too was laid low by a sniper's shot that had hit his shoulder. He called out and pointed to a sniper high in the mast of the enemy ship. It was a difficult climb at any time to reach that sniper, but after the rigours of battle, it was almost an impossible task. Our young man shinned up the main mast and was brave enough to climb from one yard to the next until he had crossed over onto the other ship." There was a pause as Mould added tension to the story. He stood near one of the blazing torches so that his face was lit by its dancing light.

"Directed by Mr Barraclough from the poop he found his way through that nightmarish tangle, I don't think any of us fancied his chances of surviving let alone reaching that sniper. At last, he reached the spar where the sniper sat. Caught by surprise the sniper turned and fired his half-loaded carbine with the ramrod still down the barrel. The rod flew through the air like a whaler's harpoon and it could have skewered our man, but he managed to dodge it or he almost managed to dodge it."

"I fell off the spar if the truth is known," Ben said. There was a ripple of laughter.

"It opened a long wound across his cheek and it was the first time I needed that sewing kit; it was not the last. I am ever grateful to that young man for leading me safely through several tight spots and dangerous places until we found this safe haven."

"Well, I've no idea who you are talking about," Edward said. Emily playfully slapped his shoulder.

There was a round of applause for Mould's story, but before he could sit down Dorothy joined him in the middle of the light.

"I love to hear your stories... but as it is my birthday, I have a request of you all, I would like to hear how you rescued by parents from the pirate gang's nest and how Uncle Edward was shot in the leg."

There was a sudden intake of breath from everyone watching. Ben glanced around his friends. "There are some stories that are best left in their box; it's not a day to remember, there are too many old wounds."

"It was my mother's favourite story, she used to tell it to me whenever I asked."

"Let's leave it for another time," Edward said.

Dorothy looked for a moment as if she was about to sulk or break into tears, but she flopped down next to Emily who threw her arm around her shoulder. In that simple act and split-second, Ben saw Ruth, she would never be caught crying. He remembered once she had fallen from a tree they were climbing; she grazed and cut her leg. She sat perfectly still on the ground, for a moment he was shocked and afraid that she had hurt herself and that she would cry, but as cold as ice she wiped away the trickles of blood from her leg and said to him, 'don't look so scared, I'm fine.' He knew differently and guessed that later she would shed a few tears.

Dorothy looked deep into Emily's eyes, "I feel as if there are secrets you all share, but you don't share with me. No one ever mentions my mother and yet they all knew her."

"You've nothing to worry about my precious, we're all one big family, and our main concern is to make sure everyone is happy," Emily whispered. "Some secrets are best left alone, there will be the right time to share them."

When the sun had set behind the distant hills and everyone was too tired to dance another step, the guests sat in a circle around one of the fires.

"Thank you, everyone, for the best birthday party ever," Dorothy suddenly chirped up.

Ben suddenly dashed away, he returned a few minutes later looking very smug.

"Well, young lady, I have another present for you," he said with his hands behind his back.

"Oh, please don't tease, what is it?"

Ben handed her a large mysterious envelope, which she eagerly opened and out glided a large ticket; she read it, and then read it again as if in disbelief.

"It's a ticket for the ballet in Lancaster at the Grande," she yelled at the top of her voice and immediately threw her arms around Ben's neck. "Oh, thank you, you said we could go one day."

The Winds of Change.

"I've booked the best box in the theatre so that a few of us can go together."

On the morning of the trip to the theatre in Lancaster, Fletch drove the beautiful landau coach from the Levante's stable so that they could all travel in style. Once it reached Cartmel, everyone was excited and several town's folks gathered to admire the vehicle.

"Quickly, all of you come and look," Dorothy shouted. She ran along the drive to one of the four matching chestnut horses to stroke its neck. "They are beautiful, Fletch," she called to him.

"And so are you this morning, Mistress, in your fine gown."

Walter was the first to climb in; closely followed by Dorothy; they wrestled a moment as they tried to fit through the doorway together.

"Can I come and ride to Lancaster with you?" he pleaded.

"No, don't be silly, it's only for us adults."

"You're not an adult," he said angrily.

"Mr Burrows, I'd like the honour of driving you today, Brendon and Bruce have volunteered to ride as guards. We are concerned that with Quigley still on the loose, that you might need some security," Fletch said seriously.

"Thank you, Fletch; I'd feel a lot happier with you all along. What will you do when we are in the theatre?"

"I'm sure we can find something, Skipper," he said with a broad, mischievous smile.

"Well, keep out of trouble; I don't want to have to bail you out of the gaol."

"Ho, ho, don't worry Skipper, you know me well enough by now."

"Yes, that's the trouble."

"What a beautiful morning," Emily observed as she waited to board the carriage. "Will we get there on time?"

"Don't you fret none ma'am, we'll have you there on time. We've even checked the tides to follow the mail coach across the sands," Fletch said joyfully.

As soon as they were all assembled, they boarded the carriage and eagerly set off. Brendon and Bruce mounted on horseback rode behind them; they were looking forward to an evening in the city.

They reached the crossing place at Kent's Bank just as the mail coach made its way onto the sands of Morecambe Bay. The ancient route across the bay saved a great deal of time, and the mail coach used it almost every week, but the sands were notoriously dangerous; quicksand, a deadly tide that slipped in as quietly as a wandering spirit, which had trapped many unsuspecting travellers.

"The mountains look so beautiful from here," Dorothy said. The beauty of the area could really be appreciated from the sands; far in the east was the broad unmistakable head of Ingleborough, still snow-capped majestic poking through a coronet of white clouds. Nearer still were the stern crags of Warton, and Arnside and to the west were the Cartmel fells surrounded by glorious woodland.

"Make haste, Mr Fletcher, it would not be an inauspicious beginning to our adventure were we all to drown," Edward called out.

"It would certainly be our last adventure was that to happen," Ben said and then laughed so much that he almost choked.

"I thought that perhaps I would be drowned whilst sailing the high seas, but never while riding a carriage across the sands," Fletch called out.

"Look at the sands, they seem flat from the shore, but it has little wrinkles and waves like the sea," Dorothy said still leaning out of the window.

Their coach suddenly splashed through a stream that meandered across the flat sand as the wheels struck harder sand everyone held onto something for dear life.

"Come in, Dorothy, or you'll be covered in sand," Emily said.

"I read a rather tragic, but slightly amusing story of a farmer and a magician who tried this crossing some years ago," Edward said.

"Is this one of your made-up stories," Dorothy asked suspiciously.

"No, honestly, their vehicle became stuck in the sand, the farmer had the good sense to unhitch the horse which he then mounted and rode to safety. The magician, however, was afraid of losing his stage props and so, he stayed with the wagon believing that when the tide came in the wooden wagon would float. The tragedy of it was that neither wagon nor the magician was ever seen again."

"That's a fine story to tell with us when we are midway across the bay," Emily said. She nudged him in the ribs.

There was a sense of relief all around when they finally reached Hest Bank and the horse's hooves could be heard clomping on the hard surface of the landing. The coach lurched as it went onto the roadway to a loud cheer from the passengers.

To the casual observer, the scene on the streets outside the theatre must have looked like complete chaos. There seemed to be hundreds of people just milling about without any obvious purpose. Some were there merely to gawp at their wealthy neighbours in their finest outfits; some were trading, selling all kinds of trinkets and wares. Fighting their way through this throng were coaches and carriages of every possible

The Winds of Change.

shape and size their drivers cursing and swearing as they tried to clear a way through.

Ben's party had to push and shove their way into the theatre where the foyer was just as chaotic as the street outside had been. Straight away, it was obvious that it was an evening of flowing gowns, sparkling jewellery, and starched, stiff collars.

"How do we know where to go?" Edward said completely exasperated.

Luckily, there was a seating plan on the wall and Ben took note of where they should be.

"If you brought us here more often, we would know where we were supposed to be!" Emma snapped excitedly.

Ben led the way up the steps, along a dark passageway and then out into their open box, which had a particularly good view of stage and theatre. The place was buzzing with excitement and chatter. Opposite their box at the far end of the stage, there was another equally Grande box. The city's Mayor, his family, and the same Town Sheriff that Ben had met at the gaol had already taken their places. They looked to be in high spirits as they sipped champagne from tall glasses.

Dorothy squeezed into the corner seat where she could look down and see the stage perfectly. They had all dressed for the occasion; the women had visited their favourite shop in Dalton and had had new gowns made. Jenny felt a little self-conscious in her fine lilac and lavender outfit, but she knew that she would treasure this moment forever.

It was a first for Edward and Ben to wear formal jackets and bow ties; they definitely looked uncomfortable constantly pulling at their collars and adjusting their ties.

"Stop fidgeting you two, you're like children," Emily snapped, she too was obviously excited by the occasion.

Suddenly the orchestra played an opening note, and a hush slowly fell over the audience. The lanterns and lights were dimmed or extinguished and there was an eerie expectant silence. As the curtains opened, a single oboe played a soft, haunting melody and in the centre of the stage stood a couple entwined in each other's arms. From then on, the audience was caught up in a magical, romantic fantasy world woven, created, and choreographed by some of the finest performing artists in Europe. It was rare that the ballet visited regional theatres, but they were experimenting with a new production that they hoped to perfect before showing it in London or Paris, which was in part why it was such a special evening, not even the royalty had seen it.

Ben was fascinated just watching the expressions on the faces of Dorothy and Emma; they were completely absorbed in the story unfolding on the stage and transported into its fantasy world; their expressions reflected every emotion of each scene. The entire audience was spellbound, and although there were the occasional ripples of applause or sighs of appreciation, mostly they sat in silent wonder. The music ended with a flourish and the lights began to come back to life.

Ben glanced across the theatre at the other large box and he was stunned by the sight of his old one-time flame Annabelle. She looked up at the same time, gave him a coy smile, and raised her hand just enough for it to be an acknowledgement. She sat very near to the sheriff and although she carried on her conversation with him, her eyes never left Ben. Guiltily, he glanced at Emma just to see if she had also seen her, fortunately, she was so busy discussing the recent performance with Jenny and Dorothy that she had not had time to look up. He touched Edward's leg and nodded in the direction of the opposite box. Edward looked back at him slightly puzzled and when Ben looked again, Annabelle was gone.

Minutes later, she bustled into their box, squeezing between the rear seats.

"Hello everyone, I didn't know that you were all ballet fans," she giggled and touched Edward's shoulder "my word Edward you are a sly old fox."

"You have friends in high places these days," Emma said. Obviously, she had seen her without letting on to Ben.

"I always did have, my dear," Annabelle said condescendingly "What do you think of Mistress Taglioni's performance? I've seen her many times; her part in La Sylphide was exceptional."

Somewhere a bell rang out to warn everyone that the second half was about to start.

"Sorry must dash... wonderful to see you all again." She stared hard into Ben's eyes. "Man of culture as well as of action these days." She was off before anyone could respond.

"Did you know she would be here?" Emma said angrily.

"Of course not, how could I? To keep it a secret from you all, I asked your mother to book the tickets for me."

"That's how Annabelle knew that we would be here, she's been staying at The Grange for the last few weeks."

"This Taglioni dancer must be very famous," Dorothy said to try to break the tension. "She must have a very glamorous life, I'll bet she's wined and dined by all the rich and famous."

The Winds of Change.

The lights faded away again and once more the music started and the performance began, but Ben noted that Emma was not as engaged in the performance as she had been and kept glancing across the theatre to the opposite box.

The performance ended with rapturous applause, flowers thrown by the audience seemed to fill the stage. The principal dancers took it in turns to accept the plaudits of the audience and then, Miss Taglioni took centre stage and the theatre erupted and showers of flowers were hurled towards her.

Dorothy was on her feet cheering wildly, throwing her arms in the air in excitement, she almost lost her balance and fell over the balcony. Fortunately, Ben was on hand and firmly took her arm and pulled her to safety.

It was cold outside, their breath hung around their faces as they spoke. Ben waved to Fletch to bring the coach forward.

"Everything all right Skipper?"

"Yes, thank you, let's get going, it's damn cold tonight."

They all snuggled together to keep warm.

"I'm glad we brought so many blankets, it could be a cold ride home," Emily said.

"We need to wait until dawn for the tide to flow out again; I've booked places for us at an inn close to the landing," Ben said.

"So how was the ballet for you?" Emma asked.

"I particularly enjoyed the music." Was Ben's only commitment.

"I thought it was wonderful, I'll remember it forever," Dorothy said.

All the rest of the journey they hummed the main musical theme, with Edward occasionally adding a baritone *la-la-la*.

The main lounge of the inn was warmed by a log fire that blazed merrily as they entered. The landlord was delighted to welcome them; he offered mulled wine and boiled beef with fresh bread made that afternoon especially for them.

"Everything is prepared as you ordered Lieutenant. So how was it, the ballet that is? Never been to such a thing myself," the landlord said.

"It was quite a spectacle; the ladies seemed to enjoy it."

"Aye well, that's all that matters, keep 'em sweet and yer dinners secure, I always say."

The following morning they were able to cross the sands back to Cartmel and a hearty breakfast.

7. Cartmel

Ben was riding out on his latest acquisition, a seventeen hand chestnut hunter, a stunning looking beast. Bent low, clinging tightly to the animal's sweating neck, he was exhilarated by its speed and power as they thundered up the hill. He tried to slow as he reached the fell-top, but the horse was fired up and it wanted to keep running, it skipped nervously letting off steam when it came to a slithering halt almost sending him over its neck. He sat for a moment to get his breath back and to admire the stunning beauty of the landscape, its patchwork of colours were a constant source of pleasure for him. It was not often that he had a chance to ride out alone, but Emma had taken Dorothy and Walter on a shopping expedition to Lancaster and now he wished that he had brought his watercolour paints with him. He cantered down the hill, enjoying the drumming of its hooves on the dry ground and then onto the road that led into the market square in the centre of the village.

It was a pretty town square, dominated by the priory that had watched the slow ebb and flow of the village for over six hundred years. As he entered the square the postmistress was frantically waving a letter at him from her doorstep.

"Coo-ee Lieutenant Burrows, a letter for you," she called, "I've no doubt that it will be from somewhere exotic. I can't help being inquisitive and wondering from where it hails," she said excitedly.

"Thank you, Mrs Cott, Yes, I was wondering about that too," Ben said getting down from his horse. "I suppose the best way to satisfy our curiosity is for you to give the letter to me so that I can open it and we can then ascertain its origins."

"Oh yes, of course, silly me," she said in a fluster. She was quite beguiled by Ben and always lost her composure whenever she saw him. To satisfy her eager curiosity, Ben broke the seal.

"Madeira, it's from, Captain Mitchell on-board our good ship, Pelican."

"Madeira, even its name sounds exotic and mysterious," she said dreamily, she tried to picture the place. "Is it a place you have visited?"

"Yes indeed, Mrs Cott, on several occasions, a green and pleasant land dominated by a volcanic mountain that reaches through the clouds, not currently active I might say."

"I would dearly love to travel," she said, she smiled at Ben as if she was half expecting him to offer to whisk her away to somewhere more exotic.

The Winds of Change.

"I have some watercolour paintings of the island, I made them the last time that I was there; I'll try and remember to bring you one."

The postmistress was satisfied with that and raced off to tell everyone that her post office was receiving mail from 'far-flung exotic places' as she would later describe it.

Ben led his mount into the drive of Edward and Emily's house. He was greeted by Glenda, Emily's housekeeper.

"Mr Burrows, what a splendid surprise, the mistress is out in her vegetable garden. I think Mr Barraclough's in the parlour, his leg's acting up again. Shall I bring tea?"

"Yes, that would be very welcome."

Edward met Ben at the door. "This is a surprise, nice to see you," Edward said. The entrance hall was filled with the fragrance of fresh-cut sweet peas a flower that was Emily's favourite.

"How's the leg?" Ben said.

"I can't get it comfortable; I think it eases it when I walk about. I've taken to using a stick. Do you think it makes me look more dignified or just older?" Edward said as he held the stick out to pose with it.

"Older, I think," Ben said with a grin.

They went into the parlour and sat down, Ben knew Edward well, and this room was such a reflection of him. He was always a meticulous dresser, his uniform, his clothes and his room were all the same, everything put away in order, neat and tidy.

Ben opened his letter he could feel the man's inquisitive stare as he impatiently waited for news. Finally, Ben looked up and put his friend out of his misery.

"Well, that seems good, Mitchell says that everything's going well, but the convicts are as ravenous as the proverbial plague of locusts, they are eating everything in sight. They were hit by a storm off Ireland, which the convicts did not enjoy and meant that most of the day's meals were washed off the decks."

Edward shrugged. "I still don't like it," he said gruffly. "Pelican was never built for such an awful duty."

"It can't be helped," Ben said. "It pays well, I suppose, but by the time we've covered our costs, there will be very little gain in it. Let's hope that his voyage to the Spice Islands and India will bring us more profit."

"Well, at least, Mitchell has his wish to follow Drake's epic voyage of discovery around the world. If he reaches India and then manages to get back here, as I'm sure he will, then the whole expedition will be a hugely profitable one."

"He says in the letter their next port of call is to be St. Kitts, I expect he is going to visit his family. His brother has a very profitable plantation on Nevis. Although I think he was at odds with him when we were last there."

"They've got the Horn and the Magellan Straights to face after that. I would have fancied it at one time, but not now," Edward said. He grimaced in pain as he moved his leg.

"You need to get that leg fixed. Is it worse than before?"

"Sometimes it feels as if the damn thing's on fire."

Glenda arrived with the tea; she gave Ben a broad smile as she passed the cup.

"How are your children?" Ben said as he took the cup.

"Doing fine thank you, Mr Burrows, Jed's working with, Mr Douglas up at the old Fell Cottage, George is still part-time at school, and Mavis is working as an apprentice milliner in Dalton as well as doing her schooling."

"I'm glad they're doing well," Ben said.

"It was a special day when you took us all in," Glenda said with a small curtsy.

Ben handed the letter to Edward and sat back to enjoy his tea. The room had a natural tranquillity; it was very typical of Emily to make somewhere feel that way. The surrounding dark oak furniture had a lingering smell of Edward's cigars; the room was laid out similar to the old parlour at Fell Cottage that reminded Ben of his teens with the Lintons and his memories of such happy times.

Edward handed back the letter. "I suppose we just have to be patient."

"Yes, I'm not very good at that," Ben said.

Edward chuckled a moment, "yes, I remember your impulsive acts getting you into trouble more than once."

At length, they wandered out into the garden, where they were greeted by orderly, almost regimental lines of hollyhocks, and lupins all waving colourful flowers in the soft breeze.

"Have you ever seen such a well-behaved set of plants in all your life?" Edward proudly said.

Emily emerged from between the stems of a cohort of tall sunflowers; her face was tanned and her rosy red cheeks glowed in the sunlight, she had her hair tied up by a headscarf and wore one of Edward's shirts tied around her slim waist with a length of cord.

"Ben!" she exclaimed and threw her arms around him. "You were a bit of a stranger this last month. You'd better have a good reason for staying away."

The Winds of Change.

The three of them sat together on the swing and it seemed like old times at Fell Cottage.

"The garden's looking spectacular," Ben said. He was pleased that the couple were so very obviously happy together.

"Thank you, kind, sir," she said with a mock bow, "and this year we've made room for even more flowering plants as well as extra vegetables. I mentioned last time we were all together that I needed help with the digging; well, Brendan and Bruce arrived the very next morning armed with spades and dug over the long section near the wall," Emily said.

"I hope Edward's doing his share."

Emily exchanged a glance with Edward.

"I suppose so, we work as a team, I grow the vegetables, and he eats them."

"Synchronised teamwork, like the best-run ship," Edward said with a broad grin.

"We've consulted a specialist about his leg," Emily said in a concerned voice.

Edward shifted uncomfortably. "He says, that there's a specialist in London who might be able to operate on it. He thinks that when the musket ball went into my leg, it split into several pieces and although some came out the other side, there might be a bit still in there and that's why I'm still getting the pain."

"Some no-goods make knife cuts in the lead so that it deliberately breaks up when it hits a target," Ben said.

Emily took hold of Edward's hand. "The doctor said that if the fragment moves it may cut off an artery or cause internal bleeding which might end up with him losing the leg."

There was a pause in their conversation; the only sound was the creak of the swing's ropes and the songs of the garden birds.

"This is a wonderfully peaceful place," Edward whispered, he hardly dared to break the silence.

"It's certainly a contrast to our past lives," Ben said.

"At long last, we've received word from Mitchell," Edward said changing the conversation.

"I trust he fares well," Emily said.

"He has reached Madeira and he is heading for St Kitts and then he'll round the Horn. I made him some charts for his journey from some that were in the old shop, but I didn't have any for the Pacific Ocean, so he will have to rely on the ones provided by the court. Once he's dropped the convicts off in Van Diemen's land, he's heading for Ceylon and

India, where he'll have to wait for the Monsoon winds on their way south to blow him back to the Horn of Africa and then home."

"Hopefully that's where we'll see a better profit from his sea-miles. Spices, silks, I'm excited at the thought of what else he might bring home."

"You make it sound easy, but it can't be such plain sailing," Emily said. "At least you both had the sense not to take the journey."

Ben and Edward exchanged a knowing glance.

"Don't look like that, Emma would kill you if you were to put to sea again," Emily said scowling at them both. "How's Dorothy doing?"

"Very well, she dotes on Walter and he follows her around like a lost duckling."

"Have you told her yet?"

"No, I'm waiting for the right time."

"Good God, man, you need to tell her before someone else does," Edward said.

"I can't, she still thinks the world of Ruth. I don't know how to tell her, I'm afraid that she'll somehow blame me."

"Well, let's be honest, it is your fault."

"Edward! How can you say that? Ruth brought about her own sad demise," Emily said as she jumped angrily off the swing.

"Edward's right."

"No, never! You suffered years of self-recrimination for her selfish act. You've nothing to be guilty about. What did, Captain Mitchell say at your court-martial? He said that you were only guilty of honour. You covered for her and made excuses for her and nearly went to the gallows for her. You've nothing to regret on that score," Emily said. "Where is the rest of your tribe?"

"Shopping, they'll be here with the mail-coach later this afternoon."

Later that afternoon, back at his farm, Ben sat alone at the kitchen table waiting for Emma to return. He was trying to clear the clutter of thoughts that seemed to be filling his mind, there was always so much to do and think about with the farm. His thoughts were suddenly disturbed by Jenny bringing in a new batch of butter from the dairy.

"Hello," she said with her usual chirpy voice, but then stopped to look at him, "Are you alright? Your complexion is quite grey."

He smiled at her. "I'm afraid some of my old wounds have finally caught up with me, maybe it's the onset of old age, but I seem to have endless aches and pains these days."

"It's the cold weather and old age," she said giggling.

"My shoulder aches like the devil has a hold of it."

The Winds of Change.

She placed her hand where she knew instinctively the pain would be; after all, she had been there the morning he had been shot in the back. Through the material of his shirt, she could feel the rough scar tissue on his back. She shuddered when she thought of the dread that had gone through her mind as she heard the shot and then saw the blood seep through Ben's clothes.

Her hand felt warm and soothing to him, he placed his hand on hers.

She never loses her magic, he thought; *somehow, she always manages to make me feel better.*

"How many years ago was it that we were with Mace's gang?" she said.

"It must be at least twenty, maybe more."

"We must have looked a dreadful sight as we crept through that town."

"Yes, do you remember we bobbed in and out of the doorways like frightened rabbits," he said smiling at the thought of it.

"If that old musket the constable shot at us had been more accurate or in better condition, well then I don't suppose that Reverend Baxter's household would have been able to repair you."

She hummed a little tune as she waited for the kettle to boil.

"I've missed having Walter about this morning, he says the funniest things. I wonder if he will be a farmer, or will he go to sea like you did when he grows up?"

She poured the tea and carefully unwrapped the butter for Ben to inspect.

"It's looking good," he said. He was about to pinch a taste of it, but she smacked the back of his hand as though he was a naughty child.

"We can't keep up with the demand for it, Tim is thinking of talking to you about extending the dairy."

"Hum, well it seems as if you have already mentioned it, I'll pretend I Don't know."

She took hold of Ben's hand and stared into his eyes. "Do you ever think of that winter we spent together in the snow?"

Ben toyed with the butter a moment. "I suppose that every time it snows it brings back a few memories; I couldn't have survived without you."

They were standing very close to each other, so close that Jenny could feel his breath on her face. From beneath his shirt collar, he pulled a leather thong with a tiny rabbit's foot attached.

"One of your gifts that Christmas," he held up the rabbit's foot, "has saved my skin all my life and has always brought me good luck."

For a moment, it was as if a magnet was pulling them together, but somehow Ben pulled back and went back to his chair. Jenny smiled contentedly and drank her tea.

8. A New Vicar.

After Easter that year, Mr Bright the vicar of St Anthony's announced that he was retiring and he had already requested a replacement, who was due in the parish the first of the following month.

To wish him well they held a party at the manse and as soon as he departed, the women of the parish worked hard for three days preparing the manse for the new vicar to arrive and of course, the topic of conversation for those three days was the new man.

"Well, I understand that our new vicar is not a married man," Glenda said in a rather critical tone.

"Ha-ha, so those with unattached daughters will be regular callers I presume," Emma said. She was busy trying to remove some unpleasant looking stains from the hearth.

"A man of the cloth is no great catch unless he has an independent wealth of his own. Do we know if he is looking for a wife?" Emily asked.

"Well, that's not the issue, should the vicar be single?" Glenda asked from behind the cupboard where she was polishing the floor.

Emma smiled. "They are all single at some time, that is until we enlighten them and make them realise how necessary we are to their well-being."

Glenda raised her head. "Some of them never get the message."

Emily was curious, "So what age is this, vicar?"

Mrs Potts checked over her shoulder to see who was listening. "I did see his application by way of a letter; it said he was twenty-nine years old. Not that I was being nosey, but the letter just happened to fall off the table and by chance landed open upon the floor, I couldn't help but see some details."

"Oh, very interesting, in his prime as you might say," Emma said.

Glenda stood up. "Men are never in their prime; they start off as small boys and progressively retard from there. The older they get the further away from their prime they are."

"I think you have quite a jaundiced view of men," Emma said.

"If you'd had my experiences with men, you'd know why," Glenda said, she smiled and shook her head in that knowing way.

By the evening, they were very pleased with their efforts, and the house was ready for their new vicar. Mrs Potts made a tour of inspection before finally passing it off as fit for purpose. She was something of an odd woman who always seemed to wear the same dress, which she protected from the ravages of housework by a wrap-around-apron. To keep her hair tidy she wore a pure white mop cap with a lace trim around its edge that fitted snugly on her head. Although she could seem fierce, she had a generous heart and her cooking was legendary.

On the day that he was due to arrive, there were several locals gathered to greet him; small boys had been strategically placed along the lane with the instruction that as soon as they saw someone approach they were to hotfoot it back to the manse.

The kettle was constantly on the boil as endless cups of tea were made and drunk. Quite a few of the parishioners were not sad to lose Mr Bright, who they said had only had one thing on his mind for the last two years, which was his approaching retirement and so they were looking forward to a younger man as vicar.

Fresh cut flowers decorated every room of the house. Just before noon, the boys came charging back excitedly announcing the vicar's arrival. Everyone gathered in the garden to catch a glimpse of him.

Mrs Potts nervously took hold of Emily's hand. "I do hope I get on with him."

"You'll be fine, once he's tasted your wonderful cooking he'll be putty in your hands."

A flat cart towed by a heavy horse that would have been more at home between the traces of a dray slowly plodded up the lane. The new vicar, who was dressed in a very sombre black coat held an umbrella above his head to protect himself from the sun. Behind him on the back of the wagon, was a tidy pile of travel trunks and a few household goods, including a rocking chair.

"He's younger than I thought he'd be," Edward whispered out of the corner of his mouth. "Looks like he intends to stay, even Emily couldn't pack that much stuff."

"Hmm, I seem to recognise him," Ben whispered back. He studied the man and he was sure they had met before.

The vicar closed his umbrella before he stepped down from the wagon. He was tall and handsome, his face was positively beaming with pleasure and there was an expression of sheer delight when he saw the gathered crowd. In fact, he was almost moved to tears by the welcome. To cover his embarrassment and to help control his emotions he made straight towards Emily.

"Mrs Linton, I'm so glad to see you again, I would have recognised you anywhere."

She was taken aback by the greeting and tried desperately to remember where she should know him from. "I'm Mrs Barraclough these days," she said simply.

The Winds of Change.

"My sincerest apologies, I'd not heard that you had remarried," he beamed at Edward, "and you are Mr Barraclough." They shook hands. He moved on and quickly approached Ben.

"Ben Stone, you don't remember me." He studied Ben's face and inspected the scar on his cheek. "I remember your arrival here, skinny and pale. If I remember rightly, you had a gunshot wound in your back and by the scars on your face; it looks like you've been in one or two scrapes since.".

"I'm Ben Burrows now," Ben laughed. He found that he was taken in by the man's excitement and joy.

The vicar giggled childishly. "How life twists and turns, I'm David Hardwick, I was David Toons when I lived here as a youth."

Emily's jaw dropped as she studied the new vicar's rather pale face. "Oh my words, now I remember you; you were with us for about three years," Emily said, "I'm so sorry for not recognising you."

"That's perfectly understandable, but it was longer than that, I was here almost seven years. I had such good luck after leaving here, and thanks to Linton's teaching and example, I was able to make the best of my new life."

The party moved indoors.

"I thought I recognised you, but I was not sure and I could not put a name to you," Ben said.

Emma and Dorothy stepped forward to meet him.

"This is my wife and our ward."

David shook their hands in quite a dainty way. Emma was intrigued by the man's story and linked up with him to escort him into the parlour.

"Is it a coincidence then that you have returned here?" she asked candidly.

"To be truthful, it's a long story, but I was so inspired by, Linton, as we all called him, that when I heard that Mr Bright was to retire I applied for the post immediately. I've been working quite near in Malham, but this seemed the obvious choice for me. I'm so looking forward to seeing the church again, and the cottage I have a wealth of happy memories about the place."

"We've taken the liberty of engaging, Mrs Potts for you as housekeeper; she has worked at the manse for many years."

"You are so very kind, I'm sure she will be perfect. It seems that we all have a great deal of catching up to do, just to know who we all are." He laughed slightly embarrassed but soon recovered his composure.

Emily felt immediately that he was going to fit in. The postmistress shook his hand and almost curtsied to him as she explained her role in the community.

"My dear, Mrs Barraclough, do you still reside in Fell Cottage?"

"Alas, no, there was a fire a few years back which gutted it. We live down in Cartmel, where I run a little school."

"Marvellous, you were such a good teacher; I'd say you were gifted at it."

It was obvious that the new vicar had something on his mind. "I'd love to see the church before tomorrow's service. I remember it as such a tranquil place."

"Very well, I'll escort you there myself," Emily said, she was still trying to place the man.

It was only a short walk and there was an air of anticipation as everyone marched up the hill. Edward tried to put on a brave face, but his limp was quite pronounced and it was obvious that he was in pain. Emily took his arm and helped him as much as she could. They paused by the gate and Hardwick smiled benevolently at his new flock.

"Wonderful, it is just as I remember it. Stepping through these gates again is the culmination of many dreams," he said tearfully. He pulled a large white handkerchief from his pocket and loudly blew his nose.

Ben held the church door open for the vicar. Hardwick paused and seemed to take a deep breath before he entered. Once inside, he took another deep breath as if absorbing everything about him.

"This is perfect," he said, his face seemed to light up the entire building.

"Is this is your first appointment?" Edward enquired.

"Not quite, for about a year I've been assistant to the vicar at St Mathew's in Malham. I've done military service too; I was a Padre with the Yorkshire Regiment at the Battle of Waterloo."

He caught sight of the bullet hole in the lectern and the little statue of St Anthony, that had lost its finger, sheared off by the bullet that was intended for Emma.

"Oh, it looks like there have been some very interesting events here too." He touched the small stone hand. "My, my, I do believe I've come to the right place, I feel at home already."

The party returned to the manse where Mrs Potts and Mould were waiting with refreshments.

Eventually Ben and David found time to speak together.

"Whenever I could, I followed the events here and also your adventures in the navy which have been widely publicised. I must confess that when I read about Linton's demise, I was heartbroken, such a shame he was certainly one of a kind. I also heard about your wedding day, Reverend Baxter, who performed the ceremony is a well-known

The Winds of Change.

columnist with the Times I suppose that's how our saint lost his finger," David said.

"Yes, I'll tell you about it sometime."

"Mrs Linton, oh, I mean Barraclough looks very happy; I couldn't imagine her with anyone else but Linton."

"Mr Barraclough and I sailed together. He's just right for her; he's a damn fine man."

The next day, the church was full to capacity, everyone expectantly waiting to see and hear their new spiritual leader. The old wheezing organ had recently been replaced by a new one; Ben had commissioned a leading London organ builder to provide a suitable instrument. To the delight of the organist and the congregation, its music filled not only the church but also the surrounding meadows with song.

"My first sermon to you all is a rather fitting one because I intend to use the parable of the Prodigal Son." As usual, his smile was radiant and the whole congregation warmed to him. The timbre of his voice was almost perfect for the church's acoustics.

"There are several candidates here, including myself, who have travelled far away and lived a life somewhere else, but there is… dare I say, an almost mystical aura surrounding this place that draws its lost children back to it." He was like a snake charmer hypnotising his congregation with his soft, comforting tone. It was not a strong, deep manly voice such as Linton's had been, it was more like a refreshing light breeze that wafted around the congregation.

After the service, the whole congregation was invited to the manse for tea. Mould was on hand to help Mrs Potts and to organise the other volunteers. The fine weather allowed the congregation to spill out into the garden and stroll through the well-kept rose garden.

"Well done, Mr Hardwick, a most enjoyable sermon," Ben said.

"Why not call me, David; I remember it was always first name terms when Linton was here."

"Yes, very well, welcome back to the Fell Farm Family, David," Ben said and shook his hand again.

"I hope we will become great friends," David said.

"Yes indeed. You may remember Tim; he works in our dairy in Alithwaite. You must come and have dinner with us one day; we can catch up on old times."

"So, what I heard about the shooting at your wedding was it true?"

"I don't know what you heard, but yes, unfortunately, a sad affair."

"I'm being very nosey, but was she a jilted lover," he whispered the words under his breath.

"No, not at all, it is far more complicated than that, she was ill and her mind was affected by laudanum."

"It must have been hurtful to all concerned, especially your bride."

"I think that we are over it now."

"I see that you have a son too, that's a blessing."

"What about yourself, why no wife?" Ben enquired.

"I've never really found the right woman. I saw such awful sights as a padre in the army, I'm sure you must have seen dreadful things when fighting on board your ships. I had several very sombre years afterwards, I became a little bit of a recluse. Fortunately, I too managed to put the past behind me."

"I saw you at Linton's grave this morning," Ben said.

"Yes, he was a one-off, I was seeking inspiration, over the years I thought about him and about life here so often, and it always brought comfort. I occasionally wrote to him and he would always promptly reply."

9. Surprise in the Churchyard.

Reverend Hardwick settled into his new parish very quickly and at times, he felt as though he had never left. He had felt great sorrow when he saw Fell Cottage in its burnt-out state. Most of it had fallen down, a few blackened roof timbers were still visible and reminded him of a well-picked carcass, but most of what was left was now almost totally covered by ivy and other trailing weeds.

Up with the lark one morning, he was in a very determined frame of mind; his heart was set on making a difference at St Anthony's. Mrs Potts made him slow down, to eat a hearty breakfast, reprimanding him for being in such a hurry.

"It's not good for a man to be off without his breakfast… the jobs will wait for you," she told him.

"My mind is running wild with ideas; I can hardly sleep for them."

"Ideas are all well and good, but nothing ever came of having an idea on an empty stomach."

"I want to stamp my mark on the place; if I am only half as successful as Linton was I will be satisfied." He ate an egg then wiped his face. "I love our little church; there are so many happy childhood memories here with the Lintons and the other children of that time. As much as the church building has been well maintained, it seems to be lacking something; as yet, I'm not sure what."

"Well eat your breakfast first."

"I've got a burning compulsion to give as much back as I can to this place, I already feel at home here. Linton's philosophy of life and his example has inspired me ever since the day that I first arrived at Fell Cottage. I pray that I can set an example too," he said passionately.

Mrs Potts eventually cleared the table. "Now off you go," she said as if talking to a small boy, "Lunch will be at twelve-thirty and don't forget Mrs Clarke will be here at two o'clock to talk about the Sunday-School."

He sang boldly as he marched up the road towards the church and felt full of zeal for the tasks ahead. He could not resist stopping to pick a few ripe, shinning blackberries to eat on his way.

He sang at the top of his voice as he pushed open the gate into the churchyard, but then he suddenly realised that there was a strange eerie stillness about the place. Usually, the jackdaws were squabbling in the trees fighting for a place amongst the branches, the sound of their beating wings and hoarse calls filling the air, but not this morning. With a racing uncertain heart, he cautiously stepped along the path. As he neared the church, he caught sight of what he at first thought was a bundle of clothes near the church door, sometimes people did leave things to be handed out to the poor.

When he reached the bundle, he was shocked to realise that it was not a pile of old clothes, but in fact, the body of a woman. He said a very quick prayer and knelt beside her to see if she was still alive. To his relief, he could feel a very weak pulse. He tried to lift her, but she was too heavy and he knew that he could not carry her very far.

What shall I do? I need to fetch Mrs Potts, no, I need to fetch the doctor, and then bring Mrs Potts here.

He made the woman as comfortable as he could by placing his jacket beneath her head and then ran as he had never run before back to the manse yelling out the name of his housekeeper all the way.

Mrs Potts was out in the garden picking peas for their tea. She saw the vicar running like he was being chased by the devil and she immediately went into a state of panic.

"Oh, Mr Hardwick what on earth is the matter?" she called long before he reached the garden.

"Quick, Mrs Potts there is not a moment to lose, there's a woman in the churchyard and I fear that she is barely clinging to life. I have no idea what ails her. Please go attend to her, I'll ride into Cartmel and find the doctor."

While Mrs Potts hurried to the churchyard, he rode as fast as he could into Cartmel. Edward was just leaving the post office as Hardwick clattered along the street. He stepped out into the road to see what his hurry was.

"Now then, David, what's to do?"

"I must find the doctor, there's a woman half-dead in the churchyard."

Edward was never one to panic. "Don't worry, I'll fetch the trap and meet you up there. Emily is teaching her class this morning, but she'll come along when I tell her."

Edward went into his house. "Glenda," he bellowed from the hallway "there's an emergency up at the church; you and Emily are needed, go find her please."

As always, he was as solid as a rock in a crisis, it was something that he seemed to thrive. He knew where some of the crew were working and headed for them.

"Bruce," he called over the paddock wall.

"Ahoy there, Mr Barraclough, what's the hurry?"

"Over to the Skipper's as quickly as you can; tell him I need him up at St Anthony's straight away."

Within an hour, they were all gathered in the little churchyard.

The Winds of Change.

"Do we know who she is?" Ben said.

"No idea, but she looks familiar," David said.

They moved her inside and placed her on a makeshift table. The doctor examined her. "There are no wounds, there are some old injuries, I think she has had a broken arm at some time which has not set properly, but she is very thin, she may not have eaten for days."

They gave her a drop of brandy, which seemed to revive her a little.

"Child," was all she said.

"What's your name?" Emma asked.

"Child"

"Is your name, child?"

The woman shook her head and began to sob.

"Let's take her to the manse," David said. "Mrs Potts go prepare a bed for her and make some tea."

Ben and Bruce searched the churchyard looking for clues as to whom the woman was and why she was there. Tim and Jenny arrived and joined in with the search.

"I've not seen her about anywhere, I'd guess that she's about our age," Ben said. After searching the churchyard for a while, they decided that there was nothing to find.

"There's nothing here, come on we'll go to the manse," Ben said.

Behind the church by the old cottage, Brendon and Ian Douglas were helping Jamie to move their herd of Galloway cattle to their fresh grazing in the lower pasture. They had no idea of the drama that was unfolding on the other side of the church. Quite often, their route would take them past the old burnt out, cottage and they would talk about their early days there. Suddenly, as they were walking Ian went down on one knee as if stalking some prey, the others followed but were not sure why. Ian held his hand up to keep everyone quiet, and then stealthily moved forward as if he was on the trail of a deer out on the fells. He dropped to his knees again and remained perfectly still. Brendon was about to ask what they were doing, but Jamie silenced him with a movement of his hand.

Like a big cat stalking its prey, Ian moved gingerly forward one step at a time. He was almost up to the wall of the cottage when he paused again. A diminutive figure crept out from amongst the rubble. The child had a knitted shawl around its shoulders and straight dark hair that had been cropped short in a crude fashion.

"Don't be afraid, wee lassie; I'll do ye no harm," Ian cooed.

The child, with eyes as big as dinner plates stood still unsure what to do. She almost bolted when Jamie and Brendon stepped towards her, but Ian held out his hands to her and she remained.

"Now where has she sprung from?" Jamie said.

They all knelt in front of her so that she would not be intimidated by them.

"What's your name my darling," Brendon said.

The girl did not even try to speak she just stared at them.

Jamie pulled a piece of bread from his rucksack and held it out to her.

"Are you hungry, little one?"

The girl took the bread and ate it greedily filling her mouth. She started to cough and Jamie offered her his hip flask, she took a swig and then coughed even more.

"Was that whiskey?" Brendon said.

"Aye, we feed it to the bairns all the time, it can't harm them."

"Well, I never believed that wee bairns came from beneath gooseberry bushes, but now I'm not so sure," Ian said.

"We'll take her down to Emily's with us, she'll know what to do," Jamie said.

Brendon held out his hands to the girl and she went to him, he picked her up and carried her on his broad shoulders. The girl was at first a little frightened, but after a few paces, she began to enjoy the ride.

When they reached the manse they were surprised to see Edward standing by the gatepost; he looked very serious and studied the girl. "Did you find her by the church?"

"She was by the old cottage. Do you know anything about her?" Jamie said.

Brendon helped the girl back to her feet.

"I fear that we may have her mother inside, Hardwick found her outside the church, but it doesn't look good," Edward said.

Jenny took the girl with her into the parlour. "Here my little precious sit on your Aunty Jenny's knee."

The girl snuggled up to Jenny and almost instantly fell asleep. They placed a blanket over the two of them and stirred the fire into life.

Upstairs Emma and Emily were trying to make the woman comfortable, but there was little that they could do.

Mrs Potts arrived with a bowl of warm milk and bread. "This might help the little love to come around a bit."

When the doctor arrived, she had slipped into a deep sleep.

"There's not much I can do now; we can only wait and pray."

The Winds of Change.

The vigil went on for several hours, but inevitably, the woman gave up the ghost and died without revealing anything of her circumstances.

"What shall we do now," Mrs Potts said tearfully mopping her cheeks with her apron.

"Our first concern now is for the child," David said.

They sat in the parlour discussing what could be done. Emily was sorely tempted to volunteer to take the child in, as she had done so many times in the past, but before she could speak out, Jenny surprised everyone.

She put down the child, grabbed Ben by the sleeve, and almost dragged him into the kitchen closing the door securely behind her.

Ben could see that she was in an anxious state. "Tim and I have prayed so often to be blessed with a child," she said passionately. "The Lord has brought the woman here because he knew the child would be welcome and find a home."

Ben looked a little aghast at her, but before he could speak, she placed her fingers to his mouth. "I know what you are going to say," she said with tears flooding down her cheeks, "I know that I can never have a baby, but I've never dared tell Tim nor have I ever given up hope. I miscarried at just twelve years old; the women that attended me said I was lucky to be alive, but that I could never have another." She wiped her nose with the back of her hand, and then Ben gave her a handkerchief. I've no idea who the father was because I'd been used by so many men. You often asked me why I stayed with Mace; he rescued me from the brothel my parents sold me to."

"Tim would have understood, he's a kind man," Ben said.

"Tim was so determined that we should have a child, I didn't dare tell him; how could I shatter his dream?"

Ben nodded and embraced her. "You'll make wonderful parents," he whispered in her ear.

They joined the others where Emma gave Ben a very suspicious glance.

"I would like to keep her and bring her up as my own," Jenny said engulfing the child in her arms.

Tim looked aghast at her for a moment, but then he smiled and touched Jenny's hair. "Yes, we'll look after her and we'll bring her up, she'll certainly have plenty of milk to drink."

"If you are sure, and no one objects, well then, I think it would be an ideal solution," Emily said.

"I think that we need to make enquiries to see if she has family nearby. Someone may know who the mother is and why she came here," Edward said.

"Then why did she come here if she had another family?" Emma said.

The doctor entered the room; he had been with Mrs Potts preparing the body for the undertaker.

"The woman died of malnutrition I am certain of that, but she has had a poor life; there were some old injuries, bruises, cuts and the like. You may bury her as soon as the undertaker has finished with her. Would you like me to arrange for the child to be taken into the workhouse in Lancaster?"

There was a gasp of horror from Jenny.

"Definitely not, Doctor, her future is secure with us, we'll look after and care for her," Tim said. "We'll bring her up as if she is our own."

The doctor nodded his acceptance and left.

"We shall baptise her; it will be my first baptism here. We will thank the Lord for her and for her future," David said.

Jenny had been adjusting the child when she pulled a scribbled note out from beneath the shawl, she handed it to Emily.

Emily read it. "It says that the child is three years old, but it doesn't say her name."

"I'll call her Eve, I think it's very fitting," Jenny said.

Emily continued to read the note. "The mother was called Alyssa… goodness me, I remember her now she stayed with us and was one of the last to leave when Linton became too ill for us to run the orphanage," Emily said.

David turned pale. "Oh heaven forgive me, I remember her too, both here and when I was working in Malham, I saw her there. She was still single, but I'm going back over ten years, maybe fifteen," he said. "If my memory serves me right, she attended the funeral of one of her adopted parents, but I don't remember any details. We did speak, she recognised me from here, but I'm sorry to say I did not have very much time, I was busy helping with the ceremony."

Mrs Potts brought tea for everyone.

"Such an unnecessary tragedy," Emily said, "if only she had come to us earlier."

"We don't know her circumstances or what eventually brought her to our door," Edward said.

"When she is old enough, can she come to your school, please, Emily?" Jenny said.

"Of course she can," Emily said, she gently touched the child's face "and I think that little Eve will be a star pupil."

All the way back to their cottage Jenny held Eve tightly in her arms and whispered to her.

The Winds of Change.

"What on earth are you telling her?" Tim said as they pulled up outside their door.

"I'm telling her what a wonderful time we are going to have. She's going to get all the love that we should have had when we were children."

"We don't have a bed for her."

"We'll find something."

Jenny stirred the fire and then sat Eve on the hearthrug wrapped in a blanket. She could hear Tim dragging something in from outside and the occasional curse as he hit a problem. He appeared in the doorway with a large wooden crate.

"This will make a very suitable bed for her," he said, he looked pleased with his find. "It even has sides like a cot."

Jenny studied it for a minute. "Yes, we will make a mattress of straw and blankets and you can put it on blocks to make it clear of the floor."

Emma knocked on the door and peered in.

"I've brought some soft wool blankets for Eve."

She could see the pleasure and satisfaction in Jenny's face as she handed them over.

"You'll make a wonderful mother and she'll be a new playmate for Walter, he can't wait to see her," Emma said.

It took several weeks for Eve to settle in. The food and love given to her by Jenny worked wonders, she was soon feeling at home, and although she had been quiet at first she soon came out of her shell.

Ian and Jamie called in one day with several packages.

"What's all this," Jenny asked.

Jamie handing over the packages and with a broad smile across his face he said: "We wanted to help, so we arranged for Emily to buy some clothes for Eve."

Eve became a little bit emotional and tears ran down her face as she opened the parcels. "That was a kind thought," she whispered, "I'll call her, she's helping Tim in the dairy. She'll be under his feet no doubt." Tear stained but glowing with happiness she hugged them both.

Emma and Dorothy called in too, and it was not long before Walter arrived from the paddock where he had been with Ben.

"It's like having a little sister," Walter said.

"It's time that you had a sister or maybe a brother." She dug Ben in the ribs with her elbow. "Yes, we should have more women around here, we're outnumbered," Emma said with a bright smile.

10. Kidnapped

On the morning of Emma's birthday, he unveiled his very special present to her. A brand new bright yellow gig, he had commissioned it to be specially made for her. It was locally made, with a weatherproof hood that could be folded back on sunny days and iron suspension springs beneath the bench seat to try to improve the ride over the bumpy roads.

Emma hugged Ben when he brought her out from the kitchen to see it.

"It's a wonderful gift, thank you."

"Now you can do your shopping when I'm busy with other things," Ben said.

"You mean that you can get out of our shopping excursions."

Ben found a letter pushed under the door, he read it in secret while Emma was busy in the kitchen.

"Have you seen the post today?" he asked Emma.

"No, I've not seen anyone."

"I need to speak with Edward this morning, but I'll be back this afternoon. If you use the gig, don't go too far; remember Quigley is still on the loose."

"Are you alright?" Emma said.

"Yes, of course, no problem, I'll see you later."

Ben rode over the fells to Edward's house with the letter hidden in his jacket pocket. Emily greeted him at the door and asked how everyone was. "We'll be over later to celebrate Emma's birthday," she said.

Ben sat opposite Edward in his parlour and waited for Emily to leave them alone.

"What's your problem?" Edward said.

"How did you know that I had one?"

"I know you too well my old shipmate, come on out with it."

Ben took the letter from his pocket.

"This was pushed under the door this morning. I'm to go alone and meet a man named Tobias Drake, he'll be able to tell me where to find Quigley," Ben said. "I'm to meet him in an inn named 'The Slaughtered Lamb,' in the town of Ulverston at eleven-thirty this morning. I Don't want you to tell anyone else, especially not Emily, she'll worry too much."

"It could be a trap, I'll follow you at a distance, cover your back sort of speak." Edward was worried, it sounded too suspicious and seemed

The Winds of Change.

too unlikely to be true but he thought Ben was grasping at straws and knew that it was no use trying to talk him out of going.

" Maybe you are right. I shall have to take that risk, but I must be alone, I dare not jeopardise this meeting by having someone with me in case it spooks this man, Drake."

Edward could see Ben's mind was set.

"Be careful," Edward said.

Ben set off, the weather was very changeable and suddenly a squall blew along the coast, it was wet and miserable with a fine, almost invisible drizzle that wets one through to the bone. Ben pulled the brim of his hat down as he headed into the wind. He pushed hard despite the weather and he was soon in Ulverston. He left his mount with the ostler at the inn; it brought back memories of his uncle's inn in Bingley where he did just that job as a boy. He paused as he thought about meeting Ruth there for the very first time, *I'd only be about six,* he said out aloud.

The interior was as drab and as dingy as the outside was. There were only two other men in the room apart from the old man behind the bar reading his paper; one was playing cards, some kind of solitaire, while the other sat and watched him over the top of his tankard, neither of them looked over to Ben nor did they even acknowledge that he was there. Ben bought a flagon of ale and took a seat near the window. He could see the almost deserted street through the rain-streaked leaded glass. A wagoner with an oilcloth cape was cursing his young assistant as he tried to roll the wet, slippery barrels from the back of his wagon. Another old character leaning heavily on a stick trudged along the street; there was no joy in his movements, his painful joints, making every step feel as though he was being tortured.

Ben was beginning to get impatient and when he heard a local church clock strike twelve he decided that for some reason he had been sent on a wild goose chase. He checked his pocket watch just to confirm the time and then decided not to wait any longer. He nodded to the old man behind the bar as he left, but there was no response; Ben wondered about checking to see if there was still any life there. The ostler greeted him with a cheery smile as he walked his horse out for him.

"Rain's stopped," the lad said.

Ben walked his mount out of the inn's yard and back onto the street.

The lad was right, at least the rain has stopped, he thought. He was about to mount up when a familiar figure dressed in a bright blue coat, carrying a matching umbrella, walked along the road towards him. By the sway of her hips and her feline grace, she was instantly recognisable.

"Why, Lieutenant Burrows, Ben, what a pleasant surprise." Her bright and cheery voice seemed out of place in that dull grey street.

"Annabelle, what are you doing here?" he said suspiciously.

"Don't look so surprised. I might ask you the same question. Are you following me, Ben Burrows.?"

"Certainly not, I was due to meet with someone, but they've not shown."

"A clandestine tryst perhaps?" she smiled a knowing smile. "My favourite milliner is along here, I call whenever I'm in the area. Perhaps, you would be so kind as to escort me; there are quite a lot of undesirables here these days."

"It's they who need to worry about an encounter with you, they should be wary if they were to have any sort of dealings with you."

"Always the tease," she laughed throwing her head back.

There were several people on the street, Ben scrutinised them all as they passed, in the hope that they were the ones he was to meet. He could not help the occasional glance at her too, she was a very attractive woman; her stylish clothes and relaxed walk made her quite alluring.

"Ha-ha, here we are," Annabelle said. She placed her hand on the door handle but then paused a moment. "How is the family? I think it is Emma's birthday today if my memory serves me right." She stared hard into his eyes, and casually straightened his collar, flattening it with the palm of her hand. "Do you ever think of our night together? I do, even when I was with my husband, I was usually thinking of you."

"I must be going," Ben said with a courteous bow.

"You're still a very handsome man, Ben; I wish I had beaten Emma to you after you managed to put Ruth behind you. I hate not getting what I want. I'm sure we'll be seeing each other again," she said. Her words had a threatening undertone to them. Without a backward glance, she entered the building.

Ben waited a moment before riding back to Cartmel.

Emma and Dorothy were busy in the kitchen the bond between them had grown very strong; they were spending a great deal of time together and their friendship strengthened with each shopping spree. Emma could not stop staring out of the window at the new gig.

"It's a beautiful day now that the rain has gone, it's high time we put my present through its paces," Emma said. "Come on, let's put on some fitting clothes and go for a drive." She wiped her hands down her apron and ran upstairs to change. It took them three-quarters of an hour before they were ready. Outside, Emma ran her hands almost lovingly over the smooth paintwork of the gig.

The Winds of Change.

"There are new tea rooms in Dalton," Dorothy said with an excited grin, "and I hear that the place has quickly become something of a fashionable hot spot. The milliner said, that the well to do ladies of the district who wished to while away a little time, with some serious gossiping are flocking to it. Let's go there. Can we please?"

"Edward and Emily are coming over this evening, so, we need to be quick wherever we go. Let's go back in, I need to put my bonnet on," Emma said.

"Mr Mould, Dorothy, and I are thinking of taking the gig into Dalton. We won't be too long. So would you harness it up for us?" Emma said. "Walter is with Jenny somewhere."

"Are you sure that it's wise you going off on your own mistress, what with Quigley still on the loose?"

Dorothy pecked his cheek. "Don't worry, we'll be fine," she said. She stood in front of the mirror in the hall looking radiant as she tied the ribbons of her bonnet.

"I'll harness up Bonney for you, but I don't know what the Skipper will say," Mould muttered under his breath and sagely shook his head.

Emma gave Mould a reassuring smile. "I think we'll go via the old cottage and see if, Mr Douglas is there, he and Ian will look after us."

As they were about to leave Jenny arrived with Eve and Walter.

"She wanted to wave goodbye," Jenny said. she ran her hands over the woodwork of the gig. "It's a wonderful gift, perhaps we could all go out for a picnic sometime."

"I like the sound of that," Emma said."Do you want to come with us now?

"I wish that I could, but I'm churning butter. We only took a break to wave you off"

"We'll be back for tea," Dorothy said.

Mould waved them off, but he was not happy and he dreaded to think what Ben was going to say. He told himself that he was being foolish, they often went out and they always came back. He decided that while the pony and Ben's mare was out he would clean out the stables. Just as he picked up the rake and began to rake the straw, Eve and Walter arrived with Jenny.

"They would like to watch you, please, Mr Mould," Jenny said.

"Watch me, nay, they can do better than that, they can help me," he said, and handed the long shaft of a rake to Eve. The children loved it and were soon tugging away at the straw with Jenny keeping a close eye on them.

Mould took a short rest and sat on a hay bale: "So Jenny, how do you like being a mother?"

"Tiring, I thought Walter was a handful, but this one is into everything, I've to watch her non-stop."

"At least she'll have a good start in life, better than we had I'd say."

"Yes, you are right about that, she is lucky to be surrounded by people who love her. Tim dotes on her, he's ever so patient with her, even when she's in his way."

As the little mare tripped lightly along the road, it seemed quite proud of its new load. Emma and Dorothy chatted; Dorothy was delighted to have the chance to wear her new outfit, a Tweed jacket and skirt hand made in Barrow. The thought of meeting the women of Dalton excited her and reminded her of outings in the Caribbean with her mother.

"How different life is here compared to when I lived in Jamaica. I often went carriage rides with mama, we had picnics and sometimes we would go to one of the plantation houses and just chat." She smiled as the memories flooded back. I realise now that she was simply getting out of the way of my father. It was so hot, and at times, the winds were so dangerous that we had to take shelter in the cellar sometimes for days on end."

"It must have been frightening; I hate gales and high winds."

"One day, one of my father's servants was killed when a stone tile blew off the roof and almost cut his head clean off. What a dreadful mess it made."

"I struggled with the heat when I visited the Caribbean with Ben on our adventure with Pelican."

"You stowed away… how wonderful to be so in love," Dorothy said dreamily. "How did Ben react when you turned up, was he angry? I don't ever remember seeing him angry."

"He took it much better than you might have thought he would, it was not such a big gamble really, I think I knew him well enough to risk being so bold and I think he was glad I was there. It brought home to me just how dangerous the life at sea is, I suppose it gave me an insight into his past and perhaps, a better understanding of him," Emma said.

"I remember one time Papa was furious," Dorothy said with a grimace, "the cane was ready to be cut, a new crusher mill had been built and everything was ready when a hurricane struck. Everything was flattened and the new mill was blown down, the mule that was driving the mill escaped and it was several days before they caught it again. It took ages to fix the mess and part of the crop was lost, papa stomped about creating as much havoc as the winds had done. We hid out of his

The Winds of Change.

way because he was carrying his crop and anybody nearby was feeling it. I remember he hit one of the slave girls with it so hard that it tore through her blouse and opened a wound across her shoulder; mother had one of the housekeepers to look after her and to dress the wound. If Papa had known, he would have been livid. He always told me not to think of them as people, but to think of them only as creatures sent by God to serve us."

Emma turned off the main road and headed along a leafy lane where dappled sunlight played along the road.

"We'll not go straight to town; I want to go by the old Fell Cottage," Emma said, "the orchard will be full of blossom at this time of year."

As they crossed a stone bridge, Dorothy brought the pony to a standstill.

"Whoa," she called gently pulling back on the reins. "This is where my mother died isn't it."

"Yes, I'm afraid so. It was an accident, her horse stumbled, and she was thrown over the edge."

"She was crazy when she was on that stuff."

"Laudanum?"

"Yes, it made her very unpredictable; I used to be frightened for us both when she took it."

"Come on, I think, Jamie Douglas and Ian should be working up at the old homestead today."

"I do love Jamie," Dorothy said with a smile, "he has a lovely accent. I think his ghillie is a little bit odd at times." She paused a moment. "I still don't understand why my mother made such an effort to get to your wedding."

"I can't answer that, I didn't know that she was in the country," Emma smiled at her, "Ian is different, but he's a good man, and when Quigley torched the cottage, it was he who saved Emily's life."

Dorothy hopped down. "I think you changed the subject then. Please, let me have a moment."

She picked some wildflowers from the roadside, Emma climbed out of the gig and joined her. They sat side by side on the bridge's stonework. Together they released the flowers, slowly letting them drop from between their fingers down into the stream.

"My father,"

"Sir Arthur?"

Dorothy gave Emma a curious glance. "Yes, of course, who else; he used to knock her about at times. He called her horrible names, but she never did anything to deserve it. He had a fancy-women all the time, painted women with large exposed breasts and loud ridiculous laughs, the foulest thing was he didn't care who knew."

"Did he ever harm you?"

"No, I was too quick for him and anyway I had a little Negro girl who helped me dress and usually if I did anything bad he would hit her; I hated him for that. As soon as I heard him shouting, we got out of the way, I once hid her under a pile of hay in the stable. Oh, there was once I tried to protect my mother from him," she paused a moment, "he threw me to the floor, but he was so angry with himself that he went off in a huff and we didn't see him for several days and when he finally returned he reeked of cigars and cheap perfume."

"You know that I was at school with your mother. We were in Switzerland together." She paused a moment. "The three of us were friends; we were thick as thieves, your mother, Annabelle, whom you met at the Christmas party and me. Annabelle married my brother the same year that I married my first husband. It was quite a surprise to find my old school friend as my sister-in-law." She stopped a moment as the memories flooded in. "There was always a lot of rivalry between us, Annabelle was a very jealous girl and liked stirring things up for the rest of us. But even so, we were good companions and shared all our secrets."

" I'd met Annabelle before the Christmas party, once, maybe twice in Jamaica, she always used to upset mother over something. They'd never allow me in the room when they were talking. When we came back to England, we lived with Mama's aunt in Skipton and Annabelle visited her a few times, the last time was… to tell her that Ben was getting married. She was totally distraught, she was angry and hurting all at once. It was only a week or so before she died." She looked sad but her mood suddenly brightened.

"Was the King really at Mother's wedding?"

"Oh yes, Sir Arthur's family is very well connected, in fact, I think that they have Hanoverian blood in their veins. Both Ben and I were there too."

"I didn't know that, did you know each other back then?"

"No, not at all, Ben was there with, Captain Mitchell because their ship was to take the married couple to Jamaica. Your mother invited Annabelle and me just to show off I think."

For a few moments, they sat and watched the river tumbling over the rocks below them.

"It looks so peaceful now," Dorothy said. "It's a long drop, and oh, all those boulders; she must have been in terrible pain after her fall."

The Winds of Change.

She paused a moment and then fixed Emma with a penetrating glare. "Was it really an accident?"

"I think, that she had taken so much laudanum she never felt a thing." Emma took Dorothy's hand. "Come on, let's go to the cottage."

As they stood up Emma looked at the causeway flagstones. "Look you can see where her horse skidded, its iron shoes scored the flagstones."

Eventually, they reached the little church on top of the fells.

"I wonder if Mr Hardwick is about?" Dorothy said. "We should call at the manse and see if Mrs Potts has been baking, her biscuits are the best in the county."

"The cottage isn't far, Jamie should be somewhere about."

They turned into the familiar driveway bringing back a flood of memories for Emma. "The first time I came here was to invite everyone to our Hunt Ball, Emily was very excited at the prospect, it was really just an excuse to invite Ben. However, it was also a great excuse for us all to have new dresses made."

Emma was saddened when she saw the old cottage, its burnt-out shell shrouded in weeds looked very sad.

"Where is everyone? Come on, let's look in the old dairy," Emma said.

They crossed the yard and then had to fight their way through the nettles and weeds that had taken over there. The wooden door creaked and complained as Emma pushed it open, several birds fluttered into the air from where they had been roosting. It was gloomy inside, just a few thin shafts of light cut in through gaps in the brickwork.

"Jenny and Tim worked really hard to restore the dairy which had not been used for decades, they were so delighted when they first managed to put it back to work."

"Did you all live here?"

"I never did, but it was Emily's home for many years. As you know, she ran an orphanage here with her first husband, Reverend Linton. He was a wonderful gentleman and an inspiration to us all. Ben was brought here after the constable in Settle shot him in the shoulder."

"Oh my goodness, he seems to have had a few close shaves," Dorothy said.

"Jenny once told me all about it; she said they were with a gang of ruffians, Ben had been kidnapped, which was when she first met him."

They waited a while, Dorothy picked some wildflowers, and Emma showed her the orchard where they used to swing from an old apple tree but Jamie was nowhere to be found.

"I didn't know that Ben knew Jenny before they came here."

"Jenny was never here with the Lintons, she stayed with the gang of outlaws, it was about ten years before she met up again with Ben and that was on what is now Compton island; she was with the same gang although they had moved on to piracy by then."

"It seems that all my friends have secrets they've not shared with me, I hope that there are not any more lurking in the shadows for me."

Emma stood a moment looking around the gardens and decided to change the subject. "He'll be busy with the cattle somewhere; they seem to be his favourite pass-time these days."

"Well, I'm famished, let's go; we can see them later," Dorothy said.

They chatted as they drove, not paying any attention at all to their surroundings. Apart from each other, all they could hear was the crunch of the wheels on the gravel lane and the jingle of the horse's harness. It was quite a shock when the lane was suddenly blocked by two horsemen dressed in long black coats and masks across their faces.

Unafraid, they pulled to a halt. Emma stood up in the gig. "What's the meaning of this?" she called. She was trying to be brave, hoping that her bluster would have the right effect.

Two men came out of hiding from behind them and grabbed Dorothy by the arms. She screamed and put up a spirited fight, punching and wriggling but it was to no avail, the man held her tight until she was forced to stop. Emma turned to try to help her but strong arms wrapped around her waist, and she too was dragged into the lane. She broke free and struck out trying to punch the men, but one of them moved behind her and threw his arms around her stilling her.

"My husband will deal with you. Let us go now or he'll be very angry."

"Shut up woman, or I'll be very angry," he said mocking her. His breath smelt of stale ale and tobacco.

Dorothy bit the hand of the man holding her and managed to escape, but it was temporary and he caught her after a couple of paces. "Do that again you bitch and I'll teach you to bite me."

A wagon hauled by two heavy horses appeared from out of another lane, it had a canvas cover and high wooden sides.

"Tie their hands and get them in the back of the wagon," the driver called, he was obviously the leader of the gang.

Dorothy was going to protest again, but Emma shook her head to say no.

"This is an organised plot; we'd best just go along with it."

Emma secretively dropped her golden locket on the floor of the gig, knowing that Ben would recognise it and somehow know something was amiss. One of the men took hold of her arm, but she shook it loose.

The Winds of Change.

"Don't you dare," she warned him defiantly. The man released his grip and gave her a hard push towards the wagon.

"Get in, or I'll break your arm."

Emma was about to speak, but he raised his hand as if to strike her and she thought better of arguing with him. She climbed into the back of the wagon and leant against its side, and then cuddled up to Dorothy. The rear canvas flap was closed and laced shut with cords.

"What should we do?" Dorothy whispered, despite her fears her voice was steady.

"We should be brave and although they can physically beat us, we don't let them take our dignity or humiliate us. Courage is the order of the day, just as Ben would expect of us."

One of the men climbed into the wagon and sat down on a box by the opening; he tied their wrists together with a length of oily rope. Once he was satisfied that there would be no more escape attempts, he pulled the flaps together again and retied them. It was dark with the flaps closed and Emma and Dorothy sat even closer together. Emma eased the rope to allow Dorothy to get her hands free.

The wagon rumbled on down the lane bouncing and bumping over the many ruts and loose rocks. There was a bone-jarring crash that knocked their guard off his perch; he shouted a string of abuse at the driver and then crawling on all fours he climbed back to his seat.

Through a rip in the canvas, Emma tried to get her bearings, she could only make out that they were in a lane with a high-sided hedgerow, which she knew could have been any one of many in the area.

"Where are you taking us?" Dorothy asked the guard. She could not see him in the dim light but she felt that he was staring at her. "What do you intend to do to us?"

"Shut yer cackle," was all that he snapped back at her.

They made themselves as comfortable as they could, but the treacherous roads shook them about occasionally jolting them so hard that they let out a cry. The guard opposite them kept shouting curses at the driver, but it made very little difference.

Emma moved closer to Dorothy so that she could whisper in her ear. "Did you notice anything odd back there?"

"What do you mean odd, apart from these thugs kidnapping us?" Dorothy said.

"I thought that I could smell perfume... expensive perfume."

"I doubt if this lot even wash let alone use perfume."

"Yes, you are most likely right, it was probably nothing."

11. Off the coast of Argentina.

Half a world away, Pelican, was off the coast of Argentina striving to make headway through high winds and mountainous waves of an Atlantic storm. The crew was working hard to maintain their course and although the ship was built to withstand such weather, it creaked and groaned as it was tossed about. The convicts below decks in their improvised cells were frightened by the amount of noise and movement; they clung on for dear life afraid that they would sink.

Early one evening in the Captain's dayroom, Mitchell was enjoying a meal with his senior officers; it was a good chance to catch up on the day's events. Dr Harvey the ship's surgeon was giving his report.

"To conclude gentlemen, we have six crew and twelve prisoners in my sickbay. I fear that I will have to deal with delivering a child soon, it's a long time since I've had to use those skills," he said with a grin. "I've been a ship's doctor for twenty-five years, most of that time with you, Captain. This is the first time that I've had the pleasure of bringing a new soul into the world; sadly my duties have usually been to see them on their way out to the next place."

"Perhaps we should nickname the ship, *The Stork*," Hardy said, he laughed loudly at his own joke. The young lieutenant had settled in with the crew and felt quite relaxed at the captain's table.

"Well, I'm pleased to say that we are making good time, despite the number of storms we've sailed through," Mitchell said.

"I estimate that we should reach Tierra del Fuego in time for Christmas, which of course is midsummer here in the southern hemisphere, and should be calm weather," Snow said. He had replaced Ben as Mitchell's navigator and was relishing the challenge.

"Thank you, Mr Snow, we still have a great distance to sail, but if we can be in the Pacific by the New Year, then I'm sure we will arrive at our destination by late February or March."

"We've had numerous outbreaks of violence and a great deal of bullying amongst the convicts. Mr Hardy and I have managed to segregate the worst offenders, but it's like a powder keg down there, the least spark and it could blow up," Brand the marine's captain said. He very rarely showed any emotion and usually delivered his report with a deadpan face, but on this occasion, he was obviously concerned.

Mitchell looked up from his meal and then thoughtfully laid down his cutlery. "It goes against the grain with me, but I have orders to flog any prisoner, man, or woman, who creates any problems for us. Consequently, I've instructed, Mr Melvin to prepare his red bag and make a new cat," he said glancing briefly at Booth the Judge Advocate. "I still find the task of shipping and transporting felons an onerous one and a bitter pill to take after so many years of service for crown and country trying to prevent slavery, but it is sweetened by the thought of

The Winds of Change.

finally having the chance to circumnavigate the earth. By the time we return to England, we will have completed a voyage like no other, few have managed it and the wonders we will see are beyond description," he said and smiled at everyone.

Booth shifted uncomfortably in his seat and cleared his throat. "We have to maintain law and order, Captain, and although I can understand your discomfort with this task, please remember that you are helping those honest and trusting people back home to go about their business untroubled by these degenerates."

"And what of this... new colony?" Mitchell said.

"It has only just been established, this will be only the second consignment of convicts. It is quite isolated, worryingly the land around it may not be easily cultivated, but apparently, there is a unique type of pine that grows there which is ideal for making boats."

"Let us hope that the convicts don't build boats to escape in," Hardy said with a smirk.

"They'll need to be accomplished shipbuilders to make anything big enough to escape that place," Snow said.

"So how will you keep them fed?" Mitchell said.

"There are other areas more suitable for agriculture; of course, there are fish to be caught and some wild game." He did not sound convincing.

Out on the quarterdeck the following morning, Mitchell studied the coastline, trying to get some bearing as to where exactly they were his charts were very sketchy. Even though he got along well with his current officers and crew, he missed Edward's sound judgement and advice; he could always rely on him to assess situations accurately. They had sailed together since their time as young midshipmen. Edward had never shown any ambition to advance further than the rank of Lieutenant, but he had always shown support for Mitchell through his various promotions up to becoming a captain. During the past few years, he had also had Ben's natural skill and ability as a navigator to rely on and although he had every faith in Snow's skills, he would have preferred to have Ben fulfilling that role.

"I think we'll drop anchor here and search for water," Mitchell said over his shoulder to Snow. He snapped his telescope shut. "Take depth soundings, there are very few marked on my charts. We are near the River Plate; the Good-Ship Agamemnon was lost here a few years ago, she ran aground on sandbanks."

"Aye, aye, Captain. It's certainly a wild-looking country," Snow said.

"It reminds me a little bit of the North Yorkshire coast," Hardy said, "those giant boulders could certainly make a mess of any ship straying too close to them." He pointed at a series of black rocks jutting out of the sea surrounded by frothing, boiling waves.

Snow gazed questioningly into the sky. "I wish this weather would make its mind up, one minute we're almost becalmed, and then in the next moment, a squall is pushing us towards the coast. I don't think I've ever seen a sea as dark in colour as this one."

As they neared the coast, they could see that there were a few patches of sand, a few bays that looked promising but mostly the shore was hard black, barren rocks that the sea mercilessly pounded. A variety of sea birds circled around the masts calling noisily.

"If they shit all over my clean sails I'll shoot the lot of them," the bosun called angrily.

Mitchell strolled towards the quarterdeck rail. "Mr Hardy, kindly organise your boat crews and go search for water," Mitchell bellowed down to the deck. "Mr Brand, six of your marines as an escort if you please."

"Ahoy, Captain," Snow called to Mitchell from the deck below. "I've secured the prisoners below apart from eight men to help with the water butts."

"Let go, the bow-anchors," Hardy called to the bosun.

As the heavy anchors dropped, their cables hummed loudly as they rushed towards the sea, there was a splash as they hit the water, and when the anchors bit into the seabed, they brought the ship to a halt.

"Clear away the boats, Mr Hardy," Mitchell ordered.

The crew was busy; sailors were furling the sails to make sure that the onshore wind did not push the ship onto the rocks. The boats hung above the decks ready to be hoisted over the sides as soon as the ship settled.

They took four boats, but the journey ashore across that indigo blue water was not an easy one; the strong current and high waves hurled them towards the beach with frightening speed. With some relief, they managed to avoid the rocks, but only three of them landed safely on the shore, the fourth was turned at an angle and hit the beach sideways which turned it over spilling out its crew and the water butts.

Snow was watching from the quarterdeck. "Tricky place to land," he said thoughtfully, "Oh no, one of the boats has capsized… looks like it's alright, not much damage, they've righted it."

Mitchell trained his telescope on the landing party. "Brand will sort it out."

The Winds of Change.

With three of the boats safely hauled onto the beach, they managed to right the fourth and pull it up the sand to safety.

Brand quickly took charge of the landing party. "Sergeant, take six men and see what's over that ridge."

The men cautiously set off in search of water. Bailey the ship's scientist had also gone ashore in his never-ending search for new plants and animals. Luckily, there was a path away from the beach. It was overgrown with weeds but there was a hollow in the ground that suggested that at one time it had been well used. Some metres back they found three small, badly rotted fishing boats that had been pulled out of the way of the waves.

"These have not been used for years," the sergeant said. He pulled at one of the boat's timbers; with a crack, it came away in his hand. Further, along the path, they were greeted by the inhabitants of a cluster of stone-built huts. Brand's men warily approached them with their muskets loaded. The natives, about fifty in number, wearing sealskins and brightly coloured headdresses made of feathers and coloured beads began a welcoming chant and dance. The sergeant sent word back to Brand for him to come forward. The natives were friendly and were obviously accustomed to seeing Europeans, and although they did not have firearms, they knew what they were and asked Brand if he could shoot a few seals for them.

Brand using sign language explained his need for water to them and they were happy to oblige. They also wanted to trade and offered to sell him salted fish, fresh vegetables and trinkets made from seashells.

"Sergeant, go and bag these four seals that are basking on the rocks. We can make a good exchange with these natives."

It took about an hour for Brand to return with news of his find to the ship. Six convicts were transported to the shore to help with the loading of the water. They were certainly happy to be out of the confines of their cells. Two of them were violently sick as they crossed the waves to the shore, one was so ill he was left in the boat.

Once the barrels were filled and carried back to the boats, the villages came to the beach to help load them. It gave them another chance of bartering goods with the crew. Eventually the last of the barrels were loaded. Gill the purser, traded iron tools and knives from his stores for the fish, vegetables, and various pieces of native craft.

He stepped back into the ship's boat. "Thank you... we'll see you again some time," he said pleased with the day's trade. One of the natives placed a decorative seashell necklace over his head.

As they were about to head for the ship, four of the convicts from the work gang made a desperate and foolish break for freedom.

"Halt, stand, or be shot," Brand called after them.

It was obvious that the men decided that it was too late to turn back and kept on running.

Brand turned to his marines. "Aim... fire!"

The musket shots echoed loudly around the rocks, the villagers screamed and ran for cover; two of the convicts went down as limp as leaves amongst the boulders. The other two stopped dead in their tracks and raised their hands high above their heads. Slowly they turned around and walked back to the beach, the pain of failure was plain to see on their faces.

The marines frog-marched the men back to the fallen men and forced them to carry them to the boat. The first boat took the two corpses back to the ship. Booth oversaw the return of the bodies, he asked the doctor to confirm that they were dead and then asked to see the Captain.

"Come in, Mr Booth," Mitchell said.

Booth was carrying a large ledger, which he placed on Mitchell's table.

"Two fewer mouths to feed, Captain. I will need your signature," he pointed to an open page in his ledger. "Just here if you please, it keeps my records straight."

Mitchell offered him a seat as he read the page.

"They were committed for minor crimes, it seems a waste of life," Mitchell said and sat opposite Booth.

"You should make an example of the other two; a good flogging will remind all of these good-for-nothings that this is no joyride."

Out on deck, they were making ready to sail; hoists were attached to the yardarms to lift the water barrels from the boats. The crew seemed to be enjoying this change of task and there was a great deal of banter between them as they hauled on the ropes to work the hoists. Shouts from the bosun triggered the usual tramping of feet on the deck which signalled that the capstan was being put to use to lift the main bow anchor.

They began to sing *'Haul away the bowlines the bowlines, haul away the...'*

Mitchell called his steward. "Tell Mr Snow and Mr Melvin I'd like a word with them."

A few moments later the two men returned with the steward.

"Mr Melvin," Mitchell said to his bosun, "do you have your red bag handy?"

"Aye, Captain I do."

The Winds of Change.

"Twelve lashes for each man, in one hour. Mr Snow, arrange for thirty prisoners, no children, to witness this event." Mitchell looked at Booth. "That should suffice I think."

The two prisoners were tied onto gratings with their arms stretched out wide almost as if they were being crucified. Their shirts were removed, and a gag placed between their teeth. The prisoners brought out to watch were chained together in a line and secured to the deck so that there was no chance of an escape.

Brand gave a discreet nod to the young drummer boy who then began a slow solemn drumbeat. Melvin stood in the centre of the deck where everyone could see him; he opened his red pouch to release the cat. He had spent all night carefully making it; it had a rope handle about two feet long and an inch in diameter. Attached to this were nine tails made of cord that were a quarter-inch diameter and about two feet long. The whole thing weighed just under a pound and could put the fear of the devil into any man.

The bosun glanced towards the captain.

"Do your duty, Mr Melvin, without a doubt these men deserve what they are about to receive," Mitchell said.

Melvin prepared himself; this was not a chore he undertook lightly. He straightened the tails and then flicked them over his shoulder; it seemed as if the whole crew held their breath as he brought his arm over in a wide arc. The tails whistled loudly and cracked like gunfire as they hit flesh. The man wriggled and tried to scream, but the gag silenced him, his back, flushed a bright scarlet.

Each stroke was counted off by the bosun's mate and accompanied by a roll of the drum. After four strokes, blood and sweat ran freely down the convict's back there were a series of deep cuts in the exposed flesh. After twelve strokes, his back resembled raw mincemeat. The man slumped as if the life had gone out of him; only the wrist and knee restraints prevented him from falling to the deck.

"Doctor Harvey, please inspect the prisoner," Mitchell called down to the deck below.

The ship's surgeon stepped forward and lifted the man's head to see if, in fact, the man was still alive. He stood back for the bosun to throw a bucket of water over the man, to revive him. There was very little response, the man was either unconscious, or he had the good sense to feign such a state.

Melvin called from the deck to the Captain, "Shall I proceed to the next man Captain?"

Mitchell looked to Harvey for guidance.

"The man's unconscious, but I think he'll survive, Captain."

"Repeat the punishment for the other prisoner," Mitchell said. He glanced at Booth, who had turned a very pale grey and Mitchell was satisfied that at least he was not enjoying the spectacle.

The next convict who had seen the fate of his fellow cellmate was screaming and struggling against his bonds, pleading not to face the cat.

Two Marines tied him securely to the railings and the bosun swung his cat again, after three lashes the convict collapsed as if dead. The doctor looked at him and signalled the mate to throw water on him. Coughing and spluttering the man regained his wits just long enough for the cat to strip lengths of skin from his back. Once the punishment was finished, the other convicts, who had been there to witness the event, went back to their quarters in a very sombre mood.

Two days later, there was a new sound to be heard aboard one of Mitchell's ships, the sound of a newborn baby. It caused quite an amount of interest.

"How are the mother and child?" Mitchell asked the ship's doctor.

"Doing well, not a good place to start life," Harvey said.

"No, it is not. Has she been given a cot for the child? What has she named it?"

"The, it, as you called the child, is a very pretty girl and she has been named Peggy Louise."

Mitchell nodded his approval. "Make sure the mother receives extra rations and the child is well looked after, she, after all, is innocent of any wrongdoing."

Three days and two hundred miles further south, Mitchell and Snow were peering into a dense fog that blanketed the ship with a strange eerie silence.

"We are in an area noted for its storms and lashing rain, and of all the bad luck, we are virtually becalmed on a flat expanse of ocean that we can barely see," Mitchell said angrily.

Snow did not answer; he stared up into the sails as if praying for them to billow out.

"Perhaps, Captain with this fog being so dense it is a blessing that we are almost motionless, the coast here is notoriously dangerous, and neither of us has any experience of the sea around the Straits of Magellan."

Despite Booth's objections, a number of the prisoners were brought out on deck to take their daily exercise, something Mitchell insisted that they do.

The Winds of Change.

"Mr Booth it is not just an attempt to try to keep them healthy, I know from years of experience managing a ship's crew that the men need something to look forward to, something to break the monotony and keep them busy. This change of routine for everyone will help stop the boredom that can lead to all kinds of troubles."

A slender young woman with a fair complexion and long flowing auburn hair slinked towards the quarterdeck steps. One of the marines stepped in front of her with his musket across his chest barring her from approaching the captain.

"Are we lost, Captain?" she called, her flirtatious voice seemed to be mocking him.

Mitchell was taken aback for a moment, but then he realised that she meant no harm. "Now don't you be fretting, we're on course, and we'll get you there," he called back.

"It's just that if we are lost, well then we don't mind," she giggled. "Perhaps I could cast a spell on the wind; after all, I'm being deported for witchcraft."

There was something about the woman that Mitchell found dangerously alluring, he smiled and nodded to her, and she gave him a mischievous wink and then spun away dancing across the deck humming to herself.

"I've not been able to take any readings for two days now Captain," Snow said, "We are drifting southeast away from the coast but there is very little else I can say."

Mitchell was still watching the woman rather than listening to Snow. She danced on tiptoe across the deck spreading her arms left and then right, occasionally she would spin in a full circle spinning her skirt out and exposing her shapely legs. He was reminded of a gipsy girl who had once entertained the crew dancing to exotic, lively flamenco music, except she seemed to provide her own music.

When the sun finally showed between the clouds, both lieutenants hurriedly took readings to try to establish their position.

"Mr Snow, do you have our exact position now?" Mitchell asked.

"Aye, Captain, I do, we are fifty-four degrees thirty-nine minutes south, and sixty-four degrees and twenty-four minutes west."

"Very good, Mr Snow, your time with, Mr Burrows was well spent."

Snow smiled. "Some of the experiences with him were useful, but alas many were a little too close for comfort."

"Well, at least they rescued us from the damn French last time we were out."

As the tide changed so did, the weather; the sails filled almost to their limit, and the ship bent to the wind and cut through the waves. However, the fine sailing was short-lived when a sharp squall from the south threatened to turn into a severe storm, it made them sail for shelter in the lee of a rugged headland.

"We're almost in the Straights of La Maire, Captain, we are ready to go around the Horn," Snow said excitedly. "We're about five leagues off Cape Diego, with Tierra Del Fuego off our starboard bow." He pointed to the place on his chart.

"It's very much like the Scottish islands or the fjords in Norway," Hardy said. He was dressed in oilskins to try to keep warm in the suddenly bitter cold wind. "I thought it was summer here now," he shouted over the sound of the wind.

"Yes, I think officially it is. This is an amazing land; everything here is on such a grand scale," Mitchell replied. He was scanning the shore through his telescope admiring its raw beauty.

A grey-headed albatross tipped its enormous wings and circled the ship banking around in a great arc. Everyone stopped to watch the spectacle; it, in turn, was watching them with idle curiosity.

"Do you think that it has ever seen a ship before?" Hardy said, "It's very curious about us."

Bailey the ship's scientist watched it through his telescope. "I hope that it's a good omen, Captain. What a magnificent sight," he whispered as if afraid to let the bird hear him. Wherever he went, he carried his sketchpad and constantly made notes and drawings of the wildlife they encountered, but he was too enthralled by the sight of the bird to be able to sketch it.

There were many more sights as they sailed along the coast of Tierra del Fuego to the tip of South America; one that caught everyone's imagination was a huge sealion basking on a rock in the middle of the Straight. It looked up and bellowed its defiance at them as if it was guarding the rock and trying to prevent any passage past that point. Bailey made several hurried sketches and added several footnotes to the drawings.

In the Captain's dayroom Booth, who had finally adjusted to life aboard the ship was sharing a drink with Mitchell. "The sea here seems very unpredictable."

"Yes, we have just sailed through the Straights of La Maire, it's hard, dangerous work of the crew, contrary winds and currents as well as heavy seas which constantly push us off course and for the last two days we've seemed not to make any progress at all," Mitchell said.

There was a tap on the door and Snow entered looking very worried as he approached the Captain.

The Winds of Change.

"What is it, Mr Snow you look to have the troubles of the world upon your shoulders?"

"To be honest, Captain it is actually good news, we are now fifty-four degrees south and seventy-five degrees west so we are officially in the area of Pacific Ocean."

"Wonderful news... is it not?" Mitchell was puzzled by Snow's reaction to the news.

"Wonderful indeed, Captain. We are eight thousand miles from England, but what is also daunting, we are still six thousand miles from our destination, and there is nothing but sea between here and there."

Mitchell took a moment to digest this news; he felt a sudden rush of elation and wanted to shout out his joy because after almost thirty years as a seafarer this was his first venture into the Pacific.

"Then we must check our stores and prepare for many a day's sailing." Mitchell smiled as he spoke, a wave of euphoria swept over him. "We are very much in the wake of Drake, and Cooke, those men changed the world by opening up these waters. It has been a lifelong dream of mine, and this ship could almost be a sister of Cooke's Endeavour." He lifted his glass in a salute. "Once we catch the Chilean current it will pull us north and then west." He had memorised the journey and knew every current off by heart.

Snow smiled, he was delighted that his Captain was in such a good mood. "At least we can be sure that our ship is up to the job," Snow said, "Mr Burrows made a sound purchase when he bought this ship, we'll not find her wanting I'm sure."

A few days later out on the deck, Snow was having concerns about the Captain. "Are you feeling all right, Captain? If you don't mind me saying you've seemed a little bit distracted recently."

Mitchell seemed to shake himself and gave Snow a quizzical glance. "I'm perfectly well, thank you, Mr Snow; I've not been sleeping too well." This was just an excuse, he knew exactly what was wrong with him; the auburn-haired girl's smile was haunting him day and night. "Well, gentlemen, it is time for me to make my inspection below decks. Mr Snow, will you accompany me please?"

A number of the convicts were out on the deck for their exercise time, the guards also strolled about not taking much notice of what was going on. Mitchell called his bosun over. "Smarten your guards up, they look like they are having a Sunday stroll, we can't take our eyes off the convicts."

Mitchell saw that the auburn-haired girl was further along the deck; she was perched on a gun carriage plaiting her hair. She gave him a coy glance from beneath her eyebrows when she saw him look in her direction. He tried to ignore her, but the corners of his lips curled into a smile.

Later that day they sailed into the mouth of a small bay to shelter from another gale that had threatened to send them onto the rocks.

"Drop the stream anchor. Mr Hardy, take depth readings," Mitchell said.

"Mr Snow, take a party ashore for wood and water. It would be a good idea to take Mr Bailey with you to identify the strange flora here so we know which may or may not be eaten."

They took the largest of the ship's boats with a crew of ten, and four marines to protect them against any hostile natives. The ship's scientist had two convicts as assistants, both of whom looked very unhappy about sailing in the boat on such a violent sea. They dropped a small kedge anchor; it was shaped so that it would dig into the seabed, and it was often used to haul on, to position the ship.

Snow relished the responsibility of being in charge and he was determined to impress his captain.

"Make sure you make the boat secure. Marines take point; we'll head towards those trees and look for fallen branches."

A second boat went ashore with Hardy in charge. His mission was to search for food. They were hunting geese and seals, of which there was a great deal. Almost immediately, they were able to begin hunting, shooting seals and birds on the rocks.

With many of the crew away, Mitchell made sure that the convicts were securely chained up in their cells below decks, and extra guards were posted along the upper and lower decks. The weather was turning very cold and Mitchell guessed that it would snow before the day was out. It was not long before Hardy triumphantly returned with his boat brimming with the spoils of their hunt.

"Fifty geese, twenty-one ducks, and three seals for the cooking pot, Captain," Hardy proudly called out as his boat touched against Pelican.

"Well done, Mr Hardy, we should be able to make a great Christmas feast out of your booty. Set some men on fishing too."

Snow found that the ground was not easy to cross; there were deep ravines and thick scrubland that forced them to take many diversions. At last, they found an ideal place where crystal-clear water bubbled to the surface and was easy to collect.

"Perhaps it's too far from the ship for the men to carry it back," Bailey said.

Not to be beaten, Snow cut and slashed at the undergrowth with his sword. "No, I think we'll be able to clear a path," he said.

The Winds of Change.

Bailey showed three of the men which plants were safe to harvest, and which ones they should leave alone. The rest collected firewood and tied brushwood into bundles.

Melvin the bosun was watching the weather; he was convinced that they had wandered too far from the ship. "Mr Snow, I think we need to return to the ship." As he spoke, an ice-cold wind swirled a blizzard around them, totally disorientating them.

"Make a fire or we'll freeze to death if we try and stay out in this," Snow said.

"Make a shelter from the brush we've collected, and let's pray that this blows over soon," Melvin said.

The wind howled and the snow swirled around them, at times, it threatened to blow the fire out. The crew built a shelter by stacking the stoops of firewood together and then they huddled together for warmth, but they were not dressed for such severe conditions. Snow was glad that he had thought to bring a keg of rum and a bag of biscuits; he handed out a ration of rum to each of them. It cheered them, but its effect was not long-lasting.

"Let's try some more of that rum please, Mr Snow," one of the crew shouted so that he could be heard above the wind.

Bailey snatched the mug from his hand. "No more! Alcohol will affect your resistance to the cold. Eat some of these herbs and biscuits, that will help warm you."

The man looked angrily at him, and then at his comrades as if trying to get support for his demand but the others ignored him.

It was dark before the storm passed over and although the nights were very short, it promised to be an uncomfortable few hours. They knew that they had to sit it out.

"Keep that fire burning, and keep rubbing your hands and feet," Bailey said. He was concerned about how unsettled the men were and feared a mutiny of some kind.

On Pelican's quarterdeck, Mitchell was worrying about Snow's fate. The sky had cleared and the stars put on a dazzling display of brilliant light, however, the temperature had dropped below freezing.

"Quite a spectacle, Mr Hardy," Mitchell said.

"Yes, indeed, sir, but I'm not so familiar with the constellations of the southern seas." They turned their backs to the wind and watched the shoreline.

"Do you think, Mr Snow's party are all right?" Hardy said.

"I'm sure they've just strayed too far and been caught out by the weather. Mr Snow is a resourceful man; he'll have the sense to find shelter for the night. Our naturalist has been on several expeditions in the far north"

There was a sudden strange gushing sound behind them from across the bay. A small pod of whales had entered the bay almost as if they were checking up on the ship.

"These waters are filled with wonders, I can't wait to sail to India and the exotic things we may find there," Hardy said.

By four o'clock, it was light; Snow shook the men around him to wake them. "Look lively we need to get back to the ship. Take what wood we've collected," he said.

The man who had wanted more rum had made off in the night and taken the rum keg with him, but in the freezing cold, he had not lasted long. They found his stiff remains against a boulder where he had tried to find shelter.

"I warned him about the drink," Bailey said.

"We'll leave him here for now," Snow said. He was angry with himself for losing a man for no reason. "Mr Melvin, when we return for water please make the necessary arrangements to take him back to the ship."

They returned loaded with firewood, but in poor spirits. Snow immediately reported his problems to Mitchell.

"Bad luck, Mr Snow," Mitchell said.

"I'm sorry, Captain, the weather caught us out. I did, however, find a good source of fresh water."

"Very well, we need to take on as much as we can. Tomorrow, when we are away from the Horn, we'll follow the coast north and we should then pick up a strong current taking us west towards Van Diemen's Land. I think we need to top up again with fresh meat and water before we head west."

The following day Pelican turned north to follow the Chilean coast north. It was Christmas day and after a short service of thanksgiving, the men were treated to roast goose for their dinners.

Below deck, a conspiracy was brewing led by Jeremiah Todd, a felon convicted of stealing cattle and sheep. So as not to be seen, six of his gang were squashed into the rope-locker in the bow of the ship. "Listen to me, you lot," he whispered, "we may only have one more chance of freedom before we reach Van Diemen's Land,"

"You'll get us killed for sure," one of the gang hissed, "if we are caught the best we can expect is to suffer the cat, and after watching what happened to them that tried to escape, I don't think I want any of it."

The Winds of Change.

Todd drew a crude, sharp blade from under his belt and held it to the man's throat. "You listen to me, you're a part of this now, don't think you can change your mind," he said with a menacing snarl.

"So, what do you intend to do?" One of the six said.

"I've heard the Captain intends to pull in to find water again within the next two days; when we do, that's when we'll strike," Todd said.

"Strike! For Christ's sake man there are only seven of us. There are at least ten marines and the guards plus the rest of the crew," Joe Clay said.

"Aye, and the prison guards, they'll not stand by and do nowt, they'd like nothing better than to lay into us," another of the six said.

"So, we take some hostages, perhaps the Doctor and that scientist, and then we'll send Mitchell and his Lieutenants ashore. We'll have the element of surprise on our side; they'll not be expecting anything."

"Wouldn't it be better if went ashore? What can we do with the ship? We'll be hunted down, and then hanged as pirates."

Todd thought about this for a moment. "Yes, you're right; we may find ourselves some nice native girls to keep us company."

"This Captain is no fool; he was captain of a seventy-six gun Royal Navy ship," Clay said. "I know I served on that ship with him. I've no intention of going against him."

"Leave it to me," Todd said confidently.

Joe Clay shook his head in disbelief, but he didn't say anything else. Later that day he made sure that he was alone when he spoke with the bosun.

"Excuse me, Mr Melvin, I hear you are looking for likely men to add to the crew," Clay said.

"Aye, that's right. Wait a minute don't I know you?"

"Yes, I served on the Sirius with you and the Captain, although he was just a Commander in them days."

"Report to the Captain's dayroom at four bells," Melvin said.

Clay was back doing his usual work of mucking out the lower decks when Todd grabbed his arm.

"You were talking to the bosun," Todd said menacingly.

"They're looking for more crew; I thought if they took me on, then I could help you better if I was part of the crew."

Todd stared into his eyes, after a moment he smiled and slapped Clay's shoulder. "Good thinking, but don't have any silly thoughts of betraying me or warning them or you'll find yourself dead," Todd grinned and tweaked Clay's cheek.

Later that day in the dayroom, Clay stood nervously before the Captain and Booth.

Tony Mead.

"I do remember you, Mr Clay, believe it or not, but I remember all the men that I've served with. So why are we deporting you?" Mitchell said.

"I tried the life ashore, sir, I got myself married and tried to settle down, but work was hard to find and we got into debt; the landlord of the rooms we rented threw us out on the street and we were arrested for begging and debt." He hung his head in shame. "There is no justice for poor folks, we were split up and sent to different debtors prisons and finally, it was decided to transport me, I've not heard from the wife, and I've no idea where she is."

"A sad story indeed, Mr Clay and a regrettable one." He glanced towards Booth, who nodded his approval.

"You can sign on with us and then as long as you give good service, you can work your passage back to England. There will be no need for you to stay in gaol." He looked toward Booth for agreement.

Clay looked delighted. "Thank you, Captain, Mr Booth; I should never have left the navy."

They sailed north for ten days past the huge limestone cliffs that surrounded the fjords of Chile. Bailey was in his element and worked constantly trying to log and catalogue everything he saw. One island they passed was almost obscured by the countless birds nesting on its cliffs, their noise was deafening and the smell of guano was overpowering and made their eyes water. The seas and land seemed filled with endless wonders, and even for the experienced mariners when whales and dolphins shot great fountains of water high into the air, it seemed like a magical place. On reaching a fjord that was over thirty miles wide at its entrance with green forests and open grasslands on its northern coast, Mitchell said that it seemed a likely place to restock with water and any fresh food that could be found.

Mitchell was having a bad day; he wearily returned to his cabin, threw off his greatcoat, hung his waistcoat on the back of his chair, and poured a good measure of brandy before sitting on the edge of his cot. He hated his current role of a gaoler, and although he doubted that he would ever tire of sailing this task meant that there was no pleasure in being at sea. He thought that he could detect a faint and unusual aroma, perhaps it was a trick of his imagination, he had been thinking about life back at the cottage in Cartmel and for the first time, he had to admit to himself that he was missing it, and his friends. There had been opportunities during his career to marry, but he was always drawn back to the sea and his ship. However, he had watched his old friend Edward settle into home life and he thought that now it might be his turn.

The Winds of Change.

Suddenly, from behind his privy curtain, the young witch stepped out. Mitchell went for the dagger concealed in his sea boot and pointed it at the girl.

She smiled coyly at him. "You won't need that, Captain," she purred, her voice was like warm treacle.

"What are you doing here, how did you get in here?"

She walked across the cabin and sat at the captain's table her fine features highlighted by the oil lamp in the middle of the table. "Don't forget I was convicted of witchcraft, perhaps I changed myself into a cat and sneaked past your guards," she said with a cheeky grin.

"Are you a witch?"

She opened the top two buttons of her blouse. "Do you believe in witchcraft? Would you like me to be a witch or a woman?"

Mitchell placed the knife back into its sheath; despite being aroused by her presence, he knew that he could be heading into dangerous waters. "Why were you convicted as a witch?"

She took a deep breath and glanced at his glass.

Mitchell smiled and decided that she probably was a witch. "Can I offer you some refreshment, my dear witch?"

"I thought you might never ask. You ask why was I convicted and transported; well, since the age of twelve, I have been the mistress of, the Right Honourable George Farley, who is now the Bishop of Connolly."

Mitchell brought two glasses from his cupboard and a bottle of port. He pulled the cork and poured the rich ruby liquid into the glasses; he offered her one of the glasses.

She smiled seductively at him over the rim of the glass. "He took me in when I was orphaned, I was well looked after and I had a nice place to stay with a couple who were shall we say very intimate friends of, Mr Farley. They were so intimate that quite often he would sleep with the woman and sometimes with them both. I didn't realise that he was married and had his own family until one morning his wife turned up and found us in bed together. He grovelled on his knees kissing her feet, saying that I had bewitched him, enchanted him. He said that he could not resist me due to the spells I had cast on him and the family." She took a swig of the port. "I don't think for a minute that his wife was that stupid nor was she so gullible as to believe him, but rather than lose face and the fine existence she had, she had me arrested and eventually convicted of witchcraft."

She gulped down the rest of the port, and then stood directly in front of Mitchell slowly unbuttoning her blouse until it fell open. She slowly released the bow that held her skirt and then let it drop around her ankles. Mitchell knew that he should stop her but he was mesmerised and thought *she probably is a witch, she certainly has me spellbound.*

"What's your name?" Mitchell asked his throat felt as dry as dust.

"Elvira Ann Raw," she said, her voice was as soft as velvet.

She pushed his legs apart so that she could kneel close to him and slowly she removed his shirt.

12. Come quickly…

David Hardwick was quickly settling into his new parish; his move to the countryside had drastically and visibly improved his health so that now he felt motivated and at one with the world. After hours of working in the garden and walking the fells, his complexion had lost that gentlemanly, sickly pale colour which had now blossomed into a much healthier hue with cheeks that looked like ripe apples from the orchard. He had made many new friends, but he really enjoyed meeting up with his old friends from Linton's time. Another thing that he was particularly enjoying, was Mrs Potts' home cooking. As he dressed that morning he was convinced that his trousers were already a little tighter around the waist. *Either these trousers are shrinking or I need to cut down on the food here,* he thought.

Something he had not anticipated on his appointment was a new romance that was blossoming with a local woman who helped with the flowers for the church and worked as a domestic servant for a nearby wealthy farmer. There had been an instant attraction between them and on her days off they had started rambling over the fells together, usually taking a picnic to eat somewhere on a hilltop. Dressed in a fine new suit he set off down the lane to meet her, with a skip in his step and whistling a happy song he felt on top of the world. He loved the sound of birdsong and quite often found himself doing nothing but just staring into space listening to their singing.

This euphoric feeling of happiness was brought to an abrupt halt when he saw the bright yellow gig alone in the lane. He recognised the little pony between the traces, which was happily munching on the grass verge; it had towed the gig slightly off the road to get at the tastiest grass. Some sixth sense warned him that things were not right; he knew who owned the gig, Ben had shown it to him the day before. Something caught his eye, it was the locket dropped by Emma. He picked it up to examine it. His appointment with his new friend was forgotten and he wasted no time setting off for help. Running back home he hurriedly harnessed his horse and then rode so fast into Cartmel that he lost his hat, and his horse almost lost its footing as it turned onto the cobblestones of the market square. He leapt from his horse before it had stopped, and ran straight for Emily's front door. Out of breath and shaking with fear, he hammered with his fist for attention. Edward opened the door looking quite surprised.

"My goodness, Vicar what's to do?"

"You'd better come with me!" His face was flushed and he was panting loudly. The commotion brought Ben into the hallway. David looked shocked and Ben knew instantly something was wrong.

"It's, Emma's gig, I found it deserted up the lane near the church," David held up the locket, "do you recognise this?"

"Yes, it is Emma's, let me see," Ben said. He held it tenderly in his fist for a moment. "To horse, quickly, there is no time to lose."

Without another word, he grabbed his jacket and ran out to the stable; fortunately, his horse was still saddled. He galloped off after David, who had remounted and was waiting in the road for him.

"I'll catch up," Edward called from the stable where he was saddling his mare. Emily was outside trying to think about how she could help. "Never mind your horse, harness the gig so that I can come and look," she said.

When Ben reached the gig, he dismounted to inspect it; his guts churned as he realised that something was very wrong. He tried to overcome the rising panic, *keep calm,* he thought. It was obvious that a much heavier vehicle had passed along the lane, he was no expert tracker, but he knew someone who was.

"I'll ride and find, Ian Douglas; he's with, Jamie in the top meadow. Stay here if you will, David, Edward will be along soon."

He spurred his horse up the fell lane and on the high fell top; it was a great relief to spot Jamie strutting across the meadow. As always, he wore his Douglas tartan kilt and jacket. Anyone passing would have been forgiven for thinking that they were somewhere in the highlands. Ben waved and Jamie broke into a trot to reach him a little quicker.

"Ahoy there, Ben, what's to do?" Jamie bellowed from twenty yards.

"Emma and Dorothy are missing!" He did not want to think about it, but he feared the worse, "I think they have been kidnapped," he had to fight hard to control his emotions, "where's Ian? We need his tracking skills, the tracks are still hot, and there's a chance we'll catch them."

Jamie blew three short blasts on his hunting horn, the sound echoed eerily across the meadow and into the distant forest. It was only a matter of minutes before Ian appeared running as fast as he could. Jamie was already mounted on his pony and without explanation; he set off across the meadow at a steady canter. As soon as Ian caught up with him, he took hold of the saddle strap and hung on to it as tightly as he could. It did not take long to find the others who still searching the lane.

"Away, Ian lad and see if you can pick up a sign of a trail," Jamie said.

The Winds of Change.

With his plaid tied tightly around his waist and over his shoulder, he set off like a hunting dog quartering the lane running from side to side as if trying to pick up the scent. He stopped and waved Jamie over.

"Disregarding Ben's horse and these others, I'd say there were five on horses and a heavy wagon. See here, these stones have been turned over," he pointed to others along the track. "Maybe it's a dray cart or merchant's wagon; probably with a canvas back. See here the wheels have cut into the side of the lane; it was probably standing here for a short while. I'll follow as far as I can, but it has been so dry recently there'll be very few signs."

Ian bobbed down and picked up a small tight ball of tobacco cinder from the track, he sniffed at it. "One of them smokes a pipe; he knocked it out here, probably while he waited." He sniffed it again. "This is an unusual mix, probably foreign."

The trail took them down to the main road that led into Ulverston.

"I can't find anything here; there have been too many travellers, horses, wagons, and people on foot. I don't know which way they turned maybe towards the town, but that's a guess."

As the wagon crunched to a halt, Emma could hear nearby church bells peeling the time of day. There were several other sounds too; definitely sea birds calling, the wind blowing through the trees and something else maybe it was the sound of the sea.

"Where are we?" Dorothy asked. "I recognise those bells, is it Dalton church?"

"No, I don't think so."

Their guard wound a cord around their ankles tying them together three-legged race-style, Emma guessed from the knots he used that he had been a sailor.

"We'll be here a while, so no trouble. I don't want to hurt you, but I have my orders. We'll feed you if you behave," he said and then climbed out of the wagon.

"At least we can talk freely now he's gone," Emma said

"I'm afraid that no one will find us, Emma," Dorothy whispered.

Emma was also afraid but she was put on a brave face to try to make Dorothy more at ease. A terrifying thought was that she might never see Ben and little Walter ever again. Without really concentrating on what she was saying she said, "Don't worry, your papa will not let anything happen to you," she bit her lip realising the mistake she had just made.

"Papa, do you mean, Sir Arthur?" Dorothy said, "I can't see him doing anything." She studied Emma's face a moment and then pulled back from Emma. "You didn't mean Sir Arthur did you, well then, who did you mean?"

"Oh dear, I need to tell you a story, a true story. You know I told you that I was a friend of your mother when we were teenagers; we were all at school together in Switzerland." She put her arm around Dorothy. "We were all great rivals too, and constantly played practical jokes on each other."

"This was with Annabelle and my mother; you've told me that story. I suppose that you were all learning to be ladies at the school? Was it all about etiquette and table manners?" Dorothy mocked her.

"That was the general idea," Emma said with a smile, "but the school had quite a radical approach, usually ladies of a certain position are taught very little apart from needlecraft, how to play the pianoforte and not to meddle in their husband's business. My previous school took the opinion that women did not have a brain sufficiently large enough to be able to understand politics or finance and that these matters should be left to the men. It was of course run by a man; a certain Doctor Jenkins, who without a doubt was the most boring person on God's earth, flowers would wilt as he passed them in the garden," she laughed and she was pleased to see that Dorothy also managed to smile. "However, our, Swiss school positively encouraged us to use our brains and I think most of the girls who attended it became quite outspoken, although I doubt if it made little difference to your mother, who was always very… shall we say, self-opinionated."

"Grandpa says that my mother drove Grandma to an early grave because she always did just as she pleased."

"That would not surprise me. After school holidays, we would all compare notes on what we had done, where we had been, and who we had met." She suddenly caught the smell of pipe tobacco and knew that one of the men was standing guard close to the wagon; she lowered her voice to a whisper.

"Ruth, your mother always used to brag about her assignations with a boyfriend and the fact that he was just an ostler, a mere stable boy, albeit the fact that he was a very handsome one which made it all the spicier. I suppose she told you that she had an older brother who she hated with a passion; he was a bully and a real predator."

"She told me that he was killed in an accident. I think he fell and broke his neck."

"Yes, unfortunately, there was some doubt at the time as to whether he had fallen or if he had been pushed by that handsome ostler. The boy went on the run, fearing that because your Grandpa was the local magistrate, he might hang him for the offence."

The Winds of Change.

"And so he should if he was guilty!" Dorothy said indignantly, temporarily forgetting her worries. Emma cleared her throat and tried not to be too critical of Dorothy's reaction.

"The fugitive was captured by a gang of thugs, and then almost killed by a gun-shot but fortunately he found a safe sanctuary with a minister and his extended family." Emma wondering if the proverbial penny had dropped yet as to whom she was speaking. "All too soon the ostler was once more in trouble when he was press-ganged into the Navy." She paused again wondering just how much of what she knew she should tell. "After your mother married Sir Arthur, they sailed immediately to the Caribbean ready for him to take up his new post as Governor of Jamaica. By an unpredictable coincidence, the handsome ostler, our unlucky fugitive, was working on the ship that was to transport them to the Caribbean. Your mother was excited to be reunited with her handsome ostler and while, Sir Arthur lay drunk in his cot, she arranged a tryst to reacquaint herself with her old friend."

"Wait, just a minute, what are you saying, that, Sir Arthur is not my father, but that I was sired by this stable boy?" Dorothy was puzzled, and yet she delighted that, Sir Arthur was not her father. There was a long silence; Emma could sense that Dorothy was becoming quite agitated.

"I have a horrible fear that I know who that boy in your story is… please tell me that I'm wrong."

"No, I think you've guessed the truth."

"Oh, please no, I'm too embarrassed to speak."

"What on earth do you mean? I thought you might be pleased."

Dorothy shuffled uncomfortably she rubbed her face with her hands trying to clear her spinning mind. "Yes, I'm delighted on the one hand and painfully embarrassed on the other. Ben," she paused a moment, "or should I call him, father or papa?" she paused again as her emotions tumbled over and over and made an embarrassing confession. "Are you sure? He is still a very handsome man, despite the numerous battle-scars he has picked up over the years, and of course his appalling singing voice in the church on a Sunday morning. I'm sixteen years old, and very aware of any handsome man that I might meet and perhaps I have fanciful thoughts about them."

Emma burst into a fit of giggles. "You mean, Ben, of course, my goodness, how embarrassing that could have been."

"So, why did you not tell me? Why did he not tell me all those years ago when I came to live with you, I know I was only young, but I would have understood; I think?"

"Ben wanted to tell you himself, but even after the four years that you've been with us, the time just never seemed right, I often told him that he should tell you. I don't think he thought it really mattered or for that matter, know where to begin."

"Didn't matter! Of course, it matters, look what a fool I have made of myself."

"I think what you have just told me, we can keep it as our secret," Emma said with a smile.

"Did they love each other?"

"I think that it was something of a bittersweet affair."

Dorothy sat in silence for quite some time mulling over this new revelation.

"So, that is why my mother spoke of him so often. It explains all kinds of things, for instance, why she was so delighted to see him, and some of the accusations Sir Arthur made."

"He loved her very much; they were only children when they first met."

"So was it, Ben, who killed my uncle in the barn?"

"It seems more likely that it was your mother."

"Then why did he run away?"

"To protect your mother, but she convinced him that he needed to run. I'm afraid your mother may have made him run so that people would not suspect that it was she who had killed him."

They sat in the darkness and eventually fell asleep.

13. Find Emma

Ben rode back up the lane in the desperate hope of finding some new clues. Ian ran alongside him and using his tracking skills, he scanned the ground left and right to look for any overturned stone or hoof print that might be a clue.

"It's no use Skipper, the more times you ride along here the less likely we are to find anything," Ian said. He squatted down by the roadside to take a breather.

"What else can I do?" Ben said desperately.

David joined them; he put on a brave encouraging smile. "Come into the house, I'm sure Mrs Potts will have the kettle on." He was trying to sound positive, although inside, he felt deep despair because there was nothing he could offer.

"I'm away," Ian said. "I'll circle around and see if I can pick up the tracks o'that big wagon further down the lane."

In the parlour of the manse, David offered Ben a chair, and as predicted, Mrs Potts arrived with tea for them both. She smiled benevolently at them paying special attention t her new ward. At first, she had not been too sure about the new vicar; she did not take to change easily and would have far preferred that the old vicar had stayed on. However, she had begun to warm to him and she was getting used to his way of doing things.

"What on earth is going on vicar?" she said.

"We are not too sure yet," David said, and taking a cup from Mrs Pott's tray, he handed it to Ben.

"Who can be behind this?" David said.

"I can only guess... but I'd say, Quigley, is the most likely candidate."

"Quigley... I know that name."

"He is a slave trader and general bad man; I had a run-in with him when I declined to transport some of his slaves to the Caribbean. He cursed everyone involved in the venture, but much worse than that, when I was at sea, he attacked the cottage; he was the one who burnt it to the ground. Fortunately, they caught him, but because of his contacts he managed to escape 'the drop' at Lancaster prison, and then someone aided his escape."

"How long ago was that?" David said.

"It's probably six months since his escape. He had a lot of friends in high places to organise his escape. The slave trade is a filthy business, but it has so many influential investors and they are from all walks of life; including the clergy."

"I'm truly sorry about Emma if there is any way I can help just let me know."

"You can pray for the girls and me," Ben said his emotions were beginning to get the better of him.

David put down his cup. "I wonder what Linton would have done?" he said more thinking aloud than directing the question at someone.

"I'm not sure that there would not have been much more that he could have done." Ben paused a moment. "He might call on his many contacts; he too had friends in high places, especially amongst the anti-slavery lobby. He would have taken it in his stride, no matter what happened, he had a way of rationalising everything," Ben said.

"I often see you up by his grave, you obviously thought a great deal about him."

Ben could not help a wry smile crossing his lips. "I go when I need to think and find a little bit of peace. He would be devastated now to see the cottage burnt down, but I think he'd be glad that Emily has found new happiness with Edward."

"I think everyone was in love with Emily back in those days; the girls used to compare her to a fairytale princess," David said with a shake of his head.

"I'm sorry, but I'll go now," Ben suddenly jumped to his feet. "I need to get my thinking cap on, and I need to feel as if I'm doing something."

He began a campaign of ideas that he hoped would solve the mystery of where they had been taken. His friend the postmistress suggested that he have leaflets printed and then distribute them across the county. After a trip into Barrow to the printers, Ben rode endless miles distributing leaflets concerning Emma's disappearance, he rode to Bingley to visit Lord Hutton-Beaumont, Ruth's father, another man with many connections.

David Hardwick was also a big help in contacting other clergymen as far away as Bristol asking them to distribute the leaflets. He called into the farm one afternoon. Mould greeted him at the door. "The skipper's not bearing up too well," he whispered.

David was sad to see how ill Ben looked. "I'm sorry there's no news yet, it's early days, I'm sure we'll find them soon."

"It's over a month; we should have heard something if they've been kidnapped then surely there should be a ransom note at the very least," Ben said.

"I know you are busy searching for Emma, but I'd like some moral support tomorrow at a meeting in Lancaster. Wilberforce and one or two others from the anti-slavery lobby will be there to debate the issue with several MPs and businessmen from Lancashire. In the past, you have

The Winds of Change.

expressed your disdain for the slave trade. Perhaps we could take Jones with us, you said that he was transported as a slave when he was a child," David said.

"It might take my mind off things, we seem to be getting nowhere," Ben said.

The Guildhall in Lancaster was so tightly packed that it was standing room only by the time the meeting began. David had reserved seats in the balcony and they had a good view of the podium where the dignitaries were sitting in a neat line behind a long table. Ben recognised one of the men behind the table, Wilberforce, he had seen him when he had visited Linton in Settle; probably fifteen or twenty years earlier.

There were a few comments and stares of disapproval when Jones sat beside Ben. The slave issue was still being very divisive; there were strong advocates for both sides of the argument, and of course, it was the concern for their wallets that was driving those objecting to emancipation. Many had come to hear Wilberforce speak, but there were just as many there to heckle the man they regarded as the main power behind the anti-slavery lobby in parliament.

The city's Sheriff hammered the table with his gavel to try to bring some order to the procedures. "Gentlemen, please," he shouted. Slowly the noise subsided and the Sheriff sat down looking exhausted after his efforts to quieten the place.

Wilberforce stood up, but he needed a little support from his friend the Reverend Caster. "Gentlemen, I intend to push further forward the bills that will require all slaves to be registered along with details of their origins."

There were a great many angry calls from the floor of the hall. The Sheriff was on his feet again, he hammered the table trying to restore order.

Wilberforce looked tired and needed to lean upon the table for support. "I do not believe that slavery should be banned outright, but my conscience as a Christian moves me towards it. The Quakers have set an example that I feel we should all follow. Be guided by your conscience, not your bank balance," Wilberforce said, his voice was suddenly bright and clear.

"We're already losing money since the abolition of transportation!" someone from the floor shouted; there were a great many shouts of support for this statement.

"This issue has been dragging on for too long; now is the time to resolve it. I don't think that they, the Black Africans are ready for full emancipation, yet, but with God's guidance they will be in time," Wilberforce said.

Another on the podium stood up. "My name is, Thomas Clarkson; I've been working with the abolitionists for more than twenty years, and since my good friend, Wilberforce is not as agile as he once was, I've been travelling the world trying to ensure that we do bring an end to this abhorrent trade and state. I call on all Christian people to demand the end of this filthy trade. It cannot be right to trade in human flesh, I know it is not a new trade but it is the devil's work."

"What about the slaves in this country, children in the mines and up chimneys, lives being lost in unsafe factories and textile mills?" Someone from beneath a trade union banner shouted.

"Nonsense, man, nonsense, we are not here to discuss such matters." Someone else shouted from across the hall.

"There has already been blood in the streets, the shameful murder of innocents at what has been ironically nicknamed as Peterloo. Even with the passing of the, 'Six Acts' to try and suppress reform was a fraudulent document from the offset. If you don't get rid of the corruption in Parliament and allow universal adult suffrage, there will be a revolution," the speaker was a tall handsome man wearing a neat grey wig. "The French knew how to deal with corrupt politicians and their greedy aristocracy."

"That's the Reverend, James Boyle, he's a real hell and brimstone preacher," David shouted in Ben's ear to try to be heard. "He's pushing the reformists to move faster, but he has too many enemies getting in his way."

A scuffle broke out and there were angry shouts from all sides of the room that threatened to spread around the room. Once again, the Sheriff was up on his feet trying to control things. Someone fired a pistol into the air and immediately there was almost silence.

"You mentioned Christianity, Mr Wilberforce what does your Christianity say about such things? There are bishops and parsons making money from this most devilish of trades," Boyle said. "You instigated the, Eighteen Hundred and Seven Bill, to abolish slavery, and yet fifteen years on there has been very little change."

"Mr Boyle, we all respect your zeal when it comes to matters of reform, but the slaves in places such as the West Indies are well cared for and sympathetically managed," Wilberforce said.

Ben felt that he was slowly being drawn into the discussion, particularly after the last statement. Suddenly he found himself on his feet.

The Winds of Change.

"With great respect, Mr Wilberforce, I have seen the slaves you are talking about, I don't think that you have ever seen them, and I say that your statement is a false one." There were gasps from the floor. "I know because I have seen the dreadful conditions that they are forced to work and live in. You and any other Christian man should be ashamed of condemning fellow humans to such degradation, humility, and pain. For what purpose? The sake of profit," Ben almost spit the words.

"Well done, Ben I didn't know you felt so strongly on the matter," David said.

Ben felt to be in full flow and nobody was going to stop him. "These parliamentarians are such hypocrites. Mr Wilberforce, you were a friend of, Reverend Linton of Cartmel, he would be distressed to know that the emancipation of all humans has been run aground so easily by bureaucracy."

Clarkson jumped to his feet. "Show more respect for, Mr Wilberforce, he has worn himself into the ground on behalf of this cause," he said.

"Mr Wilberforce, you are just another part of the corruption that exists in parliament, for is it not the case that you have just taken over a rotten borough near London, a borough that to all intents and purposes does not exist, just to get your seat in parliament? A borough that has no value or people for that matter; it should not be allowed." Ben turned towards the room below, "they cling to power whatever the cost and however deceitful they need to be," he turned back to the podium. "I came here in support of, Mr Wilberforce because I remembered him as a true and honest man and champion of the anti-slavery cause, but I begin to wonder what his motives are." Ben sat down his cheeks flushed and sweat dripped from his upper lip.

The Sheriff recognised Ben from their recent meeting he nodded to him. "Mr Burrows you have strong opinions, but whose side do you favour?" he said.

Ben jumped back to his feet. "The slaves!" Ben called emphatically, "I served in the navy for the likes of these," he pointed to the board, "I saw good men shredded to death by splintering wood, men blinded and maimed in the cause of freedom. With our sweat, our blood and our lives, we upheld your laws to ban the movement of slaves. All the while, you all sat about filling your bellies and swilling your wine, filling out forms and holding endless meetings at our expense. I see that we wasted our time because you have not the guts or the character to do what is right, or, Christian. You dare to call these people from Africa and such places, primitive heathens, but I tell you," Ben was leaning forward with his finger pointing straight at those on the podium, "I tell you that these people are ten times more honourable than you and the other monkeys that inhabit Parliament," he said passionately and then sat down.

"We see you have your own monkey with you," a voice from the opposition said.

Ben snapped back onto his feet. "How dare you? This gentleman's bravery," he placed his hand on Jones' shoulder, "has saved your necks, your lands, your investments more times than can be counted. He is a free man because he earned his freedom and every law-abiding man has the right to be so; he deserves your utmost respect because he has fought for it." Ben glared at the man. "What have you ever done? Show me your battle scars show me your courage. This man has fought on the decks of your ships at my side against ferocious enemies; I would trust this gentleman with my life, can anyone say that about you."

Someone called from the main floor. "Nothing will ever be done; we have no say or power in this land." There were cheers of support but just as many jeers of derision.

Ben stood up again; he leant against a wooden handrail with one hand and produced several plump acorns from his pocket; he then laid out in a neat line. "Around my lands are many magnificent old oak trees, some of which must be hundreds of years old. They stand with their branches extended to maybe sixty feet or more, they burrow deep into the earth, and their trunks are so wide that three men cannot reach around their girth, and yet..." He picked one of the acorns up and held it between his finger and thumb so all could see it. "This is how they started." There was a sudden silence as everyone stared at the acorn wondering where the conversation was going. "And so it is with this issue, we need to be patient and the growth will happen, but it is also a warning to those who wish to resist because nothing can stand in the way of progress. Unlike our neighbours across the sea we are not in favour of revolution and yet look at the huge revolutions that have taken place in agriculture, and industry, they have been reformed completely." Ben turned to look at the podium he paused a moment before continuing. "Revolution of one kind or another is on its way and no one will stop it."

A great cheer went up from supporters on both sides of the debate.

After the meeting, Boyle made his way towards Ben by pushing through the crowd that had gathered outside the hall. There were several heated debates and some looked as if they could end in violence.

"Well said, Mr Burrows, perhaps you should be in parliament. Do you have time to take a little refreshment with me at my lodgings?"

"I feel this debate may continue out here on the street for some time," David said.

The Winds of Change.

They found themselves in a deserted street and straight away Ben was on edge. His hand automatically went to where his sword should hang, but of course, he was not carrying it. He had a pistol under his coat and without letting the others know, he cocked it.

Jones sensed Ben's unease. "Is something wrong, Skipper?" he said.

Before Ben could answer, a dozen men wielding sticks charged from out of the shadows they ran straight into Boyle knocking him into the gutter. Ben had no time to draw his pistol before he too was set upon. A brutish thug with foul breath and an arm covered in tattoos grabbed him and tried to hurl him against the wall. At last, Ben drew his pistol, but instead of firing it, he used it like a club holding the barrel and hitting his attacker on the nose with the heavy handle. The thug staggered backwards, holding his bleeding nose; Ben turned and smashed his pistol down on the back of another's skull. Jones had laid out two of the men with his fists. From out of the shadow behind Ben, another of the thugs lunged with a dagger. Just in time, Ben caught the glint of the bright blade and managed to twist out of its way, but it nicked his arm, cutting through his sleeve and into the skin. With a single backhanded swing of his pistol, he knocked the attacker completely off his feet. Before Ben could follow up his attack, the man ran like a hare up the road. The rest ran away, leaving their fallen colleagues in the street.

Ben turned over one of the men with his foot. "I hate amateurs; this lot couldn't fight their way out of a fog." They all laughed and Ben checked on Boyle. "Does this happen often?"

"No, not really, but some of the pro-slavers have a lot of money to lose if these bills are passed through Parliament."

They reached Boyle's lodgings.

"Come in, we need to take a look at your arm," Boyle said.

Ben was holding his arm to staunch the bleeding, while Boyle found a strip of cloth to bandage it.

"Why don't you join us, Mr Burrows, you're obviously very useful in a fight."

"Some other time, I'm busy at the moment; my wife and daughter have gone missing I fear that she has been kidnapped, and yet we have not had any ransom note or any word at all."

"That's most curious, if it was a kidnapping surely they would want to profit from it."

"Mr Burrows has tried his best to locate them, but we seem to be drawing a blank with each enquiry," David said.

"Oh my Lord, what a mess; leave it with me, I'll see if I can do anything. If you think that I can help then please just ask. What about your arm, should I call a doctor?"

"No need, my valet has had some practice of stitching me back together. He usually enjoys the task; we crack open a bottle of brandy, supposedly to kill the pain and clean the wound, but most of it gets consumed."

14. Desperate Actions

On-board Pelican, Jeremiah Todd returned from his exercise walk to the dim, cold world of his cell, he had convinced himself that now was the right time to make his bid for freedom guessing that there may not be many others. While on deck, he had been watching the coastline and felt certain that with the right equipment they could survive in the forests along the rugged coast. He gathered his co-conspirators, but to his annoyance, only three were still interested.

"It doesn't matter about the others, let 'em rot here, we can still make a break for it," Todd said.

"Will the plan work with only three of us?"

"I think providence has just smiled on us," Todd said he pointed across the deck.

Booth was busily checking some paperwork by the light of an oil lamp. He was so engrossed in what he was doing that he was not paying any attention to his surroundings, nor was he watching where he was walking because he had strayed away from the guard's protection. Todd eased open the cell gate which was never locked while they were at sea. Carefully, he sneaked across the deck; the sounds of the ship, the waves against the hull, the creaking of the woodwork covered the sound of his footsteps. He felt a shiver of nervous anticipation as he moved into place; there was no going back now. Like a cat, he stalked up behind the judge and slipped his arm around the neck of the unsuspecting man.

Booth struggled and let out a cry that alerted the guards, but they had no idea how to deal with the situation.

"Now you just keep yourself nice and quiet and no one will get hurt," Todd whispered into his captive's ear. "You lot keep out of my way or he gets it," he said to the two guards.

Immediately, the guards locked the other cells before there was a mass escape.

"Let go of me. You'll hang for this," Booth spluttered.

The four conspirators realised that the die was cast and that their only hope if they had one at all, was that they would be put ashore. They frogmarched Booth along the dimly lit deck, much to the bewilderment and excitement of the other convicts who whistled and cheered loudly and soon they were banging their mugs and plates on the iron bars that surrounded them.

"Go for it Todd, slit the bastard's throat," someone shouted.

They pushed Booth up the steps and onto the main deck. A guard challenged them, but he had the sense to back away as soon as he saw that Todd was holding a crude blade hard against the skin of Booth's throat.

Snow was on watch and heard the commotion and when he saw the problem, he sent word for the Captain. "Wait there, don't move until the Captain arrives," Snow called. He ran and stood in front of them blocking their way.

"Are you unhurt Mr Booth?" Snow asked in a matter of fact way.

Booth gave a nervous nod hardly daring to move his head.

Mitchell marched across the deck; he had put on his full uniform and with a stern face approached Todd. "So what's this all about?" He said his voice was flat and calm.

"I want you to put us ashore!" Todd yelled.

"What is your name?"

"Todd, Jeremiah Todd."

"Well, Mr Todd I suggest that you rethink this plan of yours because it's not a very good one."

"I want weapons, supplies, and then to be put ashore."

"We can discuss that," Mitchell said without any change to his voice, "but let us start with this; if you draw a single drop of blood from Mr Booth's throat, I will keelhaul you, and then hang your remains from the yardarm for the rest of the journey. Is that clear?"

Todd felt suddenly insecure; he nodded that he understood but he did not trust himself to speak. He was so tense that he was having difficulty breathing; his hand began to shake and he feared that he might accidentally stab his hostage.

Snow and Hardy watched their captain, this was a lesson they would not find in any seafarer's manual; both of them realised that they still had a lot to learn about being a captain.

"So, where do we go now?" Mitchell said his tone was sympathetic, almost friendly. He paused a moment, he knew that he had only one chance to get this right. "Mr Hardy," he called over his shoulder, "three of your best marksmen here this instant."

Todd now looked very worried, his bottom lip was quivering slightly and he was quickly losing confidence unsure that he could carry on. His three accomplices huddled close behind him; they had completely lost their nerve. The three marines came to attention within feet of Todd, there was the usual stamping of their boots and then the clatter of their muskets as they were brought to their sides and hammered onto the deck.

Booth was feeling faint and overwhelmed by fear; he gave Mitchell a pleading look and then wet himself.

"Just put us ashore!" Todd snapped.

The Winds of Change.

"Do you know where we are?"

"South America," Todd said.

"I don't know for certain, because our charts are rather sketchy, but I think that we are off a large island, not the mainland." He waited for a reaction. "What will you do once you are ashore? There might be unfriendly natives, we are not leaving you a boat, and even if we did which way would you go?"

"What do you care?"

"I am not just charged with your deportation, but also with your welfare, and believe me I do care what happens to you. I pride myself on how few men I have lost in active service and this is no different."

"Let me worry about our fortunes."

"Mr Hardy," Mitchell called over his shoulder, "three muskets, and enough powder for fifty shots, a felling axe, two hand axes and a quarter of salted beef into the jolly-boat. You'd best add a keg of beer too." Mitchell's eyes were still fixed on Todd's face. "There is no happy outcome for this situation, you would have been better taking your chances in Van Dieman's land. Release Mr Booth, get in the boat, my men will row you ashore, but after that, you are on your own.

"How do I know that I can trust you? As soon as I release him you'll shoot us all dead."

"No, I don't break my word, I have told you what will happen," Mitchell said.

"You are setting an unfortunate precedent Captain, the other prisoners will try this method of escape, we'll none of us be safe," Booth managed to whisper.

"Then perhaps I should let him slit your throat, we will gun them down where they stand, and that will be an end to it. I suppose the paperwork will be a drudge."

Booth's mind was racing and he had a change of heart when he realised that unless he was prepared to sacrifice himself, he should go along with Mitchell's suggestion.

There was a silent pause as everyone thought about their options. Todd released his hold on Booth and with a trembling hand lowered the blade, bracing himself for the volley of gunfire that he fully expected to follow; he glared at Mitchell daring him to break his word.

Booth rubbed at his throat and gratefully nodded towards Mitchell.

The tension was broken when Hardy announced. "The boat's loaded, Captain."

"Make sure all the cells are locked and the prisoners secured," Mitchell said.

Nervously the convicts climbed down the ship's side and into the waiting boat. It was not an easy crossing there were high waves with deep troughs that tossed the little boat so dramatically that it seemed that all might overturn and be lost. The landing was even more difficult and there was the constant fear that they would be smashed against the rocks. One of the convicts leapt across the gap between the boat and rocks, he managed to cling on and to secure them with a rope.

Mitchell watched as the boat was unloaded on the rocks. He doubted if they could survive very long; there was plenty of wildlife for them to hunt, but their ammunition would soon run out. He waited for the jolly boat's return, everyone watched as the men on shore scampered away to hide in the forest.

"Weigh the anchor, Mr Snow, let us leave them to do what they will," Mitchell said.

"Aye, aye, Captain."

The shanty they sang as they turned the capstan to raise the anchor was a jolly tune about the joys of a certain Lady of Liverpool, which belied the real mood of the men. Any sort of mutiny was upsetting and this was no different, even though the mutineers were not part of the crew.

Mitchell and Booth stood together watching from the stern rail as they sailed away, the mutineers were nowhere to be seen.

"What will be their fate, Captain?" Booth said.

"I've no idea; if they are lucky they'll meet up with some friendly natives and live with them, they need to find a land bridge to the mainland because there are very few resources on this island. I don't think they realised that it was an island, maybe somewhere to the north is a narrow stretch of water they could cross. If we were ever to come back, I think that we would find that they had drunk all the ale, and then shot each other arguing over the last dregs."

"What will you put in your log?"

"The only mention I shall make of them will be that they were cast ashore after their involvement in a mutiny," Booth paused a moment. "I'd like to thank you for handling the matter in such a sober way, you saved my life and no dispute."

"Experience, Mr Booth, there is no substitute for it; no amount of book learning can equal it."

Later that day, Mitchell wrote his daily log, he mentioned the mutiny.

Against my better judgement, but to preserve, Mr Booth's life, I cast three men onto what I believe to be an island off the coast of Chile. We shall not be returning this way and it is unlikely that we will ever know their fate; may God have mercy upon them.

The Winds of Change.

We are now caught in a strong northerly current, which I am expecting to turn west very soon and then we will face the daunting challenge of the open and deserted Pacific Ocean. We are forty-two degrees south, which is in alignment with Van Diemen's Land, albeit we are five thousand miles east of that place; if we can hold a westerly course from here we should reach our destination in about a month. The weather is fair with a steady easterly breeze and we are making over one hundred miles per day.

We have managed to restock our water and there is still plenty of the fresh meat we hunted and wild herbs that were gathered, so they should last the journey.

We have lost two more convicts, they have been suffering from some malady; we buried them at sea with a Christian service on Christmas Day 1822. I am looking forward with all my heart to our journey north to the Spice Islands.

He glanced up from his desk to watch Elvira; she was silhouetted against the light of the rear cabin window, watching the sea she hummed to herself. She too was wondering about the future, she tried not to dwell on the past and wondered if she could survive or even endure life in a penal colony.

Against Booth's advice, she had now moved permanently into Mitchell's quarters and as he watched her, he realised, that counter to his best judgment, he was hopelessly in love with her; a new experience for him. There had been others in the past, ladies of title all of whom were willing to take the walk down the aisle with him, but his career had always been the most important thing in his life, except for now. She had become a regular at the Captain's table for evening meals and all his officers, including Snow, enjoyed her company, even Booth had stopped complaining about her being there.

What should I do about her when we reach our destination? I don't want to leave her there, he thought.

He watched her for a little while longer; it was his current favourite pastime.

"My steward is sulking at me because you are doing so many of his jobs," he said with a smile.

She smiled back at him and stretched her arms out in front of the wide bay window.

"How long before we reach… you know," she said.

"Perhaps a month, it depends on the weather," he said sadly.

"Then we should make the most of our time together."

She turned to face him and with an impish smile let her blouse slip to the floor.

15. Cattle Thieves.

"Come on, Mr Burrows, rise and shine, it's time to get up," Mould said in a very sober voice. "Looks like you hit the bottle again last night. I have to tell you that you'll not find a solution there you know." He busied himself picking up Ben's clothes that were scattered across the floor. "How's the arm this morning?" he threw back the curtains.

Ben groaned as the flood of light blinded him. "Leave me alone," he croaked. Reluctantly, he sat up. There were bags under his eyes and the stress and excessive alcohol of the previous evening gave his face a ghastly pallor.

"You've got company arriving this morning. There's never a rainbow without a little rain skipper," Mould said.

"The last thing I need this morning is philosophy."

"Well, the first thing you need is to be made presentable, so let's give you a shave. What will Mr Barraclough think of you?" Mould inspected Ben's bandage and made sure that the wound was clean. "It was like old times, putting a few stitches in for you."

"Drinking my brandy you mean."

"Your libations were always generous, Skipper, you always did have a good taste in beverages. Come on, let's get you tidied up."

"I'd expected some news by now, maybe even a ransom note; that would have been better than nothing at all, but there's just this damned silence," Ben said feeling totally depressed over the issue.

"I think someone is trying to hurt you, trying to disrupt your life."

Ben stared at him. "Yes, and they are bloody well doing it, you could be right, maybe it's not about money; perhaps it's something else altogether."

He stared into the mirror looking deep into his own eyes; he realised that he was afraid. It was not the first time he had been scared, he remembered the mind-numbing fear he had experienced before his first battle aboard HMS Seagull. He was part of a seven-man gun-crew manning one of the main guns. They had no option other than to wait patiently behind their gun as the French warship's guns pounded them with constant deadly salvos of cannon shot. It seemed to go on forever; deadly splinters of wood flew in all directions as the enemy's shot relentlessly hammered their woodwork. It went on until they were between two enemy ships and in a position that they could return fire. The fear was replaced by a rush of adrenaline that tingled through his veins and numbed him from head to toe; then like a robot, he went through the actions of loading and firing his gun. In many ways, this

The Winds of Change.

new situation was much worse; before, there was only his own life to worry about, but now there was much more at stake and other lives involved, he blamed himself for not making sure that they were safe.

Mould carefully whisked the shaving soap into a thick creamy lather. "What about your advertisements in the press?" he said.

"Nothing, and that's despite the offered reward for information. I've never felt so desperate, or so useless." Ben's head was tilted back as Mould lathered his chin. "We've come through a lot, Mr Mould, I got used to the fear of battle, the despair of losing comrades, and the feeling of hopelessness when we faced a raging storm with mountainous waves as we sailed the oceans, but this is something far worse. It's like a fiery hand reaching deep into me and tearing out my heart and soul."

"Take heart in the fact that all the lads are behind you and they will do their utmost to make sure we get them, ladies, back safe and sound."

Mould worked around Ben's face with the shaving soap and could not help a wry smile as he reached the various scars he'd made on several occasions when he'd had to stitch Ben back together. He slapped the razor on the leather strop beating out a rhythmic song as steel slipped along the leather. With practised ease, he honed the blade until he was happy with its sharpness and then he set to work carefully removing Ben's facial stubble.

"You know, if it is Quigley, perhaps he's not getting in touch just to tease you, make it hurt more, like twisting the blade," Mould said.

Once he had finished shaving, he pushed Ben's head about so that he could check his handiwork. "There's your new jacket and a clean shirt at the end of the bed. Breakfast will be ready in ten minutes, so shake a leg," Mould said. "I'll send this coat for mending." He poked his fingers through the hole in the sleeve made by the dagger.

Ben stood up and stretched. "Thank you, Mr Mould, what would I do without you? You'll make someone a wonderful wife one day."

Mould declined to answer; he just shook his head and went back to his kitchen to make breakfast. Walter entered, he had been helping Jenny in the dairy since first light. He climbed on Ben's knee.

"You sleep late papa, I've been busy for hours."

"I had a late-night, how are you this morning?"

"I'm not great," he said in a very mature manner. "I miss Dorothy and Mummy. Why don't they come home?"

"They will do soon, I'm sure they will."

Emily and Edward arrived mid-morning and when they saw Ben, they were concerned for his well-being.

"You must bring Walter, and Mr Mould and come to stay with us," Emily insisted.

Edward placed a reassuring hand on Ben's shoulder. "Tim and Jenny can look after things here. It'll be like old times, you'll see, everything will work out all right, I'm sure."

Emily made an excuse to go see Jenny and to give the men time to talk. After she had left, Edward studied Ben a moment. "You look a bit of a mess, you've got to shake yourself up a bit or you'll not be thinking straight. We are all worried about Emma and Dorothy, but until we have something to go on, there is no use fretting, or staring into an empty glass, that will never help."

"This is the worst time of my life, I just don't know what else I can do, we've drawn a blank with everything we've tried. Mould thinks that maybe, Quigley is keeping quiet, to twist the knife and hurt me more."

"You're a fighter, my lad, sitting idle is not your style, I know that I can only guess how hurtful it is to do nothing, but you must stay strong and ready for when we do know something."

Edward felt sorry for his friend and knew that no words of comfort would be of any real help, but he was convinced that Ben would be better moving to his house in Cartmel rather than being here on his own.

Walter, who had been at Jenny's playing with Eve, dashed in to see Edward.

"Now then young man what have you been up to?" Edward said.

"Playing, Eve is really funny; now that she has started talking, we can't shut her up."

Walter sat on Edward's knee; he stared solemnly into his eyes and with childish honesty asked, "Is my mother dead, just like Eve's?"

"No, of course not, she's fine, she's with Dorothy, but we've lost her for just a short while, she'll be back soon," Edward said confidently. "Do you remember when Sam went missing? Well, we couldn't see him but he came home and he was alright."

Ben moved to Cartmel the following day and immediately felt better; his friends rallied around and distracted him from his worries. He threw himself into the business of running the farm, he knew he had let some of his duties slip and he was determined to make amends. He filled each day with various tasks so that he did not have time to think and fret about Emma, but quite often, in the night, he found himself reaching for her and it was then that he missed her most. However, the lack of news and lack of sleep was taking its toll on him, so much so that his friends were worried about his health. Jones was given the job of being Walter's minder to make sure that Quigley did not try to kidnap him too.

The Winds of Change.

At breakfast one morning five weeks after his move to Cartmel everyone was very subdued and it seemed as if things could not get any worse when Ian Douglas came hammering on the door. They were all startled and for a moment, no one dared to open it, afraid of what the news might be.

"Ye must come wi' me, cattle raiders have taken about twenty of the Galloways," Ian said, he was out of breath, his cheeks were flushed and he had obviously been running hard.

"Sit down, take a drink of tea," Emily said.

Ian ran his fingers through his mop of fiery red hair to try to bring it under control. "I thank ye mistress, but there's no time. Douglas himself is on their trail; there were maybe six or eight of them."

"Take a drink, man, it will take us a few minutes to saddle the horses and make ready, we'll be as quick as possible," Edward said. He offered Ian his hip flask, with a sly wink. "A wee dram will help you climb the fells a little easier."

Ben had already thrown his heavy raincoat on and was dancing around the kitchen trying to put on his riding boots. "We... what we? He said to Edward. "You're not going anywhere with that leg, we might be chasing up and down the fells all day. We need you here, this may be more than simple theft."

"Ben's right Edward, why don't you go over to Fell Farm and make sure Tim and Jenny are all right," Emily said. "Walter and Mr Jones will look after me here."

Edward was obviously disappointed, but he helped saddle up the horses and made sure Ben was armed. "Bruce and Brendon are working in the lower meadow, pick them up on your way," he said.

It was drizzling as they clattered over the cobblestones of the market square and out towards the fells. Although the news was bad, Ben was glad to have something to occupy his mind. When he found Brendon and Bruce they also liked the sound of some action. "Anything's better than knocking in more fence posts," Brendan said.

With Ian hanging onto Ben's saddle strap, they rode as fast as possible up to where they could pick up the trail. It was not hard to find.

"Here look, my God, they've not tried to cover their tracks. There's plenty of evidence in this soft ground as to which way they've gone," Ian said.

Ten minutes later a rather hot and flustered Jamie ran to meet them. He straightened his jacket and tugged on his beard then knocked flecks of mud from his kilt before he spoke.

"They've camped along the next valley. There's something strange, I don't think it's about the cattle if you ken my meaning."

"What then?" Ben said.

"I sense something else is afoot. It's an ambush. I think they've taken them bonny beasties as bait for us to follow. They've penned them along the valley around a corner and some of their men armed with muskets are waiting in hiding just along the track," Jamie said, he tugged anxiously at his beard.

"We're not armed for a shootout," Ben said, "Bruce; you go back to Cartmel and bring back some of those carbines and plenty of that ammunition Edward's got under lock and key. We've plenty of time, it doesn't look as if the cattle thieves are going anywhere. We'll wait until dark before we do anything."

"Bring some food too," Jamie whispered. "I'm so hungry, my belly thinks that my throat's cut,"

"There's a wee dell runs alongside this one," Ian said, "maybe we could get behind them and see what they're up to."

Ben handed Brendon one of his pistols. "You stay here, while we go and see if we can get behind them."

Jamie placed his hand on Ben's shoulder. "Nay, Mr Burrows, Ian and I are better at this task; we've spent our lives stalking prey across the heather. You stay put here, like a cork in the bottle and we'll be back as soon as possible with what news we can gather, and our enemy will be none the wiser of our presence."

Just as they had done so many times before in the Highlands of Scotland, Jamie and Ian stalked silently across the land. Following small ravines and cuts in the landscape, they worked their way along the Valley until they reached the place where they were sure that they were behind the cattle thieves. They settled a moment to get their bearings and then using only sign language Jamie guided Ian until they were both within sight of the corralled animals.

"Looks like they are settling in for a long night," Jamie whispered. They watched the thieves lay out their blankets and built a fire.

Ben hid the horses, and then he and Brendon found a place to rest. They sat in silence a moment, but Brendon was fidgeting uncomfortably. "What's going on skipper? First Emma and Dorothy vanishing and now this," he said.

"I'm not sure, but this could be related to Emma's disappearance. No doubt, Quigley, will have something to do with it, which means that there's a chance we might find something out if we can capture at least one of these bandits."

"Some of the lads were saying that it's the gold we found; that there's a curse on it," Brendon said, his gravelly voice sounded like a growl.

The Winds of Change.

"I think the curse is on me, not the gold. I thought that my luck had changed when I found Emma and when Ruth's sad death brought Dorothy home. I couldn't have been happier, but I'm sure that this is due to nothing other than that evil-hearted bastard, Quigley, getting his revenge on me."

Bruce returned armed to the teeth with a couple of swords and three carbines. "Any news," he said. He threw down his load and offered a parcel to Ben. "I've brought food."

Ben shook his head. "We're still waiting for Jamie to report back."

There was a sudden movement amongst the trees followed by the appearance of Jamie. He sat down on a tree stump to get his breath back. "It's definitely an ambush. They've set up pickets and secured the beasts to act as bait in a trap."

"How many are there?" Ben said

"Difficult to say, but I think that there are eight of them."

"What about this other valley? Can we use it to get behind them?" Ben said

"Yes, I was going to suggest that. Leave them to stew all day and then this evening we can circle around them and surprise them from behind at first light."

"It sounds as if they've trapped themselves in," Brendon said.

"Oh aye, they're not going anywhere now, we've got 'em as tight as a cork in a bottle," Jamie said. "Talking of which did ye remember some victuals."

Later, Ian came into their camp. "They've settled down for the wait. One hidden each side of the valley, armed with muskets; the rest have made a camp further back near the animal pen. They've plenty of arms; I'd say they are itching for a fight."

"By God, they'll get more of a fight than they could ever have imagined, come first light," Ben said.

By evening the clouds had cleared away, leaving a fingernail of a moon hanging above them. Jamie predicted that there would be a ground frost by morning, he threw his plaid over his shoulder and settled down. A few hours later, somewhere out in the dark forest, a vixen called out, her eerie call, almost like a screaming child broke the silence; Jamie stirred he knew that it was time for action.

Ben's crew set off along the valley, the adrenaline was pumping through their veins, their nerves tingled and their senses were on high alert. The plan of action had been carefully worked out down to the finest detail. Ian and Jamie split up so that they could each deal with the men waiting in ambush. A smile curled Ian's lips as he stealthily approached his quarry, he felt alive, burning with the thrill of the stalk.

Tony Mead.

Like a hunting tiger, he stepped silently through the undergrowth and then froze as a twig beneath his foot snapped. He waited patiently hardly daring to breathe. *Did they hear that has the sound carried,* he thought? Once he was confident that it had not, he stepped forward again. A large fallen oak blocked his way and rather than climb over it, he silently slithered beneath it. He caught a faint sound and knew immediately his task was going to be quite simple; his quarry was asleep snoring peacefully, blissfully unaware of the danger he was in. Ian crept closer and before the guard knew what was happening, he was bound and gagged. In the dim light, the man stared in disbelief at Ian, fear and panic gripped him, he tried to wriggle free, but Ian touched the end of the man's nose with the tip of his razor-sharp dagger blade.

"Shh, be good, or I'll open your head like a warm tatty," Ian whispered giving the man an evil wink.

Across the valley, Jamie had also accomplished his task, but his target had been more alert. It had taken only a brief moment for Jamie to permanently silence him; the man fell to the ground with an expression of bewilderment, and fear across his face as he clutched at his gushing throat. The second part of the plan was to wait until dawn and then move in on the other bandits.

Ben, waited in a position where he could see the bandits' camp, by the time the first of the sun's rays were breaking through the trees their campfire had burnt away leaving just a few glowing embers. He looked along the barrel of his carbine slowly and deliberately cocking its hammer so that as soon as he could see anything other than the few shadows he was ready.

It seemed like the start of a perfect day, the filtered sunlight slowly brought the dawn chorus to life, it started with a bold blackbird proclaiming his territory and built into a cacophony of sound that was loud enough to wake the dead. A fine mist rolled down the valley. Ben signalled to Bruce and Brendon to move closer to the camp. Keeping low they advanced until they reached the little clearing. The bandits slept soundly despite the birdsong, unaware that they were a few heartbeats away from being in real peril. Ian and Jamie arrived, signalling Ben with an owl hoot to tell of their arrival, and now the bandits were surrounded. Jamie went over to one of the men who was rolled tightly in a blanket and kicked him in the ribs. The man sprung to life and although he was still half asleep, went for his pistol, he levelled it at Jamie, but before he could fire Ben shot him dead. One of the others went for his gun, but Jamie stood on its barrel and pointed the muzzle of his carbine right into the man's unhappy face.

"Move and I'll blow yer head away down the valley," Jamie said.

The Winds of Change.

They herded the frightened gang together near where their fire smouldered.

"Now then lads; you've got a bit of explaining to do," Ben said.

"Who are you?" one of the bandits said defiantly.

"Never mind, who are we, more the question is, who are you? What do you mean by stealing my cattle?"

"We're not stealing them; we bought 'em fair and square; them's our cattle."

The frightened men were searching for a way to escape, but in the face of the cocked guns, they were behaving themselves. It was too much for one of them; he made his last mistake, jumping up he tried to grab Ian. While he was still in the air, Bruce shot him, the man was knocked backwards by the musket ball, his head went back, and Ian slashed his throat wide open. The man fell dead on the ground before the sound of the shot had finished echoing through the trees. It stilled the others.

"Don't make the mistake of thinking you are dealing with a bunch of farmers here. I want some answers, or my Douglas friend there will slash all your throats. Who sent you?" Ben bellowed at them. He was trying to suppress his anger but his emotions were like red-hot snakes writhing inside his head and getting the better of him.

"Go to hell!" a particularly unpleasant looking man said through disdainful lips.

"Not the right answer," Ben said and to everyone's surprise calmly shot the man in the chest. The shot went right through him and as it came out of his back the blood-splattered his companions. Where there had been defiance, there was now, cold, gripping fear.

"You have to be Burrows," one of them dared to say, "we were told you were a mad bastard."

"You're right that I'm mad, someone has taken my wife and daughter, I'm very mad." Ben's voice was a low menacing growl. "I'll kill you all if I don't get an answer. Don't think I'm afraid to, I've already sent plenty of men to hell, they'll all be waiting there for me, so I'm not worried about sending a few more."

One of the gang looked at the one who had been the quietest and pointed to him. "He set us on! Honest mister, I don't know anything about your wife."

The man who had been pointed out hammered his fist into the face of his betrayer. Bruce was the first to react and knocked him back against a tree stump.

"Tie them up, but leave this one with me," Ben said.

Tony Mead.

Jamie put his face close to the quiet man's who he guessed was the gang leader. "You'll all hang for this," Ben said with a grin. "I'm sorely tempted to look for a suitable bough to drape you from right now. So, don't push your luck, we're only law-abiding up to a point, and we are at that place right now."

Ben dragged the man by his collar over towards the embers of the fire.

"Where's Quigley?" Ben said.

"Who?"

"I'm not in the mood for games, so I advise you not to mess with me," Ben said.

He knelt beside the fire and drew a smouldering stick from it. He blew the end until it went bright red and a single orange flame leapt to life.

"Quigley?"

"Never heard of him."

Ben blew the twig again and placed it close to the man's eye. The man's head tilted back away from the heat.

"Quigley?" Ben whispered. The red-hot end was slowly getting closer to the man's cheek. "Quigley?"

The man's nerve held, maybe he thought that Ben would not carry out his threat until the skin of his cheek sizzled and pain such as he had never felt surged across his face. He screamed and tried to roll away clutching at his burnt flesh, but Bruce knelt on the back of the man's leg to immobilise him.

"Quigley?" Ben's voice was calm but menacing.

He gently blew the stick again and then directed it at his face again. The man screamed, the colour drained from his face as he stared at the glowing stick in dismay. "I don't know where he is right now, honestly, I don't."

"Aha, so now you remember the name. When did you last see him, where were you?"

Ben blew on the stick again and aimed it directly at the man's eye. "Where and when? Or I'm the last thing you'll see."

Brendan took hold of the man's head from behind and placing his fingers on his eyelids, he held them wide open.

"I'll not miss your eyes now. Thank you, Brendan," Ben said.

"Manchester, but he was boarding a ship bound for the West Indies out of Liverpool the following day."

Ben was stunned by the news. "When?"

"It was about a month maybe six weeks ago; I don't know for sure. We met in a tavern, I've done some work for him before; capturing

The Winds of Change.

slaves, collecting debts that sort of thing. Steal some of your cattle, says he, kill as many of the crew as you can, but not Burrows. We could wound you he said, but you were to be left alive."

Bruce tied the man's arms behind his back. "This is getting very personal," Bruce said.

"We should hang 'em all now and save the justice the trouble," Ian said.

"Where was he sailing to?" Ben said.

"He just said the Caribbean, that's the truth."

Ben blew on the stick again as if pondering the situation. The bandit kept his eyes fixed on the glowing tip as Ben toyed with it.

"Are you sure? Is there anything else you want to tell me?" Ben said in a sympathetic whisper.

"No, honestly, I don't know anything about your wife being missing; he did say that his plans had gone wrong and he had expected you to be on your way to Van Diemen's Land, but I'm not sure what he meant."

Ben decided that he would not get any more out of the man, but the way he felt he could happily murder the whole gang and not feel any remorse, but instead, he reluctantly threw the stick back onto the fire.

"Brendan, you and Bruce take these no goods to the constable in Ulverston. If they give you any troubles at all, just shoot them, it'll save the hangman a job," Ben said.

Jamie and Ian were checking the animals to make sure that they were unharmed.

"I think yer beasties have enjoyed their little stroll. You get back to Cartmel and we'll bring them back to the pasture," Jamie said to Ben.

On his return to Cartmel, Ben tried to make sense of the news that Quigley had gone to the Caribbean and that he had expected Ben to be sailing around the world. When he reached Edward's, Emily had a hot meal waiting for him and as usual, they all gathered around the dining table.

"So have you any theories about this news?" Edward said.

"Only that maybe Quigley is acting under someone else's instructions, certainly somebody with a lot of clout," Ben said rather uncertainly.

"That could be the Caribbean connection," Emily said.

"What about, Tinker, or whatever that land agent was called?" Edward said.

"Ah yes, Theodore Tinker, he would dearly like to get his hands on the deeds to our lands out there," Ben said.

"I don't think that kidnapping is his style," Bruce said.

"How did he know that Pelican would be sailing for Van Diemen's Land?" Ben said.

"If he did know, well then, he must also have thought that you would Captain it again."

"It sounds like he wanted you out of the way, but how could he have organised it?" Edward said.

"He has friends in high and low places," Ben said. "It makes me wonder about Quigley's gang member we interviewed in Lancaster and his untimely death."

Fletch and Mould arrived and everyone moved around to allow them to sit at the table.

"What about that dictator we upset, Don Pedro Juan Silver, he was very much aggrieved by our actions," Fletch said.

Ben smiled at Fletch who as usual was dressed in a fine suit and looked every inch the country gent, even down to a gold watch chain that hung across from pocket to pocket of his waistcoat.

"What about Compton?" Edward said and then paused. "If he has found out that you are Dorothy's father, well then he'll be more than a bit put out, he also had eyes on our land. I think right from the off he regretted granting us it."

"Sir Arthur… you can't think that he would be involved," Ben said.

"He has the clout to pull a few strings and have Pelican conscripted, Brendon's suggestion makes sense if that is the case. He'd think Ben was away with his ship, perhaps he was only kidnapping Dorothy, maybe he still thinks she's his." Edward said. "Maybe when he realised that you had not sailed he had to try something else."

"I think that we need to visit the islands of the Caribbean once more," Ben said solemnly.

There was a long silence and in fact, no one even moved as they considered that suggestion. For all of them, the thought of another trip was a mixture of sweet and sour feelings.

"That is a very big decision for any of us to take," Edward said.

Emily tried not to show her emotions, but she was devastated by the thought of them all sailing away again.

16. Temptress

Ben rode back to Alithwaite to make sure that Jenny and Tim were safe. *Why has Quigley gone to the Caribbean?* Ben thought as he rode across the fell. He pulled up as he reached a good vantage place that gave him a view of the bay and out to sea. The tide was in and several small fishing boats were returning home.

Where are you my darling? He cried to the wind. *Captain Mitchell, it's time I heard from you too,* he thought, he trusted him to captain Pelican safely, but the long silence and wait were hard to endure on top of everything else that was going on. He tried to imagine where Pelican was; it had been almost a year since she had sailed and another Christmas had passed. The only word back from them was when they reached the Caribbean; he guessed that they might have reached their first destination; Van Diemen's Land and could be heading for India. *I'd think he'll be around the horn by now, probably basking in glorious sunshine and being served cool beverages by dusky maidens,* he thought, the idea made him smile.

When he reached the farm, there was an unfamiliar coach in the yard. It had four coachmen in matching uniforms standing beside it, one of the men held the harness of the lead horse. When they saw Ben, they jumped to attention to salute him. Under their scrutiny, he studied the brightly coloured coat of arms on the coach door, and although he thought he had seen it before, he was no nearer knowing who his visitor was. He patted the neck of one of the horses, it was a powerful creature with a sleek, glossy coat. "My you are a beauty," he said.

It shook its head making the highly polished harness jangle and then scraped the ground with its hoof as though it was answering him.

Jenny met him at the door. "You've got a visitor. While the cat's away, I don't think that you should play," she said with a disapproving scowl.

Ben looked puzzled and he was lost for an answer to her rather sarcastic comment. The coat of arms may have been a mystery, but the tall, elegantly dressed woman standing in his parlour was not. Her broad-brimmed hat cast a shadow across her lightly tanned face adding a sense of mystery and intrigue. She smiled a modest yet inviting smile that curled the edges of her rouged lips.

"Annabelle!" Ben said as he tried to cover his shock and dismay. "This is a surprise, please, take a seat. I'm sorry my valet, Mr Mould is not here to make some tea," Ben said. He felt quite flustered this visit was unexpected and she was not particularly welcome. "Can I offer you some port?"

"I'll make some tea," Jenny said; she had obviously been eavesdropping from the kitchen.

Annabelle carefully positioned herself on the edge of the sofa as if posing for an artist; her bright azure blue silk dress flowed over her body like rippling waves as she moved. The hat decorated with forget-me-nots and secured beneath her chin with a bright blue ribbon sat demurely on her head.

"Trouble should be your middle name, it follows you about like a younger brother," she said with a sweet smile.

Jenny interrupted them. "Anything else?"

"No, thank you, Jenny I'll speak to you later."

Jenny returned to the kitchen, she was in something of a huff, but she deliberately left the door ajar so that she could hear what was being said.

Ben turned to Annabelle. "So what brings you here?" his tone was not particularly friendly. "I don't have much time; I need to go over to Cartmel as soon as possible."

Annabelle smiled and refused to be hurried as she sipped her tea. "Well, since we met in Ulverston, I've been thinking about you, and the fact that Emma is absent." She smiled at him. "This reminds me of a meeting we once had in Portsmouth, how many years ago was that, I wonder," she said peering over the rim of her cup. "You look ill," she whispered, her voice was as smooth as silk.

"I've been up all night chasing cattle thieves," Ben said. "I'm really tired, what is it you want?" he was more abrupt than he had meant to be.

"It was quite a surprise when I heard from Emma's parents the news of Ruth's death. I thought Emma might have informed me, as we were all such old friends." She watched Ben for some reaction. "Timely, just when you were about to walk Emma down the aisle."

"What are you suggesting, why bring that up now?"

"You were always so infatuated with Ruth, so much so that you had no time for anyone else and you hurtfully snubbed me, well after you'd had your wicked way that is."

"I'd given up on Ruth a long time before I met Emma. I finally accepted that I was only dreaming, thinking that Ruth would ever settle with me. Previously, I didn't care, because for years the dream was good enough." He went and stood by the fireplace to lean against the mantle. "She told me so many lies and I know that she always played me for the fool, but she brought me such joy and life was always such an adventure with her that I could not shake free of her."

"So you threw her over the bridge!"

The Winds of Change.

Ben gasped at the suggestion. "That's not what happened and you know it. She was so loaded with laudanum that she had no idea what she was doing. She fired two pistols in church and fully intended to kill someone."

"I wonder who," Annabelle purred. "Trust me, I knew her like myself; she had no intention of letting Emma steal you away from her, and don't think that the bullets were meant for you."

"Steal me from her, I didn't belong to her, she gave up that right when she refused to come back to England with me."

"I don't think she saw it quite like that. She always bragged that you belonged body and soul to her. She fully intended to disrupt your wedding and I think that there was definitely murder in her heart."

"She told me with her dying breath, that you told her about Emma and me."

"She had mothered your child, she came back to England to find you; I thought she deserved to know what was happening." She said with deep indignation.

"As you say, you knew her very well, so well, perhaps, you might have known or hoped that she would do something to spoil the wedding, especially when you knew she was taking such powerful drugs."

"Oh, Ben, how can you think, even for one minute that I wished you harm. You seem to presume that everything I do is just part of an evil scheme."

"Because I know of what you are capable, and what you have done against me in the past."

"There was a time, that I wished I could make your heart belong to me. What was it that Emma had to offer that I didn't? How did she melt your cold heart when I couldn't? How did she break the shackles that tied you to Ruth? Or maybe she didn't quite manage that." She was on the brink of losing her composure.

"It was easy to fall in love with Emma, there was no pretence, no false promises, she knew my past, but never tried to judge me, above all, she was always honest." He paused a moment. "She took my breath away the first time I saw her, I couldn't think straight, and it just seemed the most natural thing in the world that we should be together. At that moment I knew that if there was heaven, then it was there and I was in it." He confessed.

She stood up and seemed to walk aimlessly about the room ending by the door to the kitchen which she closed firmly.

"So, you were just toying with me, playing me for the whore," her cheeks blushed a fiery red, "You were just taking out your frustrations on me. Is that it?"

"We were just ships passing in the night, no promises, no commitment, I needed you at that moment and you willingly acted as a dressing for my wounded heart."

She circled the room coming back to stand close in front of him.

"I wanted more than that one afternoon and night; my heart craved for you, I yearned for your touch, you left a deep scar in my heart."

"Which is why you tried to ruin me."

She kept her eyes fixed on his searching for emotion or weakness.

"I had expected you to sail with your ship, I was surprised when you did not. Do you really trust Captain Mitchell enough to bring it back safe and sound?" she sat down again.

Ben was puzzled by her sudden shift of conversation. "Mitchell is the finest of sailors if anyone can make that voyage, well then he can."

"Well to business, or perhaps pleasure; I've just come to humbly ask if I can offer you some comfort in your time of need." She straightened her dress and smoothed her gloves along her arms. "Our recent meetings all seem spoilt by painful memories of our past; I'm sure that it is those that seem to keep us apart. We could put all that behind us; start afresh, a new encounter."

He decided to take the initiative and change tack. "How did you know Emma and Dorothy were missing?"

"We are related you know; It was Emma's parents, my in-laws of course, who let me know that Emma has been kidnapped." She kept her face in the shadow of her hat not allowing Ben to see her eyes. "I'm so sorry that she is gone; really I am. It's curious though that there has been neither a ransom note nor any a trace of her." She moved back to the sofa and sat down to lift her face into the light. "Perhaps she doesn't want to be found; perhaps being a farmer's wife is not enough for her."

He knew that she was teasing him, trying to sow a few seeds of doubt in his mind, but he had no intention of letting her goad him into any sort of reaction.

"We don't know anything yet." The honesty of that short statement seemed to take the wind from his sails and he was forced to sit down opposite her.

"You'd be more comfortable next to me." she patted the cushions beside her.

"Your middle name, Madam should be, Danger!" Ben said.

Annabelle laughed loudly. "Oh, Ben, we could have been so happy, even if we had just remained as lovers, ships occasionally passing in the night as you say. All those empty years before you met Emma, I waited, like a flower waiting for the sun, I expected you to contact me."

The Winds of Change.

"It was always the wrong place and the wrong time. There was the small matter of the fact that you were married," he said.

"That didn't stop you where Ruth was concerned."

"Also, are you forgetting the fact that it was you who revealed my true identity to your father the Admiral, which almost sent me to the gallows?"

"Oh, don't blame me," she said with a wave of her hand, "that was your own fault; you can't blame me, you hurt and insulted me." She stared intently at him. "You are the only man that has ever made me cry."

"Dented your huge ego more like," Ben said.

"I was cross with you. You were so besotted with Ruth that you couldn't see what a fool she was making of you; whereas I, after our one night together, I wanted more, I wanted you. Anyway, it was she who almost sent you to the gallows by not admitting the truth of how her brat of a brother died." She put down her cup. "I've not come here to argue."

"What then?"

Annabelle crossed her legs and the dress shimmered in the light from the window, she stared at Ben from beneath perfectly shaped eyebrows. "I want you to know that if the worst happens and Emma cannot be found and you feel the need to find comfort in a woman's arms, just as you did at Ruth's wedding; I'm still available for you," she said smouldering with passion. "Ruth, Emma, and I were such close friends at school, we shared everything. Ruth, God bless her, has departed this life and Emma has vanished without a trace and so it only seems right that I should be here for you to help you grieve and to satisfy your more physical needs."

Ben was speechless for a moment but determined not to lose his composure he steadied himself before he spoke again. "Annabelle, I'm flattered; I'm sure that there are countless men out there who would grab your offer with both hands and who would think that I am crazy for not taking you up on it, but as you say the memories get in the way."

Jenny came back into the room. "Can I collect your cups?" she stood defiantly between Ben and Annabelle. "Your horsemen are getting restless and I think it's time you went home, Ben has to be in Cartmel right now."

"How dare you, you impudent girl!" Annabelle spluttered. She stood up as if to strike Jenny, but Ben moved between them.

"I think she's right, Annabelle, you should leave now."

Annabelle stood inches away from Ben staring into his eyes like a snake trying to hypnotise its prey. He managed to divert his gaze and not to be lured into her trap.

"Neither this skivvy nor anything else will stand between us one day. My lips are still smouldering from the time we met and you did have the time for me." She kissed the end of her finger and placed it on Ben's lips. "You remember, don't you? I know that you do."

She gave Jenny a bored sneer and with that, strolled nonchalantly out without a backwards glance.

"Good heavens, the brazen tart," Jenny said. "I can't believe what she was saying."

Ben slumped into his chair with his head tucked into his hands. Jenny poured him a large glass of port.

"You shouldn't have been listening to what she was saying."

"Here, drink this," she said, her voice had an unusually impatient hard edge to it, "you have to remain strong for all our sakes. The old crew relies on you; they look to you for strength and direction." She kissed his hand as he took the glass. "I can understand how she feels; you've left a trail of broken hearts and disappointed women behind you. To be honest, that includes me."

"You! No, no, no... not you Jenny."

"You remember the winter we spent together in the cold snow; we cuddled up together every night and not just to keep warm."

"Of course I remember," he whispered. "I would not have survived that ordeal without you."

"When we finally met up again in the Caribbean, I thought you had come to rescue me not Ruth, and then you sent me back here to live with Emily at the old cottage; I thought you wanted me to wait for you."

"But you found Tim and were intent on marrying him by the time I came back."

"I thought that you were still in love with Ruth and I was not sure that you were coming back."

She sat on his knee and placed her arm around his neck. Neither of them spoke for some time.

"I don't know about the broken hearts, but I've left a trail of damaged friends in my wake. Do you think I'm being punished because of my past? I brought misery to the Linton's household."

"Not according to Emily, she says that despite everything that happened, Linton told her before he died, that he had loved you like a son; those are not the words of a damaged friend."

"No, but I sometimes feel as if I've let people down. You saved my life on more than one occasion and I will always be grateful to you, you are a good friend, but Emma is my wife," he said and kissed her forehead.

The Winds of Change.

"I need to go and see where Walter and Eve have got to," Jenny said brushing away a tear.

Ben sat for a while trying to make sense of what was happening to his life. For a brief moment, it had seemed that he could have a normal, steady existence away from the turmoil of his past life. *I should have known better,* he thought, *I just hope that I have the strength to see this through.*

17. Compton Island

"I wish we could move a little bit, we've been here two days now and my legs are really hurting," Dorothy said, her voice was sad and sulky. "I'm starving too... dare we call the guard again for some food?"

"Try to be patient, dear; we'll only annoy these thugs if we pester them."

They were still being kept in the back of the wagon, and only occasionally let out for a call of nature. Emma had taken the time when she was last allowed out to take note of their surroundings, and now she knew exactly where they were; it worried her.

"Do you know where we are?" Dorothy asked.

"Yes, I do, we're hidden in a small wooded area close to the beach."

"I said I could hear the sea."

"I've got a horrible fear that we are waiting for a boat or maybe a ship," she said in a low whisper and hoped that she would not frighten Dorothy.

"Where will they take us? I'm afraid of what's happening," Dorothy said.

"It will be all right, I'm sure, Ben will find us before anything happens."

Later that day the rear flap of the wagon was lifted and they were given bread and cheese.

"Do you have some freshwater please?" Emma said.

The man impatiently threw the cover closed again and they thought that he was going to ignore their appeal, but he returned a minute later with a large bottle of water.

"Oh that feels better," Dorothy said as she greedily chewed on the bread.

"Make the most of it; so far they've not been the most generous of hosts."

As the church clock struck seven the canvas flap at the rear of the wagon was lifted again. "Come on you two get out, you're going on a little journey." It was their usual guard and he was as unfriendly as ever.

It was a relief of sorts to get out and stretch their legs.

"This way, come on we've not got all night."

They were led over a shingle beach and told to wait. Dorothy cuddled close to Emma clinging to her arm, afraid to let her go. The incoming tide shimmered in the moonlight as it raced across the sands towards them; it brought a change in the air and a cold breeze that made them shiver.

The Winds of Change.

One of their guards began swinging a lantern and very soon, a small boat appeared out of the dark. It flashed a lantern in return and then ground into the beach with a gentle crunch. The men exchanged whispers and the boat was made secure.

"Please step aboard ladies," a sailor with a French accent said. He offered them his hand as they stepped warily over the side of the boat. The same sailor offered them a seat in the boat's bow. "Please be seated," he said with a smile. They felt a little more relaxed it was the first friendly face they had seen for days.

Emma had a sudden thought of home and wondered if she would ever see it again. Dorothy clung to Emma's arm and tried to stop herself from trembling; she did not want Emma to know that she was afraid.

The sailor called to the shore, they were pushed free of the beach, and then the oarsmen rowed the boat out against the tide. At first, it bobbed and bumped against the breaking waves until they were well away from the shore.

It seemed very dark out on the water, but Emma thought that she had seen a light further out and when the moon broke free from behind the clouds, its silver light illuminated a waiting vessel.

Another twenty minutes passed before they reached the ship and with each minute Emma became more worried, she was confident Ben would find them if they remained local, but the odds of him finding them lengthened if they were to be deported to some distant shore.

They were carefully hoisted aboard using a sling, Emma and Dorothy tried to act as bravely as they could, but the sensation of being hoisted high in the air in the almost pitch-black night was quite nerve-racking. Once aboard, they were not given time to get their bearings; they were taken down to one of the lower decks. The sailor politely opened the door for them and then stepped back for them to enter.

Their cabin was clean and tidy with ample space for them to sleep and eat.

"I would like to see your Captain," Emma said.

The sailor nodded and then smiled, but said nothing.

"We'd best make ourselves at home," Emma said and flopped wearily into a chair.

Dorothy sat on the end of the bunk. "Oh, some comfort at last; to sleep in a bed of any sorts will seem like a luxury."

"Shh, listen," Emma said, she held her hands up to silence Dorothy.

There was a change to the sounds of the ship, the crew were obviously busy above them, chains rattled, timber and ropes creaked as they were hauled upon. Emma knew that they were heading out to deeper water; suddenly the waves could be heard bumping against the hull. Dorothy wrapped herself in a blanket and sat on the bunk with her feet dangling over the side and her back against the wooden bulkhead. It was the safest she had felt for days and she soon fell asleep.

Some while later, there was a tap at their cabin door a young smartly dressed officer entered. "Are you settled in, I wondered if you were hungry? Can I send you a meal," he said politely.

"Where is the ship going?" Emma said. "I demand to see your Captain."

"I'm not at liberty to say, ma'am," he saluted and then left.

A much older and less well-dressed sailor arrived with a tray of food for them.

"Where are you taking us?" Emma asked.

"It's to be kept secret. So I can't tell you that missus, but don't worry, we'll look after you," the man said with a lopsided smile.

After he left, they ate in silence for a while, but Dorothy was bursting to talk and eventually she sat close to Emma to whisper in her ear.

"What is to become of us?"

"Well, I don't actually know, but we are too valuable alive for them to hurt us."

"But no one will know where we are, how will they find us?"

"Ben will track us down, of that, there is no doubt..., but when..., I can't answer that."

After two weeks aboard the ship, they had settled into a routine and they had been allowed on deck every other day. The ship's captain had still not granted them an audience despite Emma constantly nagging the crew. Even though the ship's captain and his officers were dressed in smart uniforms Emma knew for certain that it was not a Royal Navy ship and could not guess who they were. Finally, land was sighted on the horizon and Emma was convinced it was the island of Madeira, a place she had visited with Ben. As they approached the island they were locked into their cabin and to their frustration, they were not released until they put to sea again.'

"I can't decide who these people are," Emma said.

"East Indiamen, I'd guess," Dorothy said confidently. "We often had them and their ships visit us in Jamaica. They are a bit of a law unto themselves, and because they run India, they think that the whole world belongs to them."

The young officer knocked and then entered their cabin again. "Excuse me ladies, but the Captain requests your company for dinner this evening," he waited a moment. "What shall I say?"

"That's very gracious of him," Emma said, "we will be delighted to attend."

The Winds of Change.

After the officer had left them, they stared quizzically at each other for a moment.

"Well, it's about time," Emma said.

"Well, I'm not in the mood for socialising after all this time, but at least the food might be better," Dorothy said.

Unsure what to expect, they nervously entered the Captain's day room.

"Captain Aquila Blinkhorn, at your service madam," he said and offered them a chair. This was their first meeting with him and Dorothy had to admit, albeit reluctantly, that she thought him a very handsome character.

They were both determined not to be sociable or agreeable, but after the tedious journey and fear of their destination, they felt starved of good food and company. It was quite a surreal situation; almost like eating with the enemy.

"I trust that my crew have been treating you with the utmost respect, ladies,"

"You will hang for this," Emma blurted out. She had not meant to say it aloud, but the words seemed to pop out unexpectedly. She clasped her hands across her mouth to suppress any further outbursts.

"What am I so guilty of?" he said with a broad smile, "I'm simply returning you to your rightful owner."

"I don't have an owner, rightful or otherwise," Emma snapped. "Kidnap is a crime like piracy and it carries the death sentence."

"Now, Lady Compton, please just enjoy my hospitality. I know nothing of kidnap, or piracy I'm just doing what I was bid and transporting you home."

Emma scowled at Dorothy warning her not to correct him because it was obvious now that there was a case of mistaken identity.

"You have a fine ship, Captain, a barque I'm guessing," Emma said.

"Indeed, yes ma'am, her name is The Pilgrim, you know your ships," he said, "apart from yourselves, we are carrying, iron and cloth, a strange combination; we ship whatever we are asked."

"What is our destination?" Dorothy asked.

"Compton Island, of course, we are to be met by an agent of, Sir Arthur, a certain, Mr Quigley. Once I have delivered you as per my instructions, then I have no further responsibility for you."

"Would you deliver a letter for me? Not personally, of course," Emma said with a disarming smile. "I have a contact on Compton Island that I would like to send word to."

Blinkhorn thought about it for a moment. "We will reach our destination by this next Sunday, if you give me the letter, then I will see to it that it is forwarded just as soon as you are out of my care."

To Dorothy's delight, the food was far better than their normal rations. The Captain was charming and he had many entertaining anecdotes to share with them, and despite their situation, they could not help appreciating and enjoying his wit. Despite a few slip-ups, they managed to keep their secret of Emma's identity.

Back in their cabin and as soon as they were alone, they stared at each other hardly daring to speak.

"They think that I'm your mother, surely the news reached Jamaica that she is dead," Emma said.

"Do you think that papa; oh, I mean Sir Arthur is behind this? Would he really want us back after all this time?"

"Your mother's family is very wealthy and as she and you are the sole heirs of that wealth, which makes you very valuable to him; perhaps he is short of money or is looking to the future and a return to England."

"He'll not get a penny from me after what he did to us and the shameful way he treated mama."

"Quigley is involved, as I feared, but who put him up to it? I know he had a grudge against Ben, but how did he escape from Lancaster, did Sir Arthur play a part in it and help him?"

"What do you think they will do if they find out who you are?"

"I've no idea, but with Ben's reputation, this captain is going to feel very uncomfortable about having us aboard. I must say, I don't think that he is as innocent as he makes out to be, but I don't think he is involved other than to transport us."

"Can you trust him with your letter? Do you think that… my father…, Ben will come for us? We are so far from home and with Pelican off around the world? I'm still finding it difficult to think of him as my true Papa," Dorothy whispered.

"You will get the hang of it, I'm sure. He will come, although I would tell him not to if I could, I know he will be somewhere in our wake. If this letter gets to their office on the island they will send word home."

"But how will he know where we are?"

"He will know," Emma said emphatically. "He will know, you can be sure of that. I whisper to him on the wind and by the stars… he will know."

Emma was awake early, she had sensed even while asleep that the motion of the ship had changed. The relentless sound of the waves thumping against the hull had stopped; the oil lamp above her head that

The Winds of Change.

had at times swung violently about was now still, the ship was almost quiet. Several shouted orders changed that state of affairs, now there was the sound of the crew rushing about the decks. From their chants and calls, Emma guessed that they were furling the sails, preparing lines and ropes ready to tie up and berth the ship.

It was stiflingly hot and she was looking forward to going on deck. She gently woke Dorothy. "Come on sleepyhead, I think we've arrived, where ever here is."

What will happen now, she thought, although she was trying to be brave for Dorothy's sake, she was feeling weary.

"I hope they feed us soon," Dorothy said. "I'm famished; I'd give anything for one of Mr Mould's Sunday breakfasts."

There was a polite, almost timid tap at the door, after a moment a smartly dressed young officer entered. "With, Captain Blinkhorn's compliments, will you please make yourselves ready to disembark."

"Where are we?" Emma said with a friendly smile.

"Compton Island ma'am; the Caribbean."

The ship had been secured by the time they arrived on deck and even the gangplank was in place. Blinkhorn stepped down from his quarterdeck to greet them.

"Ladies," he said as if they were his guests out for a stroll.

"Captain," Emma said in acknowledgement. "What is to happen now?"

There was a call from the quayside and a man ran up the gangplank. Emma instantly recognised him. "Quigley," she said under her breath to Dorothy.

There was a short conversation between the Captain and a very angry looking Quigley. Without looking at Dorothy or Emma, he ran back down to the quayside and sent two of his men onto the ship to fetch them.

The Captain approached them. "It seems that I am to lose the pleasure of your company and that you are to go ashore," he said and saluted. "I hope that your journey with us has not been too unpleasant."

Emma smiled she was feeling too nervous to risk trying to speak. She slipped him the letter. "The address is clearly marked. As a man of honour, I trust that you will not betray me and that you will keep the existence of this letter a secret."

The Captain took her hand: "I assure you, madam, that you can trust me."

They descended the gangplank without a backward glance. Once on the quayside, they were hurried away and immediately shown into a warehouse. Inside it was hot and stuffy Emma felt faint. "I need to sit down and I need a drink."

"Get in here," a hard-looking man with an untidy beard shouted at them.

A very worried looking Quigley appeared, he stared at Emma for a moment and then dashed off. "Come on, follow me," he said.

"I need to sit down, I don't feel well," Emma said almost sobbing.

The thug with the beard pulled her along by her arm. They exited the building into a rear alley. It was hot and dusty and smelt of rotten fish. Dorothy took Emma's arm to try to help her, but she was feeling the heat too, and she was also a little unsteady.

Once out of the alley, their guards were totally unsympathetic to their frail state and they were almost frogmarched across the street and into a small inn. The interior was drab and dark with furniture strewn across the floor it smelt of stale ale and tobacco smoke. It was just a passing visit, they were soon pushed out of the rear door, across another street, and into what seemed to be a private house. In the parlour, they were left on their own for a moment. The door creaked on its hinges as a young, very nervous African slave boy carrying a large teapot on a tray with cups and saucers entered. He was visibly shaking, the cups rattled loudly on the tray as he tried to find somewhere to put his burden. Without daring to look up, he planted them on the table and then looked as if he was trying to find an escape route.

"Here, let me help you," Dorothy said with a kind reassuring smile.

The boy nodded gratefully handed over his load and then retreated as quickly as he could, he closed the door gently behind him.

"I need this," Emma said thirstily drinking the tea, "I don't know what came over me."

"Probably the heat, I don't remember it being this hot the last time I was here."

As evening fell, they were hustled into a waiting carriage. It sped off immediately, bounced, and shook them about so violently that they were forced to cling on as they bumped along the road out of town. Occasionally, a wheel would drop into a rut or pothole with a jarring thud, and they would be thrown out of their seats.

"There is obviously some kind of maniac driving this thing," Dorothy cried as she was bounced into the air. "Slow down for pity's sake."

If the driver heard her cry, he took no notice and they bounced along for about twenty minutes until they suddenly came to an abrupt halt.

"Thank heavens we've stopped," Emma said. They listened, and tried to get some clue as to where they might be, they could hear the

The Winds of Change.

sound of the horses as they settled down after their headlong charge, but there were no other clues. Suddenly the door was opened.

"Come on, out you get," the voice was deep with a West Country accent.

It was almost dark and impossible for them to get any sort of idea as to where they were. They were bundled into a plantation house, a fine building with colonial furniture and a marble floor, obviously it was owned by some well to do person. The room felt cool, its shutters were closed, and the air was filled with the fragrance of Jasmine and bougainvillaea from the terrace outside.

"Now what?" Dorothy whispered.

"We wait; I think at last we will find out who is behind this kidnapping; other than Quigley."

There was a commotion outside and it was obvious that several riders had arrived. Muffled voices could be heard and Dorothy recognised that of Sir Arthur Compton, the man she had been brought up to believe was her father. The doors burst open and he entered in his usual brusque manner, but his face fell when he saw Emma. "Quigley, get in here now," he bellowed.

As Quigley entered, Compton grabbed his lapels and swung him around so violently that his feet left the ground. "What the hell is this, who is… what have you done?" He slapped Quigley's face several times with his open hand.

Emma and Dorothy clung to each other fearful that he might turn on them.

Compton's face was glowing red with anger. "Who the hell are you?" he shouted at Emma.

He still clung to Quigley's jacket collar and suddenly vented his anger on him. With a powerful thrust of his arm, he flung him across the room with such venom that when the man hit the far wall the wind was knocked from him. Almost senseless, he slid like a ragdoll down the wall to the floor.

"I'll deal with you later, Quigley, and there had better be some good reason for this." He stood in front of Dorothy. "Where's your mother?"

"Dead, sir," Dorothy said, "she has been dead for these last four years, surely you knew."

Compton stepped back a couple of paces, he looked mystified as he tried to comprehend what she had just said.

"Why was I not told? Why didn't you write to me and let me know? I am your father; you could have had the decency to write." He sounded quite confused; obviously, the news of Ruth's death was a terrific shock to him.

Dorothy stepped forward and although Emma tried to stop her, she angrily snapped at Compton. "Why should we tell you? You treated her wickedly, your whoring and drinking made our lives a complete misery. You gave her the pox, and it was that which killed her." She turned away but suddenly spun around to face him. "Oh, and by the way, you are not my father," she said with a great deal of satisfaction. It was as though she was slipping a knife blade between his ribs.

Compton's face changed colour several times, his anger was transformed into disbelief and confusion. "What... of course I am," he spluttered. He began to cough and it seemed as if he would choke.

Emma poured him a tumbler of water. "Drink this," she said.

Quigley tried to creep from the room on all fours, but Compton gave him a withering look that made him freeze to the spot.

"You realise that you are guilty of kidnap and that you will be brought to justice," Emma said.

"Who the flaming hell are you?" Compton said to Emma as his coughing fit subsided.

"Emma Burrows, daughter of Lord and Lady Levante, and I was a close school friend of Ruth. You are in deep trouble, this is kidnap, and at the very least you will be recalled to England to stand trial."

Compton never spoke; he stormed out of the room dragging Quigley by the scruff of his collar behind him. With flaming eyes and flared nostrils, he turned on Quigley. "How in hell's name has this happened? You've dropped me in deep trouble. This is about your vendetta with Burrows, you told me as much last time we spoke. Did you know who she was?"

"No, I swear on my mother's grave." Quigley was visibly shaking, sweat ran from his face, and there was real fear in his eyes.

"So, give me an explanation!" Compton exclaimed.

"The young girl is the right one, the other one, I've seen her with Burrows, but I didn't know who she was."

"So why did you think she was my wife you stupid worm."

"I thought... no, I had a reliable source who told me that she was the right woman, honestly, I've been misled too."

Compton marched up and down the room stamping his feet and swinging his arms about like someone possessed. Quigley tried to hide in the corner of the room wondering how he could get out of this mess.

"What about if we lose them at sea, or sell them in the slave market, they'll fetch a good price," Quigley said and then wished that he was somewhere miles away.

Compton angrily turned on him. "Perfect, you are the stupidest imbecile that I've ever met." For a moment he just stood and fumed,

The Winds of Change.

clenching and opening his fist as if he was about to strangle someone. "No, I'll tell you what we are going to do, you are going to take them up to the hillside plantation villa and wait for me to decide what should be done." He grabbed Quigley by the throat. "If you harm one hair of their heads, I'll tear the skin from your body just like skinning a rabbit. Is that clear?"

"What about Burrows?"

"I'm certain he'll come; in fact, I know that he will arrive at some time and when he does we'll be ready for him," Compton said. "I should have known that he was the father, I had my suspicions all along about them," he said almost to himself. More pensively, he said: "I wonder how and where did she die?" he thought a moment and then rubbed his hands with glee. "Her inheritance is all mine now and when old, Hutton-Beaumont kicks the bucket, I'll be a very wealthy man."

"I'll bet that's why they didn't tell you, mi' Lord, so you wouldn't go after what is rightfully yours."

"A return to England might be profitable after all. Her father should have told me, blast his eyes, he wouldn't want me to get my hands on his estate either, but I will now."

18. The letter.

Despite the support from his friends, Ben was sinking into a deep depression; he could not shake off the feeling of loneliness. Emma's disappearance had created a real void in his life and he felt that he had somehow let her down. It was over four months since he had last seen her and he seemed to be in a cavernous vacuum of unhappiness, nothing in his previous life had prepared him for it.

It was the first time in over four years that he had been separated from her for any length of time; it came as quite a shock when he realised that he could miss her so much. He would sometimes enter a room expecting her to be there; he thought at times, he could hear her humming one of those funny little tunes she loved as she worked about the farm. Sometimes, when he was in his lonely bed, he thought that he could feel her head resting on his chest and feel the heat of her body next to him.

Most evenings he spent playing cribbage with Mould; they would down some rum and reminisce about their past adventures. There was always someone, usually one of the old crew, who would call by to see if there was any news or just to make sure that Ben was all right.

Walter was also desperately unhappy; he missed his mother and Dorothy. He seemed to spend most of his day with Jenny helping her look after Eve, but he cried himself to sleep most nights and usually he would crawl under the sheets next to Ben.

Ben quite often began his day with a ride high up onto the fells he was not going anywhere, in particular, just visiting some of their favourite old haunts. Sometimes, he would take Walter, but mostly he needed to be alone. He would constantly check his pocket watch as though he had to be somewhere for a particular time or to attend an important appointment. On days that he visited Kirkley Grange to see Emma's parents, he would always take Walter with him; the boy loved to visit his grandparents and in particular, he loved to play out in the engine shed where his Lordship's snorting steam engine huffed and puffed.

"Now then young man," his lordship called to Walter from the footplate of the engine. "Do you want to add some coal? You dig about in there then and find me the best pieces." Walter looked delighted and went to fetch a small shovel he called his own.

"Any news Ben?"

"No, sir, nothing at all, I can't understand it."

The Winds of Change.

Tobias Wells, a blacksmith who had sailed with Ben on Pelican to the Caribbean, and who now helped with the engine. "Morning Skipper, how are you?"

"I'm bearing up, It doesn't get any quieter," Ben shouted over the din.

"No, but it's running well, and next month we're taking it to do some work, powering a new threshing machine, that should be interesting," Tobias said. They walked outside away from the constant throbbing sounds of the engine.

"I'm desperately sorry about yer missus," Tobias said. With a piece of rag, he cleaned the oil and coal dust from his hands. "You've no news and that must be a dreadful thing." They stood a moment. "It was obvious to us all on that last voyage that you were meant for each other. If you need my help for anything, just call."

"Don't forget to go see, grandma," Ben called to Walter above the din of the engine. He decided that the din of the engine was too much and he went into the house to see her.

As usual, she was sitting serenely in front of the large open fire with her favourite pet terrier on her knee. She smiled when he entered. "Still nothing, I presume from the look on your face," she said. "You're doing all you can, the rest is up to God. Don't blame yourself; you of all people should know that life throws these things at us and we have to deal with them as best we can."

"Thank you, yes, I know. Can I leave Walter with you for a few days? I'm snowed under with work on the farm, and I end up spending my day playing with him, instead of doing what I should be doing."

"Of course you can, we love the little chap to be here, and he even manages to distract his lordship from that damned engine at times." She placed a hand on Ben's shoulder. "Jenny brought Eve with her the last time they visited, how well she is doing, Jenny makes a wonderful mother."

"Yes, I think it was a match made in heaven."

"Annabelle has called here quite a lot lately, I'm always pleased to see her, but she was never my favourite. She is always quizzing me regarding you and Emma. When she was married to my eldest son, it was as if there was some sort of competition going on between her, Ruth and Emma, they were just the same when they were schoolgirls."

"Yes, I think that they had a peculiar relationship, more of a rivalry than a friendship."

"Will you stay for tea?"

"No, as I said I'm very busy; maybe next time."

Ben rode away deep in thought, it was late September, the days were shortening, and there was a chill in the air. The crops were all gathered in, and the fields looked deserted and bare as they waited, patiently for the spring. The year seemed to be slipping away; already the geese had started flying south, they formed great 'Vee' shapes in the sky as they passed noisily overhead. He realised, that this was going to be the coldest winter of his life.

The following day, he was determined to steer himself, out of the doldrums, and to be more positive about the future, if only for Walter's sake.

"I'll be out this morning; I'll probably ride over the fells." He told Mould.

"I've packed some bread, cheese, and wine into your saddlebags; don't stay out too long, the weather's changing fast this year."

Without thinking, he went to one of their favourite picnic places. He followed the river and found himself in a small woodland glade where two rivers met and formed a deep pool. He dismounted and sat on a boulder, this was where he and Emma had often sat together, he ran his hand over the stone as if trying to feel her presence. Across the pool, a large grey heron squawked noisily protesting at his company and then suddenly it took flight; he could hear its broad wings beating the air. There were so many memories; it was here that they first spent time together, and where one time they had sat naked in the moonlight listening to the sound of the river. Recently, only a few days before Emma's disappearance, they had had a picnic here with their friends.

He sat in silence watching the wildlife that frequented the pool. Several species of birds and butterflies dipped into the water and reminded him that life has to go on. For a fleeting moment, he glimpsed a small roe deer as it peeped out through the vegetation and then quickly took a drink. Cautiously, it lapped at the water where it ran over the stones, but then it was gone as silently as a fleeting memory.

In the tranquillity of the clearing, the dappled sunlight made flickering shapes and dancing shadows on the grass; the breeze was whispering a gentle lullaby through the leaves, and he fell into a deep sleep. It was haunted by characters from his past, they seemed to be dancing around him and then they would float down the river like autumn leaves. His old mentor, Reverend Linton appeared on the far bank. As usual, he was dressed in a sombre black suit that starkly contrasted with his white lace neckerchief; in his hand, was the broad-brimmed hat he took everywhere with him, but seldom wore. He seemed to carry it just to be used as a fan against the heat, or to drive away irritating insects. His old friend tarried a moment, the familiar reassuring

The Winds of Change.

broad grin cut a deep line across his face, it stretched so far that both ends of his lips disappeared into his bushy sideburns. He waved his hat and then evaporated away disappearing just like a mist in the sunlight. In the dream, he could see his reflection in the pool and next to him was Emma's face, he could see her clearly, and she suddenly swam across to where she loved to sit with her feet in the water and her face in the sunlight. His fingers created ripples as he touched the water and he thought that he could feel her soft skin, in that instant, Ben knew that she was alive.

He abruptly awoke feeling dazed and yet thrilled by his dream. He could not resist the temptation to step into the water. He cast away his clothes and dived into the icy cold water. The cold knocked the air from his lungs; with his heart pounding, and the adrenaline flushing through his veins, he swam out into the middle of the pool. His skin tingled with the cold and after a few minutes, he felt to be completely numb, but the adrenaline-charged sensation was overwhelming, he felt exhilarated and let out a loud whoop of joy.

His heart was more hopeful and his mind more settled as he rode back to Cartmel with his skin still tingling from his plunge into the pool. Riding down from the fell, he caught sight of David on his way to church; he rode over to meet him.

David grinned broadly at Ben. "I'm just on my way to set up ready for tomorrow's service, come with me and we'll talk," he said.

Although Ben did not feel much like talking, he went with him anyway. Sitting in the front pew, he watched David rearranged the hymn numbers on the wall. He carefully slid the numbers out of the wooden frame and then shuffling through his stack of cards selected the new ones and slid them back into place. It brought back a memory for Ben of Linton doing just the same thing, except Linton, spent a great deal of time with the task. He would sing through the first verse of each hymn just to make sure that it fitted in with his sermon and the other hymns for that day.

"This is my favourite time of year," David called over his shoulder to Ben, "and Harvest Festival is wonderful; I do so love it when the church is filled with the Lord's bounty,"

Ben just nodded without comment; he was deep in thought, thinking about his dream. "Do you believe in dreams?" he said.

"It depends on what you mean. I believe in prayer. Take for instance your problem; you are in the ideal place to get divine help. Our church is devoted to Saint Anthony, who as you probably know is the patron saint of things that are lost. Perhaps that includes people. I've been praying on your behalf, asking for his help daily."

Tony Mead.

David walked up to the little statue of the saint, patted him on the head, and then examined the hand where the finger was missing. "Maybe, one day he will find his lost finger. I've heard so many rumours and stories about what happened on your wedding day, will you tell me about it?" David said.

Ben shrugged it seemed a long while since it happened although it was only just over four years. "Not just now, David, I need to get back to Edward's."

"This will probably sound a bit bizarre to you, but, I almost envy your pain and anguish, such agony only comes about through the intense love you feel for your family," David said frankly.

Ben only gave him an ironic smile, he did not answer because the statement confused him; he headed back to his horse and mounted up.

David watched him ride away and remembered how they had first met when they were boys at Linton's orphanage. *How times have changed*, he thought, *what would Linton have made to our stories?*

Ben cantered into the market square, he was still trying to sort out David's riddle, when the postmistress called to him from across the road.

"Lieutenant, yoo-hoo," she called trying to maintain her composure and overcome her excitement at receiving a letter addressed to him. "This came earlier this morning; it's from the Caribbean. I know you still have connections there?" she handed over the letter. "I hope that it's news about your wife; we all miss her."

Ben took the letter, which was quite heavy; he guessed from the handwriting, that it was from Loughton the biologist who was working on Compton Island as an agent for the lands they owned there.

"Thank you, Mrs Cott; there is no need for lieutenant, I'm just plain mister these days. This will be from a friend of mine who looks after our business interests down there."

Ben loved to tease the postmistress by never opening the letters in front of her or letting her know the true contents.

"I hope that it's good news," she said.

"News of Emma would certainly be welcome; but any good news would be nice for a change, dear lady."

As usual, she went back to her post office very dissatisfied, she had hoped he might open it in front of her.

He entered Emily's kitchen and as usual, it was filled with the tempting aromas of cooking.

"Something smells good," he said. He placed his arm around Emily's shoulders and kissed her forehead.

"Rabbit stew and dumplings tonight for everyone," she said.

The Winds of Change.

"Aha, sounds as if Ian has been out snaring rabbits again," Ben said with a broad grin.

"Edward is in the parlour," she whispered, "his leg is troubling him again, he suffers terribly with it at times."

Ben took his usual chair near the fire in the parlour to open his letter. He carefully examined the seal to make sure that it was intact. Using the point of a letter knife, he cut the wax open. There was, in fact, two letters, one tucked inside the other and both of them secured with red wax and stamped with a seal.

Edward, puffing on a rosewood pipe watched Ben curiously. As Ben began to read the first letter, his face turned several shades of red, finally glowing bright pink. Without a word, Ben handed the letter to Edward.

Salutations, Mr Burrows,

I have enclosed this letter within my usual quarterly report so as not to raise any suspicions.

I have heard the news of your wife's abduction, and you have my deepest sympathy and I hope that the matter is resolved soon; you and Mr Barraclough are well-known figures here and many people here have been speculating about the abduction.

So, imagine my surprise and I have no doubt yours too when I say that I saw Emma quite recently here on the docks. I saw her often enough on our voyage with Pelican to be ninety-nine per cent sure that it was she, this was just prior to the news of her abduction reaching us. Even so, I thought it was mighty peculiar.

I was on the docks late one evening, I hasten to add that this is not somewhere I usually frequent, but on this occasion, I was on business; it was about dusk when I heard a muffled shout and saw a small fracas on the gangplank of an East Indiaman ship just arrived from England.

I kept to the shadows so that I was able to watch without being observed. It was then that I first spotted, Mrs Burrows, I knew straight away that it was she, there was another younger woman with her, and they were both bundled into a warehouse further along the wharf. I kept a vigil, l watching the place constantly. Mr Goodwit, my assistant, kindly helped and we took it in turns for three days to watch. One day I walked past the building and I again saw Mrs Burrows, but the light was poor and I do not think that she saw me. Unfortunately, perhaps sometime during the night, they were moved and I am ashamed to tell you that we do not know to where.

Two days later, I saw, Sir Arthur Compton near the waterfront, which is not unusual as he is a frequent visitor to the brothels there.

Tony Mead.

Usually, he calls into our office to check up on things, but oddly, on this occasion, he left for Jamaica without a word.

We have had many very unsavoury characters on the island in recent weeks, one of whom I think you are acquainted with and one I remember you having problems with as we signed on for Pelican, a nasty piece of work called, Quigley.

Before the East Indiaman ship sailed, I received a visit from its Captain who personally handed me a letter. He said that a passenger from his ship had asked that he should deliver it to me in strictest confidence. The letter is enclosed; it confirms that it is your wife and ward that are here. I have not dared take any action, Quigley's men seem to be everywhere and I am not equipped to confront them.

I will do my utmost to find more information for you, but I respectfully suggest that you should visit us as soon as convenient. In the meantime, I shall ascertain her whereabouts and try to keep her in sight and to tell her that I have written to you about the situation.

You will be pleased to know that, Captain Mitchell and the good ship, Pelican, passed safely through here some months past. He was not enjoying the task of gaoler but we did have time for a drink and he said that he was looking forward to eventually reaching, India. Lieutenant Snow was his usual self; although I do believe he did break into a smile on one occasion.
Your humble servant,
Charles Laughton.

Ben sat stunned by the news and for a few moments he just stared at the fire, inside his emotions were in a terrible sickening spin. With trembling hands, he opened the second letter.

My dear Mr Laughton, Dorothy, and I are in something of a predicament; to put it bluntly, we have been kidnapped and know not what our fate is to be. We have been transported under duress on a vessel belonging to the East India Company. We have been well looked after and we are in good health, but we are desperate to be free. Please, I beseech you; get a message to, Mr Burrows. Yours truly Emma Burrows.

Emily entered the room drying her hands on a towel; she stopped dead in the doorway when she caught sight of Ben, the look on his face told the whole story.

"My word, what's the matter?" she said. Even though she was afraid of the answer.

The Winds of Change.

Edward handed her the letter unable to speak, he went and poured two large brandies. Ben passed the second letter to her.

"You'd better make that three," Emily said. She too was in emotional turmoil, pleased that at last there was some word, and yet fearing for what it meant. She guessed that once again all her friends who she now regarded as family, would have to put their lives at risk and go find Emma.

Edward broke the silence. "So, where do we start?"

"We need a ship, a crew, and a lot of luck," Ben said in a deadpan way. "I need to speak to Mr McHenry to organise funds. Edward, could I ask you to organise our crew, maybe they will have put their sailing days behind them, they all seem very settled here now."

"You know very well that if you are raising a crew, then our old friends will not need asking twice."

Mould arrived with Walter, he could feel the tension in the air and knew instinctively that something was happening. "What's to do?" he said anxiously.

"I need you to help Edward to get the crew together; I'm looking for, volunteers to sail with me back to the Caribbean. How do you feel about that?" Ben said.

Mould shrugged and tried to hide his smile. "You're the Skipper; we'll follow your lead."

Ben smiled and slapped Mould on the shoulder in appreciation of his loyalty.

"Take a few moments to organise your thoughts or you'll run around like a headless chicken," Edward said.

Ben took Edward's advice and the next morning he rode to his favourite place high on the fells. From here, he could see the morning light glinting on the water of Morecambe Bay. Whenever he visited this place, he added a few stones to the cairn and thought of his old friend and mentor Linton.

He gazed out to sea and thought deep and hard as to what should be his next steps.

I never realised how hard it is to be the one stranded at home, he thought. *I've faced the fear of battle, sailed into horrific cannon fire, seen men mauled and mutilated, I've killed many with these hands.* He held his hands before his face as if he was looking at those of a stranger. *How many people have waited powerless for their loved ones to come home? A man is not just a soldier or sailor; he's a father, a son, a brother, and someone is waiting for him. I am not brave enough to wait, I must do something, Linton always said, work with your strengths, and however much a farmer I have become, my strengths are sailing and sadly, maybe killing.*

One of Ben's first decisions was to see Arthur Burges the auctioneer who had sold him, Pelican.

"Ahoy there, Lieutenant Burrows, long time no see," Burges called out to him as he arrived. "What can I do for you; are you buying or selling?" He rubbed his hands together in anticipation.

"I need a ship again, but this time I'm looking for speed, a sloop for preference," Ben said.

The auctioneer's office was neat and tidy and had dark wall panels between shelf units that were filled with wooden models of ships. He offered Ben a chair at his table.

"I trust you were happy with your last purchase, Pelican was it not."

"Yes, she is a fine vessel, although I have no idea where she is at the moment; she should be in the Indian Ocean by now."

"I can see you are a man in a hurry, but please be patient. Surprisingly enough, at the moment, there are very few for sale, so many are being lost at sea and fewer investors are willing to gamble and invest in a ship."

A steward brought them a glass of port. "I thought refreshments might be welcome," the man said and then reversed out of the room.

"He's a good man, been with me years," the auctioneer said. He did not look up from the pile of documents on his desk that he was leafing through.

"Oh!" he said, "this one looks promising." He leant back in his chair and scanned the information. "The Raven, a partially Bermuda rigged sloop, recently refit but not collected by its owner and is now offered for sale by the shipyard. It's held in, Clifford's Dock, on the Mersey. No crew with it and it is suggested that it needs fifteen to twenty experienced hands. Clifford is a reputable builder and I can vouch for his work."

Ben took the papers and read the information.

"Yes, it sounds just right; I've skippered a Bermuda before. When can I go for it?"

"What about the price?"

"Tell me."

"You should be able to get it for between fifteen hundred and two thousand pounds." The agent waited for a response.

"Who do we pay?"

The man smiled at the snap decision. "You'll need to pay the shipyard. I'll send word as quickly as possible that you will go to look

The Winds of Change.

at it. Of course," he smiled, "There will be a small finder's fee to pay too." The auctioneer smiled again. "Another adventure is it? Have you heard anything about your wife's whereabouts? You made out alright on the last trip, will you need backers?"

"For the time being, I don't want anyone to know of my interest in this ship. No one is to know, is that understood?" Ben said, "I'll buy it under a different name."

The man shrunk away from Ben's hot glaring eyes. "Don't you fear, Lieutenant, your secret's safe with me." He nodded his head to signify that he had received the message loud and clear. He did try a smile, but his lips did not seem to respond and he looked as if he was in pain. "I'll set up a false identity for you; you can trust me."

After a quick handshake, Ben was out of the door. His next call was his solicitor's office across the harbour. Outside the rain was bouncing off the pavement, but Ben did not seem to notice, undeterred he threw his heavy cloak over his shoulder and stepped forward as a man possessed. When he reached the familiar door of his solicitor's office, he shook the rain from his hat and cloak.

"Goodness me, Mr Burrows, what dreadful weather," Clough said taking Ben's coat from him. "Dreadful news about, Mistress Burrows, I'm sure everything will be fine."

"Thank you, Mr Clough; it's actually you that I need to speak with. Is, Mr McHenry in?"

McHenry opened the door of his office. "Come in, Ben, what a filthy day."

"I didn't know whether or not you would still be working, does that wife of yours never see you?"

"Och aye, well I think she prefers it that way. What can I do for you?"

"I'm buying another ship. Loughton has sent me a letter from the Caribbean and if the information is correct then I think Emma has been taken there."

McHenry opened the top drawer of his filing cabinet and pulled out his favourite malt whisky. "We need a wee dram; what about you, Mr Clough will you join us in a dram?"

"I'll get to the point," Ben said, "I'd like to borrow, Mr Clough again if he is willing to serve with us. He was invaluable on the last voyage. His organisational skills and clever bargaining was a huge asset, and I need things organising here at full speed."

Clough sat down surprised by the sudden and unexpected offer; he silently took a glass of whiskey from McHenry and drained the glass in one swig.

"I would be delighted to go, that is if you can spare me, sir." He directed the last part of the sentence to McHenry.

"I can manage without you for a while and you can keep an eye on my investments at the same time."

"Good, that's settled. I need you to clear me some money with the bank; I'm buying a new ship, three thousand pounds should do it and give Mr Clough enough to buy victuals, weapons and such like."

"It's a shame, Pelican is not home, you would have had a ready crew," McHenry said.

"I don't think that I will have much of a problem raising a crew," Ben said confidently.

In the driving rain, Ben headed back to Cartmel. He hardly noticed the weather his mind was so busy with the thoughts of what must now be arranged for the voyage. His journey was constantly interrupted by deep thoughts and he would halt his horse, staring into the black clouds above, and mull the problem over.

Was it her he saw, or am I just clutching at straws? I'm sure that, Loughton saw her often enough on that voyage to recognise her, the letter seems to confirm that it was her. Where have they taken her to? Can Compton have something to do with it? The letter is almost two months old, and so on until his mind felt so tortured it could take no more debate.

He was slightly surprised and very pleased to see the Old Crew assembled in Edward's parlour. As he entered the tightly packed room, they each greeted him. Fletch, as usual, was their spokesman.

Ben stood with his back to the fire to try to get warm.

"Thank you for coming at such short notice, and I'm sorry to ask this of you, but I need volunteers to sail with me back to the Caribbean."

"Very well, Mr Burrows as always you can really on us. What are your orders?"

Ben smiled he had been confident that this would be their answer, he felt quite emotional for their support.

"I've secured a ship, The Raven, but it needs picking up from Liverpool, or at least it needs paying for and then we can collect it. I hoped you, Brendon and Bruce might see to that, take Ezra and his fishing boat, it will be the quickest way. I'll sort out the finances with, Mr Clough, who has also agreed to sail with us again."

Edward was looking eager to be involved despite Emily showing her fears for the venture.

"I rely on you Edward to keep the farm in order and make sure you visit that surgeon in London about your leg," Ben said.

The Winds of Change.

"Nay, Ben, I should be sailing with you, I'll go mad waiting here for news."

Emily left the room and there was a heavy silence.

"You'd best take an olive branch with you my friend, Emily did not look best pleased," Ben said.

19. The Flight of the Raven

"Right Fletch, here are your directions to the boatyard and a letter to the bank, the ship is named Raven," Ben said. "Brendon and Bruce will go with you."

"Don't worry Skipper, Ezra's old boat will get us there in a couple of days," Fletch said confidently.

"Aye well, there's a lot at stake. Get the best price you can for this ship, but make sure you get it whatever the price."

"A good name the Raven, in Norse myths, a raven brought good luck," Brendon said.

They were loaded the last of the supplies to Ezra's boat ready for their journey.

"I'll be collecting some crew together and wait for word from you that the ship is secured," Ben said.

Two hours later, Ezra's fishing boat was sailing south heading for the Mersey.

"Be warned you lot, the Skipper says to get back as quickly as possible, we'll not be spending time in the inns," he glanced at Brendon over the top of his reading glasses. "I Don't have to tell you how serious a business this is," Fletch said. He was seated operating the boat's tiller, and as he sailed he studied the directions to the shipyard which were on his knee.

"Don't worry Fletch; we'll not let the Skipper down, not after all he's done for us."

"We're to sail along the Mersey to Runcorn, past all the main docks and find a boatyard by the name of, Clifford's."

"Let's hope it's still there," Brendon said.

"What the ship or the yard?" Fletch asked.

It was a straight forward journey from Barrow south to Liverpool, The Mersey was as confused and busy a highway as ever; ferries, cargo ships, navy vessels, barges and private merchants, all of them were involved in an intricate dance that by some miracle kept them out of each other's way. However, there was the occasional squabble as ships looking for their moorings or trying to catch the breeze would become tangled up with another vessel on the same mission. A dense cloak of smog hung around the buildings of the city and only the steeples of a large church were visible as they poked through the cloud in search of fresh air.

"I'd choke to death if I'd to live in that," Ezra muttered.

The Winds of Change.

"It's no worse than that damned pipe yer always puffing on," Fletch said.

They managed to dodge their way through this melee of vessels until they reached where the river began to narrow. Once they were past the city the air cleared and there were only a few buildings and several small wooden wharves along the riverbank. The tide was almost completely out and several ships were stranded high and dry on the river silt.

"Keep yer eyes on them sandbanks," Fletch called out.

Ezra leant over the side for a better look. "There's a two-mast sloop careened on its side over yonder."

Brendon had his telescope fixed firmly on the ship. "Look at her hull plates, they fair shine in the sun, they look fresh; it's been recently refitted I'd say."

A deep channel took them right past several ships being repaired and into a small private marina. A symphony of smells; freshly cut timber, rope, and the familiar evocative aroma of warm tar and hot pitch.

Fletch breathed it all in. "I'd say we've found our place."

"If that's our ship, she looks in good condition," Ezra said.

They moored alongside a sturdy wooden pier where a couple of sawers were cutting a large tree trunk to create planks of timber; their long blade sang as they pulled and pushed it through the wood.

"Is the gaffer about?" Fletch asked.

One of the men nodded towards a workshop on the river bank. Feeling the urgency of the situation Fletch almost ran along the pier and poked his head through the doorway.

"This Clifford's Dock?"

A tubby man, with shaggy sideburns and long grey hair topped by a cloth cap, nodded but did not get up from the barrel he sat on. "I'm Clifford what ya want?"

"We understand you've got a sloop for sale, is that still the case?"

"Are you the men from Barrow in Furness?"

"Yes, that's us. Can we look at the ship?"

"I gorra letter just this morning saying you'd be on yer way, you've made good time." Clifford leant out of the window and yelled at the top of his voice. "Tom, come here lad." He turned back to Fletch. "My lad will show you around. Its last owner sent it in here for repairs, but then the silly bugger went bust and now he can't pay. So, I'm selling it to recoup my losses. You got cash with you?"

"We'll talk about that when we're happy with the ship," Fletch said guardedly.

The lad arrived, he was, in fact, a young man in his late teens. He wore an apron covered in sawdust and a broad friendly smile. He gave Fletch a curious look.

"Show 'em the sloop," Clifford said.

Ezra stayed with his boat while the other three clambered down a ladder from the pier to the sand.

"Mind yer step it's dangerous in places," Tom said as he led the way. He picked up some driftwood that was poking out of the sand and threw it well away from the deep channel. "Pa always does a good job, he's a real perfectionist when it comes to shipbuilding; she's in fine fettle."

The ship was on a soft bank of sand, its hull was at a slight angle which made it easier to climb aboard.

The lad helped them over the gunwales. "Nice ship this, we've cleaned her belly, caulked her stem to stern and replated her." The lad jumped up onto the bowsprit and looked over the side. "Refit the chain on her bowsprit and tarred her inside and out." The young man went through a list of jobs they had finished on the ship. "She's Bermuda rigged; a real greyhound, she'll outsprint anything around here. What you want her for?"

Fletch smiled at the lad as he went below decks, but said nothing. They opened lockers and the two cabin doors to look inside them. Brendon and Bruce checked the rigging, sails, and other gear in the forward lockers. After an hour of inspecting the vessel, they seemed very satisfied with what they saw.

"Looks good," Fletch, said to the lad, "let's go talk to your Pa."

"We used only the best materials as instructed by the owners, and then they went belly up, my Pa went crazy, he's a lot of money invested in her."

They were met at the top of the harbour wall steps by Clifford. "Well?"

"She looks sound enough."

Clifford wiped his hands across his face. "She's sound enough, worth every penny of two thousand guineas."

"We were told she was going for fifteen hundred pounds," Fletch said.

Clifford hooked his thumbs into his braces. "I think we need to discuss this in a more civilised manner, and I know just the place." Off he strode without any further word of explanation.

Fletch was nervous, he was not accustomed to this amount of responsibility, and although he trusted his own judgement, for Ben's sake he wanted to make a good deal.

The Winds of Change.

They eventually arrived at a dowdy looking inn. Clifford did not hesitate, but marched straight into the dimly lit room and headed for what was probably his usual corner where he sat down in a large armchair, he seemed to fit snuggly into its wide embracing arms.

"Sit down gents, what'll you have?" He looked over towards the bar. "Molly, bring some ale for these fine gents," he bellowed. "Now lads, did you say it was cash?"

"I didn't say anything."

"But will it be cash?" Clifford insisted and then looked about as if he was about to tell them a secret. "If it's a cash deal, then I can probably do you a better deal, although not the price you said."

"What's the ship history?" Bruce said. they knew all about it really, but he was just testing the man for honesty.

"She was built in Bermuda in 1795, one hundred and seventy tons, seventy-three feet stem to stern, twenty-one feet wide, with a nine-foot hold. Foremast carries a square topsail; the navy classed her as a Bermuda Schooner although she was built for a private owner the navy used her for five years. She carries eight swivel guns." Clifford reeled off the facts.

"Thank you, that's enough for now," Bruce said.

"Our agent, Mr McHenry, said that the price was fifteen hundred pounds," Fletch said.

A tall woman smelling of lavender brought the ale, she neither commented nor smiled at the men but just thumped the tankards down on the table, and went away.

"A woman of few words, quite a blessing I say. Most of 'em has too much to say," Clifford said chuckling aloud. "Now then gentlemen to business."

"We have a banker's note, but we can bring you cash if you'd prefer," Fletch said.

Clifford pondered a moment. "If it were cash, I could make it two thousand pounds, not guineas." He lifted his eyebrows and winked at them.

"I am allowed to negotiate with you, so I say we split the difference and go for seventeen-fifty, and that's my final offer," Fletch said.

Clifford blew out a heavy sigh. "Ale woman, make it snappy," he called over his shoulder. He studied Fletcher a moment. "You sure you got all that money?"

"Why would I be here if I couldn't pay," Fletch said, he was losing his patience.

"Guineas," Clifford said through his teeth.

"Pounds sterling," Fletch replied.

There was a pause, Clifford scratched his sideburns, took a swig of his ale and wiped his mouth with the back of his hand.

"Well, I'm shooting myself in the foot and my children will likely as not go hungry this winter, but get the cash and we'll call it a deal." He spat in his hand and held it out. Fletch did the same and they shook on it.

"Where's there a bank around here?"

"It's a way off, but you'll find it if you follow this street, mind because there's a few twists and turns until you reach the market square and the bank stands there."

"What about your lad showing us the way?"

"No need, you'll find it, he's too busy." He took a deep swig of his ale. "You're not thinking of sailing it between the three of you."

"No, we'll send back to Barrow for our lads."

"Do you want another drink before you go?"

"No, thank you, we'll go find this bank while it's still light," Fletch said. He gave Clifford a polite nod and left.

It was raining heavily when they left the Inn. "I don't trust that chap," Bruce said. "He has shifty eyes."

Fletch turned his collar against the rain. "Bruce, you go back to the boat and sail her back to Barrow with Ezra, me and Brendon will find the bank and some lodgings for the night here."

Bruce agreed and ran along the harbour to where Ezra was moored. Although he had not always enjoyed the overpowering heat of the Caribbean, he thought that he would exchange this weather for it anytime. He noticed Clifford's son peering out at him from behind the workshop door.

"Where's my Pa?"

"He's still wetting his whistle in the alehouse over yonder."

"Aye, that's his favourite pastime these days. Did you agree on a price?"

"Yes, I'm off back up north to fetch our crew."

"Good luck, I'll make the ship ready."

The sloop had moved slightly as the incoming tide floated it off the sand. Ezra was beneath a shelter he had rigged up using sailcloth, but when he spotted Bruce running towards him he stood up and called out, "Is there a problem?"

"No, Fletch has gone to find a bank; the deal went through as smooth as silk, but we need to make haste back to Barrow for the rest of the lads."

The Winds of Change.

They punted the boat back out into the river and turned into the breeze to take them back out to sea. It took over two hours for them to be clear of Liverpool and the Mersey estuary.

"This is going to take some time," Ezra said. "We'll have to tack, the winds all in the wrong direction."

Back at Fell Cottage, Ben paced the parlour floor angry with himself and the world in general. "I can't stand much more of this waiting about," he grumbled.

Jenny and Mould arrived with some tea.

"Now come along, Mr Burrows a drop of tea will help, sit down, you've not kept still for weeks." He guided Ben to his chair.

"If the lads buy this sloop, how will you man it?" Edward said.

"We've no time to train a new crew; I'll try and find some of the old crew from Pelican they didn't all sign on with the Captain," Ben said.

Edward stood up and trying not to limp too badly poured drinks for everyone.

Ben looked at Emily, she was looking concerned and he knew she was afraid that Edward would try to insist on sailing with him.

"Someone has to look after things here, no disrespect to you Emily, but even with Jamie and Tim's help, the farm is too big," Ben said. "Edward, your leg is giving you too much grief for you to travel with us."

Edward was about to protest when Ben cut him off. "We've so many responsibilities here, you must stay; hire as much labour as you need to help with the livestock." He thought for a moment. "It will be Christmas before we are back that's if it is an easy voyage."

"Don't fret my dear," Emily said. she placed her arm around Ben's shoulder.

"My whole life seems to be balanced on this one throw of the dice, if she's not there, I don't think I want to come back alone."

"Ben, please don't say that there is Walter and little Eve," Jenny said, "We are all your family."

"Yes I know, and I'm grateful for all your concern and help, but I need to find Emma. Will you look after Walter for me Emily?" Ben said.

"You know you don't have to ask. You just worry about getting Emma and Dorothy back safely."

Fletch and Brendon worked their way through the maze of streets until they eventually found the marketplace. A few hardy traders were sitting out the rain beneath makeshift shelters, but there were very few people to buy their wares. Fortunately, the bank was still open for business. The armed guard at the door let them in, but as they entered he gave them a warning glance to let them know that he was going to keep his eyes on them.

Fletch shook the rain from his hat and straightened his jacket as he approached the counter. He was feeling rather important and pleased that he had worn one of his many new suits. With a smile, he placed his valise on the counter.

The bank clerk gave him a rather bored smile. "Yes, can I be of assistance?"

"I have here some documents; a letter of introduction from the bank in Lancaster and a money order made out to pay cash. I also have a letter from, Mr McHenry our solicitor in Barrow in Furness."

The man looked down his nose at Fletch as he opened the documents. As he read the letter, he shifted uncomfortably twisting his head and neck as though his collar was far too tight. The was a sudden transformation in the teller's attitude. "Could I invite you into a private room to discuss this," he said coming from behind the counter and leading them towards a large highly polished mahogany door.

Fletch shrugged and followed on with Brendon looking very confused at the man's sudden change in attitude. *What on earth is in the letter,* he thought.

The room was warm and inviting, a fire blazed cheerily in the hearth. Fletch grinned like a Cheshire cat when he was offered a high-backed chair of ruby-red leather. As they sat down, another character bustled in. He was a very dignified looking with a grey wig that reached down to the collar of his three-piece suit; below his nose was a large waxed moustache and a small pointy beard dripped from his chin.

"May I welcome you to our bank; my name is, Sir Arthur Randolph the main trustee of the bank. We have been expecting you; your bank in Lancaster sends a glowing report of your company credit. We would be delighted to offer you our services should you ever require them, I also have excellent connections for investments in the Far East and the Caribbean should you require such advice."

Fletch nodded and handed over the second letter which was from Ben although Edward had signed it giving clear directions as to what he wanted.

"My employer is detained, but as you can see I'm authorised to draw up to three thousand pounds in cash. We only need about two thousand."

"It is a very large sum, what are you to do with such an amount?"

"We're purchasing a ship from Clifford's yard. Do you know the man, is he trustworthy?"

The Winds of Change.

"Indeed he is, perhaps he is a little brusque, but I can assure you his finances are good and his honesty has never been in doubt. He has banked with us for many years. He is what we call, cash poor but asset rich, his marina and wharves are worth a small fortune."

"That's good news. The ship is ready to sail away, but the rest of our crew will not be here for a couple of days so we'll need lodgings and then we may need to hire some crew."

"Mr Fletcher, may I make a polite suggestion? I would advise that if you are to take lodgings tonight, it might be safer to collect the money tomorrow, or indeed bring, Mr Clifford here. I shall gladly advance you something for your night's lodgings if that would be acceptable."

Fletch stroked his chin and glanced at Brendon. "Sounds fair to me," Brendon said.

"Very well, Sir Arthur, I suppose that it makes good sense."

"Is it your first ship?" Sir Arthur asked politely. He waved his teller over. "Bring these gentlemen some beverages."

"No, sir we've served a long time for his Majesty in the navy, but we have our own ship which is currently on the Sheriff of Lancaster's business, transporting felons and such like from gaol to Van Diemen's Land."

The banker was obviously impressed. "Perhaps I might make another suggestion, you should look for lodgings well away from the docks some of those establishments are very unsanitary." He scribbled on a piece of paper. "This is a very reputable establishment, the manager is a friend of mine, show him this note and you will be well looked after."

Back out in the unrelenting rain, they headed blindly through the city until they spied the hotel. A uniformed door attendant guarded the well-lit foyer.

"This is it," Fletch said.

"To be sure it's far too…, I don't know the word, but we'll not be comfortable. Let's find a bar, somewhere we can have a few bevvies," Brendon said with a wink and naughty smile.

"Ah, Brendon, the skipper will flay us alive if we get into any trouble."

"Mr Fletcher, have you ever known me not to be on the straight and narrow?"

Fletch did not answer but he was filled with dread. "Very well, but we don't drink."

The statement 'we don't drink,' was a bit like asking a fish not to swim. They entered a smoke-filled and very noisy inn and without looking around, they went to the bar. The barmaid smiled enchantingly at them.

"Now then my pretties, what will it be?" Her voice was soft and alluring.

Fletch had taken the precaution of not having all his spare money in the same pocket so that he was able to just spill a few coins onto the bar. They took a deep satisfying swig of their ale and as Brendon wiped the froth from his lips, he turned to look around the room. The faces around them were not hostile but one or two faces seemed to be taking a great interest in them; the rest seemed not to care. They had several more drinks and then fortified their ale with whisky.

"You be looking for somewhere to stay maybe?" She said almost in a whisper as she served them another drink. Fletch, who was now a little worse for wear thought her lips looked in need of a kiss. Two drinks later, he tried planting his lips on hers, but she was too quick for him and dodged sideward. "There's a price on these lips my boy, and until you've paid it, you need to keep your distance."

A weasel of a character stepped in front of Fletch. "You leave my girl alone mister or else."

Brendon grabbed Fletch's arm dragging him away and out of trouble.

"You're a fine one, it was you warning me not to drink," Brendon said.

"I was only teasing."

"Come on, we'll find somewhere else."

They spilt out onto the street, neither of them too sure-footed, at least the rain had stopped; the fresh air soon sobered them up.

"Why don't we go sleep on the ship, I know it's not ours yet, but it will be tomorrow," Brendon said.

"Which way, I've lost my bearings a bit?"

"Come on, it's downhill this way, that must lead to the docks."

There was not a soul about, but suddenly, a cat leapt into the middle of the alley from a brick wall, it studied them a minute through glowing eyes and then scaled the far wall and was away.

"Phew, that made me jump. At least it's sobered me up."

All was quiet; there was only the sound of their footsteps. They talked about their forthcoming journey. "You can always rely on, Mr Burrows to find some action for us," Fletch said.

"Aye, but I'd rather we were not on such a mission, the Skipper's been heartbroken since we lost Emma."

"I'd not like to be in, Quigley's boots if and when he catches up with him."

Two characters appeared from out of a side alley and Fletch instinctively knew that someone was behind them too. They may have

The Winds of Change.

looked unarmed to the casual observer but they were veterans of too many scrapes to be unprepared.

"Now then lads, what's to do?" Fletch said. He slipped his hand up the back of his jacket where he had a blade tucked into his belt. Brendon had a ten-inch iron pin with a ball end that weighed almost four pounds tucked in his coat.

"There be a toll for travelling this 'ere alley, so empty yer pockets and let's see what yer got."

"You don't want to see what I got friend," Brendon said with a smile, his teeth glinting in the moonlight.

The man behind them threw himself onto Brendon's back locking his arms around the Irishman's neck. With a loud yell, Brendon threw himself back against the wall; he felt the man's breath on the back of his neck as it was knocked from his body.

One of the other two flashed a pistol, but before he could cock it, he was dead. Fletch had drawn his blade and accurately thrown it with all his strength into the man's chest. Brendon lashed out with his iron pin and hit the remaining man full on the temple with it and he too went down as dead as his friend was. The one Brendon had crushed against the wall lay in a crumpled heap in the gutter but he suddenly managed to recover a little and pulled a blade. He stabbed wildly out at Brendon, but it missed him by several inches. With surprising agility, the man was on his feet and made an overarm swing of the blade towards Brendon. Again, his attack was thwarted as Brendon parried the blow with his pin and then swiped it in a backhanded motion that landed its heavy ball on the man's chin, instantly drawing blood and sending the man crashing to the floor again.

"Come on let's pile 'em up here. I suppose we should tell the constable, but it'll mean questions."

Brendon lifted the bodies and stacked them against the wall. "Someone will clear them up with the rest of the rubbish from around here."

Squalls of freezing rain driven by a powerful wind were blowing the little fishing boat ever nearer the dangerous sandbanks of Morecambe Bay. Ezra clung to the tiller as Bruce tried to heave the sails over to change tack, but even his mighty strength was not enough. They could see the lights of Lancaster and knew that they would be lucky not to run aground on their present course. Twice they knew they had hit the bottom, but each time another wave lifted them clear and soon they were in sight of Barrow's harbour wall.

Tony Mead.

With some relief, they sailed into the harbour. The weather eased enough for Ezra to moor his boat and for them to set off in search of Ben. They did not have far to go, as he was returning from another visit to Mr McHenry's office.

"Glad you're here, how did it go?" Ben said.

"It went well, skipper, the ship looks in good fettle and it'll be as fast as a greyhound," Bruce said.

"Good, everyone back to Edward's. I've done some recruiting already I think I can have them ready by tomorrow," Ben said the action made him feel much better.

"You've been busy, we've only been away six days," Ezra said.

Emily felt to be quite at home as the old crew gathered for a meal. She welcomed Tobias to the table she remembered him from the crew of the Pelican.

"I understand you are helping, Lord Levante with his engine," she said.

"Yes, the man is obsessed, but I'm sure he's got the rights of it, steam power is the way forward."

When Clough arrived with his luggage it finalised the crew.

"Well gentlemen, I'm sorry not to be going with you, I dread to think what mischief your skipper will get up to without me." he raised his glass "Here's to your voyage and your new ship, The Raven." Everyone raised their glass for the toast but there were mixed feelings and not everyone was happy about the voyage.

The following day they crowded aboard Ezra's boat and after a few tears from Jenny and Emily, they headed out to sea with the tide. A stiff following wind pushed them south along the coast until once more they reached the mouth of the mighty River Mersey. With the boat so overloaded, they had to make sure that they steered well clear of any other ships, and it was only due to Ezra's fine seamanship that they managed to navigate safely through the busiest parts of the river.

"There she is," Bruce yelled. He was standing on the boat's prow clinging to the jib-line.

When Ben saw the ship, he instinctively knew that it was the right one for the voyage; there was something about it he liked; defiantly it had character, with its black-painted gunwales and its shinning hull, it made an impressive sight. Fletch was waving frantically from its deck, there had been time for him to check the ship out and he was very pleased.

He blew a sharp trill on his bosun's pipes as Ben stepped aboard. "Welcome aboard, Skipper," Fletch said enthusiastically.

The Winds of Change.

"She looks fine," Ben said. His whole body was tingling with excitement as he stared about the deck.

Fletch led him below deck. "Wait until you've seen your cabin; whoever had this built was not short of money."

"Is she paid for?" Ben said.

"Aye, that she is, first thing this morning we paid the shipwright off. I took the liberty of drawing a little extra cash from the bank, I'm sure we'll need it for crew and victuals."

"Well done Fletch, I've left Mr Clough in charge of buying stores for the journey, he'll be ready by the time we get back."

The cabin was a decent size and it reminded him of his accommodation on the San Justo, a prize ship he had captained during his time in the Caribbean.

"If you've settled our account, then we can sail today with the tide?" Ben said.

There was a call from outside and a small boat bumped gently against the hull. "Permission to come aboard, it's me Clifford the shipwright."

They met him on deck. "You've made a fine job of the ship," Ben said.

"Thank you, I assume you are, the new Skipper. I'm pleased to meet you."

They shook hands, and Ben led him down to his cabin and offered him a seat.

"The original owners had plenty of cash, you can see from the furnishings nothing was spared."

Mould was already making himself at home and from somewhere he found some glasses and a bottle of rum.

"I've got a favour to ask of you," Clifford said. "My son would like to sail with you. He's a fine carpenter and if you don't have anyone in mind for that post he would serve you well." He sipped his rum. "I don't want to lose him, but I've spent my whole life here and I want him to see something of the world; there's plenty of time later on for him to work in the yard."

"I'd be very happy to take him; I've got a good iron smith for him to work with aboard."

When the tide was favourable Raven inched out into the main river and there was a certain amount of nervous tension as they were released from their towboat and were set free in the Mersey.

"Steady as she goes," Ben called. He stood alongside Fletch who was manning the helm.

Their foresail top was already filled by the breeze and as they hoisted the two triangular mainsails the ship seemed to take a deep breath and then sprinted across the waves.

"Reminds me of the San Justo," Fletch called, he gave Ben a broad smile, "let's hope we have more luck with this one than that."

"We didn't steal this one, maybe that will be the difference," Ben said.

As her sails filled and stretched with the wind, they all realised that this was a very different ship from anything else they had sailed.

"She is like a greyhound!" Ezra called out.

As soon as they cleared the congestion of the Mersey and were out on the open sea everyone began enjoying the ride. With her sails at full stretch, she leant over before the breeze and cut through the sea as easy as any fish. At first, the crew seemed to be clinging on for dear life; they were unused to such speed, but very soon, there was a broad smile on every face.

"Fletch, make sure the lads check out her spares, ropes, lines and cables before we reach Barrow, we can order anything we need there."

20. Van Diemen's Land

Although Mitchell and Booth's relationship did not get off to a good start, the recent turn of events had brought about something of a truce between them. The hostilities of the past were forgotten; they even shared the occasional glass of port in the dayroom and Booth was always at the Captain's table for his evening meal.

"I'm curious about something, Captain; I thought the captain of this ship was to be a Mr Burrows, or at least that was the name I was given to expect," Booth said.

"There is a Mr Burrows, the gentleman who owns this ship," Mitchell said taken slightly off guard. "When we were informed that the ship was to be commandeered and converted for use in the transportation of convicts, Mr Burrows, who had only recently married at that time was adamant that he would not put to sea again. So, after some discussion, it was decided that I should Captain Pelican for him. Mr Burrows was my navigator during our time in the Royal Navy and since our retirement, we have remained good friends. He saved my life on at least two occasions and in fact rescued me from captivity with the French from the island of Martinique ."

Booth, as usual, had several documents in his hand; he held one out for Mitchell to see. "Look you, it is signed by non-other than, Sir Walter Ridsdale, The Lord Chief Justice."

Booth passed the document to Mitchell for him to read.

"Are private ships often commandeered for this duty?" Mitchell said as he read the paperwork.

"No, not often, but as you can see, Pelican has been specifically recommended for this duty and voyage."

"Very curious, I wonder why and where the order came from."

"I'm afraid, that I am not privy to such information, but I can say that the convicts or at least a number of them were not randomly selected for the voyage as would be normal, but picked by the Sherriff of Lancaster."

Mitchell looked up with interest. "Were you not curious about that?"

"I don't get paid to be curious, I simply follow the orders of my superiors; it makes life far less complicated."

"Do you know which men they were?"

"No, I have records of which gaol the prisoners are sent from but that is all."

Mitchell pondered the implications of Booth's words, he thought about Ben and Edward's visit to Lancaster Prison, and the man they interviewed who was murdered before they could ask him any further questions.

"I fear that this may be some kind of conspiracy against my friend and colleague Mr Burrows."

"Conspiracy, what do you mean? I hope that you don't think that I am part of this intrigue," Booth said indignantly.

"No, of course not, I'm sure you are innocent of any involvement, but I think that you have been duped the same as I have. Who can be at the back of it? My concern now is what was their plan, why did they want him out to sea and once they know that their plan has failed what else might they do?"

Booth looked agitated; the revelation had obviously been quite a shock to him. "I don't like this at all, there is too much corruption in our society, I shall seek out the truth, of that you can rest assured."

"Could this Ridsdale character be part of it?"

"No, I doubt it; he will have been advised by someone and asked to approve the deed without giving it a second thought. I shall send a letter with you for a colleague of mine, his name is Ambler who is a great friend of the anti-slavery lobby but more importantly, he is incorruptible, if some sort of conspiracy has been brewed, then he's the man to dig it out."

Mitchell was struck by a sudden thought. "What about the men we put ashore, could they have been employed to cause trouble on the ship?" he said.

"I'll check my log to see if they are the ones specifically selected. If it has been some kind of plot, well then I've been taken for a fool too, I'll not rest until I have some answers. At least they are out of harm's way now." He allowed himself a wry smile.

Mitchell braced himself against the rolling ship for a moment and then went back to his cabin with a very troubled mind. Elvira was watching the sea from the rear window; she loved the way the ragged, wind-driven waves tumbled and collided as they broke against the ship. She smiled as soon as she saw Mitchell but she immediately guessed that there was something wrong.

"Sit down," he said more harshly than he meant to say, "why did you end up on this ship?"

She looked nervous and tears started to run down her cheeks.

"I was going to tell you, honestly I was."

"Tell me what; are you part of some intrigue?"

"Before I left prison," she straightened up and moved to the edge of the chair. "I was told, that if I wanted to receive a lighter sentence then I should seduce the ship's captain," she sobbed and dare not look at him.

The Winds of Change.

"What, how do mean, so this has all been a sham... a lie!" Mitchell almost exploded.

"No, please hear me out. You are not the captain I was told to seduce, his name was," she was finding it difficult to think straight.

He took her arms and shook her. "Burrows, was it Burrows?"

"Yes, that was it. I only found out your name later after we'd met. I was relieved; truthfully, this has not been a sham or lie. Please believe me," she wiped her face with the hem of her skirt. "I love you," she whispered. "You're the best thing that has ever happened to me, and although we must soon part, I'll never forget our time together or your kindness. I just wish that we had met at another time and place."

Mitchell let go of her arms his emotions in tatters flapping in the breeze like a shredded sail. He had not wanted to believe the evidence before him, and now he was not sure what to think. His heart wanted to believe her his common sense said beware.

Snow smartly saluted Mitchell when he arrived back on the quarterdeck. "Land Ahoy, Captain, and may I inform you that we are within sight of our destination, Macquarie Harbour."

The penal colony was situated in a lagoon on the west coast of the island, far away from any other settlements. They entered through the jaws of the lagoon and Snow soon realised that there was a need for caution. "There seems to be a great many rocks and sandbars, Captain, we should be very wary."

Mitchell wondered if it might be safer to send the convicts ashore in the ship's boats rather than trying to dock near the town.

"I don't like the look of those sandbanks and rocky outcrops," Mitchell said. He snapped his telescope shut. "Mr Hardy, please ask, Mr Booth to attend me here."

Although the azure sea was peaceful, heavy black clouds were forming over the island's mountains and Mitchell knew that a storm was on its way.

"Keep a weather eye on those hills, Mr Snow; we could be in for quite a blow."

There were a couple of forlorn-looking wrecks on the shore, the wooden vessels with their backs broken, their hull timbers rotting and exposed to the elements like the carcass of some poor creature, were an obvious warning. An island sat in the middle of the entrance to the lagoon, its craggy rocks looked menacing; if the wind was to get up then they could be blown onto its shore and Mitchell had no intention of being the next victim of its dangerous rocks.

"Mr Booth, I need a pilot to take me through this dangerous-looking water, or I'll be forced to use my boats to ferry your convicts ashore. I'm not even sure that it is navigable, I don't have a single chart for this area."

Booth gazed at the rocks and the wrecks. "I think that you are wise, Captain, perhaps you could send a boat to see if a pilot is available."

Hardy took a small crew and the pinnace, which was equipped with a sail to see if he could find a pilot. The town was in complete disarray and it took almost an hour to find someone in authority. Eventually, a pilot was found and Hardy shipped him back to Pelican.

"Welcome aboard," Mitchell said as he shook the pilot's hand. "Can you safely get us in closer?"

"Don't fret Captain there is a safe strait that will get us in close enough to land on the beach."

"Prepare to disembark," Hardy bellowed down into the hold.

Mitchell breathed a sigh of relief when at last they dropped anchor but he was also feeling very sad that he would lose Elvira. He had fought with his conscience as to what to do about her. In the quiet of his cabin, he held her close. "I Don't know what to say, I can not think of any way that I can help."

"Don't be sad Captain, we've had happy moments together that we must see as a bonus of some kind and be thankful for them." She rolled a few belongings into a blanket and was preparing to leave when there was a sharp rap on the door.

Mitchell protectively pushed her behind himself. "Enter," he said suspiciously.

Booth entered carefully checking over his shoulder to make sure that he was seen as he did so. He handed Mitchell his log, which was open, Mitchell read the carefully written last entry several times before he dared to comment.

"All you need to do, Captain, is sign it, the surgeon has already seen it and approved it," Booth said.

"Are you sure? I'm dumbfounded as to what to say," Mitchell said.

"Say nothing... it's the best that I can do to repay you for saving my life." He turned towards Elvira. "I don't ever want to see you again in these circumstances, and keep below deck until after you sail."

She looked confused and tried to see what the paperwork was about. Mitchell signed and Booth picked up his log without another word and left.

"What was that all about?" Elvira asked not sure what to do.

The Winds of Change.

"You are officially dead. You've died of a fever off the coast of Brazil where you were buried. Mr Booth has given you your freedom in exchange for... my saving his life, I suppose."

"So I don't have to go ashore here," she said unsure as to laugh or cry. "Is it true, am I free?"

She squealed and threw herself into Mitchell's arms. "Will you take me back to England?"

"Will you marry me?" he blurted out as much to his surprise as hers.

She looked deep into his eyes as if trying to see into his soul. "Will you love me forever?" she whispered.

"Until hell freezes over."

"Oh, yes please, I will."

They stared at each other for a minute. "But what will I be called now? I need a new identity."

"Elvira Mitchell," he said simply.

"I can't yet," she desperately looked about her for inspiration. "Wooden boat, ropes, mast, compass," she reeled off everything she saw.

"Compass," Mitchell said.

"Compass, Elvira Compass." She threw her hands up in despair.

"No, not compass; we are travelling north from here, what about Mistress North, Elvira North? I think it sounds to have a genuine ring to it."

"Not the most glamorous name, but maybe soon we will be changing it again," she said with a sly wink.

Booth had gone ashore but he was back before the last of the prisoners were ferried to the mainland.

"Captain, the conditions here are dreadful, there is a shortage of food, but ridiculously there is a shipment of supplies sitting on the docks a hundred and fifty miles away. The settlement has very few facilities, and the isolated geography of it is making supplying it almost impossible." He threw his hands up in despair. "Coupled with that, the infertility of the surrounding soil is making growing food almost impossible; which means that most of the inhabitants are already suffering from malnutrition and scurvy. I thought things would have improved since my last visit three years ago."

"Are you asking if we'll fetch the supplies for you?"

Booth nodded humbly, "Yes if you could please, the settlement here is on its knees."

He placed a scroll on the desk. "I've managed to find some charts for you, they are a bit antiquated, but never the less I believe that they are accurate.

He felt obliged to help out and knew that he could not leave them stranded without food. "You will have to come with us; they'll not just hand these supplies to me."

Mitchell called for his steward. "I want Lieutenant Hardy, and Snow in here as soon as possible," he said as he spread out the charts on the table. Mitchell was annoyed about the delay this was going to cause, but after Booth's magnanimous gesture it would have seemed very churlish to refuse to help out.

"How soon can we sail, Mr Snow?"

"The bay is deep enough; we do not have to wait for the tide, I'd estimate that we can put to sea in three hours."

"Make it two; we are to fetch supplies for this God-forsaken place."

"Should we begin to remove the cages from below decks?" Hardy asked.

"We can certainly begin to clear the lower hold and deck; I don't know how bulky a package of supplies we are to transfer. I'll be glad to see the back of them."

A southerly wind threatened them as soon as they reached deep water. Its punishing ice-cold gusts whipped through her rigging and tore at her sheets. Pelican needed to muster all her inbuilt strength to survive.

"Ice is building upon her masts, Mr Hardy; if we are not careful she'll capsize with the weight." Mitchell was shouting to be heard over the din of the wind. "Get some men aloft with axes and clear that blasted ice."

With the wind behind them, the ship seemed as though it was being thrown forward into the dark indigo waves; several times her bow was fully submerged and the ice-cold sea flooded across her decks. Tragedy struck, when two men were swept out of the rigging and lost overboard without a trace.

Below decks, Booth was clinging on for dear life, his grey face was covered in his last meal, and he felt as though he would die. Mitchell looked in on him. "Stay in your bunk until it stops."

Booth simply groaned an answer; he had no intention of doing anything but that.

Back in Mitchell's cabin, Elvira was beginning to wish that they had put her ashore. She felt as though her brain was swirling about and drunkenly bouncing about inside of her skull.

"How do you endure this?" she whispered.

"What are you referring to?" he said with a broad grin. "I can endure looking at you for a whole lifetime."

The Winds of Change.

At that moment, she put her hand to her mouth and lost what little remained in her stomach. He carefully washed her face, straightened her hair, and placed her in his bunk.

"Try to sleep, the weather will change soon." He sat on the edge of the bunk holding her hand.

They found the new harbour and port of Hobart in chaos, many of the temporary buildings had been blown down by the gales, two ships had run aground and Several convicts had escaped into the forest.

Booth was fully recovered and trying to cover his embarrassment with efficiency.

"I'll go ashore, Captain, and make some arrangements to pick up our supplies, that is if they are still here."

When Booth returned it was not with good news. "Our supplies are here, but the wharf cranes have been blown over and everything is going to have to be carried and loaded by hand."

Snow and the purser had been ashore to assess the situation. "This is going to take some time I'm afraid, Mr Booth," Snow said.

"Very well, Mr Snow, thank you for your report," Mitchell said, "I'm going to give the crew some shore leave, we've got a difficult journey ahead and I'm not sure when the next opportunity will be. The longshoremen here can manage the loading."

"There's a good beach down there," Hardy said, "what about building a fire pit and roasting a couple of those pigs?"

"Good idea, I don't think this town has much to offer, we'll put ashore some ale and rum and take a break," Mitchell said with a confident smile.

Later that evening Mitchell and Elvira were walking along the sand after finishing the feast. The weather had suddenly improved and it was as warm as a Spring evening. "I'm nervous about meeting your friends back at home," she said.

"Why, they will love you?"

"I've nothing to wear... apart from this old blouse and skirt."

He had not thought about that, she would need some warm clothes for England. "I'll see if the purser can muster you something for the time being, and then when we reach the Spice Islands we'll find you something there I'm sure."

Two days later and with the crew in high spirits, they were sailing back around the coast to the penal colony. Mitchell called a meeting of his officers in his day room.

"Gentlemen, I have an announcement. As you are all aware I have had a special passenger sharing my cabin for the past few weeks and she will be returning to England with me." He paused to study their faces but no one showed any reaction. "The official story will be that Elvira died off the coast of Brazil. She is to change her name and we are to marry as soon as is possible."

Now there was a reaction, everyone cheered and congratulated him.

"Wonderful news, Captain, I can't wait to see what Edward and Ben have to say, they'll be delighted I'm sure," Snow said.

The sailmaker had managed to alter a shirt and trousers for Elvira, it was not a very flattering outfit, but it made her look a little less conspicuous. She approached Mitchell, and Snow on the quarterdeck in her new attire.

"So how do I look?" she did a twirl, and although she knew that it was hardly glamorous, she thought that she knew how men's minds worked and that he was bound to say that it was fine.

Mitchell studied a moment, he cleared his throat, and for a brief moment, thought about being complimentary, but decided not to insult her intelligence; honesty was the best policy. "We need to find something when we dock in Ceylon, there will be something more suitable I'm sure; it has a large British colony."

"Your friends will think that I'm just some whore you've picked up along the way."

Mitchell was lost for words. However, Snow, who was usually quiet and reserved reacted to her comments. He was delighted that Mitchell was so happy with his newfound love, but he had been slightly offended by her remarks. He found that he was forced to make a comment.

"If you'll excuse me, ma'am... Captain," Snow said hesitantly, "Those we refer to as, The Old Crew back in Cartmel would never make such a judgement. Please believe me when I say that, you will fit right in and be accepted, just as I was." Snow looked embarrassed but he was pleased to have said his piece. "The place just seems to attract what they jokingly refer to as pilgrims; an assortment of waifs and strays. After all, at the end of the day, we are all lost souls looking for a place to rest."

Elvira smiled at him. "Thank you, Mr Snow, I'm not sure how to take that, but I'm sure that you meant well by it."

They were all saved further embarrassment when the lookout warned them that they were back at Macquarie Harbour.

To meet the needs of the next leg of their journey extra barrels of water were loaded after the provisions were put ashore. Hardy and the purser worked tirelessly to ensure that the changeover went well. Mitchell impatiently supervised from the quarterdeck wishing that they could eventually set sail. Snow approached him carrying a bundle of charts, which he laid out on an upturned crate.

The Winds of Change.

"Are you alright Mr Snow? I've never known you speak out before," Mitchell said when they were alone on deck.

"My sincerest apologies Captain," he said with a bow of his head. "I'm sorry if I was clumsy with my words, but I just find that I am truly missing life and our friends on the farm." He cleared his throat to continue. It was almost painful to relax and speak plainly to his Captain. "I've never had a real family; not one that I could say that I missed when I'm away. You both seem so happy together; I just wanted to tell her that she should have nothing to fear about meeting our friends. I'm sure you will have a wonderful life back in Cartmel should you decide to stay there."

"We're a long way off there yet; Mr Snow, I understand what you mean. I do agree with you, it's the first time ever, that I wish I was back home." It was rare for them to have an informal chat and Mitchell thought that he might share an idea with him. "A few weeks before we sailed, Edward and I went to look at a fine house on the outskirts of Grange over Sands. That Scottish solicitor of Ben's informed me about it saying that it was due to come on the market; I could picture myself living there." He placed his hand on Snow's shoulder. "Now, what do you need to show me here?"

"There is a group of small islands about halfway; they are inhabited, so, therefore, we may be able to find fresh water, it is only a very minor detour to reach them."

"Good work, Mr Snow, we shall look for them, but it's a huge ocean and they are very small islands."

Finally, two days later, all was ready for Pelican to put to sea. There had been a great many forms to sign and exchange, which meant that Booth was the last to go ashore. He paused before he climbed over the ship's side and extended his hand towards Mitchell.

"Thank you for your diligence Captain and the efforts you have made to make this a successful mission despite your distaste for the task. I wish you good fortune on your next leg of your journey and a safe return to England. There is a great deal of paperwork for you to carry home for us if you can wait to pick it up."

As the new dawn spread its light across the sky like a blossoming flower, Pelican put to sea. The sea was fairly calm as the fresh light caught the aquamarine wave tops. Mitchell proudly stood on the quarterdeck; at last, he felt as though he was master of his ship again.

21. Captivity.

Emma and Dorothy had no choice but to reluctantly settle into their new life and although they were prisoners, the grand old plantation house was very comfortable, it had a large garden that they were allowed to walk around albeit was always under the watchful eye of one of their gaolers.

As they walked, they could talk in private. "This reminds me of a house we had in Jamaica, the gardens were beautiful and I have so many very happy memories from there," Dorothy said.

"I love the flowers here, they are so colourful and the fragrance is so intense. You must miss the life you had then."

"No, not really, mother was often unhappy and before we left, Sir Arthur was a real tyrant."

"Come on let's get back, we've dinner to make."

There had been no objection from their captors when Emma had offered to take over the household duties of cooking and cleaning and so, each evening she would make them all a meal. There was an abundance of fresh fruit and vegetables for her to experiment with, and although she was not allowed to go to the town market for them, one of the guards seemed to enjoy the task of shopping and bringing her food daily. It took her mind off the problems at hand and she even talked two of the guards into repairing the old brick oven so that she could bake bread for them all.

As they worked in the kitchen one morning Dorothy felt uneasy, she was concerned about Emma who seemed a little withdrawn. "Are you alright? Recently you've seemed different."

"I'm with child," Emma whispered.

Dorothy had to put her hand to her mouth so as not to make a sound, the look in her eyes said everything.

"We've been away for nearly four months," she whispered from between her fingers.

"Yes, I thought it was the stress of what we've been through, but I'm changing in shape just as I did when I was having Walter."

"Should we tell our guards?"

"What can they do… no, I think we'll keep it our secret for as long as possible."

"They are going to notice soon," Dorothy whispered.

"Not until it is very obvious, don't forget that they are men and only have two things on their very simple minds."

"What's that?" Dorothy asked innocently.

The Winds of Change.

"Food and you know."

"Oh yes, I know what the other is."

There were usually five guards, a mixed bunch of scruffy individuals, the same sort of characters, that would be found in any dockside bar. They spent their time playing cards or dice; very occasionally, there would be a fall out amongst them but nothing too serious and the incident was soon forgotten. They were always courteous towards Emma and Dorothy and even tried to temper their language whenever they saw them. One of the guards was always positioned at the back of the house just to make sure that neither of their prisoners tried to make a run for it. Occasionally, Quigley would arrive and the atmosphere became tense, he usually brought with him another two mean-looking henchmen who were very different in character to the usual guards.

Most evenings, Emma and Dorothy took their evening meal to their bedroom safely away from the men. They locked and barricaded the door with a chair wedged under the handle. From their window, they had a clear view of the bay, so they took it in turns to watch ships arriving and departing.

Although the house was old, it had character which appealed to Emma. She wondered about the last residents; from the furniture, she guessed that they were not wealthy but she could tell that there had been children, probably quite a few by the number of cots in the bedrooms. She held her stomach a moment gently rubbing it, and thought of Walter and Ben. Dorothy was sleeping peacefully snoring like a puppy, so Emma moved her chair out onto their veranda so that she could look out across the bay. She wished that Ben would sail into the harbour and realised that she also missed all the lads of the old crew. It was a peaceful scene, she watched the stars trying to remember the names of the constellations. On a clear night or when they had been at sea, Ben would point them out to her and explain how he used them to navigate his ship. Eventually, she fell asleep dreaming of happier times.

Quigley arrived early one morning; his face was bruised and he was in a foul temper. He sat down at the kitchen table where Emma served him with bread, ham and a juicy thick slice of fresh pineapple.

"What is to happen to us, Mr Quigley?" Dorothy asked.

Quigley shifted uncomfortably on his chair, he took a deep drag on his pipe and blew the smoke into the air.

"It looks like your living the life of kings here, all this food. To be honest, if it was up to me we'd sell you, someone will pay a handsome price for a lass such as you." He puffed on his pipe again. "Some farmer might want you for his bride; mind you, he'd work you like a donkey, and put as many bairns as he could into your belly." Although Quigley laughed at his own joke, he was not as confident as he sounded, he was losing sleep worrying about Ben, he knew that he would surely arrive and then there would be hell to pay.

Emma and Dorothy had altered her dress to make her growing bulge less obvious; the last thing she wanted was Quigley to know her state. *It would be something else he could use against Ben,* she thought.

That afternoon Quigley rode away and the guards seemed to relax; they were obviously afraid of him and felt much better after he had gone. One of the guards, in particular, changed noticeably when Quigley was away, he was a bit of a loner, and he was usually the one covering the back of the house. Emma had watched him and she was more afraid of him than she was of the others, quite often, she noticed his evil lecherous eyes secretively preying on Dorothy.

"I don't like Quigley," Dorothy said, "Will he decide our fate?"

"No, he's only a pawn in this, I think we are waiting for, Sir Arthur to make his mind up as to what should be done."

"He'll not harm us, he'll not dare."

"But no one knows that we are here apart from his thugs, and of course the crew of the ship that brought us here." Emma looked about them to see if anyone was within hearing distance. "We must take our chance when we can and run to the town. I think that I can remember where Ben's agent lives, if we can reach there, then we'll be safe."

"I thought we might have heard from him," Dorothy said.

"Well, that all depends on whether or not the ship's Captain kept his word and delivered my letter."

"Might he have betrayed us to Quigley?"

"I sincerely hope not, or Mr Laughton's life is in danger too."

One evening after they had all eaten, a serious situation blew up between the guard they called the loner and one of the other men.

"You cheating bastard," one of the men said and pulled a knife from his belt. Amidst the commotion the table was overturned, bottles and drinks were scattered as the men squared up for a fight. One of the others who seemed to be the leader when Quigley was away, stepped between them to stop the fight. "Put that blade away or I'll shove it up your arse so far it'll cut the roots of yer hair," he said menacingly. There was a tense moment, but the men backed off, the loner stormed out and disappeared around the back of the house.

"Sorry about that, ladies," the leader said with a crooked smile. "He'll cool off by morning."

For the rest of the day and into the evening the atmosphere around the house felt strained.

The Winds of Change.

"They all seem in a bad mood," Dorothy whispered. They were seated on a swing on the veranda watching the sunset across the sea.

"Let's hope that they stay that way, it might give us a chance to escape," Emma said with a smile.

"So long as they don't take it out on us, if I had the strength I'd fight them all," she sighed. "How are you feeling?"

"Oh, I'm alright, I've done this before you know," Emma said putting on a brave face. She did not feel very brave; she desperately missed Walter, Ben and the farm. The fear of having the baby here alone was giving her nightmares.

Dorothy tugged on Emma's sleeve. "Someone's coming."

A lone figure approached on horseback, he rode right up to the veranda before one of the guards challenged him.

"What do you want, clear off this is private property." The gang leader carried a musket in his arms.

"Good day neighbours," he tipped his hat to the women. "I'm buying some land further along the valley; I thought I might introduce myself and I'm just being nosey as to who might be my neighbours, I suppose."

"Well go be nosey somewhere else, we don't take kindly to people being nosey here."

"Well, I'll be off then, sorry to disturb you." He tipped his hat again and turned his mount around to trot off down the drive.

"I wish we could have asked him for help or something," Dorothy whispered.

"Don't worry, he got the message, that was Ben's agent."

"Why didn't he say something?"

"It would have been the last thing he had done, he'll send word now, Ben will be here soon."

"He is very brave coming here, he must know how dangerous these men are."

Laughton blew a sigh of relief as he reached the safety of the road. Since receiving the letter from the sip's Captain he had spent as much time as possible trying to find them, it had taken time but one day his luck changed and he watched Quigley leaving town with two of his thugs. He discreetly followed them from the town and worked out that this was where they were being held. He had not dared speak to them but he guessed that Emma would have the sense not to give him away. He felt relieved that they seemed safe and in good health, he would send word to Ben as soon as was possible.

They sat awhile, enjoying the warm evening air and very soon, Emma fell asleep satisfied at last that help was on its way.

Dorothy decided to leave her in peace and to take a walk, the guards were nowhere in sight and she had a wonderful sense of freedom. Following the old garden path which took her directly towards the setting sun and then in a wide arc towards the back of the house, she wondered about Walter and Ben. S*hould I call him father, papa, or Ben* she thought? *The old crew will be worried about us, especially Mould and Fletch and little Eve will be pestering Jenny to see us.* She stopped and watched the last of the sun as it slipped beneath the horizon. Suddenly she realised that she had strayed too far and she was out of sight of Emma, she turned to return but her path was blocked by the loner.

"Now then my pretty, what are you doing here?" he leered at her like a hungry hyena.

"Nothing, I'm just walking and minding my own business."

"Maybe, you were looking for me; I've seen you look at me with those big blue eyes, and I think you must be as bored as I am. Perhaps, we could bring a little comfort to each other."

He moved towards her, but Dorothy sidestepped him and skipped off the path onto the lawn. He laughed at her attempt to escape.

"Want me to chase you a little, do you?"

"Go away."

"I could chase you into the woods if you like, we could pick nice flowers." As he spoke, he reached out and squeezed Dorothy's breast. Her response was immediate, she gave him a backhanded slap that was so hard his teeth crashed together, and it was a wonder that his eyes kept in their sockets.

She was off like a rabbit; she lifted her skirt to free her legs and sprinted for safety. He recovered quickly and chased her across the lawn and with a flying tackle; he brought her to the floor. He was giggling insanely and she could smell the stale tobacco and beer on his breath. He tried to force his hands up her skirt. She kicked and writhed as she slapped and punched him, but somehow she could not scream; the sound was locked in her throat. Suddenly his hands were between her thighs forcing them apart, digging into her flesh, ripping at her clothes seemingly unstoppable. At last, the scream escaped and it echoed around the garden.

Emma suddenly roused from her nap, there was a feeling of dread coursing through her veins; she knew immediately that something was wrong. She heard another scream and dashed around the house somewhere along the way she grabbed a heavy length of firewood. In the dim light, she could see the two figures writhing on the ground. Like a lioness defending her cubs, she attacked without any thought for her

The Winds of Change.

own safety. She swung her arm left and right beating the man about the head until he rolled over battered, bloody, and lifeless.

Emma fell to her knees to hug Dorothy. "Are you alright, my poor child, what has this monster done."

Dorothy was shaking but managed to return Emma's hug. "Don't worry, I'm alright he didn't get far."

The rest of the guards arrived carrying lanterns. For a moment, they stood in a circle around Emma, as though they were not sure what to do.

The gang leader turned her attacker over with his foot and then knelt down to feel for any sign of life. Without any emotion he said. "Now you've done it." He stood up and wiped some tobacco from his lips. "He'll not bother you again miss."

One of the others felt for a pulse, he shook his head. "Dead as you like, what do you want to do?"

"Quigley will not be pleased; he seemed to like this creature. We'll bury him in the woods and tell him he just went missing, that way everyone's happy."

Emma made to object. "You can't just hide his body."

"What else would you have us do? We didn't like or care about him; he was bad news, good riddance is what I say. Quigley is hardly likely to turn you over to the constable; however, he might want recompense for his lost man. I think we'll do as I said." He gave them a wink and a nod. "You two just have to go along with whatever we say; best say nothing, least said soonest healed."

22. Sail Away

Raven was ready to sail; her black and gold painted hull made a spectacular sight as she waited with her wings of canvas folded and aching to stretch and put to sea. There had been a great deal of interest in her from the moment she had first docked; crowds had gathered along the harbour wall to see her. Some said that she looked like a pirate ship, while others thought that she was more like a hunting dog that was waiting patiently for the off. It had been difficult to keep their mission secret, and it seemed as if the whole of Barrow knew what was happening, which Ben found rather worrying. In less than two weeks she was provisioned and her crew was assembled.

Mould prepared Ben's Merchant Captain's uniform not his old Royal Navy tunic, but the one that he had made for his voyage on Pelican five years before.

"Best check to see if this still fits you, after all those homemade meals, and Mrs Barraclough's pies," he said as he helped Ben into the jacket. "Hmm, a wee bit tight, but a few weeks at sea and it will fit perfectly again."

Mould began organising the rest of Ben's clothes, while Ben sorted through his sea chest; he picked up and inspected several objects and then he stopped and looked questioningly at Mould.

"I'm afraid that I've just taken it for granted and not asked you; but will you steward and cook for me as usual? I only ask because you seem very content here these days and I think something is going on between you and, Mrs Cairns at the Grange."

"You don't need to ask, Skipper, you don't think I'd trust you on your own, do you? The other business can wait."

Ben carried on rummaging through the contents of his sea chest. He had a few precious personal items that he always took to sea; his chronometer, his navigation equipment that had belonged to Philip Burrows, his matching pistols, and his engraved sword, which had been a gift from Captain Mitchell to him for his bravery during a battle against French ships in the Caribbean. They were all carefully placed in the chest, along with the blue ensign that Captain Mitchell had presented him with to raise on his prize ship, San Justo. His charts and logbooks were squeezed in on top of his spare clothes. His lucky rabbit's foot given him by Jenny he tied around his neck under his collar and then he placed Emma's locket in a suede bag and laid it on top of his other goods. *I'll give her this as soon as I see her,* he thought. When he was satisfied that he had remembered everything he closed the lid and sat a

The Winds of Change.

moment to gather his thoughts and to say a prayer for the success of their journey.

At breakfast that morning, the atmosphere was strained. Emily was doing her best to hide her emotions and although Edward was bitterly disappointed at not being able to sail with Ben, he was doing his utmost to make their last meal together a pleasant time.

"All being well, we'll sail with tomorrow's afternoon tide. I'm meeting the crew later this morning, so, if you'd all like to come down and look over the ship," Ben said. "I'll be staying on board until we cast off."

He took Walter onto his knee. "Now young man, you have to be brave and stay with Aunty Emily until I bring mummy home."

"Will you bring Dorothy too?"

"Yes of course, and I'll bring you a surprise present too."

"Will it be an elephant?"

"No, I don't think so."

"Good, because we don't have enough straw to feed one."

"Just come home safely Ben, that's all we want," Emily said.

Ben and Edward studied the ship from the shore; the sunlight bounced off the sea and silhouetted the ship against the distant hills. Edward glanced skyward; his experienced weather eye told him that there would be good sailing for the next few days at least.

"She's a fine-looking vessel and no mistake," Edward said he felt a slight pang of jealousy.

There was an awkward silence. "I'll miss your council, Edward," Ben said without taking his eyes from the ship.

"You've captained a ship before without me; you'll be fine, there's not a better navigator anywhere than you."

"I know my limits, I can't instil discipline in the crew as you do, I am not as good a ship's officer as you are," Ben said.

"I think you underestimate yourself, and you have your crew and their loyalty; what more could any captain want. Go find Emma and Dorothy, bring them back safely so our family is back in one piece. Oh, you might bring some of those fine cigars we both enjoy and a few bottles of Port if you are planning on calling into Madeira."

Ben smiled. "None of the old crew needed asking twice to sign on for the voyage; in fact, I don't remember asking them at all, I suppose that I took it for granted that they would all sign up."

A skiff drew up to the harbour wall with Fletch at the helm. "We're all ready and waiting for you, Captain." He stood to attention and saluted.

Ben had a nervous moment as he stepped into the skiff; his emotions were twisting and turning with the excitement of sailing but the sadness of leaving home. He was confident that he would find Emma and Dorothy and that they would be well, but he was unhappy at having to leave Walter even though he knew that the boy would be well looked after.

As he stepped onto the deck the shrill sound of the bosun's pipe to welcomed him aboard; he took a moment to breathe in his new ship, the familiar concoction of smells, a mixture of tar, fresh-cut timber and the earthy smell of the new ropes made him smile. His head cleared and suddenly he felt master of his destiny and at ease with the world.

Emily and Edward were ferried over in the next boat and were helped aboard by Fletch and Brendon. Edward gave Ben an approving nod, he liked what he saw of the ship, almost instinctively he knew that it was a good vessel.

Ben felt an electric buzz of excitement as he descended into the bowels of the ship. He knew that his crew were collected together waiting for his arrival. The low timbers of the deck meant that he had to bow his head slightly before he could proceed. In the light of a dozen flickering oil lamps, he saw their expectant faces and in that instance, his doubts and fears vaporised.

"Welcome aboard, Captain," Ezra said a broad grin on his face. He offered Ben a chair.

Ben looked around and said: "Who's missing?"

"Just, Mr Clough and Fletch who is escorting Emily."

Fletch offered Emily a hand as she rather unsteadily descended the steps to the lower deck.

There was a noise above them on the deck and then the sound of someone else coming down the steps. Clough made a dramatic entrance as he flew down the steps two at a time; he looked very pleased with himself. He wore a new navy-blue tunic which he had had specially made for the voyage. His tailor had really gone overboard with the design and embellished the lapels and cuffs with gold braid.

Bruce stood up and saluted. "Admiral on deck jump to it lads."

Emily smiled at Clough and said: "Ignore them, you look very handsome."

"What news, Mr Clough?" Ben said.

"Everything is complete, Captain," Clough said with a broad smile. "I've purchased fifty of the new design rifles, they are being loaded now. Not all the British army regiments have them yet; some are for our own use, but they will fetch top money in the colonies. The fresh stores will be here tomorrow morning and we can sail with the following tide." Ben

The Winds of Change.

was once again pleased with his purser there were only a few last-minute adjustments to be made.

"So, what is so special about them?" Bruce asked.

Clough had researched the new weapons and he was pleased to be able to show off his knowledge. "Well, the most important feature is that they are much more accurate than the old muskets, they are lighter, easier, and faster to load using cartridges that have powder and ball wrapped together. Experienced riflemen can fire at better than three shots per minute."

Emily looked concerned; the talk of guns reminded her that this was not a trip around the bay they were planning but that they may be heading into danger. She took Edward's hand. "Oh my, it will be so quiet when they leave again; I'm so used to you all being under the feet. It will be a sad moment when you sail, although I know the journey is essential, I still wish I didn't have to lose you all."

"We'll be there and back in no time with this ship, and we'll bring you all gifts just like when I used to sail before. Most importantly I'll have our family back together," Ben said.

As everyone was leaving the ship, Jenny threw her arms around Ben's neck and discreetly felt under his collar, she smiled at him when she found the leather thong around his neck that meant he was wearing her the good luck charm.

"It seems a lifetime ago since you gave me this charm, I'd never go anywhere without it," he whispered.

"Come home safely, we all love you," she said.

Walter had been charging along the decks pretending to be firing the canons and fighting off pirates but when it was time to leave he clung to Ben's neck and had to be coaxed back to dry land.

"Come home soon papa," Walter said tearfully.

"You be a good lad… look after everyone… I'll have Dorothy and your mother home in no time at all," Ben was struggling with his emotions; this was, without a doubt, the most difficult, and painful parting of his life.

It seemed very quiet that evening when Ben sat in his cabin unloading his sea chest. His precision navigational instruments he laid out across the top of the desk. In a bright red wooden box, was his most prized possession, the most cutting edge technology of the time, a John Harrison chronometer. The watch inside the box was wrapped in soft suede which he carefully peeled away to reveal the face of the clock. It came into his possession when they took a slave ship as a prize; he remembered the thrill of being trusted by Mitchell to captain her back to Jamaica. The wealthy ship's captain who was probably its owner had filled his cabin with all manner of luxuries most of which were sadly lost when the ship ran aground. Ben carefully wound the watch and wiped the lens with a soft cloth, he would set it at noon the following day and then use it every day to help calculate their position and plot his course.

There was a tap at the door and Mould entered. "Everything all right Capt'n, would you like some supper?"

"No thank you, Mr Mould. How's your galley?"

"It'll be fine once I get everything in its place. I'll make some fresh bread first thing to make sure the brick-oven is working as it should."

Mould looked at the watch and smiled. "We nearly lost you and that damned watch when St Justo blew up."

"Aye, and I still have the scars to prove it," Ben said with an ironic laugh.

"Your mother-in-law loved that story when Fletch told it, but I don't think that she ever believed the bit about you flying through the air like a comet as Mr Snow described it."

"No, I don't think that she did."

"Well if there's nothing else I can do for you, Captain, I've got an early start."

"Goodnight, try not to burn us down with your new oven," Ben said.

His sparsely decorated cabin suddenly seemed very small and lonely. He felt the tide shift and the ship began to swing around on its forward anchor it reminded him that their journey was almost due to begin.

To prepare himself for the voyage, Ben went through his usual rituals; he made sure that the various sea-charts were in the order that he would need them, and then he took the two matching pistols from their heavy wooden box. Although he hoped that they would not be needed, he cleaned and primed them, just in case. He pulled the hammer back and enjoyed the precise click-click as it locked into place. They were antiquated weapons, which had been passed down to him by his namesake and mentor Philip Burrows, who in turn, had been presented with them by, Admiral Hawkes, after the battle of, Quiberon Bay in seventeen-fifty-nine. Despite their age, they were deadly accurate and proven servants. He wiped the barrels with a soft cloth before placing them respectfully back in their nest.

Usually, before a voyage, Edward and he would share a bottle of port, smoke a cigar, and perhaps reminisce about their early adventures. They had a great many shared memories and they used to joke that if they had been married they would not have spent so much time together.

The Winds of Change.

He lit his cigar and sat back blowing a great cloud of aromatic blue smoke at the ceiling timbers. He had tried to put Emma to the back of his mind so that he could concentrate on making the ship ready, but at that moment, she haunted him.

On deck later that night, he watched the moon snuggle down behind the mountains; he noticed that there was a chill in the air and guessed the tide was turning. Out across the choppy water, he could see the first light of dawn as it slowly chased away the stars. The town was just beginning to come to life, somewhere a dog was barking and someone was out extinguishing the lights along the harbour wall. He watched a lone angler sit down with his rod and line on the harbour wall to wait just as Ben was doing for the incoming tide.

Like an athlete before a marathon, he was going through his race plan, he had found a place just aft of the main ship's wheel where he felt comfortable and knew that he would spend his on-deck hours there. He ran his fingers over the gleaming polished wood of the wheel and with the cuff of his jacket sleeve he polished one of its brass fittings.

Fletch had been watching Ben from the shadows, they had been friends and shipmates for almost twenty years. They had saved each other's lives and fought side by side against many foes and he too felt the pain and sadness of losing Emma and Dorothy and he was determined that at whatever the cost he would help bring them home safely.

"It is a fine morning to sail," Fletch called.

Ben suddenly realised that he was not alone on the deck. "Yes, high tide will be about seven-thirty make sure that we are ready to sail," Ben said. He went back towards his cabin. "Oh, Fletch, thank you and the others for your support."

Mould adjusted Ben's cravat for him, gave his jacket a final brush, and made sure his waistcoat was pulled down straight. "Fit for an audience with the Admiralty," he said. "You look the part, Captain, the men will be pleased."

Out on deck, Ben knew that it was not just the crew watching him, but also several observers from the harbour wall. He took up the place he had decided upon and took a moment to enjoy the sensation of being Captain of his own ship again.

"Mr Clough, are the supplies aboard?"

"Aye, aye, Captain."

"Mr Fletcher, convey my order to let go forward and aft. Mr Coombes send your men to their stations. I want to see those sails filled to bursting."

Tony Mead.

He allowed himself a brief glance back to where his friends were waving from the harbour wall.

There was new anticipation and excitement aboard Raven as the main capstan began to lift the anchor, and the sailors unfurled the sails. As usual, the singing of their shanties filled the air.

>'When I was a little lad,
>My mother told me,
>Away, haul away,
>O, haul away together,'

23. The Spice Islands.

"Light on the Larboard bow!"

The sudden shout, brought the ship's crew out of the stupor it had slipped into after endless, monotonous days at sea. The constant heat was draining everyone's strength and tempers were becoming frayed. Everyone stopped their tasks and looked out into the silent, black night thankful that at last land was in sight.

"Mr Hardy, please convey my apologies to the Captain for disturbing him, but I'm sure he'll be delighted to know that I'm sure we've reached Ceylon."

By the time Mitchell appeared on deck, dawn had broken and a distant blue haze on the horizon promised them land. He stood a moment to enjoy the fresh cooling breeze; closing his eyes, he said a prayer of thanks. It was as though he had made two journeys of discovery, one as the ship ploughed through unfamiliar water and the second with Elvira where he felt that he was in just as unfamiliar territory. There was no question in his mind as to whether or not he had done the right thing; however, he could not help wondering about their future together.

"Well done gentlemen," Mitchell said over his shoulder; he was using the ships large telescope to scan the horizon. "I'd say your assumptions are correct and by the silhouette of the land, we have indeed reached Ceylon." He rubbed his hands together with delight all doubts cast from his mind.

There was a buzz amongst the crew; the thrill of visiting such an exotic and fabled island made them restless. Pelican's officers gathered on the quarterdeck as soon as they heard that land was sighted. After the uproar of the crashing waves and howling winds they had experienced for the last six weeks, every one of them was ready for a break.

"I think that the last few weeks since we left Van Diemen's Land have been the hardest sailing of my life," Mitchell said.

"She'll need some work doing when we reach port." Snow said. "She's a tough old bird, there's no denying that, but the weather we've experienced, it was almost too much for her, her builders in Whitby would be proud of their handiwork but they had no idea she was to face such diabolical weather."

The ship's doctor arrived on deck just in shirtsleeves; his face was flushed and he looked to be suffering in the heat. "Good morning, Captain," Harvey said, "you look well."

"I'm feeling in tip-top form and the sight of land is very welcome Mr Harvey."

Harvey stood close to Mitchell so as not to be heard by anyone else. "The crew are exhausted, we've had more than our usual accidents, I've ten men in the sickbay; two broken arms, a broken foot, the rest suffering fatigue. However, due to your good captaincy, none are suffering the sailor's curse, scurvy."

"They'll get plenty of rest here; I predict our stay may be a lengthy one with the number of repairs that are necessary."

After leaving the west coast of Australia, they had encountered enormous seas. The mountainous waves had flooded across the decks spilling into the holds and tearing at the rigging, at times it had threatened to capsize them. Even the most experienced of the crew had feared the worst as they were tossed like matchwood by the ice-cold waves. Part of the mainmast had broken free and was lost overboard, but worse was to come; as they neared the small atoll of the Cocos-Keeling Islands in the mid-Pacific, they struck a reef that was not shown on their sparsely detailed chart. It was only a glancing blow, and the ship's tough hull had survived the collision but it was obvious that it had been damaged. There was a steady seepage of water into the lower hold, and the bilge pumps had been working flat-out to try to keep up with the leak.

When the sun finally blossomed that morning, it lit up a lush green island that seemed like paradise after so many weeks at sea.

"Can you smell it, Mr Snow? There's no finer smell, than land after a long voyage," Mitchell said.

"I can see the lighthouse at the mouth of the bay," Hardy called out from his vantage point halfway up the forward mast.

The ship was surrounded by birds as they entered the sheltered bay, they circled the masts calling and screeching as if welcoming the new arrival. There were several other square-rigged sailing ships already at anchor, they were mostly merchant ships, clippers and barques all except for one heavily armed frigate that belonged to the East India Company.

"Looks like a busy place," Snow said.

"Aye we need to find a flat sandy beach to run aground on," Mitchell said with his eye to the telescope.

They were met by a small pinnace under sail and oar power; it manoeuvred so that it was running parallel with them.

"Ahoy there, permission to come aboard?" A young officer called. Mitchell immediately recognised him as he clambered up the side of the ship.

"Captain Mitchell!" the officer exclaimed, he was surprised and delighted to see his old captain.

The Winds of Change.

"Well, well, well, if it isn't Lieutenant Rhodes, my words you look very well young man," Mitchell said.

"I am indeed well, thank you, sir."

"We need to careen the ship, get her on her side to inspect underneath; we struck a chunk of coral some weeks back and we've had all on to keep her dry."

"I know just the place, Captain. This is a fine ship, I had heard that you had left the service and obviously, you are not sailing for the Royal Navy now."

"We have a lot to catch up on Lieutenant."

They were guided away from the main anchorage towards an ideal stretch of beach.

"There is not very much tide variation here, but within the next hour you should be able to get in closer to the shore road, and then once the tide recedes she should sit down quite comfortably," Rhodes said.

"We are looking to do some trade, can you help with contacts?"

"Of course I can, I live here now, with my wife and small family, two children. I can organise you a gang of workers, there are some skilled shipwrights here."

"Congratulations, about the family that is," Snow said.

"Mr Snow, thank you. I seem to remember that we only met briefly, you were just joining the crew as I left." They shook hands.

"Perhaps, Captain, you, and your officers would like to join my family for a meal, once you are settled."

"That would be delightful," Mitchell said.

He took Rhodes by the arm and led him away from the others. "Perhaps you can help me in another way," he said almost secretively. "My fiancé has had the misfortune to lose her dunnage; her truck was swept away and with it all her clothes. Could your wife take her to find new ones?"

"She'd be delighted, any excuse to go shopping."

There was a slightly worrying crunch as the ship's keel first touched the beach. Pelican had been built in Whitby on the Yorkshire coast as a collier ship and designed with a strengthened hull so that it could be beached for the purpose of loading and unloading her cargo.

Once the tide had receded, and the ship was out of the water the damage was obvious. Mitchell and his officers were on the sand beside the ship's hull.

"We were lucky the damage is not much worse," Hardy said rubbing his hand over the dented section of the hull.

"We have some very skilled carpenters and shipwrights here, they'll patch you up and make it good as new… if not even better," Rhodes said confidently.

Mitchell rubbed his hands together. "Very well, thank you, Mr Rhodes." He was having difficulty containing his excitement; this was the place he had always dreamt about visiting. "I think that it is time to fill our holds. Mr Gill, you know our budget," he said with a leer. "Go make us all ridiculously rich. Mr Snow, get this ship fixed and seaworthy, we're a long way from home."

"I'll leave you now Captain," Rhodes said. "I'll contact our local shipwrights and make sure that the work begins immediately."

"Perhaps you might call here this evening… please bring your wife too."

Later that evening a carriage arrived on the road near the ship.

"Looks like we've got visitors, Captain," Hardy said.

A long wooden gangplank had been erected by the local carpenters to make carrying materials out to the ship easier. The visitors used it to approach the ship.

"Captain may we come aboard; I've brought Mrs Rhodes to meet with you," Rhodes called from the gangplank.

They sat around the huge oak table in Mitchell's day room, all its windows were wide open to try to keep it cool.

"I'm sorry we can't offer you a meal until we restock our supplies we are reduced to some very meagre rations, but I do have some very fine Madeira wine to share," Mitchell said. "I'll go fetch my fiancée; she'll be so pleased to meet you all."

Elvira was a little bit reluctant at first. "Look at my clothes, they are rags; what will they think."

"I've told them we lost your trunk overboard, they'll love you, I promise."

When Elvira entered, there were a few shocked faces. The men, of course, jumped to their feet.

"May I introduce, Elvira North, my fiancée?"

"Oh, you poor dear," Mrs Rhodes said, "They told me you'd lost your entire luggage, how dreadful, but don't worry there are some fine shops here and they stock wonderful garments and materials." Which broke the ice and everyone relaxed and then sat down again.

Mrs Rhodes could not keep her eyes from Elvira she gave her a wink and smile. "We can have some wonderful expeditions; I cannot wait to show you around. I get such little female company."

The Winds of Change.

"I was expecting to see Mr Barraclough or Mr Burrows," Rhodes said. "You never sailed without their company."

"As I said we have a lot of catching up to do. Mr Barraclough was wounded and has needed to convalesce, Mr Burrows was well the last time I saw him. He is also married with a family and a farm."

"Really I can't imagine him fitting into that sort of life. Do you remember this incident, Captain," Rhodes said rubbing his disfigured nose.

"Aye, I do, it was your first encounter with Mr Burrows. He got you into a bit of a scrape that time."

Mrs Rhodes gave them a quizzical look. "So, this is the Captain that you've told me about so many times." She gave Mitchell a questioning stare. "His adventures with you, sir, are his main topic of conversation around the dinner table."

"I would have thought it was more about his adventures with our Mr Burrows, that was his main topic of conversation," Mitchell said.

"Was it he who broke your nose?" Mrs Rhodes said.

"Oh no, in fact, he saved my life; it was a brute of a slaver we were trying to apprehend that inflicted me with this." He rubbed his disfigured nose.

The rest of the evening was spent in pleasant conversation and although Elvira felt conspicuous in her rags, Mrs Rhodes hardly seemed to notice.

"I hope you will stay long enough to see some of the natural treasures of the island," Mrs Rhodes said. "I was not sure that I would like it when we first arrived, but I don't ever want to leave now. The creatures and flowers here are straight out of a fantastical story."

"I intend to fully rest the men, we've still the Horn of Africa to face and then thousands of miles across the Atlantic before we are home," he smiled as he spoke, "plus, I have read a great deal about the Indian subcontinent and we may never get here again, so, I want to make the most of it."

"Oh, you certainly should Captain, I've never been so enthralled with anywhere in all my life as here."

Three days later, Mitchell's breath was taken away when Elvira and Mrs Rhodes appeared back from their shopping expedition. They were dressed in light cotton and silk flowing gowns that were a westernised version of the sari. He also noticed that there was a line of porters all carrying bundles on their heads behind them.

He nodded to Mrs Rhodes and then took Elvira by the hands.

"You look extraordinary my dear," he beamed as he spoke. "You're stunning, both of you look like birds of paradise."

Tony Mead.

Mrs Rhodes giggled embarrassed by his comments. "I usually go for more conservative attire, but your dear new friend, Mistress North, talked me into being a little more adventurous with our garments."

"Well, I think that in future you should maintain this adventurous look, it certainly suits you," Mitchell said with a huge smile.

Slowly the ship changed character; the carpenters and shipwrights worked on her hull inside and out. The ship's holds were filling up with; barrels of spices, packages of fine materials, bolts of cotton, colourful silks and of course, Ceylon's green gold, tea.

"You've been busy Mr Gill, I thought we'd lost you at one point," Mitchell said.

They were huddled together in the hold between several bundles and barrels inspecting the goods.

"It took me three days to reach the tea plantations, my word; I've never seen anything like them. Stunningly beautiful, and incredibly well organised. The plantation owner, Arthur Holmes, a chap originally from Bolton in Lancashire of all places, looked after us royally," Gill said.

"I hope there will be plenty of profit when we retail everything."

"Don't worry about that Captain, I researched what we should buy before we left England and if we can make England with everything unspoilt, then we will all be very rich, once it is sold on."

"I want some of this top gun deck leaving clear, I'm going to have the carpenters replace the twenty-four-pound guns, these seas are filled with pirates."

There was a great disturbance one day when several elephants arrived carrying goods. None of the crew including the officers had ever seen such creatures and some had thought that they only existed in myths. Bailey the scientist was out with his sketchpad and tape measure. He sketched them from every angle, taking careful measurements of all their dimensions, slightly more worryingly he was fascinated by their dung and carefully pulled it apart to inspect its contents.

After a month of hard work, Mitchell decided that it was time to take a break from the niggling problems and worries of getting the ship stocked and seaworthy again. He asked Rhodes if he had any idea for a special excursion they could take. Three days later Rhodes returned riding an elephant and leading four others each one with a splendidly decorated howdah swaying hypnotically on their backs.

"Mr Rhodes, what a surprise, I know I said something special but what's this?"

The Winds of Change.

"There is a famous holy shrine dedicated to Buddha, it's not too far from here; I thought we could travel there, it will take us a few days. I've been before and I'm sure you'll think it worthwhile," Rhodes said.

"If Mr Hardy would like to join you on your excursion, I'm pleased to stay with the ship," Snow said.

Bailey was hovering nearby. "May I accompany you, this place is like paradise, I've never seen such flora."

Elvira screamed with delight at the prospect of an elephant safari. It was agreed that a small party should go and so food and supplies were packed onto the elephants and away they went. The strange swaying motion of the animals took a little to get used to even for the sailors. At first, the strange motion made everyone cling to something, terrified that they would be thrown overboard. Elvira sat closely behind the elephant's mahout and somehow managed to communicate with him despite the language barrier. It all made for an interesting, good-humoured, and entertaining journey; Bailey was so enthusiastic about recording all he saw in his sketchbook, that on many occasions he was almost lost out of the howdah.

"Try and calm yourself Mr Bailey," Mitchell called out to him.

"I cannot, there are species here that I've never seen before, not even in illustrations."

When they entered the ancient kingdom of Kandy, they were eventually greeted by the awe-inspiring vision of a beautiful stone temple built beside a tranquil lake that supported a huge amount of wildfowl. The water's surface shimmered in the sunlight and huge flowering lilies added spectacular colour to the scene. The area was surrounded by steep, lush green hills that ascended up into cloud-circled mountains.

"Breathtaking," Mitchell whispered so as not to break the spell.

They set up camp outside the main town on the shore of the lake; five large pavilions were erected for sleeping, eating and to provide shade from the scorching sun.

"We should visit the shrine," Rhodes said, "I must ask you to be very respectful; we, the British, are not very welcome here. There are many issues; to say the least, our past governance of this place has been quite shameful,"

He led a party on foot to visit the shrine. Some monks dressed in saffron robes greeted them and gladly gave them a guided tour around it.

"Welcome Mr Rhodes, we are pleased to see you again with your friends."

"Thank you, my friends are visitors and traders, it is their first visit to the island."

"They are very welcome to join us."

They finished the tour with a visit to the holiest of the relics in the shrine; Buddha's tooth encased in a series of golden boxes.

Elvira giggled when one of the monks placed a red swirling dot in the centre of Mitchell's forehead. He, in turn, made a generous offering of five gold coins; the head of the monastery was delighted by the gift.

Back in their camp, they waited for a meal to be prepared.

"Let's take a walk," Elvira said, "just the two of us." It was the first chance Mitchell and Elvira had had to spend time together away from the ship.

"What were you to do after you had seduced Mr Burrows?"

"Nothing, I was just to let it be known that you, or rather, Mr Burrows had been unfaithful to his wife, create some scandal I suppose."

"So, who was it that asked you to do this?"

"Well I'm not sure really; it was all a bit mysterious, but I got the impression that it was a woman giving the orders. There were two of them came to the gaol, a man, who was dressed like an undertaker in a black coat and tall black hat and a well-dressed woman, she was obviously high-born and with influence."

Elvira linked arms with him and they walked at ease with each other. They decided to take a walk along the shore of the lake and then towards the foothills. Suddenly they were intercepted by a monk frantically waving his arms at them. The man stopped and once he had his breath back, he placed his hands together and made a deep bow.

"Please forgive my intrusion," his English was quite good. "You must not walk in this grass."

"Oh I'm sorry, is it holy grass?" Mitchell said innocently.

"Oh my, no, it has many snakes... cobras are deadly, and although they are shy, if you stand on them, then they will follow their natural instinct and strike at you; their venom will kill you."

Mitchell went a little pale. "Thank you for your warning."

"My Sangha name given to me by the elder monks is Banyu, which roughly translates to English as water because I was born here beside the lake." He smiled happily at them pleased to share his information. "If you are wishing to walk, then I will find happiness in escorting you and perhaps I can keep you safe. I would also like the opportunity to be speaking in English with real English people."

"Thank you Banyu, we would be grateful and delighted by your company," Elvira said and returned his bow.

The Winds of Change.

He beamed his pleasure at them and handed a ribbon of saffron yellow cloth to Mitchell; on it was a painted symbol similar to a ship's wheel. "This chakra is a sacred symbol of our faith, it is said to be over two thousand years old and it will help protect you on your journey home."

"I am very grateful, Banyu, thank you." Mitchell paused a moment to look at the symbol. "Mr Rhodes told us that we are not welcome here. Is it true?"

"Everyone is welcome to our temple, maybe not so to the rest of Kandy." The monk paused as if he was gathering his thoughts. "There have been many invaders over the centuries, kings have come and gone without destroying the land and people, but when the British came, they made many changes, most of which caused hardship for the people. They also imprisoned the King of Kandy, and were discourteous to his family and to our religion." The monk looked sad. "We are different, but that does not make us lesser than you, our culture is thousands of years old, in fact, please forgive me because I mean no disrespect, but it is far older than yours. We grew a great deal of coffee and many spices here, but now it is mostly tea, I understand that there is a great thirst for it in England. You call it Ceylon from the Portuguese words for the island, but we call it Lanka, which simply means island."

They walked in silence for a while, suddenly the monk turned to them. "Please keep to the paths; I fear I must return now it is time for prayers. May your God keep you both safe."

They stayed at the camp for three days and fortunately, no one was bitten by anything other than a few insects. On their last evening, the tranquillity was completely shattered when a local Maharaja escorted by his vast retinue came to the lake to pitch camp. A caravan of elephants, camels, horses and Sherpas brought brightly coloured marquees and tents which were soon erected.

At first Mitchell's party felt a little bit intimidated as the Maharajs's men pushed them back to make way for their tents. In the dust and the heat, it was inevitable that tempers were frayed, but an envoy came to settle the situation.

"Greetings, Captain Mitchell," the envoy bowed deeply with his hands together as in prayer, "my Prince, the most Regal and Royal Maharaja Amithnal, sends you his respects and offers his most humble apologies for any disruption to your camp that we may have caused."

Mitchell bowed unsure of what protocol to observe, he settled for a smile.

"Our Prince invites you to a banquet in your own honour this evening."

Mitchell gave Rhodes a questioning glance who gave him an approving nod of his head.

"Please, thank him for his kind offer, we will be delighted to attend," Mitchell said.

The envoy left and there was a buzz of excitement around the camp.

Rhodes watched the envoy walk back to his own camp. "It's quite an honour, but I think he must want something, in all the time I've served here he has never approached me over anything."

"Perhaps he just felt obliged after pushing us about, anyway we must all be on our best behaviour," Mitchell said.

That evening as they prepared to attend the banquet, Mitchell watched Mrs Rhodes help Elvira put on her make-up and a new sari. He thought about how she had first looked like a vagabond in tatters when she came aboard, the transformation was as remarkable as a fairy story.

"What do you think, Captain, will she pass muster?" Mrs Rhodes stood back with a proud grin.

"Well I don't have much choice do I, but yes she will do."

Elvira threw a large cushion at him. "Sailors, what do they know?"

Mrs Rhodes looked slightly shocked at the banter. "Oh, I will miss you when you leave next week." She smiled at them both. "I must go and get changed myself now if you don't mind."

Mitchell took Elvira by the waist. "Well, Cinderella, you will go to the ball."

Later that evening Mitchell's people walked the short distance from their camp to that of the Prince. As they approached their excitement grew as music and the smell of cooking filled the air. Elvira clung to Mitchell's arm, he could feel that she was trembling slightly.

"Are you all right?"

"Wonderful, never better... I hope our life together will always be this exciting," she whispered.

"You look fabulous, I was reluctant to make this voyage, but I'm so glad that Ben gave me the chance to sail."

The Prince, surrounded by armed bodyguards came to greet them, he was in his mid-twenties; a neatly trimmed beard and dressed in fine colourful silks. There was a bright orange turban on his head with long flowing silks that almost reached the floor.

"Welcome, Captain Mitchell." He bowed as he spoke. "Welcome to our island, or perhaps your island, you British like to claim things."

The sarcasm was not lost on Mitchell, but he chose to ignore it. "Thank you Prince Amithnal, we are greatly honoured to be here and to receive an invite to join you. May I introduce you to my party," he

The Winds of Change.

identified each member of his party, his officers first and then, "this is my fiancée, Elvira,"

"Charmed," the Prince said taking her hand. "You are exactly how one imagines a typical English Rose... perhaps not in a sari but beautiful all the same." He reluctantly released her hand. "Come, please we, have an evening of entertainment and good food to share with you."

"He's a bit of a charmer, I'll wager that I'm not the first woman he has leered at," Elvira whispered.

There were entertainers of all types; jugglers, fire eaters, acrobats and musicians. Mitchell's party sat down on silk cushions around a large low table beneath a multi-coloured canopy. Servants suddenly appeared bearing trays of food. The meal seemed endless as course after course was served. A troupe of dancers and musicians performed both classical and folk dances for them.

When the eating and dancing was finished, another richly dressed young man joined them, he looked angry and his sullen expression worried Mitchell.

"This is my younger brother, Prince Sanjeeva," Amithnal said. He did not give the impression that he was pleased to see his younger brother.

Mitchell nodded to the young man who gave him a curt nod in reply.

"Forgive my brother, he is young and dislikes foreigners."

"Especially, British foreigners, I suppose," Mitchell said with a wry smile.

Amithnal smiled, "you are a man of the world, Captain, you know how these things are." He clapped his hands and called "Music... there should be more music."

Mitchell watched Elvira as she swayed from side to side completely immersed in the music.

"So, when will you marry, Captain?"

"I hope that I can fulfil that duty as soon as we return to England."

The prince's eyes were fixed on Elvira. "You are a lucky man to have such a beauty, I have several wives but none as fair as she."

Mitchell smiled at the Prince. "It was fate, we are lucky to have found each other."

"Then I am very envious of you, she has immense beauty of both mind and body I think." The prince leant towards Mitchell to whisper to him. "If you wish to leave her here, I have a place in my harem for another beauty such as this."

"It has taken me a lifetime to find her, I don't want to lose her now."

"Perhaps there is some other trade we can negotiate while you are here, but not tonight, tonight we shall feast, dance and make merry," Amithnal said clapping his hands to draw attention.

As they walked back to their camp in the early hours of the morning, the monk Banyu came out of the shadow of a tree; as usual, he greeted them with a low bow with his palms together.

"Forgive me, Captain," he said almost in a whisper. "You remember I spoke about the vipers in the grass and how you need to be very careful when walking." He looked around and then whispered. "The princes are like the snakes waiting in the grass, they are not what they seem, they are raising an army to overthrow the British."

"Why are you telling me this?"

"Because, I am afraid for you," Banyu said. "The younger Prince is capable of despicable acts, he may try to kidnap you."

"Thank you Banyu, we will heed your warning and be watchful."

Back in the camp, Mitchell called to see Rhodes.

"Pardon this intrusion Mrs Rhodes, but I need to speak to your husband."

They stood away from the tents near a fire that was just smouldering, Mitchell stirred it with a long stick he had picked up.

"My new friend, Banyu, warns me that our jovial host this evening is planning an insurrection and may have an army already assembled."

"Yes, we know about it, but they do not have the weapons they need, nor do they have the manpower to be a real threat. We have spies in his camp and we keep a close eye on him; his younger brother is something of a hothead and he is the one most likely to do something. Just make sure that your ship's weapons are guarded, I'd hate for them to get hold of a couple of cannons to add to their arsenal."

"I think we need to post sentries here tonight."

The following morning the prince and his envoy rode into Mitchell's camp.

"Good morning, Captain," Amithnal called brightly. "Is it not a beautiful day?"

Mitchell offered the Prince a seat. "Is this business or pleasure?"

"Both really, it is a pleasure to see you again, but also I wish to speak to you." The prince dismounted and sat close to Mitchell.

"Will you take some tea?" Mitchell asked.

Before the Prince could answer, Elvira, joined them.

The prince stood and bowed to her. "You see, Captain, I was correct it is a beautiful morning."

Elvira smiled at him, returned his bow but said nothing.

The Winds of Change.

"Captain, I am a businessman and much as my brother dislikes the British I can see that there are a great many benefits trade wise for our two nations." The Prince took a taste of his tea. "I understand that your country has an insatiable appetite for tea, and I have several great plantations. The problem is, bureaucracy, and I don't like paying taxes to anyone."

"So what are you suggesting?"

"Perhaps we could work a deal between ourselves. We could offer you tea and spices at a very discounted price in exchange for the things we need."

"Such as what?"

"We are constantly being threatened by other Maharajas, some here on the island but also from the mainland. I need your modern weapons to defend myself against these men. You would make vast profits back in England from our trade."

"It sounds an interesting proposition, but my holds are already filled, and we are sailing as soon as we reach my ship. I'm not sure my friend, Mr Rhodes, would approve of me trading weapons."

"What would be the harm if he didn't know."

"The problem is that this is not my ship and I'm accountable for everything, plus I have a very tight-fisted pursur who would demand details, but I could return with a ship of my own."

The Prince's face lit up. "Yes, that might be a good idea."

At that moment Rhodes approached them, immediately the Prince stood up.

"Please excuse me, Mr Rhodes, I am overdue for a meeting," the Prince said. he backed away and mounted his horse.

"So, what was that about?" Rhodes asked.

"Nothing really, he just wanted to buy guns from me."

Rhodes looked shocked. "And so, what did you say?"

"I said that I might return with a ship of my own."

Rhodes looked slightly aghast at him.

"Don't worry, Mr Rhodes, I needed an excuse not to trade and yet, I wanted him to think that there was a chance. I don't want him trying to steal from us."

The monk Banyu came to say farewell. "May your journey be a safe one and perhaps we will see you again sometime."

"Thank you, yes it would be a great pleasure to visit here again."

When they returned to the ship, Mitchell was pleased to see that everything was finished and they were waiting for the next high tide to refloat it.

"How goes it Mr Snow," Mitchell asked as he arrived back on deck.

"Fine, Captain, the lads here have made a good job of everything." He pointed at the deck cannons, "We've six twenty-four pounders and nine swivel guns ready for action. Do you think we'll need them?"

"The route we must follow to take advantage of the trade winds is notorious for pirates," Mitchell said warily. "There has been a great deal of interest in our ship, and what we have brought aboard; the pirates may already know of our bulging holds, and be waiting for us. I'd rather err on the side of caution, so, I want us to do a final gun drill and small-arms practice just after we leave the bay. Also, I've learnt that the local prince is thinking of an uprising and maybe after our weapons, so be on your guard."

"Aye, aye, Captain, I'll make Mr Brand and Mr Melvin aware of your orders. I hope you had a pleasant expedition, sir."

"Yes indeed, you should try it sometime Mr Snow."

"You sent me on a couple of expeditions with Mr Burrows, and they were not always comfortable experiences," he said with an uncharacteristic grin. "I'll get to the gun practice immediately."

The crew were rusty when it came to hauling the six-ton guns into place for firing and then hauling them back for reloading. The bosun bellowed orders and after a hot and very sweaty morning, things were running smoother. The ship seemed like a training camp as the men were put through their paces and finally they fired off several rounds from their muskets and the small swivel guns mounted on the ship's sides.

In the quiet of his cabin, Mitchell lay relaxing with Elvira. She knelt behind him massaging his neck with aromatic oils purchased in the nearby market.

"Thank you," she whispered.

"What for?"

"For this, for all of it, I've never had such a wonderful time and whatever happens," she paused, "when we get back to England I want you to know that I've loved every minute of our time together. Riding elephants, almost getting bitten by cobras," she chuckled, "and meeting the wonderful monks at Kandy; the memories will never fade."

"What do you plan to do when we return home?" he whispered toying with her hair, wrapping a few silky strands around his finger.

"That's up to you."

"The offer of marriage still stands?" Mitchell said. "Or, I could leave you for the Prince, he was very interested in you. I could probably get a few barrels of cinnamon in exchange."

"I could enjoy life here, not with the Prince Amithnal, we should wait until we reach England, it might not seem such a good idea to you by then."

The Winds of Change.

Mitchell was a little concerned by her answer. "Do you think that you will change your mind once you are home?"

"I'm sure that I will not change my mind, I would love to marry you."

"Very well, it's settled, I even know the perfect church for the service."

Just to tease him, she was slow to answer. "Yes... I think that would be very agreeable."

They reluctantly set sail on a hot sultry afternoon. Using the ebb tide to tow them out to sea, Mitchell had hoped to slip away unnoticed but the sheer quantity of noisy seabirds circling the masts prevented them from sneaking away.

Mitchell was pleased with the look of his crew; the time they had spent on the island with lots of fresh food and without the rigours of life at sea had made a difference to their general health. "The crew are looking fit," he said to Hardy.

"Indeed, yes sir, I don't know what we are to expect between here and rounding the Horn, but I'm sure that it will tax even the hardiest of them."

As they reached the harbour mouth, they could see Rhodes, his wife, family and their elephants waving goodbye from the headland. The crew cheered loudly, those up the masts waved energetically back. Sadly, all too soon they were out of sight of the land and back out to sea where dreadful loneliness like a damp winter's mist seemed to descend upon them all.

The first day's sailing was uneventful and allowed the crew to readjust to life at sea again. However, on the second afternoon, there was a surprising call from the lookout.

"Sail ho, three points off the starboard bow."

Mitchell guessed that his hunch about pirates was correct. "It seems that we have company, Mr Snow, muster the men, my regards to Mr Brand, ask him to prepare his marines for action."

"A sloop Captain, she's not flying any colours," Hardy called, he had raced up the shrouds to get a better vantage point from partway up the mainmast.

Elvira was on the quarterdeck enjoying the refreshing sea breeze.

"I want you to go below, find my steward and move to the doctor's quarters, you'll be safe there," Mitchell said firmly but calmly.

"I can fight pirates," she said boldly "I want to stay with you."

"I can't fight pirates if I'm worried about you. I have the lives of all my crew to worry about, I want to get us home in one piece; I can't do that if I'm distracted."

She could see that he was adamant and although she wanted to stand and argue, Hardy led her away before she could say anything any further.

"Mr Hardy," she protested, "I thought you'd be on my side."

"Trust me, ma'am, you really don't want to get on the wrong side of the Captain over this, and you would certainly not want to be in the way if this thing comes to a boil. I'll take you to stay with Mr Harvey; he may need your help in the infirmary if we do engage these pirates."

Snow calmly watched the ship approach, he had been in several battles and skirmishes, he thoughtfully rubbed his chin with his open hand. *No matter how many times I do this, the waiting is always the hardest time,* he thought. He clicked his pistol hammer into place and carefully checked that it was primed; he had made the mistake of not checking it once before and that had almost cost him his life.

Mitchell was busy as ever going through his own mental checklist of what needed to be done before the enemy was engaged. "Captain Brand, keep your men out of sight for the moment," he said. now he was calculating how long it would be before they were in cannon shot of each other. The pirate's sloop was a much quicker and more agile ship, it could manoeuvre itself into position anywhere around them. It suddenly turned to run parallel with them and Mitchell knew what to expect. There was a sudden puff of smoke that was immediately carried away on the wind, followed by the sound of a gunshot; the shot screeched through the air towards them but it fell well short raising a plume of water.

"He seems a might nervous, Captain," Snow said.

"She's still out of range of our twenty-four pounders, so unless she is carrying something much bigger we are safe for the time being," Hardy said.

"Take in the mainsails, Mr Mervin, if you please," Mitchell said calmly.

Sailors climbed aloft and began hauling on the lines to lift the heavy sails. The ship slowed. "Hold her steady," Mitchell said to the helmsman.

Now there was nothing to do but wait and see what the pirate ship intended to do. The sloop changed tack and fired another two shots, which again fell short.

"Run out our guns, Mr Snow, and let's place six swivel guns on the stern, she may try to cross abaft."

Below deck, Elvira sat curled up with her knees under her chin, she was not as brave as she had thought and when the sound of the next volley of shots reached her she began to tremble.

The Winds of Change.

"Why doesn't he shoot back and drive them away?" she asked Harvey.

"The Captain knows what he's about; you just stay near that bulkhead, the timbers are thickest there."

"Sail ho," the lookout called. "Two ships Captain."

Hardy stood next to Mitchell on the quarterdeck. "The old wolf pack trick, I think," he said as he watched the new arrivals through his scope, "One keeps us busy while the others sneak ahead."

"Mr Snow, I think it's time to bring down their mast; three shots ought to do it."

The gun carriage wheels rumbled across the deck as their crews positioned them, once secured the men waited nervously for the command to fire.

"Ready, Captain," Hardy called. This was his first real action and he was feeling the tension and excitement that went with it, his heart raced and his blood seemed to be fizzing around his body.

Mitchell waited a moment, he studied the few sails that were still working and judged the sway of the ship to make sure that the shots were fired when the ship was holding steady.

"Fire!"

Snow and the other gun captains yanked on their lanyards and the guns fired, the recoil bounced them back across the decks. The crews clung desperately onto their ropes to try to prevent the guns from rolling back across the deck.

The shots screeched across the open water and hit home with devastating force. The sloops main mast shuddered and then slowly toppled over dragging its sail into the water.

"Hold your fire," Mitchell said, "I don't want to sink her out here. Perhaps remove her other mast, Mr Snow."

"Aye, aye, Captain."

The three guns barked their message again; one of them raised a plume of water on the ship's waterline but the other two took away the smaller rear mast leaving the ship powerless. It was soon obvious that the first shot which had looked to have fallen short had indeed hit below the waterline and the sloop which was already out of balance began to capsize.

The other ships were not put off by this feat of remarkable marksmanship; they continued to close in on Pelican, but they were out of sight of her guns.

"The Pelican is a good old ship, but she is not agile, I think we will have visitors soon," Mitchell said.

Brand lined his marines on the weather deck. "Fix bayonets, prepare to repel boarders."

One of the small slopes was crossing Pelican's bow and suddenly turned so that she collided with the bigger ship, but because Pelican was hardly moving the little sloop was almost undamaged. Suddenly a swarm of pirates armed to the teeth climbed up Pelican's side. They came over the top of the gunwales screaming their war cries and waving their blades above their heads, but the marines stopped them dead with a volley of musket fire. More pirates had climbed in through the open gun ports on the lower gun deck and were fighting with the gun crews.

Elvira had changed into her sailor suit and overcoming her fears, she leapt to her feet. "We must do something to help," she cried. *Now I've found someone, I'm not going to lose him,* she thought. She armed herself with a cutlass and she was surprised how it felt in her hand; its rough handle felt brutally cold, the hammered steel blade that was chipped and stained seemed to glow with blue light; it felt natural and somehow it filled her with courage. She and the doctor attacked the pirates on the gun deck from behind. She swung her blade like a Viking Shield-Maiden; left then right, yelling at the top of her voice she hacked and chopped her enemies, the splatter from their wounds ran down her face and soaked her blouse. As soon as these pirates were dealt with and unafraid of what they might find on the deck above, she led the gun crews in a brave charge up the steps.

They were met by a confused melee of fighting pirates, sailors, and marines and it took a moment to understand what was going on. The deck was slippery with blood and was difficult to cross, but Elvira was determined to make sure that Mitchell was safe. This sudden appearance of reinforcements so demoralised the pirates that they fled back to their own ships. They clambering and tumbling over the ship's side some of them leaping into the water.

Elvira stood panting, she leant heavily on her long cutlass blade and said a prayer of thanks. As soon as she saw Mitchell, she threw herself into his arms. "I thought you might need help." Her voice was shaking with excitement; she had never been so exhilarated. Mitchell held her at arm's length for a moment, to make sure that the blood splattered across her face, arms and blouse was not hers.

"You brave girl, but you must be crazy, you could have been killed," he said dragging her close to him.

"So could you," she whispered.

"Damage report please, Mr Snow." He looked about him, Snow was usually almost on his shoulder. "Mr Snow," Mitchell said.

The Winds of Change.

Elvira rushed to Snow's side; he was sitting on an overturned barrel. "Are you injured?" she said kneeling beside him.

He opened his coat to reveal a blood soddened waistcoat. "I'm sorry Captain," his voice was strained. "I seem to be slightly incapacitated." He toppled over into Elvira's arms.

"Get him below, Mr Harvey, do your utmost to save him," Mitchell said.

Hardy had been keeping an eye on the pirate ships, which had all collected together as though they were having a meeting. "I think that they've had enough," he said gratefully. "Even so, I'll get the gun crews to reload the deck cannons, perhaps send them a few volleys from the stern swivel guns, to give the men more practice."

"Good work, we need to be vigilant still," Mitchell said. "My dayroom in twenty minutes with a full report of any damage any casualties if you please, Mr Hardy."

Mitchell shook Brand's hand. "Well done, Mr Brand, I think your men saved our bacon."

"Don't worry about that Captain; we were saving our own necks too. I reckon they underestimated our firepower and experience, they've probably just had merchants to deal with in the past."

"Join me below in my day-room."

Elvira was still out on the deck, she stared down in disbelief at her blood-splattered rags. She smiled, the corners of her lips curled slightly, but then the smile grew and grew until it was a broad grin. She had not just a feeling of pride, but a feeling of freedom; each swing of her blade, each cut she inflicted had somehow seemed to sever her from her old life and open up a new beginning. Tears ran down her cheeks but they could not wash away the grin. She suddenly realised that her upper arm felt heavy and numb its muscles were strained and tired from the exertion of fighting. She turned to stare over the ship's stern to watch the pirate ships that were still shadowing them; she was surrounded by swirling gun smoke and almost deafened by the noise of the swivel guns firing at the distant ships and knew that she could find the courage to do anything now.

Mitchell came on deck to look for her.

"You still here?" he asked. "You should get changed; you look like a butcher's apprentice."

"I'm watching those ships. Do you think that they'll attack again?"

"Hard to tell, I intend to lose them as soon as the sun goes down."

"Go check on Mr Snow for me please."

In his dayroom, Mitchell threw off his jacket and gratefully accepted the glass of port poured by his steward.

Elvira arrived still splattered with blood. "The doctor says he'll pull through; the wound looks worse than it is."

Mitchell smiled at her he sensed that she wanted to say something. "Why don't you go get changed, you've been very brave today, it can be tiring."

"No, I want to help; I can take a watch until Mr Snow is recovered. I've got ears and eyes to watch for danger."

Mitchell could see that she was still exhilarated by the battle, still high on adrenaline, he knew that feeling well and how addictive it could be.

"Very well, I'll make Mr Melvin the bosun aware of the situation. There will not be a moon tonight, and looking at the clouds in the sky it will be as black as it can be. Before dark, I want you to make sure that there is not a light showing anywhere, check the lower-deck gun ports make sure that they are tightly closed, and extinguish any unnecessary lights; we'll change course and hope that we lose them."

"Mr Hardy, warn the crew that after dark there is not to be a sound, our choir of angels must stay silent as the grave tonight."

24. Against the wind.

Although most of the journey had been against the wind, Raven reached the Caribbean in record time. After a brief stop in Madeira to refresh their water supply and to purchase a cask of their favourite wine, Ben drove the crew hard to catch the trade winds and cross the Atlantic. After dramatic storms and ferocious winds, they suddenly found that they were sailing into hot, sultry weather that drained them of any energy they had left. Heavy dark clouds tumbled across the sky and the sea seemed to be nervously boiling ahead of a coming squall. Amongst the ship's company, there was an electric, nervous anticipation buzzing like a live wire in a storm. There was not the usual banter and mischief amongst the men; they were single-mindedly focused on the job at hand.

Gazing out across the waves Ben was deep in thought when Jones came and stood beside him.

"You alright Skipper?"

"Yes thank you, Mr Jones, I'm sorry I'd not seen you there, my mind was elsewhere."

"That's understandable, you have my sympathy. It brings to mind our first meeting; we chased that slaver through the night, at first we could only follow the stench that surrounded it, but you were clever enough to anticipate where he would be."

"I don't know about clever, I've never thought of myself as that. We've shared many things since; I like to feel that we've become good friends."

"Indeed we are and I'll always be grateful to you for letting me be the one to open the hatch and free those slaves. You gave me back my self-esteem; without a doubt, it was a great gift," Jones said.

"Come on, we've a meeting below deck."

There was a sense of urgency and drama in the crowded dayroom as Ben unrolled and spread out a chart on the table. Holding one corner of the chart with his compass and the opposite corner with a pistol, he carefully pointed out their position. He mopped his face with a handkerchief before he addressed the gathered officers.

"Pay attention gentlemen," his voice was calm hiding the turmoil that was within him. "This is Compton Island," he ran his hand over the chart to flatten it down; "most of you know it from when we liberated it from the pirates over ten years ago."

Fletch moved the lamp so that its light shone on the chart. "Sorry Captain, I couldn't see."

"Here to the north, is Free Town, the main town for this island. There are still only three towns; the rest is mostly sugarcane. As you probably remember, Edward and I were both granted land here." He pointed to an area away from the main town.

"I remember shifting them huge boulders off your land with black powder," Bruce said with a chuckle. "Captain Mitchell was furious with us."

"Aye, but it cleared the land for that farmer." They all laughed.

"Settle down, I have to admit that it was funny," Ben said and allowed himself a smile but then could not help adding. "The power of the blast knocked us all off our feet.

"Are we going to dock in the harbour?" Jones said.

"No, definitely not, when we attacked the island that first time, we moored here," Ben pointed to a small bay on the opposite side of the island away from the towns. "It's a safe bay with a sandy shore and we should not attract any attention. If Quigley is here I don't want him to know that we have arrived." Ben stopped a moment to gather his thoughts. "It's a bit of a climb, but we can get into town from the beach in about forty minutes. We should reach the bay by mid-afternoon tomorrow, we'll wait there until evening, and then Jones and Brendon will come with me to find Mr Laughton our agent."

"Truthfully, what are you expecting to find here Captain?" Ezra asked. "We've brought enough firepower to start a war."

"Aye, you're right, because I don't know what we'll come across. Laughton wrote that he had seen, Emma, so maybe we can pick the trail up from here. When we meet up with him, he may have more news. If we come up against Quigley and his cut-throats we'll need all the armaments we can muster."

"We need to deal with him once and forever this time," Fletch said adamantly.

"In the meantime, I want every man to practice with the new rifles, loading and firing ten shots each. I want us to be ready for anything. Any questions?" Ben asked calmly. "Very well gentlemen, back to your stations. Mr Jones, prepare those rifles and organise the men, we're still far enough out so as not to be heard from the land. Mr Fletcher, you will take control of the ship in my absence."

When Ben took his mid-day readings, sailing conditions were good, and he felt confident that the mission was off to a good start. As always, he carefully wrote the weather conditions and the ship's position in his daily log. To try to keep his mind occupied he played with the letters of the words adding great scrolls to them. It did not divert him for long and all too soon, he was thinking about where Emma and Dorothy were.

The Winds of Change.

They were still over a hundred miles from the island; the very tip of its volcano could just be seen as a dark blue blip on the horizon. The storm had blown away leaving the sea flat and calm. It gave them plenty of time for their target practice. A boat was lowered carrying a barrel for them to use as a target. For over an hour there was the constant crackle of rifle fire, Ben took his turn and sampled the new rifles.

Clough joined him and took his turn on the shooting range. "What's your opinion of them?" he said weighing one of the rifles in his hands.

"Much easier to handle, and far more accurate than the old muskets, let's hope we don't need them," Ben said pensively.

Satisfied with the firing practice, Ben retired to his dayroom. Fletch who was acting as the first officer was taking his duties very seriously, and each day as Ben made his log entry he would give his report.

"So far so good, we've got a good crew, even the new lads are working well," Fletch said. "We've three in the sickbay; a broken arm and the other two drank too much last night, they'll get extra duties when they've sobered up."

"This ship is a dream to sail," Ben said. "I calculate we have made one-hundred-and-thirty miles against the wind this past day. How's the shipyard's lad doing?"

"He's a good worker, willing to learn and seems to have fitted in well with his mates." Fletch paused a moment, "he reminds me of you when we first met all those years ago on Seagull. He's brave enough to try anything, even if he can't do it, he'll give it a go."

"We've come a long way since then," Ben said with a sigh. "I sometimes forget, just for a moment, what this trip is about, I feel rather guilty for enjoying it."

"I must admit, Skipper this farming life we have now is a bit like wearing the wrong sized boots, sure we manage, but our best fit is here with the smell of tar and shift of the tides," Fletch said almost wistfully.

"And what about all the fine suits you've taken to wearing?" Ben said with a smile.

Fletch dusted down the sleeves of his jacket. "I'm not saying that it's all bad, but sometimes I miss our old life."

They went on deck and stood beneath the triangular rear sail, above them. Even the ship seemed to have a sense of urgency, the straining canvas ballooning out to capture as much power as it could from the wind. Despite the good time they were making, Ben felt frustrated by how long the journey was taking. A pod of dolphins had joined them and they were joyriding in the bow waves. It reminded Ben of Emma, she had been so excited when it had happened on Pelican.

"That's a lucky omen if ever there was one," Fletch said as they watched the pod circle the ship.

"Bring her about Mr Fletcher, we'll take the starboard tack for a while," Ben ordered.

Clough approached Ben with a slightly worried look on his face. "Captain, we are running short of water, beer and fresh victuals; during our mad dash south we've made good time but we need to restock again. I've never known such a hungry crew."

"They are used to the soft, plentiful life ashore but there'll be plenty of time for victuals later, Mr Clough. Thank you for making me aware of the situation," Ben said.

There were a few hectic moments as the crew worked the ropes and then ducked beneath the sails as they swept across the deck to change tack. As the ship came about, the wind seemed to freshen and for a moment, they seemed to stall almost to a standstill. The whole crew seemed to catch its breath and for the briefest of moments all seemed peaceful.

"Land," Fletch said sniffing in a great lungful of air, "that unmistakable fragrance, even out here you can smell it," Fletch said.

Clough sniffed the air. "I can't smell anything," he said.

"Cos you's a landlubber," Fletch said, "it takes years of having yer nostrils pickled by the sea before you're a real sailor and can smell the land."

"Unless yer off Fleetwood and the herring fleets have just arrived," Bruce laughed and held his nose.

Ben slapped the timber of the gunwale rail. "I like this ship," he announced as if he had just come to some decision.

"The crew's found her a good Mistress; they're very pleased with her, she's been well designed," Fletch said. "I must say whenever I'm on deck I can't help thinking of our adventure on the San Justo. She was the only other ship with this style of rigging I've put to sea in."

"Land ahoy!" the lookout called down from his perch high on the foremast.

"I'll be below should you need me," Ben said. He needed a few moments alone; his emotions were in a tangle. Now that they were almost at the island, he could hardly contain his agony, the torment of what might await them was almost too much to bear.

Mould could sense Ben's suffering; he prepared him a large brandy something they had shared many times over the years.

"Here you are Captain, this will take the edge off it," he said, "I've prepared your other jacket for you, it's cooler." As usual, he fussed

The Winds of Change.

about making sure Ben looked the part. They both downed the fiery nectar in one.

Ben dined alone in his cabin that evening and wished that Edward was with him, he missed his friend's counsel and wisdom. He allowed himself a large cigar and a glass of his favourite Port which he hoped would somehow mystically unite him with Edward's spirit. He tried to sleep, but he could not drag his eyes away from the hands of his clock slowly sweeping their way around towards the dawn.

At first light, they were within a few miles of the bay with its wide sandy beach; it brought back a great many memories to many of the crew. They had landed at this very place to try to save Ruth and her husband Sir Arthur from pirates that ruled the island at that time.

Mould tapped at Ben's cabin door. "Begging your pardon, Captain, but I thought you might like something to eat and maybe a shave before you go ashore."

"What do you think, Mr Mould, are we on a wild goose chase?" Ben said as Mould scraped the shaving foam from beneath his chin.

Mould pulled Ben's head to one side forcing him to make a face to allow the cutthroat blade to pass safely across his throat. "I say, you need to be patient and see what Mr Laughton has to tell us. Someone will know her whereabouts I'm certain of that."

At sunset, Ben impatiently launched himself over the side of the boat onto the soft, pure white sand. "Make sure that no lights are showing," he said to the coxswain as the boat headed back out to sea.

They were dressed in dark clothes and armed with pistols and swords. When they reached the top of the sand dunes, they were lucky to find a path that led through the high sugarcanes. On the edge of town where there were very few buildings; it was pitch black, but Ben knew his way. Nearer the town, braziers were blazing along the streets, and the smell of street cooking was very tempting. There was the sound of music from a quayside tavern and a few people walking the streets.

"A bit different to when we first arrived here," Jones whispered to Ben.

A well-dressed couple out for an evening stroll passed them, the man politely tipped his top hat; Ben, acknowledged the man with a salute which was a force of habit, but he wished that he too had just tipped his hat. "Very different," he said under his breath.

They found Laughton's office and were delighted that he had not gone home for the night.

"Mr Burrows, what a wonderful surprise, and, Mr Jones, Brendon, goodness, I was just thinking of you all. I have composed another letter to you because I was wondering if you had received my previous letters. I never saw your ship dock."

They shook hands and Laughton found chairs and drinks for them all.

"We have moored on the far side of the island. Do you have more news?" Ben said unable to wait for Laughton to sit down with them.

"Indeed yes, sir," he quickly slipped out of the room and closed the shutters to his office. "I don't want anyone to disturb us." He proceeded to pour himself a drink, adjusted some paperwork and then sat down.

"Get on with it man," Jones blurted out.

"I've seen them,"

Ben breathed a sigh of relief. "Where are they?"

"They are being held in an old plantation house over near David's town. It's a new settlement only formed this last year, it is run by Quakers and growing rapidly."

"Yes, yes, but who is with them?" Ben asked impatiently.

"There's a gang, it's certainly run by Quigley, but I'm not sure how many of them there are."

"Guess!" Ben exclaimed.

"Seven, maybe eight I'm not certain, plus he has several crewmen from his ship, they billet here in town. Quigley is up to his old tricks here, there seems to quite a few slaves on the island again. He has a sloop that he uses; it's moored out there now."

There was a long pause as Ben tried to decide on a plan of action, usually, these things came to him easily but there was so much to consider.

Laughton poured more drinks for them all.

"Your tenants are doing well, they had another baby this year," Laughton said. "They still talk about you blowing up those rocks on the land," Laughton smiled.

"It sounds as if we need support," Ben said ignoring Laughton's chatter. "We need to send for more of the crew before we take on Quigley,"

"We've got a local constable now, perhaps you should contact him."

"If I know Quigley, then I'm sure the constable will be in his pay. No, I think we will handle this."

Ben was excited; finally, he felt that they were within his grasp.

"Are there sugarcanes around the house?" Ben said.

"Yes I think so, they don't farm it, but every spare plot is used by someone."

"Very good, we need to return to the ship," Ben said.

The Winds of Change.

"I have a lantern you can use, light it once you are away from the town. The waterfront bars are quite busy these days and get a bit too lively at times. Since Quigley's arrival, there have been a few disturbances; the townsfolk are becoming impatient with the Mayor and Sir Arthur over it."

"Thank you, we'll meet along the road towards David's Town at dawn," Ben said.

Outside again they crossed the main town square; Ben was pleased to see that the old church, which had been derelict when they first visited, was now fully restored.

Jones stopped a moment to stare at it. "Hey, Skipper do you remember waiting over there by the church wall for Jenny to bring us news?"

"Yes, she was very brave that night, Mace would have killed her if he had known what she was up to."

They stumbled their way back along the path through the fields of sugarcanes to the ship. Ben never said a word until they reached the ship. His main fear was that Emma would not be there; perhaps they had moved her.

Back on the ship, he ate a light meal and pondered the situation. *Now is not the time to rush things,* he thought.

Out on deck, he rallied everyone to him. "Fletch you sail into the harbour; Quigley has a ship there, capture it. If everything goes sour, sail to St Kitt's and tell Captain Mitchell's family what has happened. He might be able to help,"

It was still dark; Ben wanted them in position on the road before dawn. His crew looked like an invasion force, armed with rifles, pistols and swords.

Laughton was already waiting for them; he flashed a lantern to signal them.

"You're an early bird Mr Laughton," Ben said.

"I couldn't sleep; I'd forgotten how nerve-racking it can be, with you lot."

They all smiled and Brendon slapped Laughton on the shoulder. "You'll do for me; we'd all forgotten too, farming work has made us all soft."

"Ok, keep the noise down," Ben said. His mood had changed the adrenalin was soaring through his veins and he was totally focused on the task ahead. He had felt this way many times in the past before a battle or skirmish. Now he was like a hunting dog that has picked up the scent of its prey, he was totally focused.

The sun crept over the horizon and they stopped for just a moment to enjoy its beauty and find their directions. They all crouched down by the roadside.

"The house is about half-a-mile down the road on the left," Laughton whispered.

"You can stay here if you wish, Mr Laughton, no one will think the worse of you, we know you're not a fighting man," Ben whispered.

Just then, they heard the sound of hooves behind them towards the town. Ben signalled them to hide amongst the sugar canes. The sound of singing reached them; the two riders were obviously under the influence of the previous night's alcohol. Ben signalled Brendon and Bruce to deal with the riders. They let them pass and then pounced. Brendon had no trouble dragging his man off his horse and to the ground, but Bruce's victim's horse was spooked by the attack; it spun on the spot, throwing the rider from the saddle, he landed in a pile at Bruce's feet. Fortunately, they managed to catch both horses before they bolted.

Ben sat one of the men upright and pointed his pistol at him.

"Is Quigley in the house?" Ben said.

"Sod off, who the hell are you?"

"I'm your worst nightmare." He cocked the pistol and pushed it hard into the man's face.

The man gulped loudly as the gun's cold muzzle hurt his cheekbone, but even so, he paused. He mentally weighed up his fear of Quigley on the one hand and against the immediate threat from the pistol; he decided to cooperate just a little. "Maybe he is, I don't know, he was yesterday."

"What about the women?"

"Yes, they are there, more trouble than they are worth."

Ben breathed a sigh of relief.

"Tie them up; dump them in the ditch and we'll collect them later. No wait, better still, get them on their horses; Mr Laughton you can take them back to the ship."

"But I thought I'd be able to help here."

"You certainly can help; I don't want anyone finding these two, and I can't spare the others."

He could see the disappointment in his friend's face, but he felt better knowing that Laughton was safely out of the way of what he guessed was to be a dangerous journey to come.

With the sun clear of the horizon, the day was already heating up. They could see the house, a square-built wooden building with several

The Winds of Change.

outbuildings; most looked like they were ramshackle old stores; perhaps they were where the cane was crushed when it was a plantation house.

"Very simple, Brendon, Bruce, you both go around the back, Mr Jones, you and Ezra take the left and Tobias and I will approach the front. Whistle or something when you're in place. Be careful and remember Emma's life could be at stake," Ben said.

"Perhaps we should wait until this evening, it's too hot now," Brendon said. "I know that you are impatient to find Emma, but it would be best to wait and watch; we don't know how many of them there are."

Ben pondered the situation a moment and realised that he was being hasty.

"Very well, a few more hours won't hurt and as you say it gives us time to assess the situation better."

25. Life goes on.

Every morning, come rain or shine, Walter would drag Eve by the hand and run up the hill to their special spying place, as they liked to call it. From there they could stare into the distance and whisper to the wind, *I wish you were here, please come home.* They had laid out a selection of magical objects, something like a shaman would use to help project their message, it was mostly seashells that they had brought from the beach, several pieces of oddly twisted driftwood, dried seaweed and their prize possession, a lamb's skull. After a while, they would shout and leap about, as though they were performing an ancient pagan ritual casting magical spells to bring the family back together again. Eventually, when they were out of breath from their exertions, they would wander back to the kitchen ready for some breakfast.

Jenny watched them from the kitchen doorway and added her prayers to their dance. She often felt as though she would like to join in with this ritual, not because she believed it would help, but it would be nice to occasionally let off steam. She felt lost without Emma and Ben, and she missed seeing him in the morning, he would always brighten her day. It meant a lot of extra work for her in the dairy now they were gone. The Douglas' had willing agreed to come and help with the small dairy herd, but they were often tied up on the fells with their shepherding duties.

"We'll get through lassie," Jamie said, "But it's a little like pushing a pig backwards up a ginnel when the others are not here."

She was feeling tired and although Tim was a great help, she had her hands full with looking after the children and the dairy. Fortunately, Edward and Emily were regular callers and ever since Eve's arrival, David Hardwick had become a regular visitor too. Most days he found some excuse to visit, at first they thought nothing of it but after a while, there seemed to be more to the visits than just casual interest.

One day they were all sitting out in the barn watching the children play.

"You said that you thought you knew the mother," Tim said.

"Well, I don't think that I exactly knew her." David seemed to squirm a little and looked uncomfortable.

"You told Ben you did," Jenny said. There seemed to her something suspicious about him always being there, and she was determined to get to the bottom of it.

David shifted awkwardly; he was obviously embarrassed and blushed like a child. "I don't remember... saying that," he stammered,

The Winds of Change.

"I thought you might have recognised her too, Tim, you were at Fell Cottage in those days."

"No, I don't think that I remember her. You said you'd seen her recently at your last parish."

"Yes... perhaps so, but that was some while since. Why all the questions?" He seemed unusually flustered. At that moment, Eve fell headlong over an upturned bucket and he was first to dash to pick her up.

Tim and Jenny exchanged a curious glance but never commented on the incident until after David had gone. The cattle were in for milking and Tim was perched on a stool behind one of his favourite animals. "I wonder if David wanted to keep Eve; perhaps he is lonely."

From somewhere behind another of their herd, Jenny replied. "No, he has his new lady friend... there is something more to it than that, I'm sure of it."

They both finished the animals that they were milking and then met up with their buckets by a large urn they used for storing the milk.

As Tim poured his creamy treasure, a sudden thought struck him. "Perhaps, he knew her better than he is letting on... could he be the father, is that what brought her here?"

"Do you mean that that is why she turned up at the church that day... was she looking for him? Oh yes, that would make sense, because there is no other reason for her to be here."

"Well, she did spend time with the Lintons, but maybe she knew that she was dying and wanted to make sure her daughter was looked after," Tim said.

They sat in deep thought for a moment, Tim decided to steer the conversation in a different direction.

"I can understand now why Ben fretted so much after losing Emma and Dorothy, it must have been so painful; I'd be heartbroken if I was to lose you or Eve."

Jenny put her arms around him. "She's growing up fast, she'll be as tall as me soon, that is unless Walter wears her little legs away with all the running about that they do."

"She has been a godsend for more than us; Walter would be desperate if it was not for her to keep him occupied."

"Come on, we've lots of jobs to do."

In Cartmel, Emily and Edward were worrying about Ben's voyage and when, if ever, they would see Mitchell and Pelican again, but they now had something else troubling them.

"I can't concentrate on my classes at the moment," Emily said.

"I can't concentrate on anything right now," Edward replied.

Sitting in their kitchen, staring at the table they both felt as though their lives were on hold; every day they waited for news and yet for fear of the worst, they hoped that there was none.

Each day, Edward walked across the village square to the post office to try and keep his leg moving and of course to check if there was any word from anywhere. He hated using his walking stick but without it, he struggled after only a few paces. He opened the shop door and waited for the familiar tinkle of the bell above his head and then the appearance of Mrs Cott.

"Good morning Mr Barraclough, how's the leg today? I see you seem to be resting on your walking stick more each day," the Post Mistress said.

"I'm fine, thank you," he lied.

"I have a letter from London for you today; it arrived with the late mail-coach yesterday. I was going to bring it over later; I want a word with Mrs Barraclough about the church flowers."

Edward took the letter and tucked it inside his jacket. "Thank you, ma'am, I'm sure Emily will be pleased to see you." He hoped that the issue of the flowers might distract her for a while.

Back in the kitchen, Edward held open the letter. "Finally, I have word from London, the surgeon has agreed to try to remove the piece of shot from my leg, but now we must wait for an appointment. Oh, and by the way, Mrs Cott will be across to discuss the flowers for the church. Well, at least we are a little bit closer now."

"How long is it since Ben sailed?" Emily said.

"Six weeks this Sunday."

"Will they have reached the Caribbean by now?"

Edward thought a moment before his answer. "If the weather has been kind and they've made good time, well then I would guess that they are there. His new ship made an impressive sight as it left, I'm sure it will be lucky for him."

"I hope that they are home before Christmas, it seems so empty without the lads about, and it would be unbearable if we knew nothing about their whereabouts by then."

"I don't know where Pelican will be; if the winds have been kind to them, then she will have already reached Van Diemen's Land."

"Your old Captain was not happy about the task, but I think that it filled a void for him. Perhaps on his return, he will know better which direction his life should take. I hope he stays here with us; perhaps we can find him a wife. There are plenty of farms for sale, Ben was thinking of buying more land."

The Winds of Change.

"Mitchell used to be a bit of a ladies man. When we were younger and went ashore, he always had a pretty woman hanging off each arm, but nothing serious. I thought he might join his family down in St. Kitts, but their last few meetings did not go very well, he doesn't get on well with his older brother who I think now runs their plantations."

"And what of Mr Snow, he seems an odd character at times, a bit of a loner I'd say."

"He is just a little bit self-conscious; a mighty fine officer, he became a fine navigator after working with Ben for a while. I've no idea what he will do on their return; maybe he will stay here too."

"I've been wondering about rebuilding the old Fell Cottage, it was home to so many of us; we could make it home for everyone again."

"Let's get everyone home first before we think about that."

Ten days later the letter from the surgeon in London arrived and they made plans to travel to see him.

"While we are there, perhaps we could dig around a bit, overturn a few stones and see what crawls out, maybe find out who it was that conscripted Pelican. I think that there was something fishy about it, seeing everything that has gone on since," Edward said.

"We have only one priority, and that is to get your leg seen to," Emily said as she packed the final items of clothing into her trunk.

"I really am missing the Old Crew."

"You miss your evening port and cigar with Ben more like."

Edward had to smile at that comment because it was true; Emily knew him so well, but that was not the only reason of course.

They reached London after an arduous journey that took almost two weeks because of the bad weather.

26. The Reckoning.

The hours dragged slowly by as they waited in the heat of the day. Ben snoozed beneath the shade of a tree and tried his best to be patient. The various scenarios of what might, or could happen, ran like liquid mercury through his dreams, w*hat-ifs,* stacked up like a huge pack of playing cards that flipped over one after another, relentlessly being dealt in a never-ending game.

"Wake up Skipper," Fletch said, shaking him by the shoulder.

Ben looked surprised to see him. "What are you doing here? I told you to stay with the ship."

"Sorry, Skipper, but we... I, that is… I needed to know what was going on; Laughton brought your prisoners back to the ship and he told me where to find you."

Ben checked his pocket watch and he was surprised just how long he had been asleep. "Very well, check your weapons and may the Gods be with us this day."

"Some good news, Skipper; I think I spotted Emma an hour or so ago in the garden," Bruce said.

"Then it is time for action, but nobody shoots whatever happens, not until I say so; is that clear."

"Well, I hope we get a chance to try out these new rifles," Bruce said.

"Yes, well, I hope that we don't," Ben said.

They put their plan into action and made sure that they had the building surrounded before Ben made his move. It was a hot sultry evening as he stepped out onto the track, beyond the house he could see a dramatic electrically charged storm tumbling ever nearer from out across the sea; bruised, heavy clouds twisted and flowed towards him. The setting sun was behind him, his shadow stretched along the track almost to the house, but nothing distracted him as he boldly walked along the dusty track; the gravel crunched noisily beneath his feet and he was certain that it was so loud that it would alert anyone in the house. With each step, he became warier; he doubted that Quigley would come quietly and in one way that was a very satisfying thought. After only a few steps, his shirt was discoloured with sweat. Despite the heat, he had a cold, empty feeling deep in his gut.

Within twenty feet of the house, he stopped. "Quigley," he bellowed, and despite his dry mouth, the sound carried to the house. "Let the women go and I'll spare you."

There was a single gunshot that echoed all around him and filled the sky with startled birds screaming and squawking. The bullet raised a

The Winds of Change.

plume of dust in front of him and then it hummed past him like a mad wasp as it ricocheted off the hard ground.

Ben called out in a steady voice. "Don't be stupid, we've got you surrounded. Come out with your hands up."

Another shot hit the ground much closer to Ben's legs, but he never flinched and undeterred started walking towards the house again.

"Go away Burrows or I'll kill 'em both," Quigley shouted from the house.

"Harm them in the slightest way and so help me, you'll regret it." Ben was losing his patience and yet he knew that he must be calm.

"You can't do anything to me; I've got the law on my side."

"Since when has the law approved of kidnap? Anyway, I'll not be handing you over to the authorities; we have our own way of dealing with dregs like you."

Suddenly there was noise to the side of the house and two of Quigley's gang made a dash for freedom. Two shots rang out and the men went down in the dust, they rolled over screaming with pain. Brendon had fired and deliberately hit them in the legs; they were still screaming as he and Bruce dragged them out of sight into the undergrowth.

There was a long pause, bracketed by rolls of thunder as the storm edged nearer. Ben's nerve held as he strode forward towards the building; with each step, he expected Quigley to fire again. He looked to be unarmed, but his pistol was tucked in his belt behind him and he wore a long-bladed skean-dhu down his boot.

"Stop right there, Burrows," Quigley shouted out through the open doorway.

Reluctantly, Ben stopped, he was close enough to see inside, but there was no light in the room and although he thought that he could make out some shadowy figures, he was not sure.

"Come out, Quigley stop hiding behind the women's skirts; face me like a man, this quarrel is between the two of us."

"Take a hike, Burrows, if I take even a step out of here, your lads will do for me for sure."

"No, absolutely not; this is me and you, no one else."

There was a long pause and then suddenly Dorothy and Emma stepped onto the veranda, but they were not alone, Quigley was sheltering behind them and holding them by the hair. Emma gave Ben a weak, encouraging smile; she cocked her head slightly, trying to tell him that she was all right. The relief Ben felt at seeing them was overwhelming and he had to take a minute to compose himself.

"You got a sword, Burrows? I guess you've got a pistol down the arse of yer pants and a dagger down yer boot."

Quigley drew a heavy sword from his belt, which was no ornamental blade, but a dented and battered length of dark steel scarred by countless battles. Waving the sword in one hand whilst clinging onto the women's hair, he stepped out of the shadows. "I hear you fancied yourself as something of a swordsman at one time; get a blade and we'll see how good you are." Quigley sneered disdainfully as he spoke.

Fletch stepped forward with his sword unsheathed. "Let me have a go at this dastard." His face was flushed with anger, his eyes blazed with hatred as he advanced on Quigley.

Ben stepped in front of him; he placed his hand on his shoulder and gazing deeply into his eyes took the sword from him. "Thank you, old friend, but this is my fight; just make sure the women are safe."

Quigley let go of their hair, but as he did so, he cut a length of it, just to show how sharp his blade was; he held it up for Ben to see trying to goad him into a rash decision. Dorothy ran towards Ben but Emma intercepted her and taking her by the arm, she led her away to stand with Bruce.

"Are you both alright, Mistress?" Bruce asked.

"Don't worry, we are fine," Emma said, but all her attention was on what was happening between Ben and Quigley. Fletch placed his arm around Dorothy trying to comfort her. "Don't you worry none, he can handle Quigley," he whispered.

Ben fumed furiously inside, but he realised that Quigley had not hurt them but he was just trying to provoke him.

"Just checking that my blade is nice and sharp for you." Quigley ran his thumb along its edge. "Now, Mister navy lieutenant, let's see what yer made of!"

"You'll pay for that insult to my wife, I'll make sure that you suffer," Ben spoke through gritted teeth.

They circled each other on the dusty track, and all the time the tips of their swords were like partners dancing a swirling jig. Suddenly, Quigley leapt forward, he slashed left, and then right with his blade, Ben stepped back just far enough to be out of immediate danger. He had been in this situation many times and his confidence was high but his heart pounded so loud he thought his adversary might hear it.

He parried the next blow and blocked the one after that and as the blades grated across each other, there was a shower of sparks. With his spare hand, Quigley drew a dagger from his belt and then with swirling arms, he lashed out with his dagger and then his sword again. Ben skipped sideward out of the way, but perhaps he was overconfident and

The Winds of Change.

he stumbled over a loose stone and fell into a semi-kneeling position with one knee on the ground. Quigley grasped his chance and swung his blade as hard as he could. Somewhere in the background, Emma screamed, it distracted Quigley for just a split second. Fortunately, Ben had the sense to roll over again and out of reach of the swinging blade. With a lively leap, he sprung back to his feet glowering at Quigley, and then nonchalantly he bent over to knock the dust from his trousers. As he straightened up, he drew the dagger from his boot.

"Nice move, Skipper," Brendon shouted.

Ben was forced to smile at the comment; it seemed to break the tension.

Fighting with two blades was more complicated and it took far more concentration, now they parried and stabbed with both hands.

"Give it up, Quigley, standing and fighting was never your strength," Ben teased.

Quigley realised that there was no way for him to win, he felt his arms were weakening and he knew that he was quickly tiring. Even if he managed to win the fight, he guessed Ben's loyal crew would surely kill him. They began to circle again, but this time, Quigley had a purpose to his movement and when he had the open driveway and the sun to his back, he suddenly turned and ran like a hare. However, his luck deserted him and before he reached the road, he ran straight into more of Ben's crew. He tried to dodge them, but they grabbed him and upended him wrestling him to the ground. Picking him up by his feet, they dragged him squealing like a piglet back along the driveway and no matter how hard he wriggled and cursed, he could not break free. They threw him in a heap in front of Ben.

"So, now what should I do with you?" Ben said.

"Hang him," Fletch said. "There are plenty of good trees here."

Quigley was still not quite finished, he jumped to his feet, and throwing his arm around Emma's neck, he backed away. "You either promise to hand me over to Sir Arthur or so help me, I'll break her neck."

"Break her neck and I'll gut you like a fish hang and you from a tree for the crows to feast on your innards," Ben said.

Quigley knew he had very little chance of escape, but he was willing to take a risk. He threw Emma forward towards Ben and made a dash for freedom; there was a single shot that shocked everyone and Quigley fell to the ground screaming and holding his leg.

"These new rifles are very accurate, just as Mr Clough said they were," Fletch said with a broad grin. "He'll not run about now."

"Do you remember me saying something about not shooting?" Ben said.

"Oh, now you mention it," Fletch said with a broad grin, "I think that I do remember something like that, but the lads had already had a go at those other two. I didn't want to miss out on the fun."

Ben embraced Emma and Dorothy; they held each other for a long time.

"I thought I would never see you again," Ben said, his voice trembled and he stumbled over the words.

They hugged each other so tightly that they had to stop for air.

"We knew you'd find us somehow, we never gave up hope that you come for us," Emma said tearfully.

Quigley was still writhing on the ground.

"Well, Skipper, what shall we do with him? I'm rather enjoying watching him squirm," Bruce said.

Emma knelt down at the side of Quigley and picked up his dagger; it was a tense moment; everyone held their breath. She pointed the tip of the blade at him and there was a moment's hesitation before to his relief, she cut his trouser leg to allow access to the wound.

"We need to stop the bleeding," she said and tore a length of cloth from her skirt and tied it as a tourniquet around his leg just above the wound.

"You're lucky," she said, "the bullet has gone right through."

"Well, I don't feel very lucky," he grimaced.

Ben placed the tip of the sword against Quigley's throat. "You mind your manners and the nice lady might just save your miserable life."

The first of the rain bounced around them in the dust, a flash of lightning lit the scene, and they all dashed under cover of the veranda.

"Brendan, go fetch Mould, and tell him to bring his sewing kit and some brandy," Ben said.

Dorothy stepped back out into the rain filling her lungs with the new fresh air. "Smell that, what a wonderful smell," she said and danced a few steps.

They dragged Quigley screaming onto the veranda and out of the rain.

"We need to fix his wound or he'll bleed to death," Fletch said.

At last, Ben had time to check Dorothy and Emma; it was then that he noticed that she was not her usual shape. Gently, he placed his hand on her stomach, they exchanged a glance, and she smiled and nodded. His hand felt glued to her, and without regard for anyone else, he dropped to his knees and placed his head against her stomach as if listening for any sound from within.

The Winds of Change.

Someone found the oil lamps and lit them bringing life to the gloomy room.

Dorothy sat next to Ben. "So, papa, what should I call you?"

Ben glanced over at Emma.

"I had to tell her, I had to explain!" Emma exclaimed.

Dorothy turned angrily to Ben. "I'm very angry with you for not telling me," she said. "I had the right to know, it seems that everyone else knew, and now I feel such a fool."

"I didn't mean you any harm, just the opposite; I suppose I was being a coward by not telling you." He took her in his arms. "It never seemed the right moment, we were happy as we were. I saw no sense in rocking the boat."

Mould arrived with some of the crew. "I'm delighted it's not you that I'm repairing for once," he said to Ben. He looked at Dorothy and then Emma and read the situation. "The truth is out I suppose," he said with a knowing nod of his head.

"Mr Mould, I thought that you were my friend; why didn't you tell me," Dorothy said tearfully.

Mould declined to answer; he shook his head and unrolled his canvas sewing kit. Quigley was lifted onto the table and pinned down. Mould carefully exposed the leg; he made a few tutting noises as he prodded the wound.

"Now then, Quigley, I'll make this as painful as I can for you." Mould pulled the cork of the brandy bottle with a loud pop. Quigley held out his hand for a drink.

"It's for me, not you, it steadies my hand," Mould said with a grin.

Mould pulled a flask of ship's grog from his pocket. "Give him a good swig of this, and then hold him down. I can't work on a moving target." He poured more alcohol over the wound and then pulled back the flesh to make sure that there was nothing in there that should not have been there. With his tweezers, he removed a tiny piece of rag that the bullet had carried into the wound. "You see that," he held it up. "That's what stops the wound healing and kills you."

Ben felt exhausted he went and sat in an old wicker chair out on the veranda.

Emma brought him a bottle of wine and a cigar. "These were on the table; you look like you need it. She'll get over it," Emma whispered, "it has been a very trying time, she's been very brave, but I think it's all too much for her now. Did you miss me?"

"Of course I did, I was like a rudderless ship drifting with the tide on an endless sea."

They brought Quigley's men in for Mould to stitch up, but it was too late for one of them who had already bled to death and the other was quite delirious through the loss of blood.

"Mr Laughton, there is some business, we can conclude before I leave. We need to inform the magistrate about these two."

Laughton looked anxiously at Ben. "You know that Sir Arthur has set himself up here not only as Governor of this island but also as Chief Justice. With his suspected involvement do you think it wise to approach him about this?"

"Well then, we're not likely to get much justice here." Ben thought a moment. "Very well, we'll take Quigley back to England, I have a reliable contact there, and Dorothy's grandfather needs to be told about what has gone on, maybe he can deal with, Compton."

The rain had blown over and now the air was filled with the sounds of wildlife, chirping, croaking and squawking their delight at the fresh, cool, damp air.

"What are your orders Skipper?" Bruce said.

"Get everyone back to the ship and let's get away from here, we should make England for Christmas."

Clough joined them. "Mr Burrows I was wondering if we might move the ship to the harbour, our holds are almost empty and we need to restock."

"No, I'm sorry, Mr Clough, but the fewer people who know we have been here the better. We can restock in Madeira, or if we are desperate one of the other islands.

Back aboard Raven, there was a great deal of applause and cheering as Emma and Dorothy climbed over the sides onto the deck. Clifford the young carpenter dashed forward to help Dorothy and there was a brief moment when their eyes locked together and they were speechless.

"Here, ma'am let me help you," he managed to say. She, in turn, offered her arm and it was obvious that something slightly magical had flowed between them.

27. Christmas Day 1825.

For several days leading up to Christmas Day, there were endless flurries of light snow that floated through the cold mist veiling the fells it drifted against the walls and settled on the hilltops making them resemble giant iced cakes.

In the early morning hours of Christmas day, long before sunrise, Jamie, and Ian slept beneath their woollen plaid blankets and heaps of straw in a briar out in the pasture; they were exhausted after days of bringing their flock down from the fells in time for lambing.

Jamie reluctantly woke up and peeped at his pocket watch. "We should make tracks down to Emily's," he said, and then snuggled down in the straw pulling his blanket tighter around his shoulders. "She'll be disappointed if we don't make it for Christmas dinner."

Ian appeared from beneath a heap of straw. "I need to wash up if we are to eat at Emily's." He dug his way out and then excitedly threw off his clothes. "I love Christmas dinner at Emily's; it reminds me of my childhood." In the cold air, his breath hung in a great cloud around his head

Jamie laughed aloud. "Aye, we'd some fine celebrations at Castle Douglas when we were lads."

Completely naked, Ian dashed out of the shelter of the briar into the snow; he let out a whoop of joy and with a single punch smashed his way through the ice that topped the water of one of the drinking troughs. He threw the freezing water all over his body; it was so cold that it felt to be stinging him.

Above him, several rooks and magpies flew from the trees noisily complaining about being disturbed. They called and then began arguing amongst themselves as they circled and tried to find their favourite perch.

"We can nay smell like beasts of the field, especially on Christmas Day," Ian shouted drying himself with a handful of dry straw as he danced about to try to keep warm.

"Well, I hope you'll be getting dressed before we go to dinner, or Edward will be throwing you out by your lugs, and your smell will be the least of your worries."

Ian studied the pasture around them. "We've brought these beasties down, just in time to beat the snow. Look how it drifts against the walls, another week and we'd struggle to find half o'them."

Tony Mead.

Lady Levante was far too upset by the disappearance of Emma and Dorothy to organise her usual Christmas Shindig at the Grange, and so, Emily volunteered to host the meal in Cartmel. The kitchen also needed an early start to make sure the food was cooked in time and Mrs Cairns, her Ladyship's cook had been drafted in to help. With her hair tied back under her mop cap and her white starched apron tightly tied around her waist, she had it all under control; it ran with military precision, which meant everything would be ready for their guests and in plenty of time. Despite so many of the usual participants being away, Christmas day promised to be as much fun for the children as any other year.

"We have to make it right for the sake of the bairns," Emily said. She was busy peeling potatoes, dropping the skins into a pale for the pigs and the rest into a large cast-iron pot on the stove.

"I know, but it doesn't seem much like Christmas with most of the crew still away. It wouldn't be so bad if we knew what was happening," Glenda said.

"I do hope that Mr Mould comes home safely; I was rather enjoying his occasional company in my kitchen at the Grange," Mrs Cairns said. She allowed herself a secret smile.

Emily gave Glenda a sly, knowing wink. "Mr Mould certainly knows his way around the kitchen."

Mrs Cairns gave Emily a curious glance over the top of her spectacles.

Emily went to see what was happening around the house, several days before the event, Jenny, Eve, and David had joined forces with Emily to decorate each room with coloured ribbons, wreaths of holly, and candles. Outside, the men had made a huge bonfire it was stacked up and the Yule Log was ready to be lit at noon. She smiled with pleasure knowing that all was ready apart from the food and the guests who would soon arrive.

Invited friends, began to arrive and soon there was a festive hum about the place as people mingled and chatted. Reverend Hardwick and his fiancée, Clair, arrived after he had delivered morning prayers at the little church; he had been looking forward with childish enthusiasm to this event for weeks and he was guilty of rushing the morning service so that they could be one of the first to arrive.

Already, tempting, delicious smells were pouring out from the kitchen making everyone feel hungry. Two large geese were slowly cooking, rotated by a mechanical contraption in front of the blazing kitchen fire; it was Edward's job to keep winding up the clockwork device. He watched with glee as the birds slowly began to roast and turn

The Winds of Change.

a golden brown adding their aroma to the festival of smells coming from the oven.

Emily watched him and smiled. "That was always Linton's job, we've not used that thing since I don't know when." She said.

"Is there anything we can help with?" David said.

"Oh yes," Emily said. Immediately, they were conscripted into helping with the tables.

Walter was getting under everyone's feet as he and Sam dashed around the house looking for presents, occasionally he would look out of the window to see if Eve was arriving.

Jenny and Tim arrived later. "Sorry that we are a bit late, we had to milk this morning, but at least we've brought some freshly churned butter with us. Eve has driven us mad running around pleading with us to get ready for the party." Eve's frustration had driven her to tears on several occasions that morning, but all was made right when Jenny finally announced that it was time to leave.

At noon precisely, Lord and Lady Levante arrived; they brought gifts for everyone and a guest, their daughter-in-law the very beautiful and immaculately dressed Annabelle Levante.

Lady Levante took Emily aside. "I hope you don't mind me bringing Annabelle, but she said that she was on her own this Christmas, and she was a friend of both Ruth and Emma." Her ladyship looked downhearted for a moment, "Her husband, my son, was killed in action alongside Emma's husband, somewhere in Austria, but of course, you know that. I felt slightly sorry for her."

Emily helped Annabelle remove her fur coat and hat. "This is quite an unexpected surprise," she said.

"I knew you would be pleased to see me," Annabelle said gracefully. "I thought that you might have news about Ben."

When Jenny saw Annabelle, she was furious, but said nothing, so as not to spoil the day, she went off to help in the kitchen.

However, there was another much greater surprise install for them all.

Raven was perched and ready for action, in the darkness, it bobbed impatiently on the waves waiting for the tide to turn. A gentle breeze that kept varying in strength was blowing onshore as though it was trying to hurry them home. Apart from the creaking of the ship's timbers and rigging all was quiet. On deck, a small group of weary and inpatient travellers stood silently watching the distant shore. As dawn crept slowly in and the sky with washed grey clouds lightened, the familiar shape of the snow-capped hills and a few lights in the town beyond the harbour welcomed them; it was all that was needed to lift their spirits. Huddled together on deck they waited for the tide to change.

Dorothy moved closer to Ben and took his arm. "When can we go into port? I'm bursting to see home again."

"Not long now, I'm waiting for the word from Mr Fletcher. High tide is ten o'clock, but we can probably enter just after first light at about eight-thirty." He flicked open his pocket watch and read the time by the light of the stern lantern. "About an hour."

"And so, Papa, what shall we do then?" she said cheekily.

"Less of the papa, I've not decided yet about that," Ben said. "We'll have a Christmas Dinner, somewhere, after that I shall lock you both up and throw away the key so that you don't get misplaced ever again."

Emma took his other arm. "I can't wait to see, Walter; I feel so guilty, I can't imagine what everyone went through when we first went missing."

"It was a couple of weeks before anyone noticed," Ben teased. He received a slap on the shoulder from Emma.

The minutes dragged slowly by, and then suddenly. "Haul away lads," Fletcher bellowed and everywhere burst into action; the crew trimmed the sails, weighed the anchor, and sailed Raven towards the harbour. Emma and Dorothy wept as the ship slowly eased into the harbour.

"Mr Fletcher, despite the hour, it's time to fire the cannons. I want five shots to ring out around the fells."

"Nearly home," Emma said, "I never doubted that we would make it, but at times I wondered if we would ever get here."

"I can't wait to see Walter, I bet he will have grown two feet taller than when we last saw him," Dorothy said tearfully.

Emma tried to straighten her crumpled dress and to hold back the tears. "Oh, I must look a mess," she said, shaking her hair from beneath her hat.

Ben went below to where Quigley was being held.

"How is he?" Ben asked the doctor.

Quigley sat up in his bed. "I'm dying and you'll be committed for murder."

"Think yourself lucky to be alive, there are many folks on this ship who would like to see you swing from the yardarm."

"Go to hell Burrows!"

"I probably will, the only downside of that is that you'll be there too."

"Just hang him now Skipper," Fletch said.

"Not until he tells us who put him up to this."

The Winds of Change.

"I have friends Burrows, high placed friends who'll fix you for good."

"Just tell me what I need to know and then maybe we can release you."

"Ha, do you think I'm that stupid, I'll never tell you her name." instantly he knew that he had said too much and bit his lip.

"Her name, what do you mean her name? I thought it was Compton that put you up to this?"

Quigley sat on the deck in the corner of his cell and refused to speak.

"Let me alone with him for a few moments, I'll make him talk," Fletch said.

"We'll leave him to stew until we get ashore, everyone's desperate to get home."

"In the meantime, Mr Fletcher, fire five shots from the deck guns, if you please."

High above the coast, on the windswept fells, Jamie Douglas could hardly believe his ears; the thunderous boom of cannon fire echoed around him. It meant just one thing to him; at least one of their ships was home, but which one.

"Come on, Ian my lad, we need to get down to Edward's."

Even in Cartmel, the sound could be heard, and pandemonium set in as everyone excitedly gathered together.

"Who is it? Jenny said, she could hardly contain her emotions and began sobbing.

"I think it will be Ben, I'm sure he said he would fire five shots," Edward replied.

"I counted five… I definitely counted five," Emily said. Her emotions were in such a spin that she lost her usual composure and began weeping.

Six thousand miles away, beneath a glorious bejewelled sky, Pelican was on her way home and making good time. Driven along by westerly trade winds and dragged by the strong current running from the Horn of Africa across the Atlantic to the coast of Brazil, it almost seemed as if the ship sensed that it was going home.

Mitchell had just finished an inspection of the lower hold; the weather around the Horn had been difficult, but as usual, Pelican had brought them all through safely. After the violent weather they had faced heading north from Australia, the Horn for once seemed an easy passage. He was desperate to get back to England and start a new life whatever that might be, he was not short of options. Elvira clung to his arm and hummed a haunting tune, she was also thinking about her return to England and what might await her there.

"What time is sunrise?" she whispered. She leant hard against him and stared at the stars above as if trying to read her fortune.

"About two hours, the watch will change on two bells and we will turn due north to head for England."

"It's Christmas Day," she whispered. "I have a very fitting present for you once your watch is over."

"Well, I shall be only too pleased to receive your gift," he said with a smile. He cast his mind back to his last Christmas day in Cartmel and how wonderful it had felt to have a family Christmas at home rather than being out to sea; Mitchell's thoughts were disrupted by the arrival of Lieutenant Hardy.

"Season's greetings sir, ma'am," he smartly saluted them both. "Good news, Captain, we've just reached five degrees west, forty degrees south, so we've officially circumnavigated the world, of course, we are many degrees south of our start point but even so."

"Thank you, Mr Hardy, I do believe that such news warrants an extra rum ration for the lads this evening, and I have a bottle of Madeira wine that has been waiting for this very occasion. Perhaps you will join us for Christmas Dinner and to pay homage to such a fine wine," Mitchell said with a satisfied smile.

"I would be honoured, sir. Actually, Captain the men have asked if they will be allowed some revelry at noon, seeing as it is Christmas day. The cook says that he has salted beef and pork in his larder and that he would be prepared to put on extra victuals if you would permit it."

"Very well, inform the cook that a holiday festival is permitted and no expense spared. The men have worked damned hard on this voyage and we shall all be glad to be home."

After Hardy left, they stood in silence a while watching the constant rise and fall of the waves. Elvira turned to Mitchell. "What is our future? Will you leave me, will you be ashamed of me, and cast me off like an old coat?"

Mitchell studied her a moment, he was still very much in love with her and the question was a surprise and made him smile a little. "Why do ask that? My friends will welcome you like a lost sister," he said passionately. "I could never imagine you as an old coat."

She carried on regardless of his quip. "Will you tell them about my past and how it is that we are together?"

"I'm sure that they will be curious as to who you are, and how we met, but they are my friends and they won't pry. You'll fit right in and they will make you feel at home."

The Winds of Change.

She hugged his arm. "This is the first Christmas that I've ever felt free."

"It's the first one that I've ever felt loved," he whispered in her ear.

She noticed Snow standing alone against the stern rail and she was curious as to why he always seemed to be on his own.

She stepped lightly across the deck. "May I join you, Mr Snow?" she said.

"My pleasure, ma'am," he said. He touched his hat and bowed towards her.

"I'm pleased that you have recovered from your battle wound. You seem to be fully recovered now, but do you have much pain?"

"Thank you for your concern, ma'am, I am indeed well on the way to a full recovery." He paused and straightened his tunic jacket. "Doctor Harvey did a fine job of stitching me back together; says he, it could have been worse, if the blade had punctured something vital inside."

She looked over to the Captain who was now deep in conversation with Hardy.

"You must have seen many such skies as this on your past voyages," she said. She flung her arms wide as though she could embrace the whole sky.

"Indeed, yes, for a sailor who can read them, they are a great comfort, the constellations are like old friends."

"Have you been with the Captain for a long time?" she asked turning towards him.

"Quite a lot of years now, I imagine it is over ten years. Strangely, I was first sent to his ship by my previous Captain who wanted me to spy on Mitchell. There was quite a bit of rivalry and friction between the two of them." He straightened up almost coming to attention. "I hasten to say that I had no intentions of doing such a thing, but I had heard many stories of the heroic actions of his officers and it was an opportunity for me to join them."

"Mr Snow, I didn't realise that you were a man craving for action."

Snow looked slightly embarrassed. "I'm not really, but I knew that if there was a chance for me to advance in the Navy, then it was with Mitchell's crew. I seemed to fit right in, they made me welcome, as though we had been shipmates for years." He stopped abruptly; he had never spoken so openly to anyone before. He realised that she had a special way about her, almost magic, he had opened up to her as though he had had a few glasses of wine too many. It left him feeling vulnerable and open.

She could see that he was embarrassed. "What will you do after this voyage?" she said, deliberately changing the subject. "The Captain tells me everyone will be rich once the goods are sold."

"I'm not sure yet; I've had enough of the sea, I know that; I was invited to join our old crew on their farm, which seems to be my best option."

"Where are you from originally?"

"Yorkshire, Leeds actually; my father still lives there with my siblings, they own a mill, but I never took to that sort of thing, I prefer the outdoors."

"What are your plans, ma'am?"

"That rests with the Captain, life has taught me one great lesson," she said with a smile

"May I ask what that is?"

"Just to go with the tide, as you do with your ships, sailing against it, is hard work and fruitless."

A crowd gathered as Raven came to rest beside the quayside. A few realised who the ship belonged to but most were just curious as to why their Christmas Day had been so noisily disturbed. A figure that Ben did recognise amongst the crowd was Mr McHenry his solicitor. As soon as the gangplank was put in place, McHenry dashed across it.

"Welcome home!" He called out to them and even before he reached the deck, he caught sight of Emma and Dorothy. "Saints preserve us, my, my… what a sight for sore eyes you all are." Tears were flowing down his cheeks.

"Mr McHenry, I'm delighted to be here," Ben said. "We've a great deal to do, but I intend to leave much of it for tomorrow, for now, I want to get home."

"I have a message from Emily, I saw her last week; Christmas dinner is to be held at Cartmel this year everyone will be there."

"Well then, that is where we shall all head," Ben declared.

Clough embraced McHenry. "I have a lot to tell you, sir," he said.

"Should we go to the harbour," Emily said. "I did tell Mr McHenry that we would all be here this year for Christmas."

"I think they will have enough to do as they dock. McHenry will get to the ship straight away. They'll get here as soon as they can, I've never known, Ben miss a good meal," Edward said.

"Let us pray," David said, "We should pray that they have all come home and that they have returned safely to our arms."

The Winds of Change.

"I think that we should all eat something or the dinner will be spoiled," Mrs Cairns said.

Edward and Tim began carving the goose, but none of the guests had much of an appetite. They all slowly drifted outside and gathered in the warmth of the bonfire. Even Walter and Eve seemed to sense the anticipation in the air and stayed close to the adults.

David took Eve's hand, he looked at Jenny, I have a special present for you if your mama will allow it."

"Yes, of course, David," Jenny said.

At that moment, Claire came from the stable leading a Shetland pony, its back was covered in a bright scarlet woollen blanket. Eve screamed her delight. "Is it mine…really mine?" she squealed and ran in all directions at once. "What's its name?"

"You must name her," David said.

"That's a fine pony and a very generous gift David," Tim said.

"I hope you don't mind, but when we saw her earlier this month she said she wanted to learn to ride so that she could go to market with you."

"She can share a box in the stable with our other pony, they'll enjoy the company," Jenny said.

Walter led the pony around the garden with Eve sitting proudly on her back.

"So what shall you name her," Jenny said.

"Beauty, because she is so beautiful," Eve announced.

Time seemed to drag, so they threw more logs on the fire and tried to keep everyone entertained, but by mid-afternoon, they were beginning to fear that perhaps the news was not good.

Suddenly, there was the clatter of hooves and steel tired wheels on the streets of the village square. It seemed as if the whole village was out to greet them and welcome them home. The noisy crowd whistled and cheered as Emma and Dorothy stood up on the back of their flat cart.

"What took you so long?" Edward bellowed above the din.

"It took us as long to hire these wagons as it did to sail home," Ben shouted back.

Suddenly the air was split with the sound of Jamie's bagpipes playing a joyful tune and very soon, people were dancing in the street, the whole village came out to celebrate. Mrs Cott the postmistress dropped her usual reserve and threw her arms around Ben. "Welcome home Lieutenant, we have missed you and worried about your safety,"

The party moved into Edward's drive where more logs were thrown on the bonfire and drinks were flowing.

Emma jumped down from the back of the cart into Edward's open arms and they hugged like never before. Walter and Eve joined in, closely followed by Glenda and so many others that it looked like a rugby football scrum. For over an hour it seemed as if the whole village had gone mad; people were singing and dancing as more food and drink were put out on half a dozen makeshift tables.

Ben finally managed to take Edward aside. "We've got Quigley in chains, but he needs a doctor, he has a bullet wound to the leg that's not healing at all well."

Edward studied for a moment. "So what do you intend to do with him?"

"I'm not sure yet, I don't trust the justices around here. I can't so far get him to tell me who was at the back of this."

"What about Ruth's father? We could take him over to Yorkshire and hand him over there."

"Yes, I'm sure he'd be only too pleased to deal with him and to have evidence of Compton's villainy."

Annabelle was sitting alone in Emily's parlour when Ben and Emma entered.

"So, you both made it home then."

"You sound disappointed, I think you need to explain a few things," Emma said.

"I don't know what you mean," Annabelle said defensively.

Emma poured drinks for them all from the cabinet.

"Well, I think that you do know exactly what I mean," she said as she handed over the drink. "Who identified me as Ruth to Quigley?

"I have no idea," Annabelle said and stood up as if to leave.

"You're not going anywhere until we get some answers," Ben said forcefully.

"Why on earth do you think that it was me that had anything to do with it?"

"Because I know just what you are capable of, I know how low you can sink."

"How dare you!" she looked flustered. "I've never been so insulted in all my life."

"You should get out more," Fletch said over Ben's shoulder.

There was a strained pause as a few of the crew entered the room. They were also interested to hear her side of things.

Annabelle made a dismissive gesture. "Don't bother me with this, who do you think you are?"

Emma made two large steps towards Annabelle and with all her might slapped her face. The ensuing sound and scream brought

The Winds of Change.

everyone dashing in from outside. Annabelle swooned to the floor colliding with a small drinks table on the way down, it went over and its contents scattered across the floor.

"What on earth is going on," Emily shouted.

"Annabelle got in the way of Emma's hand, that's all," Ben said.

They helped Annabelle into a chair where she sat looking hurt and outraged, but she soon regained her composure and holding her hand to the bright crimson cheek glared around her.

Ben stepped in front of her. "I have Quigley aboard Raven, and he has agreed to identify the woman who misled him into thinking that Emma was Ruth and to save his own puny neck, he is prepared to expose anyone else involved in this heinous crime no matter who they are."

Annabelle tried to stand, but her composure seemed to evaporate, the effort was too much and she dropped back into the chair. "I demand to be returned to the Grange, fetch his Lordship at once."

"Do you deny the charge?" Emily said.

"The charge, what charge? You have no right to treat me like a criminal or to cross-examine me. I refuse to answer this allegation," she said arrogantly. "Especially from a band of pirates, cutthroats and farmers." She glared defiantly at Emma. "I'll also report you to the constable about you assaulting me, farmer's wife." She spat the words with real venom.

Lady Levante had been a bystander to what had gone on, but now she gracefully stepped forward and stood in front of Annabelle. "You accepted my hospitality, ate my food while all the time you were plotting against my family, and against our friends with the intent of bringing us hurt. You risked the life of my daughter and the happiness of her family for your own twisted needs." The room was silent even the grandfather clock seemed to be suppressing the sound of its works. "You will go back to the Grange now; you must pack your bags and be ready to leave and never to return, you will never be welcome in my house again. I shall speak with your father and we will have you sent away to some distant colony; in the past, you would have been committed to a convent somewhere out of the way."

For a moment, it appeared that Annabelle was about to object, but then she yielded and went to stand meekly outside which meant squeezing out between everyone, no one moved for her. Emma handed her her coat. "You'll not get away with this, I'll see to that," Emma said, "Quigley will talk and when he does you will be very sorry."

The rest of the party was a subdued affair, but even these events could not dampen the joy of the family being back together. Quite soon, they were singing carols and hymns around the bonfire. David led them in a prayer of thanks for everyone's safe return.

Ben was helping to serve drinks and food when it dawned upon him that Jenny had not made her usual fuss of him and was nowhere to be seen. "Tim, where's Jenny I've not seen her?"

"Last time I saw her, she was helping in the kitchen."

Inside the house was quiet, even the kitchen was still. Ben went into the parlour, where he found Jenny sitting in front of the fire; he could tell by the red bags beneath her eyes that she had been crying.

"What is the matter, my dear?" he whispered.

"Nothing, nothing at all."

"Come on Jenny I know you too well, it takes something of great magnitude to make you cry."

She looked up and then over his shoulder to make sure that they were alone. "I'm ashamed of myself and my wicked thoughts. I have sinned dreadfully."

Ben sat beside her and placed his arm around her shoulders. "You can tell me, no matter what it is."

"No, you'll hate me."

"Never, I'd never do that, you mean far too much to me."

"I'm so ashamed; I should be banished from here too." She sobbed and wiped her running nose with the palm of her hand. "I'm so pleased everyone is home, especially you, I really, really am." She stared into his eyes, "I did imagine, although I never wished it, I swear I never wished it, but I imagined that if perhaps Emma did not return, well then there was a chance for us to be together."

Ben took a deep breath he had not foreseen this. They sat in silence for a while. "What about Tim?"

"I know it's wicked of me, I could not ask for a better husband… but sometimes, we just can't help what we feel and think. In a way, I feel sorry for Annabelle. That day she came to the farm just after Emma had vanished, I knew she was desperate, I was angry with her because if anyone was to comfort you I wanted it to be me, but I understood her pain."

Ben kissed her forehead and tenderly squeezed her shoulder. "I'm sorry that I've let you down, I never to hurt you, or anyone, but as you said we can't help our feelings. The others will be looking for us, we had best rejoin the party," Ben said.

Annabelle was not one to wait patiently, as soon as she thought everyone had forgotten her, she sneaked out of the kitchen door. "Hey you," she called to Levante's driver "You are to take me back to the Grange."

The Winds of Change.

The carriage left almost unnoticed, and she did not relax until it was clear of the village. *I must get away quickly if Quigley identifies me then neither my position nor my sex will prevent me from being sent to prison,* she thought. *Perhaps I need to deal with him.*

At the Grange, she sent the carriage back to Cartmel, then quickly packed two cases, and hoped that all the staff was too busy celebrating to notice her. She had been mulling over what she must do and decided that she should dress in trousers, a jacket and a long riding coat that had belonged to her husband. For once, the kitchen was quiet, she knew that Mrs Cairns was in Cartmel so she doubted that she would be disturbed. Selecting several jars of food and potted meat, she filled her bag for the journey. In the barn, she saddled one of the best hunters and took another pony to carry her bags.

"Hello, there mistress, Merry Christmas can I help?" It was one of the young grooms.

"Oh hello, you startled me," she said with a broad smile.

The groom held her horse as she mounted.

"I've got to dash, a friend of mine in Penrith is very ill."

"Be careful ma'am the roads are very slippery."

She did not reply, but cantered out of the yard and away. She had thought through her options and realised that she would not be safe anywhere in the country. She had insurance of sorts; in her case was a heavy bag of gold coins, enough to buy her passage to anywhere. Hoping that mentioning Penrith would put them off her trail, she headed for the docks.

It was the early hours by the time she rode through the quiet and almost deserted streets of the town. She tethered her horses in the shadows near where Raven was moored. Although she knew that she was taking a dangerous course she felt that it was the right one. There was some commotion from further along the quay where a ship was making ready to catch the high tide and set sail. She waited and watched as a line of people formed a queue ready to board the ship.

There were no sentries on duty on the deck of Raven, Annabelle slipped silently up the gangplank and onto the deck. As silent as a shadow, she crossed the deck and found the steps down to the hold. Lightly treading on each step she tiptoed down to the lower deck. Two lanterns provided a little light, she smiled when she saw the guards slumped around a table where they had obviously been celebrating Christmas, empty beer bottles were strewn about the place. A candle in the middle of their table was at the end of its life, it flickered without giving much light its wax formed a puddle on the tabletop. She passed them by unnoticed and drew a long blade from inside her coat.

Tony Mead.

Quigley was not hard to find, she followed the uneven sound of his snoring to his cell. The keys hung beside the cell door, so she was easily able to open it. He grunted and his eyes opened in alarm but when he recognised her his face lit up with a broad smile; he must have thought that she was there to rescue him. She placed her fingers to her seductively curled lips to tell him to be quiet. In a single movement, much too fast for him to react, she placed a rag over his mouth and with her blade slit his throat wide open almost from ear to ear. He clutched at the gaping wound as his lifeblood oozed away. She wiped the blood from the blade and casually closed and relocked the cell door carefully replacing the key. *Now my darling, Lieutenant Burrows, you have no proof of anything,* she had to suppress a laugh.

She returned to the horses and leaving the hunter behind she walked her pack animal to the ship where the Captain was waiting onshore counting on and registering the passengers.

She stood directly in front of him and he needed a second glance before he realised that it was a woman.

"Can I help you, ma'am?"

"Where are you bound?"

"The West Indies, we have several calls for trade and our passengers."

"Do you have room for another passenger? I don't take up much space."

"Hm, I can see that," he said devouring her with his gaze.

She coyly smiled at him and fluttered her eyelashes seductively.

Opening his ledger he asked, "Name?"

"Florence Drake." She had no idea what inspired her to use that name.

"Not being rude ma'am but I assume you have the means of paying?"

"I certainly do… but I'm sure there could be so many ways to sort it out between us."

28. New Arrivals.

Boxing Day morning was crisp and bright, a cloudless sky and a gentle breeze made it the perfect start to a winter's morn, but its splendour was shattered when a rider galloped along the drive and came to a slithering halt outside. Almost before the animal had stopped, the rider leapt off and raced towards the door.

"Skipper," the rider called. "Come quick, Quigley has been murdered!"

Ben and his family had only just returned from the party at Emily's and had not even had a chance to get to bed. He stepped out of the kitchen door stopping for a short moment to take a deep breath of the morning air and then gave the messenger a curt nod. "Davis is it?"

"Aye, Skipper."

"So what's happened?"

"The lads guarding the ship sent me sir, they found Quigley butchered this morning, his throat is cut wide open, it hangs like a torn pocket."

Ben fetched his mount from the stable, he apologised to it for the early start; after all, it had only just been put into its stall. Mould brought Ben his riding coat, and a long knitted scarf, a present from his mother-in-law to twist around his neck before mounting up again.

"Mr Mould will you take everyone over to Cartmel, Fletch and the crew stayed over there last night, ask them to meet me aboard Raven? I'll meet you all in Cartmel later." Ben rode for the harbour.

"Any idea how this has happened?" he asked Davis as they cantered towards the coast.

"Sorry Skipper, I can't help you with that."

Ben could not help wondering if his own crew had done this, after all, they all had good reasons for wanting Quigley dead.

When he reached the ship he was greeted by three very shamefaced guards who looked as if they wished the sea would wash them away.

"What the hell were you doing?" he bellowed and then he turned on one of the men. "Has anyone put you up to this? If I find out that you were involved in this, then I promise you, you'll swing from the yardarm."

The man seemed to shrink away from Ben. "Sorry Skipper, we all had a wee dram or two it was Christmas Day after all, and we must have all fallen asleep, we heard nothing."

Ben gave him a suspicious glance. "Very well, I'll be in my dayroom until Fletch gets here."

Ben poured himself a large glass of port, he was still suffering from the day before's excesses and he thought it was the best antidote. He dropped into the chair behind the desk feeling worse for wear.

While waiting he filled his time looking over his last log entries, he had not completed them all and it took his mind off things and helped calm him down as he filled in the details of the last day at sea. It was several hours later when Fletch arrived with more of the crew, Ben heard them arrive and met them on deck.

"Follow me," he said abruptly.

They dragged Quigley's limp body out of the cell and unceremoniously dumped him on the deck. His almost severed head rolled sidewards and seemed to be grinning at them.

Fletch could see that Ben was furious. "Calm down skipper it was all he deserved."

"Don't tell me to calm down, he could have explained the mystery of who was behind the kidnapping. If I find out that any of our lads were involved they'll swing."

"Bring some lights," Fletch called. "Skipper you go back to Cartmel, I can handle things here; we'll join you there later. The why and wherefores don't really matter, everyone is home safe; that's the important thing."

Ben studied his old friend a moment, *is there something you are not telling me?* he thought.

"Very well, there's nothing I can do here," Ben reluctantly said and did as he was told, he knew that he could trust Fletch to deal with the situation.

It was early afternoon when he reached Cartmel and Edward was waiting for him.

"Have you heard the news?" Ben said. he was still feeling annoyed and frustrated that his chance of making Quigley talk was now gone.

"Aye, Mould says Quigley's been murdered. I may have an answer for you regarding something of what has gone on."

Edward led him inside, Emma greeted him relieved him of his coat and gave him a huge hug. Ben was surprised that Lady Levante serenely seated in the parlour in front of a blazing fire.

A broad smile crossed her face when she saw Ben. "I have what I consider to be an explanation for yesterday's events," she said looking very pleased with herself. "We rushed back here as soon as events began to unfold." She made herself comfortable in the chair and then continued. "Early this morning one of our hunters found its way home, it was still saddled; they have an amazing sense of direction and she has a three-month-old foal to think about. One of the grooms said that he

The Winds of Change.

helped Annabelle take the animal and another of our ponies which was to carry her baggage out last night. Bold as brass she lied to him, telling the boy that I had sanctioned the event, and that she was bound for Carnforth, a likely story I'm sure."

"No one noticed her leaving the party," Emily said.

"I think that she may have still been smarting from your confrontation. It appears that she also helped herself to quantities of food, I assume for her journey, but worse she stole gold coins from my husband's chest. I've told him for years he needed a more secure place, but he knew best, as usual."

"The hunter was alone, with no sign of the pony?" Edward said.

"It cantered down the drive and straight into its box, the groom rushed to tell us it was home."

"I was wondering if she might have met with an accident; the roads were very slippery," Ben said.

"More likely she went to the docks, murdered Quigley and boarded a ship," Emma said. "If she is involved, in the kidnapping which I suspect is the case, well then, she had a very good motive for wanting Quigley silenced."

"If that's the case the pony should be on the docks somewhere," Ben said. "I'll make enquiries as to which ships sailed with last night's tide."

"I'll make a meal, we've lots of cold meat leftover from yesterday. Will you join us, your Ladyship?"

After the meal, they all relaxed in front of the fire. Walter was very curious about his mother's condition and kept studying her rounded stomach. "How will we know what it is called?" he asked.

Eve was standing beside him as usual and reached out with her finger and daringly touched the bulge. "Will it play with us when it arrives?"

"Yes, but you will have to be very careful with it and look after it," Emma said.

Ben walked out into the garden for some fresh air and to try to think, however, his thoughts were disrupted by Dorothy. "May I walk with you?" she said.

"Of course, let us walk down to the stream, there's a bench there."

They stopped and gazed into the water for a few moments.

"Did you love my mother?" she said.

It was as if a dark cloud had crossed Ben's soul as he was reminded of Ruth, the many good times they had had were now faded memories but the feel of her wet body as she lay dying in his arms was very real. Ben kept his eyes on the water. "Yes… yes very much. From the first moment that we met as small children, I was infatuated with her; she seemed like some fairy-tale princess to me. I was under her spell and she knew it."

"So what happened?"

Suddenly, the memories flooded back and Ben felt as though he was a small boy again. "When she came home on holiday from her exclusive schools, she would come and find me." A broad grin lit up his face, "Even as a young boy, I worked as an ostler for my uncle, it was hard work at times, but at least my Aunty taught me how to read and write. When I'd time off, and your mother was home, we'd explore the moors and glens around where we lived. Your grandmother would have gone completely mad had she known about our silly stunts; sometimes the days were quite mad, we'd do the craziest of things, we would laugh and sing at the top of our voices, we'd clamber up rocks, swim in the river and just run about like wild ponies. I can still almost hear the buzz of the insects and feel the heat of the sun. Looking back, I seem to remember that the summers were always warm and sunny, although I doubt that."

"So, did you kill her brother?"

Ben let out a sigh. "Ouch, that's a bit direct," Ben said to give himself a little breathing space. "No, he fell from the hayloft and landed on the stone floor below."

"So why did you run?"

"Good question, you've been thinking about this, I can tell." He placed his arm around her shoulder. "Don't forget your grandfather is or rather was the local justice and your mother persuaded me that he might just string me up for the loss of his son. So I fled. It soon dawned on me that I had made the wrong decision but it seemed too late, so I just kept going." He picked up a thin stick to toy with. "After that, events just seemed to take over; it's a long story and it's too cold to stay out here for long."

"Emma and I had a lot of time to talk while we were away."

"Yes, I bet you had." Ben was trying to move them back towards the house."

"She told me about your wedding day."

"Oh, what did she say?"

"I knew that my mother died that day but I did not know that she almost killed the two of you."

"It was the laudanum, she didn't know what she was doing, and poor St. Anthony had his finger shot off," he said with a smile.

"She was sometimes very cruel to you I think. She spoke about you quite often particularly after you visited us in the Caribbean. She never

The Winds of Change.

gave away that she had known you before, nor did she say that you had been...lovers."

"Ooh, come on, I think I can hear Uncle Edward calling." Ben ran back to the house.

There was no respite for anyone after the Christmas celebrations were over, lambing began and a mild, dry spell allowed the fields to be ploughed in the hope that later frosts would turn the heavy clods of earth into a finer tilth.

Ben with four of his crew made the journey over to Yorkshire to Dorothy's grandfather's manor. The journey took three days and although Dorothy was excited over the prospect of seeing her grandfather she also liked the adventure of staying in a different inn each night. On their final night, they stayed in Skipton and spent an afternoon looking around its castle. That evening they sat in the public bar to eat. "It's fascinating watching everyone, and listening to them, I've not heard such strong accents before."

"This was where I came with Jenny and the gang of cutthroats she was owned by."

"Jenny!" her mouth seemed to drop open. "You knew Jenny at that time."

"Yes, I told you it was a long story." He gave a shrug. "Perhaps one day I will fill in all the blanks for you."

When they finally reached her grandfather's home they were all travel weary. They were shown into the parlour by a butler who looked every bit as old as his master. Although Ben was glad to see Hutton-Beaumont, he was sad to see that the man was suffering badly with arthritis and general problems of old age and could hardly stand as they entered the room.

"Greetings Ben, it is good to see that you have returned home safely, Emily has been sending me news of events."

Dorothy dashed forward to hug the old man.

"My words you have grown young lady," he said. "Have you recovered from your ordeal yet?"

"Yes, don't worry, I'll be fine. It was quite exciting, a little bit scary at times, but I love an adventure."

The old man laughed; "Just like your mother; she always seemed to bounce back whatever the problem."

Ben explained what had happened to Quigley to him. "I'm sure there was some collusion by the justice in Lancaster, but now we will never know for sure, unless, we were able to catch the culprits."

"We will all sleep better knowing he's out of the way," the old man said. "I thought you might have settled your score with him in your own fashion."

"It was very tempting, but that would have made me no better than him; no I wanted the law to deal with him."

"A wise choice I'm sure."

"The mystery continues though, Annabelle, Admiral Hunter's daughter, you will remember the woman, she went to school with Ruth and Emma; she has disappeared, last seen on Christmas Day and no one has seen her since. We think that she was involved and it was she who was behind the kidnappings. She took off on one of Lord Levante's best hunters, took some money and food and now he wants her to be hanged for horse theft."

"Really, that's interesting she has called here on occasion, much too flirty for me, she stayed here one summer with Ruth and I think Emma was here too; my wife did not like her at all, which was why she was never invited again. After my wife died and after Ruth's sad death Annabelle arrived unannounced to offer her condolences."

"Her father is a proud man, he'll be devastated by the news of her disappearance," Ben said.

The man managed to stand up and took Dorothy's hand. "Come, my dear, I have something to show you." He led her to one of the great bay windows. Dorothy helped him sit on a bench looking out. "This was your grandmama's favourite place to sit, she loved to look out across the park at the deer." He took a deep breath. "Dorothy, I'd like it if you came and stay for a while with me, I get a bit lonely these days and there is a great deal to sort out. Your grandmamma left several wardrobes of clothes and tons of jewellery, which you may as well have if you wish." He gripped her hand. "One day soon this will all be yours, I don't have any other living relatives and no one else to share it with." He glanced at Ben. "You must choose a husband wisely because you will be a very rich young woman."

"Oh, grandpapa please don't speak of such things; I'll be glad to spend some time here, you can show me the estate."

They stayed another two days in Bingley when there was a let-up in the weather so they rode home as quickly as they could.

Back in Cartmel Ben and Edward shared a bottle of port and they each contentedly puffed on their favourite cigars. "What do you think that your old friend meant by dealing with him?" Edward said.

The Winds of Change.

Ben waited until Dorothy was out of earshot. "I'm not sure that I care, but now that Quigley can no longer bother us I feel much safer."

"Yes, my worry now is where Mitchell is, it is a hell of a journey; our old captain is one of the best sailors I've ever known, but it is a huge challenge to circumnavigate the globe and get back safely."

"So, what happened about your leg, which seems much better?" Ben said.

"I cannot explain the difference, it is still a bit sore, but the pain has gone, every week there is some improvement."

Emily joined them by the fire. "The excursion to London was a great success, she said with a broad smile. "The surgeon was a very skilful man, we stayed in a wonderful hotel; I've never known such luxury, and I had six days of shopping, Edward's operation went well, so, all in all, it was a resounding success."

"What about you Emma, when do you think the new arrival is due?" Edward said.

"Not long, he's kicking like a mule."

"I've felt him," Walter said.

"You are sure it's a boy?" Emily said.

"I think so," Emma said and rubbed her stomach with pride. "I think it's time to go, Ben, I'm feeling tired and we need to be up early, some of the ewes are ready to lamb. We cannot leave it all for Jenny and Tim to do; they've worked hard enough while we were away."

Since their return from the Caribbean, Bruce, Brendon and Fletch had all moved into Ben's farm.

"Saddle up lads, it's time for home," Ben said.

Two days later Emma gave birth to a healthy girl who they named Beatrice; Emily said that the name meant bringer of joy.

At the Grange, they prepared for another celebration and feast.

29. The return of the Pelican.

The peace and quiet of an early April morning was shattered by a loud salvo of cannon fire; it shook the docklands in Barrow and its deep thunderous roar resounded through the streets of the town alarming its residents who assumed that they were under attack. In the streets, there was pandemonium as people dashed out to see what was happening. The shots were heard far beyond the town, in fact, the sound travelled high up onto the fells echoing along the valleys and eventually it reached Cartmel; there it brought a smile to everyone's face because they guessed the significance of the salvo.

Ben and Edward rode swiftly into Barrow; it was difficult to contain their excitement at the prospect of meeting up again with Mitchell, Pelican and its crew and of course they were interested in how profitable the journey had been.

In their cabin onboard Pelican, Mitchell watched Elvira dressing, he could see that she was not her usual self; she was hesitant and seemed to be trembling slightly.

"What's the matter?" Mitchell said anxiously. "Are you ill?"

She paused what she doing. "No... I'm afraid, I've never felt so nervous. What if they don't like me or if they tease you over me?"

He took her in his arms. "Trust me; there will be no problems at all. So, just be you and they will love you as I do."

"How can you be so certain, what if you change your mind?"

"No one knows what the future holds, and there may be some problems but we can face them together and overcome them whatever they are. Your real identity is safe and all I know is that my feelings for you will not change."

"There is just so much going on in my head, so many questions, and so many problems."

"Trust me... we can overcome anything together." He tenderly kissed her forehead. "I'm sorry I must attend to other matters, just try to relax."

He knew that it would not be too long before Ben and Edward would arrive and he wanted everything to be in order for them.

By the time Ben reached the docks, Pelican was safely berthed; he stopped to admire it with pride and to listen to the old familiar sound of sea shanties as the sailors went about their final jobs. The whole ship was alive and bustling with activity; down on the decks, ropes, lines and lanyards were all being carefully coiled and stowed away. In the rigging high above the decks, as they furled her heavy sails, they raucously sang

The Winds of Change.

with great gusto from their precarious perches. The gangplank was lowered and secured in place ready to start unloading. Mitchell, of course, was centre stage directing things from the quarterdeck, he had been checking her for damage after she had taken a battering for three days out in an Atlantic storm but there was nothing visible, her rigging, masts and hull had survived remarkably well.

It was Snow who first spotted Ben and Edward. "Ahoy there!" he called, excitedly. He jumped up onto the gunwale to wave to them and then with a broad smile he made a mad dash down the gangplank. Ben and Edward had dismounted and they were surprised when the usually restrained Snow grabbed them in a huge embrace.

"Well, Mr Snow, it would appear that you are pleased to home," Edward said.

"Indeed yes, Mr Barraclough, I have such stories to tell and there is a surprise for you as big as… as big as the cosmos."

"Let us hope it is that you made us all a fortune," Ben laughed.

"What do you need another fortune for," Edward said. "Good heavens man, we are as rich as King Croesus now, we've more gold still hidden than the crown's treasury has seen in centuries."

Mitchell met them all as they came aboard, "Well met gentlemen, it is good to see you all."

Ben and then Edward shook his hand. "Welcome home, Captain, we are very relieved to see you, we were beginning to wonder what your fate was."

"Please my friends; let us go down to the day room where I have some important news."

They all took their usual chairs around the table and were joined by Lieutenant Hardy and Doctor Harvey the ship's surgeon.

"It looks like you've looked after the old girl," Ben said. It felt good to be back aboard his old ship. Ben felt quite at home in the large cabin.

Edward poured drinks for everyone and then returned to his place.

"Excuse me a moment," Mitchell said and as he left he closed the cabin door behind him. Minutes later, he rejoined them looking slightly apprehensive. He cleared his throat and paused almost like a magician about to perform his most skilful illusion. "Gentlemen I'd like you all to meet someone." He opened the door, and looked out and then nodded to encourage someone outside to enter. Her auburn hair cascaded down onto her brightly coloured sari and even in the dim light; he was stunned by her beauty.

Elvira drummed up all her courage, nervously entered the cabin, and standing demurely before them all, expected there to be some harsh judgement. She could not have predicted the reaction. Instantly the men jumped to their feet almost as though fired from their chairs. Ben and Edward stood open-mouthed at the vision before them. For a moment it seemed as though time was standing still, no one even seemed to draw breath.

"Gentlemen may I introduce you to Elvira, Elvira North, my fiancée."

"Congratulations my dear old friend," Edward said and enthusiastically pumped Mitchell's arm.

"Well Captain, I said for you to bring home some of the wonders of the orient, but I never imagined anything as splendid as… Mistress North," Ben said, he smiled and bowed to her.

Elvira gazed back at him a moment and noticed the fine white scar that cut across his dark weathered cheek. With her confidence restored, she turned her attention to Edward. "Neither of you gentlemen needs to be introduced to me," she gave them an endearing smile. "Mr Barraclough, and Mr Burrows, I presume. I have heard so much about you both; I'm delighted to finally meet you."

Snow joined them in the cabin; he smiled at his old friend's reaction to Elvira because he knew that she had already worked her magic around them like a warm blanket. They waited for her to take a seat before they all sat down.

"So, Captain, what are your plans now?" Edward said.

"I've decided that I now have a very good reason for staying ashore, we intend to get married and live somewhere around here to be near to you all."

"That is really good news, our ladies will be so pleased to have another amongst their ranks."

"How did you meet?" Edward asked.

"It's a long story and it will have to wait; there is so much to be done before we can go ashore and we are so looking forward to meeting Emma, Emily and the others," Mitchell said. "Has anything happened whilst we've been away?"

"That is another long story and one best left for later too."

"I have gifts for everyone; after all, we did miss two Christmas days with you. I'll hire a wagon for our things and be along tomorrow," Mitchell said.

"Do you have plans for where you will stay?" Edward said.

"Not at the moment I was rather hoping that you might have a suggestion."

"I'm sure Emily will find room for you, we have plenty of empty rooms."

The Winds of Change.

Ben and Edward left Mitchell to his work of making sure that the ship was safe and more importantly secure. They arranged with a waggoner to go offer his services.

There was a new urgency to the ship's crew after they were promised extra rations if the ship was made secure before nightfall.

"Right Mr Snow, we have a party to prepare for; at first light tomorrow I want the wagon loaded with samples; also the gifts for our friends and ourselves of course."

On Boxing Day in Cartmel, preparations were being made to welcome Mitchell home, which included sending word to the Grange to invite her Ladyship to the party. At dawn, the preparations were already underway. A pavilion was erected on the lawn and makeshift tables and chairs made ready for the guests.

Emma knew that Ben had a secret but he was keeping tight-lipped about it and although she tried a few subtle ways to make him tell, he was stalwart in his resistance. Fletch and the old crew were keeping the children busy and out of the way. There was a new swing in the garden and they were all squabbling as to whose turn it was next. However, the mood became more sombre when Emma's parents arrived; they brought several hampers of food and drink. They had raided their larder and brought game, fowl and wine as well as some pies and puddings.

When Mitchell's caravan of assorted vehicles arrived led by a brightly coloured gig he had managed to hire for the occasion, the whole village came out onto the streets to welcome them home and consequently they were all invited to the party.

On their return, Elvira and Mitchell had decided that a small deception was necessary and they decided to say that they had met in India, hence the reason for her wearing the sari. It would save a lot of embarrassment for both them and their hosts.

There were a few gasps of approval and amazement as Elvira stepped down from the vehicle. She stood a moment to compose herself and to take in the beauty of the little village.

"What a charming place," she said.

"Just relax and be yourself," Mitchell whispered in her ear.

There was a shocked silence and even more speculation when Elvira linked arms with Mitchell as he escorted her into the marquee. It was Jenny who broke the spell; she gently took hold of Elvira's sleeve material. "This is so beautiful," she said, "and you are so very welcome." She then turned to Mitchell, "I hope you have brought me some of this, or there will be trouble," she giggled and everyone seemed to relax. Jenny instantly knew that she and this latest member of their circle would be friends; almost by some sixth sense, she felt a bond with the woman.

"Welcome home, Captain," Ben said.

There was a round of applause and cheers from the old crew who took turns to shake Mitchell's hand and to get a better look at the exotic creature clinging to his arm. When the commotion had died down a little, Mitchell raised his hand to get everyone's attention.

"Your attention Elvira please; I intend to marry as soon as we can," he looked at David, "We would be grateful if we can use your wonderful church."

There was loud applause from everyone and they crowded around Elvira to congratulate her.

Later in the parlour, Mitchell was in his element surrounded by his most loyal lieutenants; Elvira had been whisked away by the women, who were fascinated by her and how she came to be with Mitchell.

"So gentlemen, what now for the future?" Mitchell said.

Ben stood up, "I have something I wish to say on that matter, but because it affects everyone I think we should ask the ladies back in here."

Everyone seemed puzzled but they recalled the women and the rest of the crew back into the parlour.

"This is our best ever Christmas party; we are all together again as it should be. I have a few extra gifts."

Emma handed him a glass of wine which he gratefully took.

"We have all travelled many miles and many years to be here, the road has not always been easy. Sometimes, I for one wondered where it would lead."

"It's been damned hard at times," Edward chipped in and received an elbow in the ribs from Emily.

Ben smiled and took a sip of his wine. "I know that like me there are some of you who have had enough of the sea, but likewise some have not and so I have a few proposals."

The room fell silent and everyone was impatient to hear what Ben had to say.

"I will stay on my farm and watch my family grow, but it would be a terrible shame for our two ships to rot in the harbour. I propose that Mr Snow should captain the Pelican and take her back to trade in India; also that, Mr Hardy should captain Raven and sail to the Caribbean to look after our interests there."

He drew a large key from his waistcoat pocket. "This is the door key for a property I have in Barrow; I would like you, Captain, to have it to thank you for bringing Pelican, her crew and cargo safely home. You

The Winds of Change.

and your bride need somewhere to live and it is yours for as long as you want it."

Later that night, Ben and Edward sat before the dying embers of the parlour fire as they had done so many times in the past. They sipped their port and puffed on large cigars totally content with the way the day had gone.

"I've appointed Fletch as first-mate for Mr Snow, they get on well enough and I know Fletch was itching to get back to sea, Hardy will have Brendon and Bruce as his bosuns. I think we can leave them to their own devices."

"Yes and we can enjoy the comforts of home until these cigars run out."

"Why do you think I sent Raven back to the Caribbean if not to keep us topped up with wine and cigars," Ben said.

Edward smiled and said: "No more adventures for us."

There was a long silent pause broken only by the sound of the long case clock and the crackling fire.

End

∞ ∞ ∞

Books in this saga

~ Guilty of Honour   978-1-78719-289-8
~ Angel Island   978-1-78719-290-4
~ Return to Angel Island   978-1-78719-315-4

Other books by Tony Mead.

~ Seadogs Revenge   978-1-78507-889-7

Printed in Great Britain
by Amazon